D1610724

Phineas Kahn

PORTRAIT
OF AN
IMMIGRANT

Phineas Kahn

PORTRAIT OF AN IMMIGRANT

Simon Blumenfeld

With an introduction by Peter Mason

LONDON BOOKS CLASSICS

LONDON BOOKS
39 Lavender Gardens
London SW11 1DJ
www.london-books.co.uk

First published 1937 by Jonathan Cape
This edition published by London Books 2018

The publisher wishes to thank Eric Bloomfield
for his assistance with this edition of *Phineas Kahn*

A catalogue record for this book
is available from the British Library

ISBN 978-0-9957217-1-5

Printed and bound in Great Britain by
CPI Group (UK) Ltd, Croydon, CR0 4YY

Typeset by Octavo Smith Publishing Services
in Plantin 9.75/12.5
www.octavosmith.com

INTRODUCTION

Phineas Kahn was the second of Simon Blumenfeld's four novels, and arguably his best.

He was commissioned to write it after the success of his first book, *Jew Boy*, about Alec, a son of Jewish immigrants whose struggles with sweatshop life and poverty in London turn him in the direction of 1930s communist politics.

Jew Boy's heartfelt, down-to-earth portrayal of life in the East End generated significant interest when Jonathan Cape published it in 1935 – and the book was also successful in the US, where it was released under the sanitised title of *The Iron Garden* in 1936. His publishers were so pleased with its reception that they gave him an advance for a second offering.

The deal was a watershed for the thirty-year-old, who since leaving school at fourteen had been working variously as a cutter and presser in a tailoring firm, selling dress fabric on a market stall and helping out in his father's kosher slaughterhouse. Although he had been building a parallel life as an author – writing short stories and plays, and serving on the editorial board of the *Left Review* – the contract for a second book meant he could at last consider himself a full-time writer, and for the most part was able to do so for the rest of his life.

If Jonathan Cape were expecting Blumenfeld's second novel to follow the militant template of his first, then they were in for a surprise. *Phineas Kahn*, published in 1937, was far less political than *Jew Boy*, in fact, for large parts almost without politics at all. *Jew Boy*, it seems, had released much of the anger from his system, and its successor switched the focus to old-fashioned storytelling, allowing the author freer rein to explore his literary voice.

As its subtitle makes clear, *Phineas Kahn* is a portrait of the life of an immigrant – a Jewish merchant's son who seeks a better existence away from the stifling confines of Tsarist Russia, first in Vienna and then, for the bulk of the novel, in the more liberating atmosphere of London, where he nonetheless struggles to make ends meet in the backstreets of Whitechapel. A dynastic tale that in some ways brings to mind Alex Haley's *Roots*, it also takes in aspects of the lives of Phineas Kahn's antecedents, and of the large family he raises in Britain.

The story of Kahn was based on the life of Blumenfeld's father-in-law, Philip Stern (known affectionately as Pinya), who had journeyed from the Russian Empire to England in the late 19th century. Stern by nature as well as by name, the real-life Kahn appears to have been a rather less engaging and determinedly more religious figure than the character in Blumenfeld's book – an orthodox Jew, he spoke mainly Russian and Yiddish and little English – and in the classical Victorian mode was a rather distant father figure. Like Phineas Kahn, however, he did possess a lighter side with violin in hand, and was said to have been humming Mozart's 40th Symphony when he died peacefully in his bed, still in England, in the 1940s.

Most of the other protagonists in *Phineas Kahn* were also based on real people – Blumenfeld's wife, Deborah, whom he married in 1931, went under her actual name, and he even placed himself in the narrative, although under the assumed name of Leon. Bertha and Michael, central figures in the events that form the final part of the novel, were his sister-in-law and brother-in-law, and their tribulations, which had a profound effect on Blumenfeld, were real ones that were later played out in the public eye.

Although, as the book demonstrates, the legend of Philip Stern is a fascinating one, it is interesting to consider why Blumenfeld chose to base the novel on his wife's family rather than his own. His ancestors were Catholic olive growers in Sicily, with the surname Campofiore, meaning field of flowers. When an eruption of Mount Etna forced them to flee to Bavaria in southern Germany, the family name was translated to Blumenfeld and, through business expediency rather than any great religious conviction, they also converted to Judaism. Blumenfeld's grandfather, who became a seaman and smuggler, ended up in Turkey, and when the authorities caught up with his illegal activities towards the end of the 19th century, he moved his young family to London. Blumenfeld's father, Michael, who had been born in Odessa in the Ukraine, grew up in the East End, became a cap-maker and chicken-slaughterer, and married a Jewish woman, Sarah, who hailed from Balta, also in the Ukraine. Simon was born in Whitechapel on November 25th 1907.

Compelling though that family history was, however, it was beset by significant gaps in knowledge, and had been constructed on a fair amount of hearsay and conjecture. By contrast, Deborah's genealogy appears to have been more watertight, and therefore a better base on which to construct a novel. Although it has erroneously been suggested that the Blumenfelds were not Jewish at all, they were certainly 'less Jewish' than the Sterns, both in terms of their converted status and in their lack of enthusiasm for orthodox religious activity – a proclivity that Simon, an atheist, took one step further. The Blumenfelds were also slightly more prosperous than the Sterns, and so poverty was less of a factor in the drama of their story. All these elements no doubt had some bearing on Blumenfeld's choice.

The Stern story, then, was the more gripping of the two and served Blumenfeld's purposes more efficiently – a classic Jewish immigration tale that allowed him to explore the vicissitudes, false beginnings, dead ends, miscalculations, bad luck, false pride, abrupt partings and new starts that make up the emigrant experience.

The novel's greatest strength is that it tackles all these elements with a lack of sentimentality. Reviewing the book on its release, the *Times Literary Supplement* (*TLS*) rejoiced in the fact that Blumenfeld 'preaches no sermons' and that 'his Jews are neither jokes nor angels' – perhaps a reference to previous, more dewy-eyed literature on Jewish immigrants in Britain, including Israel Zangwill's *Children Of The Ghetto*, published in 1892.

While the *TLS* also observed that Kahn 'is someone we can understand, grieve and rejoice with, and for whose sorrow and hunger and despair we can have compassion', Blumenfeld invested his main character with sufficient flaws and foibles to make him a sometimes frustrating figure for the reader. Although Kahn's moral compass generally steers him in the right direction, it is not always easy to empathise with his decision-making as he moves across Europe and, at one point, even to New York. In a narrative peopled with rounded figures who have the normal traits of ordinary human beings (no outright villains, no saints), here is a hero with limitations, whose experiences are therefore more moving.

As the *TLS* also noted, Kahn's 'is not a very fortunate story'. Following him from the religious studies of his boyhood in a Russian village to the daily grind of adulthood in London, it is difficult to escape the sense that for every step forward he is required to take two steps back. Outlooks veer from bright optimism to deep despair in a few moments – and back from the dark of night to the promise of a new day in double-quick time. Just as a new opportunity for prosperity opens up, so it seems to be closed off, if not by some malign outside influence then by circumstance, bad luck or misjudgement. For in some ways the trajectory of Kahn's life is not so much ill-starred as ill-conceived. While his Jewishness prevents him from progressing in certain sections of society, especially in Eastern Europe, he can also be the author of his own misfortunes, making crucial decisions at crucial times that either play out badly or leave him chasing his tail. Such is the lot of most people in life, but for an immigrant the line between success and failure is often that much thinner.

When Kahn arrives in London with his wife Shandel in 1900, he breathes in what the playwright Steven Berkoff calls 'the freer air of the West, [where] he is simply an ordinary human being'. But the atmosphere is also foggy and damp, and his existence becomes even more precarious than it was before. Well away from the comforts of rural family and home, there seems to be no cushion from absolute poverty; it feels as if everything may come crashing down at any moment, much as it does for some of those with whom Kahn shares the crowded spaces of the East End.

Through sweatshop misery and even unemployment, Kahn's life becomes, as Berkoff says, 'a fierce study of the Jew attempting merely to be, and to live'. Yet this is not just an account of Jewish survival; it is a story of the survival of others, too. Kahn lives an insular life, his world populated mainly by other Jews – whether as fellow workers or bosses – and for the most part, as is pointed out on the very last page, the life of London and the wider East End is 'a culture in which he had no part'. But there are glimpses of contact with other immigrants, Irish in particular, and of native Londoners who are struggling on the same poverty-ridden terms. The soup kitchens, workshops and damp, overcrowded housing are part of a whole, and though we view them through the lens of Kahn's limited experiences, we are also afforded fleeting insights into the lives of others in the world outside.

This is enough to show us that the terrible conditions of Whitechapel and St George's are not exclusive to Jews, nor even to immigrant communities, and that there exists beyond Kahn's closed environment another East End that is also wracked by destitution and disappointment – a world that had begun to form well before Kahn's arrival and which Blumenfeld chronicles later in his novel *Doctor Of The Lost*.

While *Phineas Kahn* is about the trials and tribulations of emigration – and of the specific Jewish experiences of such – it is also, therefore, a consideration of the more general iniquities of grinding poverty in the early 20th century. Instead of saying 'Look at the terrible lives we impose on immigrants,' it asks 'Why do we allow anyone to suffer in this way?'

From this angle it can also be argued that *Phineas Kahn* is not primarily a book about Jewishness – although it educates its readers in that direction – and that neither is it about race or race relations, much as our heightened 21st century sensibilities (so often conflating immigration exclusively with race) might tempt us to think so. Anti-Semitism is certainly a background thread in the first half of the book. But it features hardly at all thereafter, nor does it take a central part in any of its main workings. Kahn is not fleeing from a pogrom, nor from any direct act of persecution, though there is always that threat. He is an economic migrant, searching, in time-honoured fashion, for a 'better life'.

That he doesn't wholly find it in London can perhaps tell us more about the dynamics of emigration than any racial matters. For various reasons – only one of which is prejudice – immigrants arriving in a host country are typically thrown into lower strata of society than the ones from which they came. In Kahn's case he was held back in Russia by being a Jew, but in London he is thwarted not so much by his race but by his position on the bottom rung of the capitalist ladder – a point emphasised by the fact that most of his exploiters – landlords, employers, shysters – are Jews themselves. Blumenfeld's Marxist perspective would have led him to consider the virtual impossibility of separating race from class: here he makes the point in his novel.

It is worth nothing that Kahn emerges from a relatively well-off home environment in Russia before descending into poverty by stages. Although he is pretty much penniless when he arrives in London, his starting point reminds us that not all immigrants – in fact very few – leave their countries as an act of absolute desperation. Certainly the history of immigration in Britain shows us that a sizeable proportion of those who have arrived from the Indian subcontinent, Ireland, the Caribbean, Africa and Eastern Europe have been from better-off segments of society back home. The poorest of the poor often cannot afford even the bus fare to the airport or dockyard, let alone the passage to a new land.

As Phineas Kahn's experience shows, the collateral damage from emigration is nearly always tougher for the first generation than it is for the next. Parents who have been used to an easier way of life at home work all hours in their new country, making sacrifices in the hope of creating opportunities for their children that were unavailable to themselves on their arrival. Kahn's efforts certainly seem to produce rewards for his offspring, who are remarkably successful given the material circumstances of their upbringing. By the end of the book we see how dramatically things can change in a generation – from desperate poverty to middle-class aspiration. Yet despite greater financial security and higher societal status, the second generation often finds there are other issues to deal with, including struggles with identity, acceptance and integration.

Sometimes this leads to a rejection of the traditional codes, values and aspirations of the previous generation, even a sense of embarrassment at what has gone before – as we see for a time with Kahn's son Michael. In *Jew Boy*, to which *Phineas Kahn* is a kind of prequel, we find a more severe reaction as young Alec lives a dislocated, directionless existence blighted by unemployment, turning him to a new kind of rebelliousness as a consequence.

Phineas Kahn, then, is a book that paints a complex, nuanced picture of the consequences of emigration, both for the first and second generations. It deserves our attention for that alone, but also for the fact that it laid down the template for other Jewish chronicles that followed, notably André Schwarz-Bart's celebrated *The Last Of The Just* (1959). We must, though, also see it as a work of art. As Blumenfeld hoped it would, *Phineas Kahn* gave full expression to his writing talents, freeing him from the shackles that *Jew Boy*, with its more carefully crafted political message, had placed upon him. It not only blazed a trail; it did so with style.

After *Phineas Kahn*, Blumenfeld wrote two more novels before the outbreak of the Second World War – *Doctor Of The Lost* (1938), a fictionalised account of the life of Thomas Barnardo, founder of the Barnardo's children's homes, and – having been ditched by Jonathan Cape – *They Won't Let You Live*, about the plight of a small-time shopkeeper (1939, published by Nicholson & Watson). After that, serious novel writing became a thing of the past, a short phase in his life (1935–1939) that was ended, apparently, with little regret.

Partly this may have been because Blumenfeld had said much of what he wanted to say, but it was also down to the fact that his novels proved to be financially unrewarding. Despite critical success, *Phineas Kahn* failed to generate much in the way of income, and his following two books were less profitable still.

By 1939 he had moved out of the East End to live in Westcliff-on-Sea in Essex and had fallen on hard times, selling his typewriter and sending requests for handouts to friends or would-be patrons. Wartime call-up at least gave him some measure of financial security, and it also opened up new avenues for his writing talents. After a period in the Royal Army Ordinance Corps he was seconded to Stars In Battledress, the army entertainment unit, where he wrote scripts for shows and got to know current and future stars of stage and screen, including the comedian Charlie Chester, for whom he wrote material once he had left the forces in 1946.

Although scriptwriting kept him going for a period after the war, Blumenfeld eventually moved into journalism, and he was involved in the foundation of two short-lived publications, *Weekly Sporting Review* and the entertainment magazine *Band Wagon*. He also worked for the fledgling *Record Mirror*, which had a much longer life. By the early 1960s he had begun to write for *The Stage*, a weekly trade magazine for the theatre and entertainment industry. He became its long-serving light-entertainment editor in 1962, a role that allowed him to mix socially with a colourful cast of extrovert characters that included the rich and famous, villains, boxers, nightclub owners and film stars.

Still politically engaged – as a communist with a small 'c' rather than as a slavish party man – and with a continued interest in Jewish affairs, Blumenfeld also involved himself in the theatre, something he had explored in the late 1920s, when he had forged links with the Workers' Theatre Movement and joined the Rebel Players, with whom he produced various plays. After the war he wrote a drama about the Aldgate-born boxer Daniel Mendoza – still unstaged – and in 1960 *The Promised Land*, written exclusively in Yiddish, was staged professionally at the Grand Palais in Whitechapel. He also collaborated with Bernard Mendelovitch and Harry Ariel on plays for that Yiddish institution before it was forced to close in 1970. His play *The Battle Of Cable Street*, written in English and set around the streets where he grew up, was premiered at the Edinburgh Festival in 1987.

When he died in Barnet, Hertfordshire, on April 13th 2005, aged 97, Blumenfeld remained a larger than life figure with his waxed moustache and colourful, immaculately tailored suits. He was also still writing for *The Stage*, having been declared the world's oldest columnist.

He was cremated at Golders Green Crematorium in North London, where a memorial plaque was placed at his request in its 'communist corner' – noting that he and Deborah were now 'comrades in life and in death'. Like Phineas Kahn, Blumenfeld 'had his ticket and was on his way', a man whose long journey had been crowned with success.

Peter Mason
Battersea, 2018

BOOK I

RUSSIA

CHAPTER I

Tuesday was market day in Zvonitz. One end of the single, narrow, unpaved street was crowded with peasants, goats, pigs and crates of poultry. Chayim Cooper heard the snuffling of animals, the squawking of hens and the guffaws of drunken moujiks behind him as he walked towards the house of his friend Yisroel, the spirit merchant.

People greeted him as he passed, men dressed exactly like himself, in long black caftans and wide-brimmed hats with shallow crowns, little corkscrew curls dangling over the sides of their ears. 'Good afternoon, Reb Chayim,' they said respectfully. Chayim nodded and walked on, humming a little tune, hardly appearing to notice them, his hands clasped behind his back. He felt like a king as he passed down the crooked street. Zvonitz lived on him – he was its bread and butter. He tried to feel humble, but in spite of himself a note of triumph crept into his wordless song.

Well might Chayim sing. He had harnessed the broad Dniester to his profit. From its very source on the northern slopes of the Carpathians, past Zvonitz and Nicolaev until it emptied into the Black Sea at Odessa, the river was Chayim Cooper's servant.

As a young man, an orphan, Chayim had evolved a brilliant idea, and had succeeded in capitalising it. He took a trip to the Carpathians, and with borrowed money bought some timber which was absurdly cheap in that region. This he floated down to Zvonitz, where he made it into a raft. He loaded the raft with produce of the district, and the current washed the outfit to Nicolaev. At Nicolaev he disposed of his cargo and sold the timber at a handsome profit. He was able to return to Zvonitz, pay back the borrowed money, and have a surplus of nearly one hundred roubles for himself.

Chayim Cooper's rafts grew longer, wider and more numerous with the years. He now owned whole stretches of forest where, at the beginning, he had been forced to seek a loan to buy a few trees. Half of Zvonitz belonged to him, and three-quarters of the Jewish population worked for him. Now, when the Dniester thawed, Zvonitz was a hive of activity. The trees were skinned, the trunks were bound firmly together with bark and the rafts prepared. In the centre of each raft there was a space about twelve feet square heaped with a foot of black earth. On top of this, a hut was constructed to accommodate the six or seven workers who navigated the raft.

Chayim's agents scoured the neighbourhood, buying sheep cheese, dried fish, Romanian wines, chalk and lime. If anyone had merchandise to send down the river, Chayim's carters collected and delivered it. A flotilla of fifteen to twenty rafts would set out at a time, each drifting a few yards behind the other like squat soldiers in Indian file. The journey to Odessa, three days by road, took a fortnight or longer, but Chayim's rates were low, and time was less valuable then; it still took unwilling pilgrims two years to reach Siberia.

Yisroel's house was a little way from the street, at the highest elevation of the village. Chayim, panting a little from the climb, stopped for a moment, turned and looked down on his kingdom. The ragged line of nondescript houses, their walls of dried mud hardened by decades of sun, their triangular roofs of brown dovetailed planks or clumsy thatches, twisted down the street and dropped behind some trees. It reappeared below, dipping to the market, where clusters of black beetles squirmed in the distance. Lower still, like a flawless steel belt, the Dniester lay placidly, joined a little way off by the thin silver scrawl of its tributary, the Zvonchik. To his right like grey stumps of decayed teeth rose the jagged turrets of an ancient fortress. A dried moat surrounded the mossy walls. The whole structure dated back from the turbulent days of the revolutionary, Stenka Razin. In winter, with the snow obliterating the pockings of age, the fortress looked like a Christmas card, but in summer it stank abominably, and the inhabitants only approached it to dump their rubbish in the moat and hurry off again.

Some two hundred Jewish families lived in Zvonitz, crowded together in the ghetto, the business and trading centre. Surrounding them straggled perhaps twice that number of gentiles, mostly lower-class peasants with smallholdings. Chayim saw the twin towers of his white house dominating the Jewish quarter, soaring above the mud huts surrounding it. It stood in the same relationship to Zvonitz now as Stenka Razin's fortress had done centuries ago. Guardian and ruler, governing not by force, but with money. Chayim looked round once more. What he saw satisfied him. He turned, and knocked at Yisroel's door.

Leah, Yisroel's wife, opened the door for him. A wide smile spread across her face when she recognised the visitor. She almost bowed him in, overwhelmed by the honour he did her household. Although he came frequently, she could never quite get used to the idea of the great Chayim Cooper coming to her house and liking it. Why, Chayim must be a millionaire at least. True, he had been poor once, but so also had been most rich men. This friendship between Chayim and Yisroel seemed as incongruous to her as a Rothschild being intimate with his secretary's valet.

'Is Yisroel in?' Chayim asked.

'Yes. Yes. Come in. Come in, Reb Chayim,' she replied eagerly, as if she were afraid he would change his mind at the very threshold.

Chayim blinked a little in the darkened room, his eyes still dazzled from the outside sunlight. Then he made out some dark blobs which resolved themselves into people and furniture. He recognised Moishe-Leib, Yisroel's eldest son, a boy of sixteen, sitting in the corner poring over a thick volume on the table. A little girl was curled up on the huge cold stove, fast asleep. The curtain that shut off the living-room parted, and Yisroel came in holding a beaker half-filled with a straw-coloured liquid. The other side of the curtain was his workroom. There he diluted the raw spirit with sixty per cent of water; the resultant vodka he sold to the Jewish innkeepers who retailed it to the moujiks. He put the beaker on the table and welcomed his guest. Leah hurriedly procured the best chair, the only upholstered one, and, dusting it hastily, set it before Chayim. He thanked her with a nod and sat down, Yisroel seating himself opposite.

For a while nothing was said. Yisroel was silent, fingering his side-locks, waiting for Chayim to speak. The magnate, however, was not inclined to open the conversation. He hummed softly, drumming on the table with his slender white fingers.

'Nu Reb Chayim,' said Yisroel at last, 'what's the news from town?'

'What news should there be?' Cooper replied. 'Kamenetz is not the capital of Russia. Now, if you asked me what was happening in Petersburg...'

'Petersburg! Have you heard something from Petersburg, Reb Chayim?'

'Well...' the magnate began. 'The Englander, Moses Montefiore, has been to see the Tsar...'

'No!' Yisroel ejaculated. 'A Jew to see the Tsar! And he actually saw him?'

Chayim nodded. 'He saw him, and spoke to him. Called him Nicholas, like I might call you Yisroel. He is a giant, this Englander, a Samson. They say the English queen won't move a step unless Moses Montefiore is by her side.'

Moishe-Leib raised his head from his book and sat up stiffly. To listen to such a conversation he could afford to neglect even the Talmud for a few minutes. His piercing blue eyes regarded Chayim so intently that the magnate could almost feel his words churning up excited channels in the boy's mind. Leah too stood transfixed in the centre of the room, her mouth slightly open. Wonder of wonders! A Jew to see the Tsar! Talk on, dear Reb Chayim. Talk on, for God's sake!

Chayim drummed on the table. He was enjoying himself. Playing the oracle was the role closest to his heart. He felt that next to being a businessman he would have liked to be an actor, although they were mostly thieves and vagabonds, Jewish gypsies. An actor. To hypnotise people. To know that not three, but three hundred or three thousand, were hanging on his words.

'Nu Reb Chayim? Nu Reb Chayim?' Yisroel interpolated excitedly, leaning forward, his hands on Cooper's knees.

'That's all I've heard,' said Chayim. 'He saw the Tsar. But something will come of it. Perhaps they will allow us to live in the capitals, Moscow and Petersburg. I am a Perve Gilde Koopetz, a merchant of the first guild, and they treat me like a criminal whenever I go there. Perhaps things will be easier now – who knows? You can be sure Moses Montefiore did not go away empty-handed. That would be an insult to the English queen, and even Bloody Nicolai knows that too...'

Yisroel tried to pump his friend further, but Chayim either knew nothing more or was reluctant to talk about it. He switched the subject on to business matters, chuckling over a deal he had just concluded in Kamenetz. Leah, no longer interested, went on with her housework, polishing the samovar until she saw pictures of the English lord in it, a huge man with side-whiskers, dressed like a German engineer. She saw the pygmy of a Tsar trembling before him like Pharaoh in the face of the other Moses. Perhaps he would do for them what the Lawgiver had done for their ancestors. Lead them out of Egypt. Out of bondage. God give you strength, Moses Montefiore! May angels stand before you and behind you, and the Heavenly Father himself talk out of your mouth!

Moishe-Leib lowered his head over the Talmud once more. Now, however, the philosophical speculations of the medieval rabbis seemed strangely dull. A dog set fire to a house with a burning brand carried in its mouth. Who was responsible for the fire? The owner of the dog or the man from whose house the dog had snatched the burning brand? The owner of the dog because. The dog. The man. Wood. Fire... And Jews would live in the capital cities. Universities. Citizens. Equal rights. Rabbi Ben Ezra said... said... said... It was useless. He had no head for the Talmud now. He closed the musty volume, put it on the shelf, excused himself and went into the street.

CHAPTER II

Stepan Skoboleff sat on the wheel of his wagon eating his dinner, a hunk of rye bread and an onion. Inside the cart, Grigori, his son, a truculent, tallow-haired boy of nineteen, was also eating. Between the shafts, an emaciated horse had its nose in a bag of chaff, chewing lazily, occasionally throwing its head up in the air with a snort, to the accompaniment of a jangle of cracked bells from its hooped beech-wood collar. But the snorting was a thin pretence, like the feeding; Kolka the horse was only half alive, a bundle of ribs from Stepan Skoboleff's farm.

Stepan was nearly seventy, a well-preserved moujik, although the years had begun to round his shoulders, throwing his huge head forward on to his chest. What little of his face was not covered by a matted growth of grey hair was wrinkled bronze. His small blue eyes were still shrewd and bright, as if laughing constantly at the hairy wart on the side of his broad pug nose.

Stepan sat on the wagon wheel trying to puzzle it all out. His toothless jaws worked up and down. Occasionally he spat out a lump of grit that had been baked in with the bread. Why did it have to be this way? He worked the whole season, sowed and reaped, planted seeds and tore up weeds, chopped wood, mended fences. From daybreak to sunset the sweat poured down his face. The earth yielded him a bountiful harvest, yet when he brought the fruits of his labour to market, sold them and purchased a fancy kerchief for the old woman, candles, paraffin, needles, thread and had one or two drinks, there was nothing left. Nothing at all. Why should it be so?

He and Grigori had been up since four in the morning heaping the cart with fresh green vegetables; the black juice of the moist earth still clung to their boots like dark blood protesting at the rape of innocent fields. Now the day was nearly spent. They had sold the whole of their load with the exception of half a basketful of eggs, but the few roubles had almost entirely vanished in the purchase of household necessities. Stepan scratched his head. One day he would get to the bottom of it. Must be these Jews. Father Vanka was right, they were to blame. Betrayers of Christ. They had crucified the Lord, and now the honest Russian peasant had to suffer. And yet, he knew Jews as poor as he was, and when a Russian bought his potatoes he gave less than a Jew. Still, it had always been this way, as long as he could remember. It would go on always, just the same. But why? This was too much of a puzzle for a poor man's head. Ivan Ivanovitch had been created to work in summer and starve in winter, alternating working with starving until he died. Then the Holy Virgin would take him in her arms and keep him well fed and warm for ever, and there would be no more worry, only rest. That would be a happy day when they straightened out his old bones for the last time. Rest – blessed word! But until the Holy Mother called him, he would have to keep on working.

His meal finished, he tied the crust of black bread carefully in a spotted red handkerchief and thrust it into a pocket of his homespun linen pantaloons to eat on the road back. He stood up and stretched himself; it had been a long day, he was beginning to feel tired. Suddenly he felt a sharp pain under his heart. He stood perfectly still hoping it would pass. Nothing like this had ever happened to him before. The pain increased and curled round his side, coming to rest between his shoulder blades like a core of red fire. He sat down on the wheel again and grasped the side of the wagon for support.

'Grigori!' he called weakly.

His son, sensing a note of alarm in the old man's voice, jumped out of the cart. Stepan's appearance gave him a shock. The broad nose seemed suddenly contracted, the wart stood out like an ugly blotch, the wrinkled skin around it a dirty yellow. The old man stretched a shaky claw towards Grigori and clutched the boy's arm, his chest heaving convulsively as if he were fighting for breath. Grigori bent over him. Twice he had to ask what was wrong before Stepan could answer.

'A pain... My heart... My heart, Grigori...'

The boy looked around wildly. There was no one about. He was torn between two impulses, hardly knowing whether to leave his father and run for help or wait till somebody came along. He broke into a cold sweat and bent over Stepan again, massaging his heart gently with a broad red palm.

'Steady, Father, steady,' he kept reassuring him. 'It'll soon blow over.'

A shadow fell across the cart. Grigori looked up. A young Jew was passing on the opposite side of the road.

'Hey, Zhid!' he called.

Moishe-Leib walked on. In his thoughts he was already in Petersburg, at the university. He must be a wonderful man this English Graf even if only half the things he had heard about him were true. He rode about in a golden carriage. Kings trembled at his glance. Perhaps he would see him one day in Petersburg... Petersburg... A rough hand caught his shoulder. Moishe-Leib turned, half expecting to see Moses Montefiore in person. He looked with amazement at the angry young moujik before him.

'Zhid!' roared Grigori. 'Don't you stop when a true Russian calls?'

'B... but...' Moishe-Leib began.

'Never mind,' said Grigori. 'My father's dying. Where does the feldsher live?'

'Hey!' A wheezy croak from Stepan interrupted him. The old man was on his feet again, close to the wagon, one hand resting on the wheel. 'Hey, Grishka!'

The boy ran across to him at once and Moishe-Leib followed.

'How is it now?' asked Grigori.

'Easier,' Stepan answered shortly. 'Come. Let's start for home.'

'Wait a minute, Father,' said Grigori urgently. 'You still look queer. You ought to see the feldsher. Maybe he could give you an ointment or something.'

'Feldsher!' growled Stepan. 'I want none of those sawbones. I've never been to one in my life, and I'm not starting now. Shto budet, to budet! What will be, will be... Feldsher! Huh! I'm not an old woman. Hop in, Grishka.'

Grigori jumped inside the cart while the old man unfastened Kolka's nosebag and tightened up the harness. Kolka threw his head back with a snort and pawed the rubble with his hooves. He could smell the fresh hay in his stall, he too was anxious to be home. Stepan put his foot on the wheel hub and raised himself from the ground, but his strength seemed to desert him in mid-air, he was unable to climb farther. He lowered himself shakily and stood still, his heart beating rapidly, the fire still poking between his shoulder blades. He shook his shaggy head, angry and disgusted at his weakness.

'No use, Grishka,' he said. 'I can't go on.'

Grigori was at his side in a moment. 'Far to the feldsher's?' he asked, turning to Moishe-Leib.

'Two minutes. Less perhaps.'

'Right,' said Grigori, putting one arm round his father's shoulders. 'Show us the way.'

'Don't be in such a hurry,' protested Stepan, refusing to budge. 'I'm not dead yet. I haven't decided whether I want to go to the feldsher or not. If there's anything a man can do, I can do it myself. I don't have to have a feldsher to put on a leech for me, and if it's in God's hands, then all the feldshers in Russia won't help. No. I'm not going.'

He sat down on the wheel again. Grigori looked at Moishe-Leib pleadingly. When his father had one of his obstinate fits, nothing could move him. Moishe-Leib shrugged his shoulders. What could he do? There was no arguing with a mad moujik. The horse whinnied impatiently.

'Listen,' said Grigori. 'Kolka wants to get home. Come to the feldsher and get something, otherwise Kolka will have to stay here all night.'

Stepan rose ponderously to his feet. That hadn't struck him. Kolka; that was different – but if the feldsher started letting blood or any of that other moonshine – 'All right,' he said resignedly. He started to walk slowly after Moishe-Leib, leaning heavily on his son. 'Wait a minute,' he cried, halting after a few paces. 'The eggs. Grishka, go and fetch the eggs.'

Only when the basket was safe on Grigori's arm did they continue towards the feldsher's, Stepan grumbling softly, cursing every other step when the pain gave an extra-sharp jab.

The feldsher Pinya, nicknamed 'Royfe', the healer, stood by his door when Moishe-Leib and the two moujiks arrived. He was a tall thin man with a straggly white beard, dressed exactly like all the other Jews of Zvonitz. A clumsy pair of glasses straddled his huge nose, although his eyesight was exceptionally keen for a man of sixty. Thirty years earlier he had seen a real doctor wearing spectacles, and adopting them as the badge of his profession, he had worn glasses ever since, taking them off only when he had work to do and when he went to sleep at night. All his family had been feldshers as far back as he could remember, and Pinya was dentist, bloodletter, apothecary, warder-off of the evil eye, weaver of charms and village barber.

He courteously invited the visitors to enter, and followed them, closing the door. He motioned Stepan to be seated on a low wooden bunk, and drew up a stool beside him. With a grand gesture he took off his spectacles, breathed on them loudly, polished them with a dirty handkerchief and put them in his pocket. Stepan watched him, fascinated; he had half a mind to ask for the glasses to look through them himself, but he thought better of it. Possibly they were bewitched; you never could tell what devilment these Jews were up to. Grigori's mouth was wide open; he stood by the side of the bunk, clutching Moishe-Leib's arm as though he were about to witness the most awe-inspiring ceremony.

'Now, tell me what is wrong,' said Pinya, talking softly in a wheedling tone as if the old moujik were a baby. 'Where does it hurt?'

Stepan did not answer. He was looking round the surgery. It seemed just like any other living-room. There was a huge stove in the corner, a table and a few chairs and an immense antique mahogany bureau against one wall almost covering it. On top of the bureau was a glass jar containing a clear liquid in which some fat leeches were wriggling uneasily. The leeches attracted Stepan. They looked like vigorous worms, would draw plenty of blood. Just a pinch of salt on the affected spot, a slight prick, and the leech would gorge till it fell off, sated. He was a fool to have come here just for that. Near the marsh at the back of his farm, they could be scooped up in handfuls.

'I said "Where does it hurt?"' Pinya repeated impatiently.

Stepan pulled his eyes away from the leeches. He answered half regretfully. 'Here – by my heart.' He traced the pain over his ribs with a thick forefinger. 'Here, in the back. But it's not so bad now,' he added as an afterthought.

'Take off your shirt,' said Pinya.

Stepan raised his arms, and Grigori, unfastening the neck tapes, slipped the garment over the old man's head.

'Lie down,' said Pinya. He placed two sensitive hands on Stepan's body and felt beneath his heart with long, delicate fingers.

'Here?'

Stepan nodded with a grunt. He felt better already. This was wasting time and money. He should never have come here. Another ten minutes' rest and he would have been himself anyhow, without all this fiddling about.

'Turn over.'

The old man turned obediently on his face and felt the smooth fingers, light as a girl's, fluttering between his shoulder blades. They came to rest on the affected spot and pressed down slightly, ever so slightly. Stepan winced.

'Here?'

'Yea, bogou! It's there all right!'

Pinya rose to his feet, and Stepan, resting on his elbows, twisted his head to watch him. He went to the bureau, and opening the door importantly as if every motion were exactly prescribed by some esoteric society of feldshers, extracted six glass bulbs. Then he took a candle from the shelf and, lighting it gravely, stuck it inside one of the bulbs. When he adjudged it to be sufficiently heated, the burning-up of the oxygen creating a partial vacuum inside, he clapped the bulb on Stepan's back where it held fast by suction, drawing up the vapours beneath the skin. Stepan let out an anticipatory yell, but instead of the excruciating pain he had expected, all he felt was a sharp tingling, a drawing-in of the skin. He was disappointed. He had no faith in a remedy that did not tug his heart out by the roots. Gingerly, his fingers felt the bulb sticking firmly to his flesh as if it were growing there. He sat up, and soon all six bulbs were grafted on to him like stiff shining limpets, three beneath his heart and three on his back. After a while the feldsher removed the bulbs and massaged the red circles with deft fingers, restoring the circulation of the blood.

Stepan got up from the bunk and slipped on his shirt. He drew a deep breath, another and another, filling his lungs. No. There was no more pain. He stretched his arms in the air, straining to the low ceiling, and brought them smartly to his sides. Still no pain. He was satisfied. He took up the basket of eggs and turned to Pinya.

'How much?'

'One moment,' said the feldsher. He crossed to the bureau, brought out a small box and returned to Stepan. 'Take this ointment,' he said. 'I prepared it myself from the very finest herbs. Rub it on your chest and back twice daily, once in the morning and again at night. The pains won't trouble you any more.'

'Spassebo,' said Stepan bowing slightly. 'Now, how much?'

Pinya thought for a moment. '... Er... For you, fifty copecks.'

'Fifty copecks?' Stepan straightened himself indignantly. Fifty copecks was two days' hard work in the fields, and here this Zhid put on half a dozen bunkes and expected that much remuneration. No wonder most Jews were rich!

'... Fifty copecks?' he asked again.

'Fifty copecks,' Pinya repeated. 'That's only for you.'

'Zhid!' Stepan bellowed, losing his temper. 'Are you mad? For me! Who do you think *I* am? Chayim Cooper?'

Pinya smiled. 'If it were Chayim Cooper it would be roubles, not copecks, for exactly the same treatment. Believe me, chelovek, fifty copecks is dirt cheap. Why, do you know there are eleven herbs in that ointment, made up in a special formula handed down in my family from generation to generation. Apart from their grinding and preparation, to buy those eleven herbs costs me nearly fifty copecks. The herbs are all I charge for, my labour I give you for nothing.'

'Well, you can keep your ointment,' said Stepan gruffly, throwing the box on the table. 'That makes us quits.' Fifty copecks! It was positive extortion. Besides, now he was himself again, he could eat this skinny old Jew. Give him fifty copecks, indeed! For what?

'But putting on bunkes!' cried Pinya excitely. 'You want that for nothing too?'

'I am an honest Christian,' Stepan replied. 'A Skoboleff never yet took anything for nothing. How much for your measly bunkes? – although I was nearly better without them.'

'Better!' cried Pinya scornfully. 'If you had come here a bit later, you'd have been carried out feet first. I, Pinya Royfe, saved you.

Give me twenty copecks – if you think you're worth that much!'

'Fifteen,' said Stepan doggedly. 'Not a copeck more!'

Pinya shrugged his shoulders. He could see he would never get anywhere with this moujik. 'Nu, loz-zein fifteen,' he answered resignedly.

Stepan scratched in his pantaloons. He had very little more than that altogether, and to go home with next to nothing, what would the old woman say? To spend money on vodka, that was understandable. But bunkes! – he would never hear the end of it. Suddenly he came to a decision. He counted out a score of eggs and laid them carefully on the table.

'There's your fifteen copecks,' he said. 'The best new-laid. Come, Grishka,' he added to his son, and followed by the open-mouthed boy, he crossed himself and stalked disdainfully from the room.

Pinya looked quizzically at the eggs, then turned to Moishe-Leib. 'Nice customer you brought me,' he said.

Moishe-Leib turned red. 'I'm sorry, Reb Pinya,' he replied, 'but I thought the old moujik was dying.'

'Dying!' Pinya laughed. 'It's only a bit of a cold. He'll live another fifty years yet – the old skinflint!' The feldsher gazed regretfully at his remuneration. 'Eggs he pays me! Now I'll have to eat veranekes every day for a month!'

He gathered the eggs from the table, put them carefully in a large bowl and shut them away in the bureau. Moishe-Leib remained hesitantly in the centre of the room. The feldsher knew all the village gossip; he was the retail news distributor. Everything came to him, he was the fountainhead, and from him sprayed in all directions the accumulated talk of the district. Moishe-Leib stayed on because he wanted Pinya to talk. He wanted to hear more about Moses Montefiore.

'Is it true about the Englander?' he asked after a while.

Pinya nodded. 'True. True. I had it from Chayim Cooper himself.'

'Then do you think something will come of it?' Moishe-Leib threw in eagerly.

'Maybe yes, and maybe no,' Pinya answered. 'Nicolai is a wily old fox. He'll promise our Moses everything, and the minute his back is turned all will go on exactly as before. Ah! If we only had the old Moses back to send him down at least a dozen plagues!'

The feldsher sighed deeply. Nothing less than a Moses could save the floundering, beaten Hebrews, squeezed and harassed from one end of the Pale of Settlement to the other... And poor Moishe-Leib! Part of that expressive sigh was for him too. Although he did not know it yet, Moishe-Leib had no reason to be uncertain about the future. His future was assured. Twenty-five years in Nicolai's army. Pinya shook his head and sighed again.

'You know they're calling up recruits in the autumn?' he said, running his long fingers nervously through his straggly beard.

'Recruits...?'

Moishe-Leib was puzzled by the apparent irrelevance. What connection did recruits have with Moses Montefiore? Perhaps the old man was hinting that he might be conscripted. But that was ridiculous, he was nowhere near old enough – not by years! Pinya's wits must be wandering, or, most likely, the moujik had upset him.

'Recruits...?' he repeated.

Pinya nodded. 'Mendel Hirsch was here this morning. The Kahal are at their wits' end. There aren't enough recruits from Zvonitz to fill the quota...'

Moishe-Leib turned pale. He knew well enough what that meant. 'So...?'

Pinya spread his hands in the air. 'So... the quota will have to be filled. If you were an only son, or had a father like Chayim Cooper, it would be all right. As it is... the quota will have to be filled...'

Moishe-Leib stumbled from the room. There was no more sunlight in the street for him. The Jewish Kahal had to produce the requisite number of soldiers, otherwise the elders themselves were pressed into service... Twenty-five years in some barbarous region; hundreds of miles from his home, his mother, from his family, from Jews. No Talmud to study, no services in the synagogue. Trifa to eat, pork and other filth. The very thought made him sick... He had heard tales of the youthful cantonists, of the horrors they had undergone only a few years back. Tiny children, little Jewish boys of eight and nine, kidnapped from their homes, torn from their mothers' arms and driven in pitiful droves to the other end of Russia. Dying like flies on the road, so emaciated and exhausted that even the Russian officers occasionally pitied them. Forcibly baptised, browbeaten and cudgelled unmercifully, fifty per cent never reaching their destination, the frail corpses discarded *en route* and left to rot beneath a few feet of earth, their bleached, undersized, brittle bones, milestones lining the wayside, enduring testimony to the glory of Nicholas I... And those same distant barracks were waiting for him too. Twenty-five years, a quarter of a century to be spent amongst hostile strangers. No wonder, when recruiting commenced, eligible young men ran away; hid themselves in black, oozy ditches, disappeared amongst the menacing shadows of dark, trackless forests, preferring bears to human vultures... The mournful song of the cantonists ran like the whimpering of a dying dog through the night of his muddled brain...

> Der ukas is urobgekummen auf Judische selner
> Seinen mir sich zulofen in die puste walder
> In alle puste walder seinen mir zulofen
> In puste Gruber seinen mir verlofen
> Weih! Oi weih...!

His heavy footsteps dragged homewards up the slope to the rhythm of the cantonists' dirge. The lament repeated itself again and again in his mind, and his heart echoed dully the lost, despairing wail. Oi weih! Woe is me! Woe is me!

CHAPTER III

Moishe-Leib's father made discreet inquiries. He discovered that Pinya was right. Pinya was always right. Moses Montefiore had left Russia in the greatest of good humours, convinced that his visit would result in some amelioration of the lot of his brethren, but Pinya and Yisroel knew better than to trust the promises of the Tsar. 'As well to tie a bell round a wolf's neck and expect him to become a calf,' said Pinya sagely to his friend. 'Recruiting will go on just the same. Take my advice, Yisroel, and get Moishe-Leib away from Zvonitz. The sooner, the better.'

Yisroel needed no further prompting. As the autumn drew closer, he arranged to smuggle Moishe-Leib across the Galician border. Uriel, the carter, waited outside the house while Moishe-Leib collected his belongings in a bundle. His sister Dvoirele frisked unconcernedly about the room; she was too young to understand or care what was happening. Isaac, his younger brother, was twelve, almost a man. His face was unnaturally sombre. He would miss Moishe-Leib, he looked up to him, idolised him almost. Now he was going away, perhaps for ever.

Leah sat in the corner swaying, little squeals of pain darting from her lips as she dabbed her swollen eyes, red from ceaseless weeping. She too had the feeling that she would never see Moishe-Leib again.

At last they were ready for the journey. Yisroel climbed into the cart while Leah embraced her son by the door, clinging to him as if she would never let him go. Then Moishe-Leib clambered in beside his father, and turned as the cart lumbered off. He saw a pathetic little group waving from the doorway. Now, even Dvoirele was crying, the behaviour of the rest of the family had at last succeeded in piercing her innocence. She wept because the others wept, although to her it was an incomprehensible catastrophe. Moishe-Leib's eyes picked her out and Dvoirele's was the last figure he saw as the cart turned the corner. Then he too broke down. Yisroel let him cry. After a while, he put a friendly arm round his shoulder and they drove on in silence.

They stopped in a wood about thirty versts from Zvonitz. Close by ran the little stream that separated Russia from Galicia. It was no more than twenty yards wide, and Yisroel knew exactly where it could be forded without difficulty. He had often made this same journey, crossing into Galicia and smuggling back contraband spirit. He left his son with Uriel and went towards the stream to reconnoitre. Soon he returned; the coast was clear. There was a guard on duty on the Russian side, but Yisroel knew him well, so there would be no danger from that source.

Uriel tied a bag of chaff round the horse's neck and made himself comfortable in the wagon. He watched Yisroel and Moishe-Leib set out on the last lap of their journey, their forms flitting like moving tree trunks through the interlaced light and shade of the forest until they disappeared. Then he heard the swishing of branches and dry wood crackling beneath their feet, then those sounds too died away and everything was quiet except for the soft rustle of leaves and the occasional call of a bird or the sleek scuffle of some small animal in the undergrowth. Uriel had a long wait ahead of him. He yawned. He tried talking to the horse, but the horse chewed stubbornly without even a nod of understanding. 'Go talk to a horse!' muttered Uriel resignedly. He made a pillow of some empty sacks and in a few moments was fast asleep.

At the edge of the clearing Yisroel took off his boots and tucked his trousers above his knees. Moishe-Leib did likewise, then under his father's direction he fastened his boots to the bundle containing his worldly goods and yoked them over his shoulders. At the water's edge the guard came striding towards them. The boy shivered with apprehension as he approached, an enormous fellow, ruddy-faced with a bushy black beard and tremendously long arms. Moishe-Leib felt like an errant schoolboy before an irate master, the stolen apples still in his hands. He gaped as the ogre drew closer, wondering what would happen next. Would the guard take him and truss him up like a chicken and throw him over his shoulder, or would he shoot him without any fuss? He hoped he would shoot. Better that way. Much better. Just a big black bang, then darkness... Yisroel stood his ground coolly and bowed as the obiestchik halted in front of them, the old man's nose almost rubbing the muzzle of the guard's cocked rifle.

'Good afternoon, sergeant,' he said.

'So it's you,' the obiestchik replied. 'What's it this time, business or pleasure?' he asked with a guffaw.

'Business, your honour,' said Yisroel, bowing still lower.

'Two of you, eh?' the guard chuckled. 'Business must be good.'

'This is my son,' Yisroel replied. 'I am getting too old for this sort of thing any longer. He will be crossing over instead of me in future.'

'Oh well,' said the guard. 'What have you got?'

'The usual.'

Yisroel produced a flask filled with vodka and gave it to him. The obiestchik pulled out the cork with his teeth and put his nose to the neck of the flask. He grinned, and smacked his lips in anticipation. 'Spassebo!' he said, his eyes never leaving the vodka. Without another word he turned his back to them, stuck the flask down the side of his boot and marched off.

They reached the opposite bank without wetting their knees. The guards on the Galician side were conveniently blind. They would get their cut on the way back. Moishe-Leib and Yisroel sat down on the grass and put on their boots, then they started for the first village, Kudrintza. On the road the boy kept shivering violently as if he had the fever. Yisroel looked at him anxiously and stopped several times to inquire how he felt. The boy nodded reassuringly but did not talk much in case his voice betrayed his extreme nervousness. This was Galicia, Freedom, yet Moishe-Leib felt as if he were marching to an execution.

In half an hour they reached Kudrintza. The Jews they passed in the village wore a pinched, hungry look, unlike the bronzed toughness of Chayim Cooper's raftsmen. Yisroel exchanged greetings with several of them, but did not stop to gossip, passing on to Reb Shalom's house.

A tall, dark girl, two long black braids hanging over her shoulders, opened the door for them. She smiled at Yisroel but dropped her eyes when she met Moishe-Leib's glance and blushed deeply. She was Lantze, the eldest daughter, about a year Moishe-Leib's senior. She had been expecting them to come and wanted to be the first to see the new boarder.

Yisroel and his son kissed the talisman on the doorpost and entered Moishe-Leib's new home. A dignified old man with a long grey beard got up from the table and greeted them gravely.

'Shalom aleichem, Reb Yisroel; shalom aleichem, my son.'

Yisroel shook his hand warmly. 'Peace be with you, Reb Shalom. With you, and with all your house.'

They seated themselves at the table, and Lantze put on the samovar. Reb Shalom's wife came in and helped the girl to prepare tea. While his father and Reb Shalom were talking together, Moishe-Leib was taking in the details of the room. It was almost like his own in Zvonitz. The huge stove hugged the wall in one corner just as at home, the table and chairs had a solid, comfortable look, the table to eat on, chairs to sit on without any frippery-frapperies. On one wall there was an illuminated Hebrew parchment, and near by a faded picture of a white-bearded ancient in a skullcap, probably some noted local rabbi. Moishe-Leib missed the upholstered chair. That had been a noble piece of furniture in his father's house. Here everything looked as though it had always been part of a poor man's home, intimately bound up with a pauper's life. He kept glancing surreptitiously at Lantze, growing hot and cold whenever he met her eyes. The only females he knew well were his mother and Dvoirele. He wondered how it would be with her...

After what seemed an interminable time, the three men retired to an inner room and Reb Shalom tested Moishe-Leib's knowledge of the Talmud. At the conclusion of a searching examination he pronounced himself satisfied, and accepted Moishe-Leib as a pupil. Yisroel sighed with relief. Reb Shalom was a pious man and a brilliant scholar; under him Moishe-Leib would grow up strong in the knowledge of the Law. He kissed his son affectionately, passing his thin, shaky hands over the boy's smooth face. Moishe-Leib was conscious only of two large, suffering dark eyes and a maze of wrinkles puckering the sockets. Yisroel looked at Moishe-Leib for a long time in silence as if to engrave a permanent picture of him on his mind. Then he turned his face away and like a very old man shuffled to the door.

'Write to your mother,' he said dully, and was gone.

★

Reb Shalom was a melumed, a teacher of Hebrew, and a scribe. With his delicate, minute writing, he traced in Hebrew the four keystones of Judaism on tiny strips of parchment that formed the cores of phylacteries, and etched the clarion call of Judah, 'Hear O Israel, the Lord our God, the Lord is One', into the interiors of mezzuzoth that were affixed as a sign before Jehovah on the doorposts of every Jewish house. He also wrote scrolls, laboriously copying by hand every word of the five books of Moses. He was busy from morning till night, writing, praying and teaching, yet his family rarely had sufficient to eat, so he welcomed the extra few gulden that Moishe-Leib would provide. Shimshon, the youngest son, a tall, slim youth of nineteen, helped his father; the elder brother Velvel, a thinly bearded ascetic-looking man in the early twenties, was still a student. Velvel's behaviour was queer at times, so the family left him severely alone, regarding him as an over-learned eccentric. Apart from Lantze there were two more girls, Rachel who was nearly fifteen, and Baile, a precocious child of twelve.

Moishe-Leib found the household strange at first. He blushed and stammered whenever Lantze spoke to him. Reb Shalom's wife, Celia, he found easier to get on with, she was so like his own mother. Shimshon, a plodding industrious youth without any great capabilities, had to be shown what to do, then did it more or less well; although he was older than Moishe-Leib, the newcomer soon took to bossing him, and Shimshon obeyed his orders good-naturedly, since it was less trouble than arguing.

On his second night at Kudrintza, Moishe-Leib discovered one of Velvel's peculiarities. The new boarder was tossing about on his bunk, strung between the borderline of sleep and consciousness, when he heard curious sounds issuing from the tiny outhouse. He sat up wide awake and listened. He recognised Velvel's voice, so he tiptoed to the back door and silently passed into the outhouse. Velvel was poring over a prayer book by the light of a flickering candle. Occasionally he straightened himself and sung an incantation in Hebrew. Moishe-Leib recognised the words, they were part of the New Year service, but the tune was strange and unearthly, quite unlike the traditional melodies of Rosh Hashanah. Velvel sang a few phrases but seemed dissatisfied. He repeated them again, varying a few notes. Pausing, as if comparing the tunes, he nodded to himself and wrote something in a book, then he duplicated the whole performance.

Suddenly Velvel became conscious of Moishe-Leib's presence. He turned slowly and the boy was immediately startled by the wild, staring eyes that seemed to burn with an unholy fire, the unsteady candle flame shading his hollow cheeks into a diabolical tautness. Remembering the hints the others had dropped about him, Moishe-Leib backed away in alarm, but Velvel smiled gently, and beckoned him disarmingly to come closer.

'You were listening?' he asked eagerly.

Moishe-Leib nodded.

'Well, what do you think of it?' said Velvel.

Moishe-Leib nodded again. The gesture might have meant anything. Velvel was encouraged. He caught Moishe-Leib's arm and showed him the hieroglyphics in the book.

'My own compositions,' he said excitedly. 'One day, cantors will sing them in the synagogues.'

He had never been taught music, but songs surged up from within him. To capture the elusive tunes he had invented his own system of staff notation: 1 was doh, 2 ray, 3 me, and so on up the scale. A big 1 was a sharp, a small 1 a flat. Whenever the music started bubbling in his head, he went to the outhouse and wrote it down. They all thought he was mad, but he was a musician. It was a gift from God. All this he explained excitedly to Moishe-Leib, who, as the recital went on, found it more and more difficult to stay awake. At last, the boy tore himself away and dropped wearily on his bunk, while in the outhouse Velvel remained tirelessly intoning new hymns to the Lord.

In the morning, Moishe-Leib told Reb Shalom what he had witnessed. The old man stroked his beard and sighed deeply.

'Yes,' he said, 'Velvel is the only strange one in the family, but the good Lord has blessed me with four sound children, so who am I to complain of the fifth? Supposing he were a cripple or dumb or blind? As it is, he is a little mad, but he is very learned and harms nobody.' ... Reb Shalom sighed again and continued: 'He was training to become a shochet, a ritual slaughterer, and had passed all the examinations with ease. On the day he was to begin duty in the slaughterhouse they brought him a chicken to kill. He put the handle of the knife in his mouth, then twisted the chicken's throat, ready to cut the jugular. Then he looked at the chicken and cried out that it spoke to him, that the chicken said: "Velvel, don't kill me!" He threw the chicken on one side and the knife on the other, and ran out of the slaughterhouse as if the devil were chasing him, and has never been near it since.'

The old man shook his head regretfully. Although he had said, 'Who am I to complain?' the conduct of his eldest son hurt him deeply, the more so since Velvel had shown promise of attaining the highest rabbinical laurels. And almost as important was the fact that he would have been earning his own living by this time instead of remaining an extra mouth to feed. It was bad enough if, God forbid, a child were physically disabled and had to be a drag on its parents, but an able-bodied man content to eat the scraps from his father's meagre table was sufficient to try the patience of a Job, especially when this Job had in addition to bring up three strapping girls, and find husbands for them!

Reb Shalom got up from the table, dismissed Velvel and the girls from his mind and lovingly fingered the sacred books on the shelf. God was good after all! If He gave sorrows with one hand, He showered blessings with the other. The old man's face dropped his worried, worldly look and assumed once more the saintly mask of the ascetic. The Holy Scriptures more than compensated for the roughness and hardships of everyday life. 'Adoishem, Adoishem, el rachoom vechanoon,' words of praise, clearing his mind of rancour. 'The Lord. The Lord. Gracious and merciful.' He selected a musty tome and turned to Moishe-Leib.

'Come, my son,' he said, 'let us try a little of this gemarrah today.'

Moishe-Leib grew more and more friendly with Lantze. They chatted unconstrainedly while she was busy about the house and went for long walks together in the evenings, and after a year of companionship, the inevitable happened, Moishe-Leib discovered he was in love.

Reb Shalom was in a quandary when Moishe-Leib asked him for Lantze's hand. If he gave his permission he would lose a pupil and a paying boarder, while if he withheld it, he would lose a son-in-law, and Lantze a husband. His parental solicitude triumphed, however, and Moishe-Leib and Lantze were married, and moved into the outhouse from which the lumber and tomcats had been hastily dispossessed.

After the customary first year of kest, during which the young husband was kept by the bride's father, Moishe-Leib tried to find a job in order to contribute something to the communal exchequer. He had had one year's board and lodging free; now, for the rest of his life, he was obliged to provide due sustenance for a wife. In Kudrintza, that was not so easy to do. His sole professional equipment was a knowledge of the Talmud, and every second Jew in the village knew as much as he did or more. Eventually his father-in-law's influence procured him some pupils who, ferreting out his meekness with childish cunning, plagued the life out of him till he could stand it no longer.

He hungered to go back to his home town. The nostalgia had been growing in him steadily, until, after four years, he almost imagined heaven to be a substitute for Zvonitz. He was hungry in a literal sense too. The combined efforts of all the wage-earners of Reb Shalom's household sufficed to provide the family with not more than one square meal daily, which consisted in the main of black bread and a communal stew of potatoes, lentils and cabbage. On Friday night and Saturday there was meat or fish, sometimes both, but not often. And Moishe-Leib wanted to be a father. He had been married for three years, but his wife showed no signs of pregnancy. Lantze was virile enough, in fact he had not the strength to appease her constant demands satis-factorily, so he felt the blame rested with him, and in turn he shifted the onus on to the vegetables. How could a man have children if he fed on grass like a cow? Meat was what he wanted, red, juicy, grilled meat, or boiled meat, but meat, meat.

Suddenly, without any warning, Moishe-Leib turned up in Zvonitz. His father looked at him as though he were a ghost, and Leah first wept with joy at the sight of his face, then wept again at the gaunt scarecrow her son had become. After the first reckless pleasure of reunion, they remembered that Moishe-Leib was still of military age, and liable at any time to be drafted into the army. They implored him to go back to Galicia, but he refused point blank, and nothing could move him. Now that he had tasted real food once more, nothing in the world would induce him to return.

As a last resource, they went to Pinya for advice. The feldsher shook his head when confronted by the anxious parents and their son. Moishe-Leib was now technically a deserter; if the boy were caught they would make it hot for him. The only way out was to prove some disablement, but Moishe-Leib, although thin as a twig, was unfortunately quite sound. Pinya was thereupon commissioned to improve on nature. He strapped the trigger and second fingers of Moishe-Leib's right hand tightly over his palm. Every other day the strap was drawn still tighter, until after several weeks the cartilages of the knuckle joints cracked, and broke completely.

When the strap was finally removed, two blue, choked fingers clung lifelessly over the palm. Moishe-Leib would never be able to use them again, he was now a bona fide cripple. Pinya received his payment, glanced down proudly at his handiwork, and said in the tone of a surgeon at the successful conclusion of a particularly hazardous operation: 'Now let Nicolai make a soldier of you if he can!'

CHAPTER IV

As soon as Moishe-Leib was settled once more in his father's house, he sent for Lantze. A corner of the room had been partitioned off for the use of the young couple, but, although it had none of the privacy of their outhouse in Kudrintza, the placid daughter of Reb Shalom did not complain. She was only too glad to have Moishe-Leib beside her once more.

The meat diet began to have its effect on Moishe-Leib. Lantze became as prolific as a rabbit. Her first two children died, but the third, a girl, survived. Her husband was bitterly disappointed. Its two predecessors had been boys; a girl was only half a child, its prayers would have no value in the ears of the Lord, whereas a boy could perpetuate his name in the afterlife and save his spirit from haunting the earth in search of a kadish. Moishe-Leib kept on eating meat and hoping for the best.

Two years after the birth of Miriam, Lantze was delivered of a boy. She called him Samuel in the fullness of her heart after the son of that ancient Jewess Hannah, because she had begged him of the Lord.

Now he had his kadish, Moishe-Leib was satisfied, but bearing children had become a habit with Lantze, and her womb blossomed continually long after they had any desire for more. The babies were undersized weaklings, and she buried them as monotonously as she brought them into the world.

Suddenly, Moishe-Leib's mother died. Leah had never been ill in her life, but one day she complained of abdominal pains. Yisroel was mildly worried, but did nothing about it; it was not so terrible or she would not stay on her feet all day and work the way she did. That was just like Leah. She suffered agonies with only an occasional complaint. She wilted before their eyes until, when she took to her bed, it was too late. She died the same evening, less than a fortnight after the first portent of death had been wrung from her lips.

The old man survived her by barely a year, and when Moishe-Leib buried his father, he found himself in sole control of Yisroel's business. Isaac, his younger brother, was married, and like every other brawny youth in Zvonitz, worked on Chayim Cooper's rafts. Dvoirele had married too, and lived in the county town Kamenetz Podolsk with her husband, a general dealer in a small way.

For several months, Moishe-Leib carried on in the old systematic fashion of his father, then he developed a taste for his own wares. At first he contented himself with sampling occasional sips of vodka, but as time went on he drank more than he sold. For just over a twelvemonth, Yisroel's edifice held out, then the painstaking labour of years crashed to the ground. Moishe-Leib had no more money, and nobody would give him credit.

Reluctantly he went to work for another spirit merchant, but found his new master's liquor even more to his liking. On the third day of his employment, at four o'clock in the afternoon, two burly workmen lugged Moishe-Leib to his house and dropped him contemptuously in a heap on the floor. At first Lantze was alarmed, but when she put her face to his, and smelled the sickly odour of sour vodka, she breathed a prayer of relief and dragged him to his bunk. He slept placidly till early next morning, a smile of seraphic content on his face, while Lantze kept watch over him, shooing off Samuel and Miriam whenever they approached too closely or seemed liked making a noise sufficient to wake him.

Moishe-Leib never went out to work again. He found a few pupils whom he taught elementary Hebrew, and spent the rest of his time studying in the synagogue. Every Saturday after the morning service, he partook of kiddush with some favoured chasidim in Chayim Cooper's house, and returned home pleasantly fuddled to sleep until the evening. The rest of the week had no meaning to him, he muddled through it haphazardly, his twinkling blue eyes jesting through six days in anticipation of heaven – Chayim Cooper's Saturday afternoons.

Lantze could not appreciate Moishe-Leib's idea of heaven. It was no use arguing with him, he dismissed her remonstrances with a joke, chucking her affectionately under the chin, or pinching her rump good-humouredly. His mind was totally divorced from the problems of this world; only two things interested him, the

Talmud and vodka. Lantze, however, had to bring up two children. She developed the peculiar mania that Samuel and Miriam were entitled to eat at least once a day. Somehow, she scraped together a few roubles, and selling her old home on the hill bought a little shop lower down in the market. There she sold paraffin, boots, needles, thread and various other commodities to the moujiks of the outlying district. So, while Moishe-Leib dedicated his life to the Law and Chayim Cooper's Saturday afternoons, Lantze scratched some sort of living from her shop, and in the intervals bore children, and just as regularly buried them.

Miriam grew up into a tall, buxom young woman, a replica of what Lantze had looked like as a girl. At nineteen, she was already married, while Samuel, a year younger, was still studying for his rabbinical degree. Miriam became pregnant almost immediately, but Lantze's joy at the expectation of a grandchild was dulled by the discovery soon after that she too was heavy with child.

Lantze was well on in the forties. For several years now she had been spared the agonies, twofold for her, of parturition. She had imagined that she was finished now for ever with laboriously squeezing children from her womb. The travail did not worry her, did not even incommode her; what made her so bitter was that her suffering had no concrete aftermath, that she had to go through nine months of sickness and pain in order to be delivered of a coffin.

She shut in her sorrow within her, brooding over it continually. She moodily watched her stomach distending week by week, until the first struggles of the embryo roused her more sharply to the fact that the child was awake inside her, clamouring for a chance to live. Every twist and turn of the rapidly growing little body seemed to reproach her, to taunt her as a worse than empty vessel, the first flutterings of new life causing her unbearable anguish.

One day, she closed the shop and disappeared. Only Moishe-Leib knew where she had gone. When his neighbours inquired of him what had happened to Lantze, he winked slyly and said: 'I think she's run away with a soldier.'

The little town of Chotin, in the adjacent province of Bessarabia, was crowded with visitors. A match had been arranged between the representatives of two chasidic dynasties. The daughter of a famous Russian tzadik was to be married to the son of an equally famous Galician miracle worker. Neither side would agree to the nuptials being held in the other's town, so the honour fell to Chotin on the border.

The Jewish quarter was crowded with rabbis, saints, tzadiks and their adoring disciples. Lantze threaded her way through the happy, argumentative chasidim, stopping only to inquire where she could find the celebrated Reb David-Moishe, the Rabbi of Chertkof. The tzadik was the eldest son of the late Rabbi Yisroel of Regen, and lived like a medieval king in Chertkof, waited on hand and foot by a crowd of retainers who lapped up his most banal utterances as priceless pearls dropped from the fountainhead of wisdom. He had been invited with his two brothers to the wedding, and Moishe-Leib, who was a devout follower of Reb David-Moishe, had told Lantze where to find him.

The chasid who opened the door for her was the Rabbi of Chertkof's personal attendant. He was a little weasel-faced man with sharp, crafty eyes. A tiny black skullcap was perched at the back of his head, and two greasy side-locks corkscrewed over his ears. He wore a long black gabardine over dark-stained satin knee breeches and once-white woollen stockings. He kept the woman waiting on the threshold while he looked her over impudently. His face dropped its usual servile expression as he noted her darned, well-worn garments, and his voice took on an imperious tone as he inquired her business.

'I want to see the Rabbi,' said Lantze humbly.

'Reb David-Moishe is very busy,' replied the lackey, without budging from the door.

Lantze took out a rouble from a knotted handkerchief and gave it to him. Grudgingly, he allowed her to enter the room.

'What is it you want, woman?' he demanded.

'I want to see the Rabbi,' Lantze repeated.

The little Jew looked her over. With a smirk he pointed at her belly.

'About that, eh?'

Lantze nodded.

'The first?' he inquired.

Lantze shook her head. 'No. This is the twelfth.'

'The twelfth!' The little rat-face broke into a sharp yellow-toothed grin. 'You don't want the Rabbi,' he spat at her with a malicious gurgle. 'It's a midwife you need!'

Lantze, without reply, resignedly fished out another rouble from her handkerchief. She was determined to see the Rabbi and the second rouble had the desired effect. The little Jew, his movements even sharp and perky like a rodent's, darted out of the room like a piebald mouse, and soon returned to escort her to the presence. The Rabbi dismissed his retainer with a wave of his plump white hand and closed the bulky volume that lay in front of him on the table. Lantze stood before the Rabbi humbly, her head lowered, her heart racing out of her bosom; stammeringly, in an almost inaudible voice, she told him who she was, and why she had sought him out.

The Rabbi rose to his feet, managing in spite of his short stature to appear an imposing figure. He was dressed like his disciple, but the garments were of better quality and scrupulously clean. He looked kindly at Lantze and stroked his thick black beard. A certain nobleness seemed to radiate from him, an animal magnetism that encompassed the woman and soothed and quietened her.

'So you are Moishe-Leib's wife,' he said in a rich voice, softly, as if talking to himself. 'Moishe-Leib is a Jew in a thousand. He is a dear soul. He has often spoken to me of you.'

A gentle smile suffused his countenance. It was difficult to think of the gay, careless Moishe-Leib without a smile. His large blue eyes were fixed on the woman, and slowly, as if in answer to a command, she lifted her head and stared straight at him. While he looked at her, she felt strong and confident. The Lord surely was in this room! Suddenly, without a word, she sank to her feet and kissed the hem of the Rabbi's gabardine, while years of accumulated tears burst loose and crinkled, at her moist grasp, his saintly garment.

Reb David-Moishe helped her gently to her feet. He closed his eyes and held his hands clasped together before him, in prayer. His body stiffened and trembled with an uncanny intensity like an epileptic before a fit. After a few moments he opened his eyes, but there was a rapt, faraway look in them.

'Go home, daughter,' he said in a weak voice, as if he had been wrestling with a spirit and was physically weary. 'Go home. Your child will live. It will be a boy. His fame will spread across the world, and his name will be on millions of lips.'

He sat down a little shakily and reopened the volume with a trembling hand. He seemed to have forgotten all about Lantze. She tried to speak to him, but the Rabbi did not answer. Radiantly, like a bride just betrothed, she tiptoed from the room.

Some four weeks later, her daughter Miriam was delivered of a girl, a plump, pink, healthy baby; and a month after that, in the middle of a blazing July, Lantze felt that her time had come. She rose on Friday at two in the morning to prepare for the Sabbath as she did every week. She dragged her heavy body about the house, performing her usual chores. She prepared the chicken, and cut dough into thin strips for the soup, and put the plaited Sabbath bread, fancifully besprinkled with black poppy seeds, in the oven. Later in the day she went into the fields and laboriously scooped up half a pailful of cow's dung. This she mixed with water till it was a thick, dark green paste, then she went on her hands and knees and painted the earthen floor of the hovel. Long usage had inured her to the objectionable smell; at least the rooms would look clean over the Sabbath. All the while, she felt her pains increasing in frequency, and the dull ache at the base of her spine grew sharper and sharper.

The next morning when Moishe-Leib went to the synagogue she was still in labour. She was resting now, in bed, and Miriam and a midwife were seated beside her. In a basket in the corner, Ruth, Miriam's baby, lay squalling with the full power of her tiny lungs. Moishe-Leib was not disturbed in the slightest by his wife's condition. He had seen her go through this eleven times before, and, for all he knew, she might have to endure it eleven times again. With God all things were possible, he reflected. He had singled Sarah out for miracles, maybe Lantze would be similarly favoured.

In the synagogue, Moishe-Leib gave himself up to the aesthetic pleasure of the liturgy. About ten o'clock there was a break in the service and a tiny wizened old man climbed on to the cantor's raised platform and, swaying from side to side, intoned in a thin nasal tenor the weekly portion of the Law. Moishe-Leib, huddled up like a Bedouin in his striped woollen praying shawl, his eyes shut, followed the verbal involutions keenly, testing every syllable in case the bulkeraye gave the wrong emphasis to a word, or sang it on a false note. The sedrah was the twenty-fifth chapter of the Book of Numbers.

And, behold, one of the children of Israel came and brought unto his brethren a Midianitish woman in the sight of Moses, and in the sight of all the congregation of the children of Israel, who were weeping before the door of the tabernacle of the congregation.

And when Phineas, the son of Eleazar, the son of Aaron the priest, saw it, he rose up from amongst the congregation, and took a javelin in his hand;

And he went after the man of Israel into the tent, and thrust both of them through, the man of Israel, and the woman through her belly. So the plague was stayed from the children of Israel.

And those that died in the plague were twenty and four thousand.

And the Lord spake unto Moses saying,

'Phineas, the son of Eleazar, the son of Aaron the priest, hath turned my wrath away from the children of Israel, while he was zealous for my sake amongst them, that I consume not the children of Israel in my jealousy.

'Wherefore say, Behold, I give unto him my covenant of peace:

'And he shall have it, and his seed after him, even the covenant of an everlasting priesthood; because he was zealous for his God, and made an atonement for the children of Israel.'

The reader adjusted his praying shawl more closely round his shoulders and paused for breath, swaying from side to side like a metronome. At that moment the beadle came to Moishe-Leib and tapped him on the shoulder. He had brought a message from Miriam. Lantze had been delivered of a boy. Mother and child were both doing well. Moishe-Leib breathed a sigh of thankfulness. Lantze he expected to be all right, the child alone had worried him. He muttered a little prayer, then he restored his whole attention to the piping of the shrouded mummy on the platform.

After the service, he went home to see the baby. It was a tiny, red, wrinkled thing, its head covered with a tangled growth of soft black hair. Swathed in a huge white shawl it lay placidly in the bed beside Lantze, protected in the crook of her right arm, its tiny face screwed up, the little mouth gasping like a fish. Lantze in a white cotton nightdress, flushed from her exertions, sat up proudly on two enormous pillows. She felt like a queen who has given birth to a long-awaited crown prince. She knew her son would live. Reb David-Moishe had said so. And he would grow up healthy and strong, and his fame would go across the world, and his name would be on millions of lips. Moishe-Leib kissed his son tenderly on the forehead and caressed his wife affectionately. The Rabbi had spoken; the child would live, he had no doubts whatever on that score. He left Lantze and his son in the care of Miriam and the stout little midwife, and with a glad heart flew to Chayim Cooper, and that afternoon he came home more drunk than usual.

The same evening, a messenger was dispatched post-haste to Chertkof to inform the Rabbi of the news. The next day he returned with David-Moishe's blessing, and a suggestion that the child be named Phineas, after the hero of the weekly portion. To Moishe-Leib a suggestion from the Rabbi was tantamount to a command. Accordingly, on the following Saturday, with all the rites and pomp of circumcision, Lantze's child entered into the covenant of Abraham and was named Phineas after the son of Eleazar, the son of Aaron, the high priest of Israel.

CHAPTER V

Little Phineas seemed determined to prove David-Moishe a false prophet. He was sickly from the start and refused to take the breast. Then, when after much patient cajoling he was inveigled into sucking the huge, purple nipples, Lantze's copious flow of milk dried up, and Phineas howled night after night with hungry vexation. Miriam came to his aid. She had enough for Ruth and to spare. She fed her own child first, then took Phineas on her lap and saw him greedily suck in her rich creamy milk till it trickled in two tiny rivulets from the sides of his mouth. Lantze watched over him as though he were the Messiah incarnate. Miriam's milk alone did not satisfy her; wherever Lantze saw a big healthy woman with huge, milk-laden breasts, she begged a meal for Phineas, and gorged him with liquid life.

Phineas put on flesh, and his cheeks bloomed with health. Now, when he howled, his lungs let out a clear, lusty cry. Lantze bounced him on her knees and made grandiose plans for his future. She lavished on him a nine-fold love, the sum of her affection for his prematurely deceased playmates. He grew up straight and sturdy, clear-eyed and nimble-witted. Lantze looked at him often and lovingly, part fulfilment of the Rabbi's prophecy. Reb David-Moishe had said... She wondered what Phineas would be, what Phineas would do. 'Dear God,' she caught herself praying repeatedly, 'let me live to see the day – the day!'

Moishe-Leib, as he grew older, grew lazier. He gave up his few Hebrew pupils, and devoted his entire time to studying in the synagogue; occasionally, and then only after a great deal of arguing, he would condescend to help his wife in the shop. Samuel was concluding his studies in Kamenetz Podolsk and appeared to have a brilliant Talmudic career ahead of him. Phineas's religious education, however, could not be neglected. That was the passport, the most esteemed passport, to any decent Jewish society. There were no schools in Zvonitz, and in any case, secular education, where the high cost was no obstacle, was decried and sneered at as being totally unnecessary for a practising Jew, which in a way was true, because the Russian schools of those days, if their teaching made any impression at all, led straight to the baptismal font. Phineas was therefore enrolled at the age of six in the cheder of Obish the Lame.

Obish was the ugliest person in Zvonitz and for miles around. He was short and stumpy, and dark-complexioned, his gross, irregular features adorned by vast numbers of warts. In addition, he had a slight hump on one shoulder blade, and the leg on the same side was two inches shorter than its fellow. Obish had a disposition to match his physical comeliness. He was the most surly tutor in the district, a martinet and a tyrant, but his methods produced good scholastic results, which were the only results that mattered to the scrupulously orthodox Jews of Zvonitz.

The school was in Obish's tiny back room. Around a long plain deal table, twelve or more children, between the ages of five and thirteen, were cooped up every afternoon for four hours at a session. Outside, the sun might smile and throw golden rings on the Zvonchik, birds might call enticingly in the woods and the springy turf be just begging to be jumped on and rolled over, but Phineas and his classmates were sentenced for a sixth of the day to the dark, airless little room.

Obish sat on a chair, raised like a throne at the head of the table. On either side of him, his pupils were ranged on two long benches in order of seniority. The more advanced their knowledge of the Law, the closer they moved to Obish, but their pride in the progress of their studies was tempered by a wholesale dread of the tutor's right arm.

Obish always started off the session with a little prayer. After that, he glanced at his immature audience in silence, first collectively, then balefully singling out quaking individuals. In silky tones he repeated his favourite quotation from the book of Proverbs. 'He that spareth his rod, hateth his son, but he that loveth him, chasteneth him betimes.' It was no small consolation to Phineas, nursing a sore backside, to know that Obish's actions were ratified and sanctified by no less an authority than King Solomon himself.

Prominently displayed from a hook on the wall hung a leathern thong, like a silky brown snake. That was merely a symbol, however, for Obish rarely used it. If a child's behaviour displeased him, he would call the culprit to the head of the table. In his humblest tone he would beg the boy's pardon, and plead with him to take down his trousers. Then the criminal would go across his knee, and Obish's broad palm would caress the soft, naked buttocks. Several times Obish's hand would go up in the air, and the boy, his eyes screwed together, his heart hanging on a string, would wait for the hand to descend. When it did come down, the boy usually howled in anticipation, but Obish would be as gentle as a mother, his hand barely brushing the victim's skin. At last, tiring of this refined torture, Obish would lay his silkiness aside and, grabbing between his thumb and forefinger a lump of the child's flesh, would twist it viciously, as if trying to detach it from the rest of his body. Then the boy would slither painfully off his knees and limp back in agony to his hard seat, upon which he was now in no condition to sit.

Only once did Phineas remember the leathern thong in use. Yossul, the carter's son, a boy of eight, had made a mistake in translation. Obish called him before the seat of judgement and looked sternly at him. With Yossul, who was something of a dunce, he had adopted a different technique. He no longer apologised to the boy, because sarcasm was wasted on him, Yossul never howled apprehensively at his sadistic approaches. He would lower his trousers stolidly without a word from Obish, and not a murmur was wrung from him till his imprisoned flesh was actually turning blue in the vice of the teacher's grip.

On one occasion, Yossul refused to allow himself to be man-handled. Obish jumped up in a towering rage. This was mutiny! He chased Yossul about the room, but the boy was too nimble to fall into Obish's arms. He taunted the teacher on his infirmity. 'Lame one! Lame one!' he called. This was to Obish like the picador's dart to a bull. He snatched the leathern thong from the wall and redoubled his efforts to catch the boy. He might have run round the table till he collapsed from dizziness, had not his wife come in to discover the cause of all the shouting. Her stout figure effectively blocked the door. Obish, seizing his chance, shifted the table broadside to one end of the room and advanced on his trapped tormentor like a hungry hyena. He threw himself on Yossul, beating him about the face and head with the leathern snake until the boy was streaming with blood. Obish's wife pulled her husband off with difficulty, afraid that he might kill the child, or else inflict some serious injury. As it was, Yossul remained sufficiently conscious to drag himself home and bathe his wounds as best as he could.

When his father returned from work in the evening and learned what had happened, he gave Yossul another thrashing. His son must be indeed a blackguard to force Obish to beat him like that! He left the boy whimpering in a corner and went to Obish to apologise for his son's misbehaviour and to beg the teacher to take him back. Obish was adamant. He had never liked Yossul, and liked him less now after the jibes at his infirmity. The very thought made him seethe. With a great show of injured pride, he dismissed the husky carter. He said he would think the matter over, but could make no promises.

Yossul's father went home in a raving temper. He himself was illiterate, so he worshipped learning all the more. He had set his heart on Yossul's becoming at least a Rabbi to compensate for the meagreness of his own religious equipment. The boy, too hurt and miserable to crawl away, was still whimpering in the corner. The carter strode over to him like an angry bear, picked him up, laid him across his knees and spanked him till his arm grew stiff.

Two days later, as a direct result of the tutor's ministrations, Yossul lost the sight of an eye. Even then, nobody cast any doubts whatever upon the wisdom of Obish the Lame, nor did anyone attempt to call into question his right to inflict such corporal punishment. On the contrary, Obish's stock went up. Yossul was expelled ignominiously from the cheder, and henceforth was treated by the adults of the village like an outcast. Yossul was satisfied too. The loss of an eye was not too much to pay for his good fortune in escaping from Obish the Lame.

Phineas stayed with Obish for three years, and steadily developed leathern buttocks. Now, when Obish called him to the throne and gave him the usual preliminary pinch before examining him on the day's lesson, it hurt him hardly at all, but just when his backside was thoroughly conditioned, Moishe-Leib died, and without many regrets Phineas said goodbye to Obish for ever.

Moishe-Leib of latter years had been in the habit of travelling to Chertkof on high festivals and other religious holidays, to bask in the radiance of Reb David-Moishe's sun. He was the court jester. He ate and drank, especially drank, and joked at the Rabbi's table, eating the choicest food and drinking the most expensive liquor. What with Chayim Cooper's Saturday afternoons, and the freedom of David-Moishe's cellars, life was one fairly continuous swill, until, on the return from one of his pilgrimages to Chertkof, he was suddenly attacked by apoplexy and dropped dead in the street before his house.

Phineas was not distraught at the tragedy. There was hardly any intimacy between the boy and his father, the gay, amiable, pious old drunkard. He knew that being an orphan would mean getting up earlier to help his mother, and performing various other odd jobs, but to offset against these disadvantages was the fact that it would also mean farewell to Obish.

Lantze, however, was determined that Moishe-Leib's death should not be allowed to interfere with her son's studies. It would be hard in many ways, now that her husband was gone, but she felt that she had a responsibility before the Rabbi of Chertkof. She would place no obstacle in the path of the Messiah's blossoming. Phineas was quite agreeable to continuing in the ways of the Law, but he refused any longer to be pinched into wisdom. He was the only male in the house, and like the late Moishe-Leib could twist Lantze round his little finger. He prevailed on his mother to allow him to pick up the rest of his education in the synagogue.

The decrepit, ill-ventilated, badly illuminated little synagogue was never empty. Like the holy flame that burned unendingly before the ark of the Law, the light of medieval learning flickered on without being extinguished. Some fanatics prayed all day, others prayed all night, others again pored over the Talmud, mumbling to themselves without ceasing. In the intervals between the services, groups of scholars gathered together and discussed abstruse points of logic. Time was of no value to them, they droned endlessly on and on. Phineas hovered like a cheeky moth around them. At first, the greybeards treated him condescendingly, but the boy's brain was sharp beyond his years; he persisted in spite of rebuffs until by dint of shrewd questioning he gained by right a place in their circles. They called him 'Rabbele', the little Rabbi, and vied with each other in unravelling for him Talmudic tangles.

At the end of three years, Phineas had sapped the best of their brains. The scattered scraps of knowledge no longer satisfied him. His mentors seemed to be going round and round in tortuous, concentric circles. He looked for wider, more clearly defined horizons. With his mother's blessings, he packed his praying shawl, phylacteries and some oddments of clothing into a carpet bag, and set off for Kamenetz Podolsk.

His brother Samuel was married and already the father of two children. Phineas did not recognise him, with his carefully trimmed beard and strange outlandish clothes, while to Samuel, Phineas in his long black gabardine, and the various other accessories of the Zvonitz ghetto, looked like a queer little barbarian. Samuel took Phineas into his private room and examined him at length. As the interrogation proceeded the elder brother grew more and more surprised at the fertility of the boy's mind. If only some of his other pupils had half Phineas's brains! He decided to take him in hand and wrote immediately to his mother that Phineas could have a home in Kamenetz Podolsk for as long as he cared to stay.

Phineas who, after the adulation of the old men in the synagogue, had half expected to take the town by storm, was disgusted to find how little he really knew. The puritan bigotry of the chasidim had confined the stream of learning to the narrow banks of holy writ; in Kamenetz, the boy was surprised to find that there was other literature in Hebrew besides the Bible and the Talmud. There were poems, and plays, and novels, and treatises on mathematics that were anathema to the hidebound little Jews of Zvonitz.

He even discovered that he could not talk Russian properly. The Jews of his native village lived and worked in a severely constricted community. With the peasants they conversed only on business matters; amongst themselves they spoke in Yiddish. It was sufficient for them to understand what the moujiks said to them and to make themselves understood in return. What their vocabularies lacked in Russian, they supplemented with gestures that were universally comprehensible. Phineas found out that a Russian grammar existed, and that the Jews of Kamenetz were bilingual, speaking Russian as correctly as the Russians themselves.

He discovered music. He joined the choir of the large synagogue and learned staff notation. Now, encircled by this living, progressive, hitherto undreamed-of town culture, his head whirled with activity. Amoeba-like, his mind reached out, absorbing new thoughts, new experiences, incorporating them in the fabric of his brain. Grammatical Russian alone soon ceased to content him, he took up French and German, being taught those languages by students in return for lessons in Hebrew.

His best friend in Kamenetz Podolsk was Nachum, an old carpenter, whose shop was in the same street as Samuel's house. Whenever he had some time to spare, he called in at Nachum's. The patriarchal old man would continue gravely with his work while Phineas watched absorbedly the gnarled brown hands gliding like tortoises over the virginal white wood, and listened to an unending repertoire of wisdom garnished with wit.

Nachum soon ferreted out the boy's love of music. He was a shrewd psychologist without ever having heard of psychology. He noticed that whenever in the lull of a conversation he started to hum a sacred tune, Phineas almost unconsciously supplied the alto harmony. Again and again he sensed in Phineas the desire to express himself in music.

Secretly, for a few copecks, the old man purchased a battered fiddle. The body was cracked and rotting, the scroll minus two pegs. Using that as a pattern, Nachum constructed a violin of varnished pinewood. One evening, when Phineas was about to leave, the old man put aside his work and wiped his hands slowly on his apron.

'Just now, Phineas, what is it you would like most?' he asked suddenly, fixing Phineas with his shrewd grey eyes.

Phineas, at the door, turned and looked at Nachum in bewilderment. The old man, a quizzical smile on his face, repeated the question. Phineas scratched his head, completely puzzled, but as Nachum commenced to hum a tune, the boy's eyes lit up. He moved his fingers in the air, like a harpist plucking invisible strings. 'Something to play on,' he said with infinite longing. 'Something to play on,' he repeated, as if he fully realised the improbability of his ever possessing an instrument of his own.

Without a word, the old man bent down ponderously and fished out the shining fiddle from a pile of shavings under the bench. Moving round to the boy, he placed it triumphantly in his arms, like a midwife presenting a mother with her firstborn.

'For you, Phineas,' he said.

The boy, too overcome to speak coherently, stammered his thanks. Good-naturedly, the carpenter pushed him from the shop.

'Come back tomorrow night,' he said, 'and thank me on the fiddle.'

Several tomorrows elapsed before Phineas could play even a single scale. The fiddle bucked in his clumsy hands like an untamed animal, and the sounds he scratched from it were like the nocturnal serenadings of a lovesick tomcat. He began to realise that learning to play the violin without a tutor and without knowledge of the instrument was no easy matter. There was one competent music teacher in town, but he insisted on being paid for his services, and as Phineas sent home every rouble he earned, it looked as though he would have to grope his way through the world of music like an explorer lost without a compass in an uncharted jungle.

Fortunately, Phineas managed to interest one of his pupils in the violin. He persuaded the young student to buy a fiddle and arranged for Motke, the music teacher, to give him lessons at a highly inflated price. As a commission for introducing new business, Motke allowed Phineas to stay in the room while he taught. At the end of every lesson, Phineas went home and practised on his own instrument what the teacher had shown the boy. By the time the student buried his fiddle for good in the attic, Phineas could read music proficiently, and held the violin almost like a professional.

Nachum was delighted whenever the boy came in to display each newly mastered piece. Ignoring the mistakes and hesitations, Nachum swore that Phineas played like a virtuoso. Listening to the music the old man felt as though he were in part responsible, not only for the reproduction, but for its composition as well. Phineas was a genius. Phineas would go far. Nachum's blood warmed at the thought that his humble workroom had given birth to such a prodigy of talent.

At the age of fifteen, Phineas returned to Zvonitz. Whoever saw him in the street stopped to look at him. Gone was the untidy little boy with long side-locks, kapota and gabardine reaching to his ankles; instead, here was a well-set-up young man of average height wearing a hard, high-crowned felt hat, a short close-fitting jacket, tight trousers and buttoned boots, the latest sartorial edict of Kamenetz in fashion, not quite ten years behind St Petersburg. A few of the ultra-orthodox regarded his clean-shaven face contemptuously as a breach of the Talmudic law; German clothes they could forgive, but a hairless face, never. They turned away from Phineas ostentatiously, and spat disgustedly behind his back. After the first week, Zvonitz adapted itself to him, all except the young girls, who without exception had fallen in love with Phineas's clear blue eyes, his handsome aquiline features and refined city ways.

In a short time, he became known as 'Phineas the Scribe'. Even Obish had to bow before his superior knowledge of the Law and his prowess as a teacher. Lantze did very little business now in her shop; Phineas was the breadwinner. Apart from oral Hebrew, he taught Yiddish calligraphy, his pupils starting from elementary courses in mastering the alphabet and continuing until they could write a complete letter. To his advanced students he taught Russian till such time as they could painfully manage to scrawl an address, then they gave up that branch of secular knowledge and rested on their laurels as educated men.

Life rolled on placidly until Uncle Velvel arrived. He passed through the open door of the little shop like a somnambulist, preoccupied with a new tune he was composing. Lantze, thinking he was a customer, rose to meet him, and recognised her brother. She embraced him tearfully, covering his face with kisses. He endured her wet welcome abstractedly, a little peeved because a marvellous sequence of notes did not ring right in his head. He had remained astonishingly youthful; although he was over fifty, he did not look more than thirty-five at the most. His beard was black without the slightest fleck of grey, and his lean, ascetic face with the wild, dark eyes, looked like the head of an El Greco Jesus.

They exchanged mutual greetings, Lantze inquiring after her parents, kindred and a whole string of in-laws. She had just embarked upon a picturesque series of personal reminiscences connected with them, projecting her long inactive mind through the murky haze of piled-up, uneventful years, when Velvel heard the sound of a fiddle being tuned. At once he pricked up his ears, becoming entirely oblivious to his sister's non-stop monologue.

'Who's that?' he asked, interrupting her torrent of words.

'Who? Baruch's wife of course!' she answered. 'As I'm telling you, she took the baby to the Rabbi…'

'One moment, Lantze.' Velvel cut her short, placing a restraining hand on her arm. 'Never mind about Baruch's wife. Who's that playing the fiddle?'

'Fiddle?' She looked up uncomprehendingly. The sound of the instrument coruscated like flashes of light through the drab little shop. She shook her shoulders resignedly; the fiddle, along with a razor and short, tight clothes, was just another of the useless gentile diversions her son had brought from town. She had got used to it, she hoped Velvel wouldn't object. 'That's Phineas,' she apologised. 'He always practises about this time…Well, the Rabbi…'

She spoke to herself. Like a wind, Velvel whisked himself away from her. He flew into Phineas's room and stood by the door watching his nephew with wide-open mouth.

Phineas turned and looked with amazement at the gaunt apparition. He was still more amazed when the intruder rushed over to him and embraced him, kissing him soundly on both cheeks. Lantze came up behind them and explained the riddle of the stranger's presence. Velvel brushed her aside gently but impatiently, and produced a pile of manuscripts. He laid them before Phineas, and with one hand lovingly caressing the boy's shoulders he interpreted the meaning of each numbered hieroglyphic. Phineas, affected by his uncle's contagious excitement, sat down and tried to decipher the melodies. He drew five rough staves on a sheet of paper and transposed the numbers into quavers and crochets. To his surprise and delight, something definite emerged. He rose to his feet and played one tune over and over again, adjusting the beat of the melody till he produced quite a creditable waltz.

Velvel exulted like a prophet come into his own, and during the next few days, when Phineas was not busy teaching, Velvel monopolised his time, not even hesitating to awaken the boy during the night to transcribe some lingering tune.

On the following Saturday, Velvel had his big chance, the real reason for his coming to Zvonitz. The cantor of the little synagogue had died, and Velvel was one of two candidates for the vacant position. The other was an old Jew from Kamenetz named Mordecai who had been employed in one of the town synagogues until superseded by a younger man. Reb Mordecai was to conduct the morning service, and Velvel would officiate in the evening; whoever proved the more suitable would be offered the cantor's job.

On the Saturday morning, the little synagogue was crowded. Reb Mordecai, wreathed in a huge, hand-woven praying shawl, swayed his tiny body on the cantor's elevated platform. He sang in a sweet tenor voice seared with the quaverings of age, but his limitations were exposed ruthlessly when he cracked down on the falsettos. His Hebrew was perfect, and his phrasing a delight to the critical congregation; the insurmountable obstacles were the top notes, but then, the knowledgeable ones reflected, if he could trill like a soprano, he would still be in Kamenetz. After all, it was useless to expect a tender pullet for the price of a tough old rooster.

Velvel was full of confidence when he mounted the rostrum in the evening. From the very first prayer he sang to the litany his own compositions. Phineas watched excitedly the reactions of the congregation. The audience for the most part listened silently, but several Jews, a small minority, shook their heads and whispered dubiously amongst themselves. At the conclusion of the service, Velvel was overwhelmed with hearty congratulations. The congregation, chattering like voluble black magpies, filed slowly from the synagogue, leaving Velvel to face the elders. The guboyim were ranged on either side of Chayim Cooper, gazing earnestly at his face for a clue from that impeccable rock. The magnate sat silently, seemingly lost in thought, then he lifted his face to Velvel, smiled kindly and shook his head. No more weighty was the down-turned thumb of a Roman Caesar. Without a word the decision had been taken. Orthodoxy had won.

Chayim Cooper, however, had no intention of letting Velvel go. He recognised in him an extremely cultured man, and Chayim Cooper liked to have the monopoly of culture in Zvonitz. Two of the plums reserved for the most brilliant students of the village were a handsome dowry and the hand of one of Chayim Cooper's numerous female relatives in marriage, which meant that the lucky ones were freed from financial worry for the rest of their lives. Chayim dangled this bait before Velvel's nose. Through a marriage broker he arranged for Velvel to wed a widowed cousin of his, a dark, buxom widow of thirty-five. Velvel was not in the least interested in money, and still less in a wife, but he jumped at the chance of staying in Zvonitz. He accepted reluctantly the wife and the money, buoyed up by the prospect of seeing Phineas every day, and of hearing his dreams assume a concrete reality on the violin.

The following March, when the ice broke on the Dniester, Zvonitz started once again to hum with activity. Soon after the periodical flood, the river traffic resumed its normal course, and Velvel was put in charge of a raft as overseer, to check what came on and what went off, to collect incoming receipts and disburse wages. He had no objection to taking a trip down to Odessa, the journey would give him a chance to work on some new tunes, and at the same time afford him a few weeks' welcome respite from his wife.

Velvel's heavily laden raft, the last of a string of eleven, floated smoothly downstream, propelled by the steady two-miles-an-hour current. The workers were busy at the sides, trying to ensnare sturgeon, and Velvel sat by himself on a barrel of dried fish, lazily contemplating the sliding landscape. Suddenly a bird darted from an overhanging tree like a flash of silver fire in the sun, and tacked a zigzag course like a yacht sailing to heaven. From it came an amazing burst of melody. The raftsmen continued fishing, laughing and swearing as if nothing had happened, and to them indeed a bird was not worth troubling about unless it were inside a pie. But Velvel sat up intently and listened. He heard a trill recurring with different variations on each turn of the flight. He got up fascinated and watched it mount higher and higher, a fluttering dark-blue speck in a light-blue sky.

The burst of song turned into dancing numbers in his head. Phrase merged into phrase till it assumed the joyousness of a hymn of praise, a melody fit for God himself. He could hear Phineas playing it on the fiddle, the ringing notes flying out like coloured sparks. This would be his masterpiece. 'Esso aini el hehorim mayuyin yovoi esri.' The psalm fitted exactly the birdsong. 'I will lift up mine eyes unto the high hills whence cometh my help.'... Now the next line. The next... 'My help cometh. My help cometh...'

The next line was never set to the soaring song, the masterpiece was never written. Velvel had unconsciously been walking on the edge of the raft; his eyes fixed on the high hills failed to warn his legs of the danger beneath, and he stepped into the river. His long black alpaca coat caught on a log projecting from the raft and twisted itself over his head like a tightly drawn sack.

It was some time before the raftsmen missed him, and when they fished him at last from the Dniester, Velvel was blue and puffed like a man swollen with dropsy. They moored the raft at the first village and sent his body back by cart to Zvonitz. So Velvel died, and his rare talent, warped and withered in the dank fetid air of the Russia of Nicholas II, was buried with him.

After the flaming beacon of Velvel's presence, Zvonitz without him seemed to Phineas abysmally dull and utterly uncivilized. He carried on teaching his simpletons by day, and playing his violin at night, but his heart was heavy with the memory of the lean, wild-eyed Jew who had come into his life like a burst of light, and vanished like the echo of a song heard in a dream. Every night he poured over Velvel's manuscripts and played the dead man's compositions. It seemed to him that Velvel stood over him always when he played, swaying his noble head to the rhythm of the music, a more than earthly light glowing in the deep dark eyes.

For the first few months after his uncle's death, he felt every night at his music a oneness with Velvel, a more than spiritual communion, as if the dead man's physical presence overlapped the boundary of the grave; but after a while his little room rang hollow and Phineas knew that he was really alone.

Kamenetz drew him once more. He returned to the county town and rented a room in Nachum's house, where he revived his connection as a private tutor. Every month he sent his mother her allowance, and two or three times a year he travelled to Zvonitz to see her.

During one of his visits to Zvonitz he experienced for the first time the early blossoming of love. Coming out of the synagogue, he saw on the other side of the street a slim young girl of about fifteen, blue-eyed, with two long, fair plaits swinging over her back. She looked at Phineas and smiled. He returned her smile, slightly giddy, then blushed like a beetroot as she smiled at him again and disappeared into a little house.

Phineas was eighteen at the time. Too preoccupied with his music and his studies, he had hitherto had neither the opportunity nor the inclination to interest himself in women. But this girl was different. Surreptitiously, he made inquiries about her. Her name was Shandel, the eldest of four sisters. Her father Berel, called 'Copper Beard' because of the sleek metallic richness of his hirsute adornment, had recently settled in Zvonitz, where his wife ran a little haberdashery store, while he piously studied all day in the synagogue. Berel, unlike his wife, who was Russian, came from the other side of the Galician border. As an alien, he lived on sufferance in Zvonitz, constantly having to run the gauntlet of the village constable's displeasure. The uradnik exacted a toll of two roubles a week from all the Austrians of the village as the price of his tolerance. If they missed a single payment, they were bundled back unceremoniously across the border. Copper Beard paid up regularly, but the uradnik came round sometimes in a drunken rage when he had swallowed all his bribes in vodka. On such occasions Berel hid himself beneath the counter until the arm of the law stormed off, but if he was discovered, he was beaten unmercifully and forced to disgorge another two roubles under pain of being repatriated on the spot.

Shandel worked in a millinery establishment in Chotin. Every Monday morning she set off for the town, and returned on Friday before sundown ushered in the Sabbath. She stayed with some relatives there, and Phineas, discovering this, managed to visit the town fairly regularly. In Chotin, they could walk and talk together without attracting undue attention, whereas in Zvonitz conversation, no matter how innocent, between two young people was illicit intercourse, almost tantamount to adultery unless they happened to be betrothed. For two years they conducted their long-distance courtship in secret, until it got to Berel's ears that Phineas was fond of his daughter Shandel. At the very first opportunity,

Copper Beard accosted Phineas and asked him whether such rumours were true. Phineas blushed and admitted that they had a solid foundation, and expressed the hope that, when his finances permitted, Berel would allow him to marry his daughter.

Copper Beard readily consented. Phineas was the most eligible young bachelor in the district, one who could command a substantial dowry if he so desired, whereas Berel had nothing to give with Shandel apart from her youthful beauty and sweet disposition. He shook Phineas's hand warmly on parting.

'My daughter is like a bolt of precious silk,' he observed sententiously. 'Not anyone is fit to possess such a treasure, but of all the people in Zvonitz, you are most surely the man.'

To all intents and purposes, they were now betrothed. Phineas no longer made a secret of seeing Shandel. When he came to Zvonitz, he first saw his mother, then went straight on to Berel's house. On one occasion he encountered in Kamenetz the coachman in charge of a landowner's phaeton. He had driven his master over from Zvonitz on the previous evening, and was returning with an empty coach that morning. On a hasty impulse, Phineas offered the driver a rouble for a lift. The coachman was more than agreeable, so late on Saturday afternoon, before dusk ended the Sabbath, the phaeton rolled to its journey's end in the middle of the central street of Zvonitz.

The Jews of the village were shocked beyond words by such vandalism. Almost by telepathy, news of the sacrilege reached Shandel's father. When Phineas came to see his bride an irate Berel met him at the door, his copper beard bristling with rage.

'Young man,' he demanded immediately, 'is it true that you travelled by phaeton today from Kamenetz?'

Phineas nodded guiltily and tried to explain that he had, without thinking, snatched the brief opportunity for a flying visit. Copper Beard waved his protestations aside. There was no excuse to justify such an offence. And a monster like that dared to court his daughter!

'Phineas,' he said angrily, 'you have desecrated the Sabbath. There is nothing more to be said. You are not for my daughter!'

He turned on his heel without another word, and slammed the door in the young man's face.

Phineas returned chastened to Kamenetz Podolsk. He threw

himself completely into his music and scholarship, his only recreation being an occasional game of chess in the evening with Nachum. After several months, the acute pain of parting deadened into a dull, intermittent ache, only cutting into raw life sometimes at night, or during the day when a figure encountered in the street awoke a smiling image of the radiant Shandel.

In Zvonitz, Shandel was very far from appearing radiant. She had no intellectual pursuits with which to engage her mind. She wasted to a melancholy wraith, sickening into a decline. At the lowest ebb of her vitality she contracted typhoid fever, and tossed in her sweat-drenched bed muttering only one word in her delirium – 'Phineas! – Phineas!'

Copper Beard had a hard struggle with his conscience. He saw that his daughter's life was intertwined irrevocably with Phineas's. He took counsel, sorely troubled, with the Rabbi, who after much deliberation advised a reconciliation. When the crisis of Shandel's illness was passed, Berel sent for Phineas. As soon as Shandel saw him, she brightened like a brimming lamp lit in blackness, and her drooping frame tautened with a new will to live. From that moment she mended rapidly and soon became her old self again.

CHAPTER VI

In September 1895, Phineas received some disquieting news from Zvonitz. It was a notice to the effect that as he was over the age of twenty-one, he would be required to present himself for military service before the starosta Oklomoff, mayor of Zvonitz, on the twenty-third of the month.

Phineas's first impulse was to pack up bag and baggage and emigrate to America. From what he had heard, it was not very difficult to make a living in the golden West; almost everyone in Kamenetz had relatives in America, or knew of friends there, who without exception were rolling in wealth. Three years and eight months of stringent military discipline did not commend themselves highly to Phineas, nor did the munificent scale of wages, forty-five copecks every four months, the equivalent of half a farthing a day, meet with his approval. Quite apart from the pecuniary attractiveness of this lordly salary, Phineas and most of the other Jews would have been ready and willing to serve Russia, had their mother country only occasionally done something for them in return. They were asked to give up their freedom, their homes, their lives if necessary, and to accept gratefully rewards in the shape of pogroms, beatings, insults, humiliations and forty-five copecks in cash three times a year.

Phineas took the document to Samuel, to ask his brother's advice. Samuel was no longer the ascetic scholar of a few years back. He had bought his own house in the best residential quarter of the city, and lived like a wealthy merchant. He still taught, but only special pupils, his one criterion in their selection being the size of the parental purse. The rest of his income he made by speculation and lending money to retired captains and colonels, who were as thick as fleas in the neighbourhood. They pledged him their pension books for a year ahead in return for their face value in cash, minus of course a good slice for interest.

Samuel pondered long on the question of his brother's military service. If Phineas failed to present himself, the nearest of kin, by the promulgation of an Imperial ukase, had to pay the government three hundred roubles in compensation. The nearest of kin in this case was obviously Samuel, from whom the representatives of the government would most certainly mulct the required sum. Several years ago Samuel would have paid the money cheerily, and regarded it as well spent; he would even have borrowed to make it good, but now he was a rich man and knew the value of hard cash. He therefore, after a long and cogent argument, backed up by copious extracts from the Talmud, persuaded Phineas to enrol as a recruit. Three years and eight months, he pointed out, was not an eternity. If he went to America, neither he, Samuel, nor his mother, would ever see him again, which would break the old woman's heart. As for the three hundred roubles, Phineas's pay in the army would not keep him in boot polish, or rifle oil, and rather than let the government confiscate his hard-earned money, Samuel would send the three hundred roubles to the barracks wherever he was stationed, so that Phineas could buy himself various privileges.

After Samuel's disquisition, the prospect Phineas envisaged was not so dreadful. America was a long way off after all, and there was Shandel to consider too. Three years and eight months was an insignificant fraction of a man's life. It would fly past like a dream, and leave him and his family without an ocean between them. Reluctantly he agreed; maybe this was for the best.

Samuel escorted Phineas benevolently to the door and shook his hand cordially before they parted. The elder brother was quite genuine in his desire to baulk the government of its three hundred roubles, but at the same time he had no intention of throwing them away on Phineas. A young man like that, he reflected, had no need for so much money; he would of course send him a few roubles now and again, but the bulk of the three hundred would stay where they would do most good – in his own pocket.

On the twenty-third of the month, Phineas and a crowd of other young men assembled in the courtyard of the starosta's official residence in Zvonitz. Oklomoff, a coarse, illiterate ex-sergeant, appeared before them, puffed up importantly like a mating turkey cock, an impressive-looking white document in his hand. Being unable to read, he passed the paper to the chinovnik who stood subserviently by his side, and the secretary read out a long list of names. As each name was called, the bearer stepped forward smartly and answered 'Here!' and the chinovnik marked off his presence. At the end of the roll-call, the starosta, his purple-veined nose glowing greasily from a recent heavy libation of vodka, made a thick patriotic speech extolling the virtues of serving His Imperial Majesty, and dismissed them as an old soldier with an unctuous blessing, after telling them where to report in Kamenetz.

At the administrative buildings in Kamenetz Podolsk it was found that there were more recruits than the quota required. According to the usual procedure, lots were drawn, the lucky holders of the highest numbers qualifying for exemption from military service. The recruits filed singly into a big room. There, each one dipped into a leathern bag held out by a soldier, and registered his number with the presiding officer. Gavriel, a nephew of Chayim Cooper, went in before Phineas. Gavriel was over six feet in height, with a red, healthy face, and shoulders like a buttress. He came out triumphantly, clutching a number only one point below the very highest possible. Phineas had quite expected that to happen. Even if Gavriel had not drawn one of the high ones, Chayim Cooper's money ensured that the medical examination would most certainly reveal that his fourteen stone of radiant muscle was in the last stages of galloping consumption.

Phineas had no luck in the draw, and no Chayim Cooper in the family. After a cursory appearance before the medical tribunal, he was passed fit for service. A fortnight of freedom elapsed, during which time Phineas had to prepare some kit, pillows, sheets, boots and various other things that the army authorities did not supply to new recruits. At the end of the fortnight, most of which he spent with his mother and Shandel in Zvonitz, Phineas reported to headquarters in Kamenetz. Along with most of the Jews in the district he had elected to serve his time with the Warsaw garrison, because of the huge Jewish population of that city and its reputation for beauty and gaiety. His bundles and those of his comrades were loaded into carts, and the new recruits set off on a little jaunt of sixteen miles to Largo, the nearest railway station. At Largo, footsore and hungry, they were squeezed into a long succession of cattle trucks and jolted along the monotonous rails for two and a half days until they reached Warsaw.

The divisional headquarters were in the suburb Novoya Praga. The new recruits were herded before officers who took note of their names and trades or professions, and detailed them to various regiments. Phineas registered himself as a musician, and was assigned to the Vengrovsky Polk, the 190th Infantry Reserve. At the regimental quarters, the recruits were again examined, weighed and measured, thumped and sworn at. Phineas and Mendel, a slim, meek-mannered inoffensive lad from Zvonitz, being of the same height, five-feet-five, found themselves in the third company, the first and second consisting of taller men, the fourth, fifth and sixth grading downwards. Thirty men were apportioned to a dormitory, and in the evening, as soon as each recruit secured his belongings in his locker, he flung himself fully dressed on his bed and slept.

At seven in the morning, a corporal woke them with a yell. 'Stavai!' – 'Get up!' Most of them rolled off their beds, but those that still slept were shaken roughly to their senses. The corporal was lenient today. In future, he explained, laggards would be hastened with a whip. He marched them off to the bakehouse, and each man drew his bread rations for three days, a long, black loaf weighing nine pounds. They returned to the dormitory and broke their fast on bread and water and salt.

At twelve o'clock each recruit received his daily meat ration, half a pound of sliced red meat impaled on a skewer, and a wooden spoon for use during dinner. The thirty men were split up into small groups of five, each in the charge of a 'dadka', an old soldier whose duty it was, for the next day or two, to guide the fledglings. His first lesson was to show them how to tuck the spoon in their boots. It was to become as much a part of their personal equipment as cap, rifle or tunic.

At twelve-thirty dinner was served in the large hall. A hundred and twenty men sat down at long tables, ravenously hungry. Each group of five was given a huge empty bowl, and one of the five was chosen to bring the dinner for that day. Mendel caught the dadka's eye and was appointed orderly. Proud of his responsible job, he hastened to the cook's quarters and lined up outside the kitchen. After a while he returned with a steaming load of borscht. All five set to from the same bowl, and in a few minutes it was scraped clean. The next course was kasha baked with hog fat. Mendel took the empty bowl and vanished into the kitchen. There were three soldiers before him when he arrived, but others kept coming and they pushed him roughly out of his turn. Mendel was too meek to object, or even swear violently in return, so he was tossed like a shuttlecock behind soldier after soldier until he found himself the last of the queue, and consequently with the last of the kasha.

He returned shamefacedly to his comrades. The other soldiers were eating a luscious brown mess running with steaming fat, while he brought to the table a hard-baked brick. Cursing angrily, the recruits chipped off lumps of kasha with their knives, but their teeth were no match for such toughness. Regretfully they dropped the kasha back into the bowl and glared at Mendel as though they would enjoy eating him instead.

A squat little pug-nosed private, Fonka, a soldier in his last year of service, seated on the opposite side of the table, watched the comedy keenly. Seeking still further to enliven it, he picked up a lump of cabbage from the floor and threw it in Phineas's face. The whole table roared with laughter. Phineas rose to his feet. He was in no temper to be laughed at after the loss of half his dinner. The impregnable kasha grinned at him – it was still of some use after all! He picked up the largest segment from the bowl and flung it full in Fonka's face. It hit the soldier just beneath the eye, scraped a lump of flesh from his nose, bounced off and fell like a solid lump of masonry on to the table. Again the soldiers roared, and Phineas, a little more pleased with himself, sat down.

Fonka, the blood streaming from his face, his eye turning blue and swelling visibly, jumped to his feet in a raging fury.

'Zhidofska morda!' he roared. 'You bloody Jew! I'll teach you to throw kasha at a Russian!'

He leaped on to the table, but before he could reach Phineas the dadka stopped him.

'Go easy, Fonka,' he said. 'Don't you dare lay a finger on him!'

'B-but look what he's done!' growled Fonka indignantly, pointing to his bloody face.

'Serves you right,' observed the dadka dryly. 'You asked for it, and you got it. But if you touch him I'll report you, then you can think about it for the next year – in jail!'

Fonka dropped back to his seat, gingerly dabbing his injured eye.

'Put on a kasha poultice!' yelled a wag from the other end of the table.

Fonka scowled viciously and subsided into a sullen silence. The laugh was on him this time, but he'd get even with that lousy little Jew, if it was the last thing he ever did.

The next day, training began in earnest. At four o'clock in the morning, the corporal roused them with a stentorian 'Stavai!' He cracked his nagaika in the air, and those that still slept, after one minute's grace, felt the sting of the whip cutting through their slumbers. When all were roused, the corporal gave a second command – 'Oomevatzja!' – 'Wash!', and within five minutes the whole of the dormitory had to complete their ablutions. Hastily they snatched a bite of black bread and filed into the frosty morning blackness.

Fonka was waiting for them on the parade ground, a wicked grin on his battered face. The sergeant major, Nicolai Grigorovitch, had had the surprise of his life when Fonka volunteered for early-morning service. One of the old soldiers was usually detailed to break in the new recruits while the higher ranks enjoyed their beauty sleep. It was regarded as a form of punishment by the unlucky ones so chosen, and they took it out of the hides of the tyros in return. Fonka leered at the recruits. He would make them all sweat, and for Phineas something extra special was reserved.

Fonka lined them up in squads and wheeled them round and round the parade ground. The recruits in their divers civilian costumes, sheepskin jackets, long coats and short coats, breeches and baggy pantaloons, presented an awkward picture. Fonka swore fluently at their clumsy manoeuvres, and at their inability to distinguish between right and left, and invariably chose Phineas to illustrate the way a movement should not be executed. Then he started them on elementary physical jerks, and whenever Phineas was squatting on his heels, a well-directed kick on the rump would send him sprawling on his face.

At seven the exercises concluded. Fonka marched them into the barracks and left them to rest for an hour. The recruits immediately fell on the black bread, and filled themselves with water and salt. All except Phineas, who was far too busy trying to mitigate the pain of his bruises to attend to any other physical requirements.

At eight o'clock they filed on to the parade ground again, this time equipped with dummy rifles. The sergeant major formed them into line and called them smartly to attention when the officer, a slim, pale, monocled lieutenant, appeared. Between them, the lieutenant and the sergeant-major made them hop about like performing monkeys, until, steaming with perspiration, they began to feel that never in the whole of their service would they be able to hold a rifle properly or obey a command with the required precision.

At nine o'clock they returned to the barracks, and an instructor twisted them about in Swedish drill until ten. At the conclusion of their drill they retired to the dormitory and rested on their beds for a while. After a brief respite, the whole platoon was gathered round Piotr, the corporal. Piotr was a born bully, a husky giant with a red face and bull neck, close-cropped fair hair and tiny, deep-set blue eyes. He surveyed the nervous recruits jovially, while they wondered what new brand of torture was in store for them.

The corporal first put them at their ease. They lolled about on the beds or squatted on the floor, while Piotr imparted to them the first rudiments of a military education. He showed them how to salute, told them exactly how to address their superior officers, from the excellencies downwards. Then he asked them the names of the Tsar, the Tsarina, the Tsar's mother and the names of various other prominent members of the Imperial family. These questions the more intelligent recruits answered fairly satisfactorily. Piotr went on to explain some of the niceties of military etiquette, and the relationship between soldiers and the civilian population outside the barracks. He warned them, under threat of the direst penalties, when in uniform, on no account to molest civilians.

'Is that understood?' he inquired politely.

A chorus of assent answered him.

'Good!' said Piotr. His tiny, roguish blue eyes travelled sharply over the recruits till they rested on Mendel. He pointed a thick finger like a boiled red sausage at Phineas's friend. 'Now supposing you were walking along the street,' he said, 'and a civilian pushed you. As a Russian soldier, what would you do?'

Mendel blushed and opened his mouth, but abashed by the focused attention of his comrades, remained silent.

'Now come along, young man,' the corporal encouraged him smilingly, 'what would you do?'

'W-well,' said Mendel, 'I... I wouldn't take any notice... I would apologise and walk straight on.'

'Would you?' commented Piotr, still smiling. 'Now come over here. I'll show you what a Russian soldier should do.' Mendel stepped forward. The corporal drew back his ham-like fist and without any warning smashed it on Mendel's face. The recruit dropped to the floor like a felled ox, blood streaming from his mouth. He lay there, one hand drawn protectingly across his face, gazing with pathetic eyes like a bewildered child at the corporal.

'Get up!' said Piotr roughly. 'Don't sham. You know I didn't hurt you.'

Mendel rose shakily to his feet, spitting out two loosened teeth, and stood to attention before his mentor.

'Now will you know what to do?' asked Piotr.

'Yes, sir.' Mendel cowered before the grinning corporal. 'Yes, sir. I shall know what to do, sir,' he said.

At eleven, for an hour, the recruits went through a course of rifle drill in the armoury. The rifles were screwed into vices, while the instructors familiarised them with the mechanism of the weapon. They tested the sights and practised on fixed targets with small shot.

At twelve they had their half-pounds of impaled meat, and at twelve-thirty dinner was served, consisting of borscht and kasha, the same as yesterday, and the same for the next six months to come. After dinner they were free until two o'clock, when a new series of marching, drill and exercises occupied the next two hours. At four, their day's training concluded, they were free to roam the barracks at will until seven.

At seven they returned to the dormitories. Now their social life began. A few settled down to cards, but the majority gathered round a balalaika player, singing mournful songs that tearfully reminded them of their homes and the loved ones they had left. When the balalaika player tired, Phineas produced his violin. He started by playing a lilting dance tune, and the recruits, forgetting their nostalgia, wiped their eyes on their sleeves and danced merrily, yelling and clapping their hands till they sank exhausted to the floor. At nine, lights were extinguished, and the whole dormitory tumbled wearily into bed.

For nearly six months, nothing but beatings and fatigues varied the daily military routine. Passover arrived, and as it coincided with the Easter festival, the Jewish soldiers were given eight days' freedom from training. Those who had relatives or friends in Warsaw with whom they could stay received leave of absence for that period, while the recruits who were without connections in the city had to leave the barracks every morning, scrounge Jewish meals as best they could, and return before ten-thirty every evening.

Mendel and Phineas did not know a soul in Warsaw. They left the barracks on the first day of Passover and wandered into the city. In the centre of the town they passed a handsome synagogue, and with one impulse moved towards the entrance, their hearts beating faster at the thought of mixing once more with homely Jews and listening to the beautiful Passover morning service. The interior of the synagogue was brightly lit and more ornately embellished than any building Phineas or his companion had ever seen. The intricately carved, gilded pillars, and the opulent richness of the curtain that hung before the ark of the Law, almost took their breath away. They stood timidly behind the last pew, afraid to push into a seat in case the beadle took exception to two such impecunious strangers. The shamas, a thin, sad-faced, grey-haired man, with a faded praying shawl over his long black frock coat, spied them from his seat on the raised platform. He came towards them at once, and greeted them hospitably in Yiddish. He asked them, in swift whispers, where they came from, to which regiment they were attached and whether they were staying in Warsaw over the holidays. When the shamas heard that they had to return to the barracks in the evening, he told them to wait until the conclusion of the service, and he would try to billet them on to a member of the congregation.

The shamas was as good as his word. At the end of the service, when the richly dressed congregants were filing from the synagogue, he approached the two soldiers. Accompanying him was a tall, middle-aged, dark-skinned man with a small square-cut black beard, whom he introduced as Reb Zalman. The tall Jew smiled and bowed courteously.

'My name is Teitlebaum,' he said.

Phineas and Mendel clicked their heels smartly and sprang to attention. 'This is Mendel Weisman,' said Phineas. 'My name is Phineas Kahn. Vengrovsky Polk, 190th Infantry Reserve.'

'It will be an honour if you will both consent to be my guests over Passover,' said Teitlebaum gravely. 'What poor hospitality I can afford is yours. Now, if you will excuse me, there is a man with whom I have urgent business. I will meet you outside in a few moments.'

He shook each of them warmly by the hand and left the synagogue.

'You will be comfortable at Reb Zalman's,' said the shamas.

Mendel rummaged in his pockets and extracted a crumpled banknote, the remainder of his last remittance from home. Phineas having nothing to offer, watched with an embarrassed air while Mendel pressed it into the shamas's hand. The shamas looked at the money, then at Mendel.

'Are you sure you can afford it, soldier?' he said.

Mendel blushed and remained silent. The shamas smiled, returning the note to Mendel's pocket.

'Thank you very much,' he said. 'I appreciate your goodness of heart. But this is a rich synagogue, the members are all pretty well off. I take from them as much as I can get, they don't miss it, and between ourselves I can tell you I've got quite a tidy "knipple". As a matter of fact, if I were not such a skinflint, I could quite easily afford to give two such poor soldiers a handsome present each; but my son is studying to become a lawyer, and I have still a daughter of marriageable age. So I won't give you any money, but a little good advice. Look after Reb Zalman. He is not a man, he is a precious jewel. Don't do anything to make me sorry I introduced you both to him.'

The soldiers thanked him effusively and left the synagogue. A few minutes later, Teitlebaum joined them near the porch and they set off for his home. They chatted pleasantly on the way, Teitlebaum nodding continuously to acquaintances. He was a Hebrew scholar and a journalist, the author of two books on Jewish problems. As foreign correspondent of several Yiddish journals in England and America, he was well acquainted with affairs in the outside world, and his culture was polyglot, assimilated in the course of his travels across the globe. After questioning Mendel, most of Teitlebaum's conversation was addressed to Phineas, in whom he immediately perceived an extremely intelligent young man.

Olga, Teitlebaum's wife, was an exotically beautiful woman. Tall and dark-haired with a smooth olive complexion, she wore, when she received her guests, a low-necked black velvet gown tightly fitted about the waist and hips, and draping in artistically bountiful flares about her ankles. She was delighted to welcome the soldiers, especially when she discovered that Phineas had lived for several years in Kamenetz, her birthplace. Her maiden name was Fischer, her father being one of the most prominent traders in Kamenetz. Phineas knew him well, by sight and reputation only, being far too youthful and impecunious to mix in the august society of the provincial nabobs.

She led the soldiers into the drawing-room. They followed her, twiddling nervously with their caps, Teitlebaum bringing up the rear. It was a huge room, tastefully decorated in the style of Louis Quinze. There was a good deal of furniture in it, but the room was so large that it did not appear overcrowded, the enormous grand piano in the centre of the polished floor seeming quite a necessary and proportionate embellishment. She saw immediately that they were unaccustomed to such luxury. Chatting animatedly, she tried to make them feel at ease. Phineas and Mendel stood facing her, gazing from her to Teitlebaum, blushing like awkward children, rooted to the floor.

'Pray be seated, gentlemen,' she said at length.

Phineas glanced round the room. The slender, decoratively carved spindles of the chairs seemed too frail to be able to support his weight with safety. He chose a huge couch in a corner, and Mendel followed him docilely. Olga seated herself at the piano, and to her own accompaniment sang in a sweet contralto a Russian gypsy song. Mendel and Phineas both completely lost their hearts to her, not as a sexually desirable female, but as the very apotheosis of charming womanhood.

After the seder, the two soldiers left for the barracks, Phineas having promised to return the next day with his fiddle. Olga had also sent with him a note for the commanding officer whom she knew very well, praying him to allow the two friends leave of absence until the end of Passover.

The polkovnik Baron Voronoff, as soon as he read the note, acceded at once to Madame Teitlebaum's request. He was something of a gallant, and a favour from such a 'krasavitza', such a beautiful lady, even though she was a Jewess, especially a request that put him to no inconvenience or expense, had only to be made to be granted immediately.

On the following day, Phineas came to the Teitlebaums' hugging his precious violin in its battered case under his arm. Most of the afternoon he practised duets with Olga in the drawing-room, while Teitlebaum was busy in his study, and Mendel was more than busy in the kitchen with Vera, the plump red-faced Polish maid. In the evening, after the seder, Phineas and Reb Zalman carried Mendel, who had drunk too much wine, up to bed, and returned to the dining-room. They reclined by the table, according to the ancient custom, on cushions, and spoke of current literature. At least, Olga and her husband spoke, while Phineas listened avidly, and made a mental note of books and authors that he must read as soon as his military service was ended.

The eight days of Passover were the happiest Phineas had ever experienced. He had plenty to eat, more than enough to drink, a bed of a softness such as he had never before known, music and intellectual stimuli. He loved to play Velvel's compositions to Olga. She would close her eyes and shake her beautiful head in time to the rhythm and, after hearing one piece two or three times, was able to improvise an efficient accompaniment at the piano. Long before the end of his stay, she was Olga to Phineas, and he used her Christian name naturally, as though they had been friends for years, while her husband was still Pan Teitlebaum. Somehow it seemed as though calling him Zalman would imply a gross want of respect. You just couldn't call him Zalman, the bigness of the man, his nobility of mind and character demanded a prefix of some sort to show how far he was above the common rut. Zalman didn't suit him; Pan Teitlebaum had the correct ring of dignity. Even if Phineas were a child of his, he could not imagine having the cheek to call him 'Father'.

On the evening of the eighth day, Phineas and Mendel bade their hosts farewell. Phineas courteously kissed Olga's outstretched hand. Mendel, afraid to take such liberties, bowed awkwardly. Teitlebaum held out his hand and Phineas grasped it firmly.

'Come and see us again,' said Teitlebaum. 'We have enjoyed your company exceedingly.'

Phineas blushed. 'Thank you, Pan Teitlebaum,' he said. 'Thank you for everything.'

The Pole smiled gently, and a flush suffusing his dark countenance showed that he understood what Phineas meant, and appreciated the compliment. He was glad that the cultural seeds he had implanted had not fallen on barren ground. He stood by the door, one arm round Olga's shoulder, and waved them farewell. Mendel looked up. From a first floor window Vera's snub nose and a section of her vividly coloured face peeked through. A plump hand appeared at the side of the curtain and waved. Mendel turned red, grinned like a schoolboy and, answering her salute, marched away with military briskness like a young officer showing off his epaulettes.

After Easter, at the conclusion of six months' rigorous training, the whole army corps moved to summer quarters under canvas in the forests of Belan, on the outskirts of Warsaw. Here the recruits were graded according to their trades or professions, and sent to different parts of the camp.

Mendel joined the labourers, and Phineas being a musician was sent to the regimental kapellmeister, Tirchov. He was a Muscovite, a squat, heavily built katzap, with a beefy red face and sharply waxed moustache. He called Phineas before him and looked him up and down insolently. 'So you're a musician!' he said at last.

'Yes, sir,' Phineas replied.

'What instrument do you play?'

'The violin, sir.'

'I suppose you know,' said the kapellmeister gruffly, 'that there are no strings in a military band?'

'Yes, sir,' Phineas answered. 'I know that.'

'Can you read music?' he shot at him.

'Yes, sir.'

'I hope so,' said Tirchov. 'Most of the "musicians" they send me can't tell a crochet from a clef. Well, we'll give you a chance. You say you're a musician. Well, I'll try you out on a solo instrument. Which would you like to play, the cornet, clarinet, flute or the euphonium?'

Phineas thought for a moment. He had always had a sneaking regard for the rich baritone note of the euphonium. He might as well learn to play an instrument he liked, as one towards which he felt no inclination. He chose the euphonium.

'Hump!' grunted the kapellmeister. 'You know it's a very difficult instrument to master. Have you ever played on it before?'

'No, sir,' said Phineas.

The kapellmeister looked more closely at Phineas. He had strong lips, good teeth, and from the depth of his chest, healthy lungs, all the physical desiderata of the euphonium player.

'Very well,' he said. 'We'll let you have a shot at it. But if you're no good, off you go to the tailors – where you belong!' Tirchov dismissed him brusquely. 'Report to me in the morning.'

Phineas saluted smartly and retired. On the following morning he reported to the kapellmeister. Tirchov put him under the charge of Gaponov, a thin, dark, seedy-looking man who wore spectacles that continually dropped down the bridge of his nose, so that he had acquired the habit of nervously pushing them up again in his free moments with a long, skinny forefinger. Gaponov was not a regular soldier. Euphonium players being scarce, and hardly ever procurable from amongst the recruits, Gaponov, a private citizen, had obtained employment in the military band. Tirchov hoped very much that Phineas would turn out to be suitable, because he could then dispense with the paid services of the euphonium player. Gaponov, on the other hand, was determined to make Phineas unsuitable by a process he had tried on several previous apprentices with complete success. He detached the brass mouthpiece of the instrument and gave it to Phineas with instructions to practise blowing through it.

For two whole days, Phineas spent his time spitting daintily with pursed lips through the mouthpiece until he became heartily sick of it. On the third day, he refused to blow any longer and demanded to be shown the fingering. Gaponov complied with bad grace, cursing his clumsiness and assuring him that his efforts were wasted, since he could never hope to become a proficient instrumentalist.

Left to himself, Phineas began to experiment with the euphonium. He soon produced scales with ridiculous ease. Encouraged, he transcribed one of Velvel's melodies to suit the range of the instrument, and practised it over and over again. In the evening, when he had established some sort of mastery over the tune, Tirchov walked by. He stopped, grimly watching Phineas, and listened. At last he walked up to him and clapped him roughly on the shoulder. Phineas turned good-humouredly, expecting to see one of his comrades, and was momentarily put off his guard by the spectacle of the irate kapellmeister. Flustered, he drew himself to attention and saluted stiffly.

'Sooken-Sinn!' Tirchov swore violently, his face turning blue with anger. 'You son of a bitch! How dare you deceive me!'

'B-but, w-why...?' Phineas stammered.

'Don't "but" and "why" me!' growled the kapellmeister. 'I thought you said you couldn't play the euphonium? How dare you lie to your superior officer!'

Phineas worked hard to pacify him. Eventually Tirchov appeared to be satisfied with his explanation. Still half convinced that Phineas was lying, the kapellmeister walked off consoled by the thought that he would soon have a cheap soloist. In two weeks, Phineas took his place in the band, and a month after that Gaponov was dismissed.

The band of thirty musicians was a polyglot combination. Most of them were Jews from the big towns, who, prior to joining the army, had had about as much inkling of music as performing seals. Attracted by the easy life of the instrumentalist, and the tips that would accrue from playing at outside functions, in parks, skating rinks and pleasure boats on the Vistula, they had registered themselves as musicians. Tirchov had immediately uncovered the deception, but so long as the recruits bribed him sufficiently, he was content to allow them to blow their heads off. At the end of three months, when Phineas was a proficient soloist, most of the other Jews were just about enough advanced to belch and grunt on their instruments like flatulent dyspeptics. The rest of the musicians were Tartars, Lithuanians, Kirghizes and German colonists, the three full-blooded Russians being in charge of the most complicated instruments, the drums and cymbals.

At the end of the manoeuvres that wound up the camp in August, the regiment returned to Warsaw. The soldiers had a fortnight's holiday, and Phineas and Mendel, reunited once more, spent the whole of their leave with the Teitlebaums.

Phineas enjoyed being a member of the band. Apart from missing the usual fatigues, they were occupied the whole day either performing or practising, and their engagements took them all over Warsaw. The instrumentalists received a proportion of the proceeds, not a great deal, but princely remuneration compared with their miserly pay, and there were always some generous souls in the parks or the pleasure boats ready to treat them to drinks.

Returning to Novoya Praga one night from a skating rink at the other end of Warsaw, the bandsmen were more than usually jovial. A young blood, out on the spree, had been pouring drinks down their gullets the whole evening. Tirchov drove back to the barracks in a droshky, but the soldiers, being forbidden by regulations to ride home from engagements no matter how far distant, marched along the hoary, glistening roads. Near Praga, Phineas, slightly tipsy still, slipped and dented his instrument. Too tired and befuddled to straighten it out, he picked himself up and followed his comrades, deciding to repair it early next day.

In the morning it escaped his memory, and the eagle eyes of Tirchov picked it out at inspection. He examined the instrument closely and questioned Phineas who was at a loss for a satisfactory explanation. The kapellmeister frowned forbiddingly. The damage was not irreparable, but regulations were regulations, the Tsar's property had been maltreated. He could of course have winked at such a slight mishap, but he had never been over-fond of Phineas who was insufficiently cringing for his liking. He took away the euphonium and ordered him to report for punishment after the parade.

Phineas was sentenced to stand in full kit at attention for two hours in full view of the administrative building, so that if he lowered his rifle for a moment he could more easily be observed, not less than two full hours having to be spent in complete immobility. By the time the torture was ended, Phineas was ready to drop from exhaustion. He swore that he would be revenged on Tirchov, and lay awake the whole night searching for an opportunity to even the score.

His chance came the evening before the colonel's big party. The *élite* of the town had been invited, and the whole band had for weeks been practising musical items, waltzes and operatic selections, to entertain the guests. Phineas, knowing how indispensable he was, determined to absent himself. Michail and Motke, two young rapscallions from Odessa, who gathered cunning as good Jews gather rabbinical lore, gave him expert advice. They made two tiny pellets of soap and poked them one in each corner of Phineas's eyes when he retired. They assured him it would do his eyes no permanent harm, although temporarily it might be slightly painful. Painful it certainly was, like hot needles pricking the corneas, and in the morning both eyes were swollen, and alarmingly inflamed.

Tirchov was almost frantic when he heard the news. He had arranged selections from *Les Huguenots* and *Rigoletto*, the colonel's favourite operas, and the euphonium had fat solos in each. He rushed over to the polkovnik, the sweat pouring down his red face. Quaking like a criminal about to be sentenced, he bearded the colonel in his study.

'Y-your excellency,' he stammered. 'I beg to report that the band will be unable to play this evening.'

'What!' shouted the polkovnik.

Tirchov wished that the floor of the study would open up and suck him into its black fastnesses. He would have preferred to be anywhere but here at this moment. He licked his dry lips nervously and shifted from foot to foot at a complete loss for words.

'Have you gone mad, Tirchov?' the colonel said in an ominously quiet voice.

'Yes, sir... No, sir!' Tirchov stumbled over hot words that were racing like a disorganised mob in his brain. 'The euphonium player, your excellency,' he brought out at last, 'the Jew, Kahn. He was taken to hospital this morning.'

Voronoff exploded angrily. 'What! One lousy Jew is taken to hospital and the band can't play without him! How many in your band, Tirchov?'

'Thirty, your excellency.'

'Sooken-Sinn! And you call yourself a kapellmeister! And you call yours a band! Why, fifteen of the bastards could absent themselves, and you should still be able to play!'

'B-but, your excellency,' Tirchov pleaded, tears in his eyes, 'he is the soloist, your excellency.'

'Then get him out of hospital!' snapped the polkovnik. 'Get him out of bed. Out of his coffin if necessary. But your band must play tonight. D'you hear? God help you, Tirchov, if you shame me before all my guests!'

The kapellmeister withdrew in a pitiable condition. He stopped in the passage and wiped the sweat from his forehead. The colonel's aide-de-camp passed, and Tirchov, clutching at a straw, explained the whole matter to him. The lieutenant laughed.

'Just you leave it to me,' he said.

In the hospital Phineas was taking his ease, sitting on a comfortable easy chair, smoking, when the young officer came in. The physician, Kauffman, met him at the door and saluted gravely.

'I have come for the soldier, Kahn, reported sick this morning,' said the lieutenant briskly.

'Oh you have, have you?' Kauffman replied. 'And pray, who may you be?'

The aide grinned, thinking the physician joked. 'I am His Imperial Majesty, Nicholas II,' he said. 'Now, joking apart, Kauffman, you've got to let Kahn go.'

'Have I?' replied Kauffman. 'Who says so?'

'Orders from his excellency, Baron Voronoff.'

The physician drew up his lean, sagging body to its full height. 'In this hospital,' he said in a dignified tone, 'I take no orders from Baron Voronoff. If a man is sick, he stays here until he discharges himself, or is cured. Here *I* am Tsar. You can tell that to his excellency.' He saluted quietly, turned on his heel and walked off.

The aide reported his failure to Tirchov. The kapellmeister pulled at his moustache distractedly. Now he was ruined indeed! He implored the lieutenant to try again, only this time to see Phineas personally. The officer, being a good-natured young fellow, promised to do his best and returned to the ward. Phineas drew himself stiffly to attention when the officer accosted him, but the lieutenant smiled cheerily.

'So you are the wandering euphonium player?' he said.

'Yes, sir,' Phineas replied.

'What's wrong with you?' the officer asked.

'I really don't know, sir,' Phineas replied innocently. 'I had a pain in my eyes, so I reported sick, and they kept me in.'

'How do you feel now?'

'Much better, thank you, sir.'

'Now look here,' said the aide confidentially. 'The kapellmeister sent me here to see you. He begs of you to play this evening. He says he is ruined if you don't turn up. Now be a sport, Kahn, remember he's a married man with five children – you might have five kids yourself one day! Now try, won't you?'

Phineas smiled. 'I'll do my best, sir,' he said.

In the late afternoon, Phineas went to see Kauffman. His eyes were clear and limpid once more. The physician examined him, could find nothing wrong with him, and put it down gratifyingly to the drops he had administered.

In the evening, the band was drawn up in a semi-circle in the courtyard of the colonel's residence. Behind the large french windows, the glaring chandeliers of the mansion glittered festively. Tirchov stood on his tiny wooden platform, his face pale with anxiety, biting the coarse little hairs on his underlip. In ten minutes the band was due to play, and still there was no sign of Phineas. At last, the euphonium player appeared. Tirchov breathed a sigh of relief, feeling as though a whole world's weight had been blown from his shoulders. He descended from his platform and went forward to meet him.

'Thank God you've come, Kahn,' he said. 'And are you all right now?' he inquired solicitously.

Phineas grinned and nodded. 'Will you give me "two hours" again?' he asked in a swift whisper.

Tirchov shook his head. 'Never again,' he said. 'Never!' He clapped Phineas jovially on the back. 'Now show the colonel what you can do!'

Phineas surpassed himself in the arrangement of the quartet from the third act of *Rigoletto*. The rich baritone song soared like a graceful bird above the courtyard... 'Figlia dell'a – mo – re, schia – vo son de'vez – zi tuo – i; con un detto, un detto sol tu puo – i le mie pe – ne, le mie pe – ne con – so – lar... – 'A word, a word in kindness spoken, will my peace of mind, my peace of mind restore...' The french windows opened, and the side-whiskered colonel, a slimmer edition of the Emperor Franz Joseph, appeared silently on the balcony surrounded by brilliantly uniformed officers and gorgeously puffed and beflowered ladies. When the last notes of the euphonium died away, there was a spontaneous burst of applause from the guests. The colonel was as gratified as if he had himself been the soloist. The band was a reflection of his own good taste. He walked down the stairs from the balcony and asked Phineas to step forward. He took out a bank note from his pocket and gave it to the musician.

'Very good, my son,' he said with a paternal pat on the shoulder.

Phineas saluted smartly. The polkovnik unbuttoned the neck of the soldier's iron-grey topcoat, and was surprised to find no gold braid adorning the collar of his tunic. He drew up his sleeve and saw no stripes on the cuff. The baron motioned to Tirchov, who came rushing over, his short legs moving like a wound-up clockwork toy.

'What's this?' said the polkovnik. 'No braid? No sergeant's chevrons for such an instrumentalist?'

The kapellmeister whispered apologetically in his ear. 'A Zhid, your excellency. A Zhid.'

Voronoff nodded comprehendingly. He had in his first enthusiasm forgotten. He turned to Phineas.

'It's a pity you're a Jew,' he said regretfully, 'I could have made a man of you.'

The colonel's remark hurt Phineas more than any other incident of the sort in the army. After that, he determined to be rid of Tirchov, and the whole gang of coarse, ignorant bullies. Several days later he went on to the soap injections again, and found himself back in hospital. Kauffman was mystified when the soldier's complaint did not respond to the same treatment as before, which was not surprising, since Phineas dosed himself with soap pellets every night. The hospital orderly, however, was not deceived.

'Look here, Kahn,' he said to him one day. 'I'm an old soldier. You may be able to fool the doctors, but you can't fool me. You're as fit as I am. Now if you want to get out of the army, I can wangle it for you for twenty-five roubles.'

'How?' said Phineas.

'Well,' replied the orderly. 'Kauffman hasn't been here very long. I can tell him that the other doctor was always having trouble with you about your eyes. He'll send you before the medical board at the Ooyasdorvsky Hospital. That's the chief military hospital of the Polish command, and once you get before them, they'll either give you a year's leave or discharge you altogether as medically unfit. Now what do you say?'

Phineas decided to trust the orderly, but his main difficulty was the twenty-five roubles. It was no use writing to Samuel. His brother would only send him in return a letter consisting of ten pages of exquisite Hebrew calligraphy crammed full of anecdotes, aphorisms and advice, in fact with almost everything except money. Mendel, however, solved the problem. He put forward the Teitlebaums. Phineas fought for a long time against the suggestion that he should sponge on friends to whom he was already so enormously indebted, but eventually, knowing how little they would miss the money, he agreed. He sent a note to Madame Teitlebaum, simply worded, but urgent. 'Olga. You can save me with twenty-five roubles. Phineas.'

Mendel returned the same evening with the money. Phineas gave half to the orderly, promising him the remainder when he went to the hospital. He was not surprised when two days later Kauffman called him into his surgery and told him he was to report at the hospital before the medical board for examination.

The hospital was a huge building situated in the beautiful boulevard Ooyasdorvsky Allee. Phineas undressed and waited with several others in a large anteroom. When he finally appeared before the panel of five doctors, he looked a sorry sight. His eyes were puffy and horribly bloodshot, and in addition he had an angry red rash on his right forearm, artistically created by Michail and

Motke through repeated applications of diluted vitriol. The doctors glanced at Kauffman's notes, and one of them, an old man with a square grey beard and black-beribboned spectacles, cursorily peered into Phineas's eyes. He nodded sagely, then looked at his forearm. He grabbed at the eruption like a botanist at a rare orchid.

'Does it hurt?' he asked.

'Yes, sir,' answered Phineas.

'You get twinges of pain when you move your elbow?'

'Yes, sir,' replied Phineas. 'That's right.'

'I thought so,' said the doctor. 'An acute form of rheumatism. Gets so that you can't bend your arm at all – doesn't it?'

'Yes, sir,' said Phineas. 'It's like that now.'

'Hum!' coughed the old man, thoroughly satisfied by the accuracy of his diagnosis.

He glanced at the other doctors for the rewards of his acumen, but nobody took any further notice of the superfluous old bore. Phineas watched the panel anxiously, keeping a rigid control over his paralysed hand. He could hardly restrain a fleeting grin when he thought how little the dear old doctor, innocent soul, would relish a cuff from that same right arm, crippled with rheumatism though it was!

The board, after a little deliberation, granted him a green billet, which meant a year's freedom for convalescence. That suited Phineas perfectly. He had already served two years and four months of his time; at the end of twelve months' 'papravka' he would only have to complete four months to end his full term of conscription. He returned to Kamenetz and to teaching, augmenting his income by regular evening engagements with a dance band.

The death of his mother changed his plans completely. Now there was nothing to hold him to Russia. The army had instilled in him such a hatred of Tsarism in all its forms, that he could not bear to live under its despotism any longer. Although he would automatically become a deserter if he did not return to his regiment after his leave, he begrudged even the last four months' service that was still due to Nicholas. He decided to marry Shandel and emigrate, to which country was not yet clear, but any place in the world would be sweeter for him than Russia, his native land.

They were married at Okop over the Galician border, in the

house of one of Shandel's uncles. The young couple sat at a long, decorated table, surrounded by relatives and friends. They ate and drank heartily, amused by the quips and sallies of the batchan who combined the offices of master of ceremonies and jester. The batchan hopped around the table with tireless energy, flattering obese old women and whispering chunks of doggerel into the willing ears of the slightly tipsy men. At the conclusion of the festivities, late in the evening, Copper Beard rose to his feet and, unfolding a red Turkish handkerchief, called for 'drushe-geschank'.

Gold and silver coins clinked fatly in it as each guest contributed his or her wedding gift. Then Copper Beard tied up the handkerchief and, stationing himself with his wife and the bride and groom by the door, said goodbye to the guests. When the room was empty, Phineas faced his father-in-law.

'... So now I'm a married man,' he remarked.

'Married – pooh!' said Copper Beard sententiously with an airy gesture. 'Marriage! What is marriage, my son? What is life? What is everything? Nothing but a dream, Phineas, a dream!'

Phineas hoped devoutly that the 'drushe-geschank' was no dream. Copper Beard, his bright eyes twinkling, mischievously guessed the tenor of the young man's thoughts. He produced the tightly knotted Turkish handkerchief and thrust it with a blessing into Phineas's hand.

The young couple left Okop on the following day and travelled to Tarnopol, staying at the house of another of Shandel's uncles, Hirsch Friedmann. Uncle Hirsch furnished them with the name and address of an acquaintance in Vienna, together with a letter of introduction. Thus equipped, the newlyweds set their faces towards the capital. Hand in hand, a little frightened and apprehensive like a pair of shabby, forlorn children, they set off on the long journey to Vienna. Vienna, the twinkling star on the distant horizon; Vienna, the city of dreams.

BOOK II

GOLDEN LANDS

CHAPTER I

They found lodgings with a Polish Jew and his wife, two rooms in a tiny house off the Kleineschiffegasse. Phineas reported to the district police in the usual way and looked around for a job. Phineas could still speak stiffish German, and Shandel's Yiddish helped her along tolerably well in her daily intercourse with such few Viennese as she encountered. The young couple determined in their pride and ignorance to make use of Uncle Hirsch's recommendation only as a last resource, Phineas being quite sure he was capable of making his own way without having recourse to strangers.

Five weeks in Vienna disillusioned them. Face to face for the first time with the problems of a highly industrialised modern city, they were soon down to their last few groschen. Such Jews as there were in Vienna had no use for a small-town Hebrew tutor, and Russian did not interest them in the least. Phineas, without the machine knowledge, the industrial equipment of the factory worker, was forced to capitulate, unceremoniously to haul down his colours.

Together they called on Dr Rappoport. Uncle Hirsch's friend had come to Vienna from Tarnopol many years back and graduated as a Doctor of Philosophy, but finding that learned degree a hindrance rather than an aid to earning a living, he had quietly shelved his doctorate and made a modest income as a corn chandler. He was still a bachelor. As a youth he had been devoted to Miriam, Shandel's mother, and when she had married Copper Beard and left Galicia, he put all thoughts of women behind him and travelled to Vienna faithful to the memory of his first and only love.

Frau Krawinkle, Dr Rappoport's housekeeper, a small, tidy, grey-haired old lady, opened the door for them and ushered them through a fresh-smelling, dimly lit shop, following a narrow passage like a pass cut through overhanging crags of cereal bins. In the little shop parlour Dr Rappoport rose to greet them. He was a short tubby man with a domed bald head that seemed far too big for his body. Large glasses were perched on his nose, two keen blue eyes magnified almost to the size of brimming saucers staring through the thick lenses. Phineas and Shandel stood embarrassed and silent by the door, hardly knowing how to introduce themselves. Dr Rappoport motioned them to chairs.

'Please be seated,' he said.

When they had taken their places, he sat down opposite them. Resting his elbows on the table he leaned his huge head forward so that he seemed all head and hands.

'Now. What can I do for you children?' he asked kindly. Phineas blushed, and coughed nervously. He took Uncle Hirsch's letter from his pocket and passed it across to Dr Rappoport. The doctor tapped the envelope gently on the table without glancing at it, rotating it slowly from end to end. 'My name is Kahn,' said Phineas at last. 'This is my wife.' Dr Rappoport nodded comprehendingly and smiled. 'You don't have to tell me who *she* is,' he said. 'I know. I knew as soon as she walked into the room. She is Miriam's daughter. Is that not so, Fräulein?'

Shandel turned red and nodded. Dr Rappoport rose to his feet, and leaning over, took Shandel's hand. 'Permit me,' he said courteously, and kissed her soft white fingers. He smiled at Phineas. 'I hope you don't mind,' he apologised. 'I was once very fond of her mother. To tell the truth, I still am, and when I look at her, I know why.'

He opened the letter and read it through rapidly, then he folded it carefully and thrust it into his jacket pocket. Sticking his thumbs in the armholes of his waistcoat, he leaned back thoughtfully in his chair.

'How are you off for money?' he said at last.

Phineas was silent, but Shandel pulled out her purse, and without a word emptied it on the table. A few coppers rolled out sadly. Rappoport felt a tug at his heart as he regarded the worldly wealth of the young couple. He remembered when he himself had come to Vienna as a youth, homeless, almost penniless and without a friend. He remembered only too clearly those early struggles, breadless days and bedless nights; how much more difficult must it be for this young man with a wife to support as well! He took a wallet from his breast pocket and, extracting several bank notes, put them in Shandel's purse.

'This will keep you going for a while,' he said. 'You can regard it as a loan until you get enough to pay me back. In the meantime, I'll see if I can't find one of you a job.'

In his own business affairs Rappoport was as somnolent and dilatory as only a philosopher could be; but after the visit of the young couple he rushed about the city with such energy that he surprised all his acquaintances, and himself as well. Frau Krawinkle, who always had difficulty in rousing him on time in the morning, almost collapsed when she heard him moving about before she had even prepared his coffee. His fierce pursuit of work was to such good effect that, in two days, he had found Shandel a job in a millinery establishment. With Phineas, however, he drew a blank. He shrank from breaking the young man's spirit by introducing him to work involving hard manual labour, and a job suited to Phineas's capacities was difficult to find. In the long run, he supposed he would have to make for him some clerical position in the shop. He had one assistant already, and the business would not pay for two. As it was impossible to sack Franz, whom he regarded as part of the fixtures, it would mean giving Phineas part of his own work to do. In that case he would be able to devote more time to philosophy. If his business suffered, what did it matter, so long as Miriam's daughter was happy and he could commune to his heart's content with the greatest minds of all the ages?

Now that Shandel went out to work, Phineas wandered about the city during the day, disconsolate and lonely. He had no eye for the beauty of the buildings, or the spacious lines of the boulevards. Such things were all very fine for well-fed idlers, a hungry man was as hungry in a prison cell as in a palace. He chafed at the thought of living on Rappoport's charity and Shandel's labour. He ran short of cigarettes, but could not bring himself to ask Shandel for more money. If she noticed his abstinence and offered him a few groschen he would accept willingly, but asking he found impossible; it made him feel like a pimp suddenly assailed by moral scruples.

At last he decided to visit the pawnshop and pledge his one valuable asset, his violin. Like the actor in *La Bohème* singing farewell to his coat, he caressed his fiddle lovingly and laid it gently in its case. He knew that once he parted with it he would never have sufficient cash to redeem it again, but sooner than keep on asking Shandel for more money for an intangible luxury like smoking, he resolved to give cigarettes up altogether. He would have an orgy of tobacco on the proceeds of his violin, and when that was gone, goodbye to the seductive, yellow-tipped enchantress for ever!

Passing a busy wayside café, his violin under his arm, he was enveloped by the rich smell of cooking. It was the lunch hour, just after one, and the stout burghers and their wives were enjoying the midday meal. He threaded his way between the jutting knees that stuck out from beneath the round, marble-topped tables, jostling the inhospitably stiff folds of their protecting gay cloths, to a seat in the corner, near the kitchen entrance. The waiter came up and greeted him obsequiously. Then he stood over him in silence, with bowed head and poised pencil.

'Yes, sir?'

'Coffee, please.'

'Yes, sir,' said the waiter. 'And?' He paused hesitantly.

'Just coffee,' said Phineas quietly, feeling like a beggar soliciting for alms. The waiter stuck his nose up in the air and bounced off with brusque rudeness to another customer. Taking up a seat with coffee at this time of the day! A coffee meant no tip, and without tips how could a man live? Let him wait. He would keep him hanging about so long that he would probably get up in disgust and leave, making room for a more substantial client. The waiter's eyes sparkled as he observed, a few minutes later, a stout, florid-faced man go towards the seat opposite Phineas. In a moment he was at the table and, with an expert flick of his napkin, brushed some non-existent crumbs from the vacant chair. The stout man nodded agreeably and sat down.

'Good afternoon, Herr Sonnenshein,' said the waiter with a pleasant smile.

The man nodded again, and with deft, podgy fingers, tucked a serviette under his chin. 'Now what have you got, Karl?' he asked, leaning back contentedly in his chair, his plump hands spread benevolently across his unbuttoned waistcoat.

Phineas listened hungrily as the waiter rattled off a string of appetising dishes. 'Good afternoon, Herr Sonnenshein!' To him it seemed now that the most desirable thing in the world was to be greeted by name by an obliging servant. He had not had a real meal since the previous evening; the saliva rose up sour-tasting in his mouth as he watched Karl place a huge lager on the table, and heap up the stout man's plate with food. The smell of the braten and the steaming vegetables tickled his nostrils, and his empty stomach rolled over and over, like an exhibition high-diver turning somersaults in mid-air. And to crown it all, the waiter had apparently forgotten his coffee.

The stout man kicked something hard at his feet. With his mouth full, and his fork speared through a lump of cauliflower jabbing the air, he turned his head sideways and glanced down at the floor. He prodded the violin case again with his boot.

'Yours?' he asked Phineas, pushing a stray lump of meat into his mouth with the tip of his knife.

Phineas followed his downward glance and nodded. 'Yes.'

'Well, how about a tune?' said the stout man jovially.

Phineas blushed and shook his head.

'Why? Can't you play?' the man demanded.

'Yes,' said Phineas. 'But not here, amongst all these people. They might not like it. The Herr Proprietor might object.'

'Poof!' grunted the stout man with a wave of his fork. 'Nobody'll object. They'll be pleased. And the proprietor is a pal of mine – a very nice fellow!'

'Right!' said Phineas. 'But remember, you asked for it!'

He took the violin from its case and rose to his feet. He had nothing to lose by performing, and this was probably the last time he would handle his beloved instrument. He closed his eyes and commenced to play. He started with Schubert's 'Marche Militaire', and followed with the 'Serenade', and his own arrangement from the *Trout Quintet*. Soon half the café was tapping softly to time with knives and forks, the other half listening intently between munchings. Even the waiters moved about with softened tread, and took orders in whispers.

When, with a flourish of the bow, he concluded his selections from Schubert and sat down, the whole café burst into a tumult of applause. The face of his neighbour was wreathed in smiles, like an impresario in a crowded house at a virtuoso's concert. The stout man snapped two imperious fingers. Karl came running over.

'Another lager,' said the stout man.

Almost as if by magic, a brimming mug of beer materialised before Phineas. He lifted it gratefully before his benefactor.

'Prosit!'

'Drink hearty, maestro,' said his neighbour.

The café was insistent for encores. Every table was now occupied, and waiters were dragging out chairs from the kitchen to fill the call for seats. Phineas finished his lager, and, a little muzzy but exhilarated from its potent action on an empty stomach, played some heady gypsy airs. At last he sat down, flushed and sweating, his eyes moist like a drunkard's. The plaudits whirled in his head. The stout man stretched his arm towards Phineas and gripped his hand in a friendly grasp.

'Bravo!' he cried enthusiastically, in a high-pitched, squeaky voice. 'Bravo! Bravo!'

Phineas acknowledged the salutation with a weary nod. His head was aching as if two conflicting gangs of noisy imps were having a tug-of-war between his temples. In a confused sort of way he became aware that the stout man had left his seat. Through a splurged, smoky film he saw him bobbing about from table to table. Triumphantly his neighbour returned, and pushing his hard felt hat beneath the emigrant's nose, Phineas saw glittering in it a heap of coins. He looked up in bewilderment.

'For you,' said the stout man. 'As a token of our appreciation.'

Before Phineas could properly grasp what had happened, another man came over to the table. Phineas's neighbour beamed as he introduced Herr Katzenfreund, the proprietor of the café. Katzenfreund shifted a chair close to Phineas, and, seating himself, came to business immediately.

'Are you out of a job?' he asked.

Phineas nodded, wondering whether all this was real, or still the result of fermenting lager.

'Look here,' said Herr Katzenfreund, 'I can't afford to pay you a big salary, but if you care to come here every day at this time to play, I'll give you a first-class dinner and a couple of gulden – besides what you can pick up. Will that suit you all right?'

Phineas, almost overwhelmed by this amazing stroke of good fortune, accepted eagerly before the proprietor could change his mind, and, his head still singing like a humming top, he shook hands with Herr Katzenfreund and his corpulent neighbour, and left the building. The next day he turned up at the café early. Herr Katzenfreund himself set before him a choice meal, and when the midday diners started to fill the tables, he began to play. As on the previous occasion, he was an instant success. Day by day he varied his repertoire, interspersing operatic extracts with Strauss waltzes, and some of Velvel's compositions, which were received surprisingly well. Phineas was happy. For the first time since his arrival in Vienna, he stood on his own feet and earned his keep.

One crowded dinner hour, at the conclusion of his performance, when Phineas was bowing to an enthusiastic audience, Karl button-holed him and led him to a corner table. A tall, broad man stood up at his approach, and inviting Phineas to a vacant chair, sat down opposite him. The stranger had a long, pale face, a bullet head covered with sparse, close-cropped black hair, curved, bushy eyebrows and a big spiked moustache that curling upwards in the same direction gave him the appearance of a stage Mephistopheles. A huge cigar smouldered in his mouth, and every second thick finger, adorned with sparkling diamonds, drummed ceaselessly on the table before him.

'My name is Max Berger,' said the opulent-looking stranger.

'Mine is Kahn,' replied Phineas, wondering what prelude this would turn out to be.

'I have heard of your playing,' said Berger. 'That is why I have come here. You are a gypsy?'

'No. I am a Russian. A Jew.'

Berger laughed. 'That's nothing. Half the gypsies in Vienna are Jews!' He gently tapped the fine grey ash from his cigar on to a tray and resumed his soft, insistent rapping. 'So long as you can play gypsy music, my friend, that's what matters – and what you've been playing just now is *real* gypsy music. I suppose you'll tell me that's Jewish too.'

'As a matter of fact, it is,' said Phineas. 'The last two items were composed by my uncle.'

'Well, well,' said Berger. 'We live and learn. But let's come to business. I own the Marie-Thérèse café in the Pratergasse – I expect you've heard of it?'

Phineas nodded, although he had no inkling that such a place existed nor the faintest idea of its location. He had been through the Prater several times, but to memorise the names of all the cafés was a job for a Viennese, not an unemployed Hebrew tutor. He nodded and smiled, as if to indicate that everybody knew the Marie-Thérèse. Berger continued with a gratified air.

'Well, I've got a gypsy orchestra, but my leader gets drunk never less than five nights a week, so I've given him the sack. How would you like to take his place?'

'I – I should be honoured, honoured, Herr Berger,' Phineas stammered. 'But will I be suitable? I've told you I'm not a gypsy.'

Berger grinned. 'Neither was the other fellow. He was a Romanian tailor, but he became a gypsy before I was done with him. All you need, my friend, are a satin blouse with full sleeves and Magyar embroidery round the neck and down the front, baggy panta-loons and red top boots, and hey presto, you're a gypsy! Now what about it? If you say yes, you can come round to my place and discuss money details later.'

'Very good, Herr Berger,' said Phineas.

'Splendid!' The thick, hairy fingers tapped Phineas's hand encouragingly. 'Come round to the Marie-Thérèse at four-thirty and we'll talk it over. By the way, what's your name?'

'Kahn.'

'Yes, I know. Kahn. But what's your Christian name?'

'Phineas.'

'Phineas... Phineas...' Herr Berger rolled the name on his tongue, and, crinkling his nose distastefully, shook his head. 'No. Definitely Phineas won't do,' he proclaimed. 'All right for an Old Testament orchestra, but no good for Tzigane. Phineas... Pini... Pilli... Pitti... Ah! I've got it – Pittilingri! That's more like a gypsy. Pittilingri – a peach of a name! Good, eh, Herr Kahn?'

Phineas nodded. 'Very good. Very good indeed.'

'You leave it to Maxie Berger,' said the café proprietor with a self-satisfied smirk. 'Why, you're even beginning to look like a gypsy. If I sit here much longer, I can swear you'll start jabbering Romany.' He rose to his feet. 'At four-thirty then, Herr Pittilingri – Auf Wiedersehen!' With a dazzling flash of his hand he tossed a note to Karl and was gone.

At four-thirty Phineas went to see Berger. In a little room at the back of the café, over half a bottle of brandy, Phineas accepted a salary of fifty gulden a week. He dared not ask for more, and Berger could not, for self-respect, pay less, although he knew that Phineas was worth three times that sum. Time enough to pay him big money when he asked for it – which would no doubt be soon enough – he reflected; in the meantime, let him serve his apprenticeship.

Shandel worked overtime that night. She was a clever needle-woman, and the two and a half yards of heavy peach satin that Phineas had brought home quickly became a blouse. Without complaining, she sat up till the early hours of the morning, laboriously embroidering it with a red, green and gold pattern of her own design.

Complete with red top boots and pantaloons, the gypsy Pittilingri turned up at the Marie-Thérèse in the afternoon for rehearsal. There were, apart from him, five more musicians in the orchestra, three of them genuine gypsies, the other two Viennese. The popular waltzes were straightforward pieces that needed no intricate orchestration or laborious rehearsals, but with Velvel's compositions the whole harmony had to be improvised. Phineas had brought with him several handwritten copies, and each musician played them over softly to himself to become familiarised with the melodies. Then they went over them together a few bars at a time, taking their tempo from Phineas, each instrumentalist suggesting bits of counterpoint as they went along. After several hours of rehearsal, that flew by in joyful experimentation, two pieces were ready for presentation in the evening, and Pittilingri and his gypsy orchestra were set for their debut before the patrons of the Marie-Thérèse.

The Marie-Thérèse was one of the better-class cafés in the Prater frequented by students, actresses, *cocottes,* smart, monocled officers and the more impecunious younger sons of the nobility. It filled up late in the evenings when the theatres emptied, and acted as a sort of club for the *habitués.* It was a spacious chamber with a lofty ceiling from which were suspended a huge chandelier in the centre and several smaller ones at the sides. The walls were adorned with a whirling tracery of fauns and Bacchantes, and riotous scenes from Parnassian legends executed in vivid colours like a Renaissance painter's pipe dream. The band played in an ornamental wooden balcony overhanging the floor. Occasionally there were cabaret turns, singers and cancan dancers, for whom Phineas was told that he would be required to arrange the music.

Phineas, surprisingly calm in face of this ordeal, started off the programme on his first night with the usual hackneyed airs. The floor below was filled with a haze of blue smoke and shining faces. A kaleidoscopic forest of humps, the stiff, puffed sleeves of the ladies, jerked up and down like tipsy dromedaries. The women in gay satins and spotted taffetas giggled like shrill, gaudy parakeets, and the officers bowed tirelessly, banging their mugs boisterously and flinging cheery salutations across the room. A solid canopy of buzzing conversation, like a curtain of corporeal texture, shut off Phineas from intimate contact with the audience beneath. He played mechanically, like a wound-up automaton, and bowed half-heartedly as each item was rewarded by a few lazy handclaps from below.

He brightened immensely when he saw Dr Rappoport enter accompanied by Shandel, a slim figure in a plain, close-fitting purple taffeta dress borrowed from one of her workmates. Her modest air and beautiful face were a welcome contrast to the highly painted complexions of the flashy ladies. She seated herself grace-fully in a corner beside Dr Rappoport, leaning against one of the tall leather-upholstered forms that ran flush against the walls right round the room. She raised her right hand and smiled a cheery greeting. Phineas bowed, and turning to the orchestra struck up one of Velvel's pieces. He threw himself into it completely; if nobody else took the slightest notice, at least he knew Shandel was listening. The music penetrated like sharp shafts of light through the fog of conversation, which, reluctant to clear at first, gradually died down to an intermittent whispering. When, in an almost complete silence, he drew out the penultimate wild note which soared into the last tenuous thread of sound, the café burst into a roar of applause. His eyes shining, flushed with triumph, Phineas bowed repeatedly to the audience, and finally made one long genuflection to Shandel's direction, like a victorious knight laying the garlands of the conqueror at his lady's feet.

For several months Phineas prospered. Berger had increased his salary of his own accord, and by this time the young couple had moved into a modest flat of their own off the Pratergasse. Phineas had repaid Rappoport's loan in spite of the philosophical corn chandler's protestations, and insisted on Shandel leaving her situation. Bloated by the late hours and lack of exercise, Phineas began to put on weight. Shandel even prodded him gently in the stomach and swore that she would have to divorce him if he got any fatter. She too was filling out, and the faintest rose began to bloom in her usually pallid cheeks.

A new tune was becoming the rage. Within a few weeks everybody in Vienna would be either humming or whistling Romanovsky's 'Valse Arabesque'. When he got the music, Phineas realised with a painful shock that it was a shameless plagiarism of one of Velvel's tunes. At rehearsal, arriving early at the café, he found only Chu-Chi the cellist before him. He was a small, clean-shaven gypsy with a mass of sleek black hair and a face to match his instrument, mahogany-coloured, with wide-set slanting eyes, broad forehead, sunken cheeks and square pugnacious chin. Chu-Chi was Phineas's confidant, the only one apart from Berger who knew his previous history and the genesis of the gypsy tunes. Phineas gave Chu-Chi the score of 'Valse Arabesque', and asked him to run it over. The gypsy read the score through rapidly and, puzzled, played softly a few bars to convince himself that his reading was correct.

'Well, what do you think of that?' asked Phineas.

'One of Velvel's,' said Chu-Chi without hesitation.

Phineas nodded. Chu-Chi's verdict confirmed his own convictions. To the ordinary man in the street troubling to juxtapose the two, 'Valse Arabesque' might have appeared as a faint reflection of Velvel's composition, but to the experienced ears of both musicians the fraud was immediately apparent. A whole melody, complete in itself, had been lifted bodily, disguised with slight variations, complemented by additions suggested by the run of the tune and converted into a waltz by regularising the tempo. Phineas glared at the score until the staves zigzagged before him like forked lightning, and the black dots danced in fantastic patterns before his eyes. The cellist's soft voice broke through his bitter absorption.

'I'm afraid, Pittilingri, there's nothing you can do,' said Chu-Chi.

Phineas flung the music disgustedly in a corner. 'Pirates!' he growled. 'Burglars!'

At first he resolved never to play 'Valse Arabesque', but inundated by requests from numerous patrons, he was eventually forced to acquiesce. With a great deal of reluctance he incorporated it in his repertoire. He played 'Valse Arabesque' night after night, and on each occasion had to give at least one encore. It followed him about in the street, errand boys whistled it under his windows, military bands featured it in the parks, itinerant musicians tore it to pieces; he even heard it in his dreams until at last it was superseded in the affections of the fickle Viennese public by another catchy tune.

The 'Valse Arabesque' period had become to him like a continuous nightmare. He had not completely recovered from those disturbing months when Chu-Chi one evening pointed out the great Romanovsky himself. Chu-Chi knew everybody who was anybody in Vienna. How he did it was a mystery to Phineas, who imagined that he must sleep no more than an hour each night and spend the rest of his free time wandering about the boulevards and restaurants. Phineas had been busy sorting out the music for the next item when the cellist's bow tapped him gently on the shoulder.

'Look down there,' said Chu-Chi. 'There's your burglar.'

'Who?' asked Phineas, for the moment completely nonplussed.

The cellist, leaning forward on his chair, indicated four men sitting together at a table beneath the huge chandelier in the centre of the crowded café.

'Romanovsky,' he whispered. 'The fat, pasty-faced man with the bald head. The fellow with the little beard next to him is Baron Rothenstein, the banker, and the smart, youngish-looking fop with the waved hair is Herr Stock, who also fancies himself as a composer because his father's got so much money that he can afford to pay music firms to publish his son's rubbish. I can't place the other exactly, but I rather fancy he's an actor.'

Phineas took in the flabby, sensuous face of Romanovsky. It seemed neither vicious nor cunning; on the contrary, it seemed like the physiognomy of a good-humoured simpleton, which surprised Phineas, since his imagination had endowed Romanovsky at least with horns. He struck up a Strauss waltz and, leading the orchestra mechanically, concentrated all his attention on the four men at the centre table. They laughed and chatted spiritedly, Baron Rothenstein doing most of the talking, his little beard wagging like that of a nibbling goat. A waiter brought over a magnum of champagne to Romanovsky. Phineas saw the liquid fill each slender-stemmed glass, and to him it seemed like Velvel's blood they were drinking. The wine effervesced as the clear water of the Dniester must have bubbled when Velvel was fighting beneath it for his life. Velvel, the student, the musician... Velvel singing half the night to his father in an outhouse... Velvel waking him at three in the morning to transcribe a melody... Velvel singing in the synagogue, music his life, his one consuming ambition. Velvel, a forgotten corpse, long annihilated by the hungry worms of the Zvonitz graveyard, the Christ-like Jew crucified to fatten fat swine, his blood bubbling protestingly in the transparent glasses.

He saw the servile Berger approach the table, fawning on his distinguished guests, his long body arrested in a low bow, washing both jewelled hands in the air before him. The Baron said something; Romanovsky grinned, and Herr Stock roared good-humouredly, poking a finger in Berger's stomach. Berger smiled, his mood was trained to be always that of the customer, he bent still lower as Romanovsky beckoned him closer and whispered a few words in his ear. The proprietor straightened himself and nodded, then, with what seemed to be oily apologies he backed away from the

97

table like a courtier departing from the presence of royalty, and Phineas saw him make his way to the balcony.

Berger's usually colourless face held a red tinge of pleasurable excitement when he confronted Phineas. 'Ah, Pittilingri,' he said cordially, rubbing his hands. 'I've got a request for you.'

'Oh?' replied Phineas. 'What do they want?'

'*They*?' said Berger. 'Wait till I tell you who *they* are.'

'I know who they are,' replied Phineas coldly.

'Good!' Berger was all smiles, too much concerned with his own preoccupations to jib at the tone of the leader's voice. 'Good, Pittilingri! Then you realise what an honour this is. They are not the ordinary lumpen. Romanovsky himself asked for some gypsy airs!' he announced triumphantly.

'Did he?' said Phineas. 'Well, you can tell him I'm not playing any tonight.'

Berger stared at him as if he had taken leave of his senses. Surely he must be jesting! He essayed a half smile, but Phineas stood before him pale and determined, his lips pressed together in a thin red line. The smile vanished from Berger's face and his bushy eyebrows drew together ominously in a forbidding frown.

'Listen, my friend,' he said threateningly, his voice never raised above a throaty whisper. 'Let me warn you. Nobody can do what you're trying to do to Maxie Berger and get away with it. Don't give yourself airs because for the past few months you've had enough to eat. Now stop this foolishness and get on with your job.'

'My job is to play,' replied Phineas. 'And that's what I'm going to do. But I'm not playing Velvel's music for that bandit Romanovsky. He stole "Valse Arabesque" from me, he's not stealing anything else!'

'Idiot! You've gone off your head!' muttered Berger angrily. 'Stole "Valse Arabesque"! Enough of this nonsense, Pittilingri!' The frown reluctantly left his face and gave way to a forced, oily smile. 'Now don't let's fall out, Pittilingri,' he wheedled. 'Just do what I ask you this once, to oblige me.'

'I'm sorry, Max,' said Phineas slowly, as if the words were being dragged out of him. 'I can't. It's impossible. I won't play for Romanovsky.'

Berger dropped at once all pretence of friendliness. 'I'm not used to being spoken to like this,' he said sharply. 'For the last time, are you going to play?'

'No,' replied Phineas.

'Very well. Pittilingri is dead. Clear out of my place!' He turned to the first violin. 'Fritz, take over!'

His expression truly Mephistophelian, even to the hectic red smears of anger on his greyish cheeks, Berger flashed a vindictive glance at Phineas and spat insultingly at the fiddler's feet, then he turned his back on him and clumped heavily down the stairs.

The Marie-Thérèse was an excellent recommendation, so Phineas felt reasonably certain of quickly obtaining another situation. He reckoned without Berger, however. The café proprietor paid a visit to the district police and gave them a short biographical sketch of the late Pittilingri. Several days later, a gendarme called for Phineas and politely asked the violinist to accompany him to the station. Phineas went along, mildly puzzled, but not unduly alarmed, since he had no misdemeanours whatsoever upon his conscience. The police inspector was perched behind a desk raised above the floor level in the ascetically sober charge room. Only two arms, a massive pair of shoulders and a round face showed above the desk, the inspector's greying moustache seeming too absurdly adult for his pink-and-white schoolboy complexion. He nodded in friendly fashion as Phineas came before him, one strong white hand thoughtfully caressing his chin.

'Your name is Herr Kahn?' asked the inspector affably, glancing at a dossier on the desk before him.

'Yes, sir,' Phineas replied.

'You are a musician?'

'Yes, sir.'

'You have been playing for some time at the café Marie-Thérèse?'

'Yes, sir.'

'Pittilingri, you called yourself. That's not your real name, is it?'

'No, sir. My Christian name is Phineas – the Pittilingri was the proprietor's idea,' he added hurriedly.

'Don't be alarmed, Herr Kahn,' said the inspector kindly. 'That's not a criminal offence. I may say I have listened to Pittilingri on several occasions myself, and although this is hardly the place to do it, I should like to compliment him on his playing.'

'Thank you, sir.' Phineas breathed a sigh of relief. These Viennese were a queer lot. Fancy calling him to the station to hand him bouquets!

'You are a Russian subject?' the police inspector continued.

'Yes, sir.'

'You served in the army?'

'Yes, sir.'

'Did you complete your term of military service?' His voice assumed a graver tone. 'Now, think carefully before you answer me,' he said.

Phineas blanched and his heart seemed to miss a beat, then to rush ahead pounding violently upwards till it pulsed in his larynx like an obstruction in his throat.

'I...Well... I did,' Phineas stammered. '... All but four months, that is.'

'Only four months!' said the inspector. 'Four months, four weeks or even four days, what's the difference? Technically you are still a deserter. You have been very foolish, Herr Kahn.'

Phineas hung his head dejectedly, a morbid premonition growing on him as of some impending catastrophe. The very air about him seemed to have become clammy and heavy as lead. When this oppression burst, he felt that with it would tumble his whole world about his shoulders. The inspector rapped gently with a pencil on the desk. He was an amiable man and found this an unenviable task since the violinist seemed quite a decent young fellow, with probably a promising career ahead of him. Why couldn't the greasy Maxie have minded his own business? Ach! The world was full of all sorts of people.

'... Hmmm! ... I am very sorry, Herr Kahn,' he said at last, 'but I am afraid you will have to leave Vienna. You may reside anywhere else in Austria, but you must vacate the city within the next fortnight.'

A fortnight! This was worse, much worse than anything he had expected. Phineas felt at that moment like a patient, imagining his ailment progressing satisfactorily, suddenly being informed by the doctor that he was about to die. This was death too, in real earnest, the death of all his dreams. A fortnight to wind up his life, pack up his bundles and move off to the Lord knows where! And Shandel! Poor Shandel. Surely this was too harsh a judgement!

'A fortnight...!' he exclaimed. 'But, your excellency, my wife...'

The inspector shook his head. 'I am sorry,' he repeated. 'Those are my instructions. That is the law, and nothing I may be able to do can alter it. Of course, there is nothing against your wife, she can stay here as long as she pleases, but you must leave Vienna within fourteen days.'

The harassed young couple went at once to Rappoport, their corpulent godfather. The genial corn chandler was as upset at this turn of events as Phineas and Shandel themselves. He strode about his little shop parlour agitatedly, his hands thrust deep in his pockets. Cosmic problems he found not one tenth as difficult: he could settle the nature of the universe and the correct apportionment of its deities with a wave of the hand and the flick of half a dozen thick, yellow pages, but he was impotent as a child in the face of this tiniest of terrestrial problems.

'Well, what are you thinking of doing?' he said at last, halting before them.

'Shandel has some relatives in America,' Phineas replied haltingly. 'They would help me if I went there.'

'America...' said Rappoport. 'That's a long way off. Have you got any money?'

Phineas gestured despairingly with his hands.

'Hmmm! I thought not!' Rappoport's right hand tugged thoughtfully at his ear. 'Well, I'll get you a steamship ticket to America,' he announced. 'If I could afford it, I would send you both, but corn chandling is almost as bad as philosophy these days. Shandel will have to stay here till you send for her.'

The young couple looked at each other, and Shandel's underlip quivered as though she were about to burst into tears. Phineas averted his head hastily, he felt like tears himself. Rappoport regarded them sadly, like a worried, kindly parent, as both their faces delineated only too clearly the tumult in their minds. What sort of animals are we Jews, he thought bitterly, that we must always have heaped on us every sort of indignity? It would be a crime to separate these two dear souls, yet his own resources were so slender that there was no option if Phineas was to go to America.

'Don't you know someone nearer home?' he asked, flinging a chance stone into the whirling maelstrom of their thought. 'Someone in Germany, in France or in England?'

Phineas shook his head, but Shandel sat up hopefully; to her this meant a new lease of life. Breathing a silent invocation, she opened her bag and rummaged amongst its contents. 'Good Lord, Dear Lord, I hope it's still there!' She searched feverishly, and at last, with a muttered prayer of thankfulness, extracted a crumpled envelope. Smoothing it out on the table, she deciphered a name and an address in London. She passed the envelope across to Rappoport.

'My mother's cousin, Rachel,' she said.

Rappoport's face became one broad smile. He banged a podgy fist on the open palm of the second hand and let forth a triumphant whoop.

'Rachel! Of course!' he exclaimed excitedly. 'Isaac Levi's daughter. Why didn't I think of her before? Rachel's all right. She'll look after you. That settles it. I can just about manage to send both of you to London. Once there, you'll have to fend for yourselves.'

Phineas bought two large valises which were commodious enough to enclose all their personal belongings, with room to spare. Rappoport came to the Bahnhof to see them off. He found a corner seat for Shandel and, just before the train steamed out, he thrust a bouquet of flowers and a big box of chocolates in her arms. He stepped into the carriage and kissed her gently on the forehead, then, as the guard's flag went up and the locomotive moved off, noisily protesting with laborious grunts and squeaks at the load it had to pull, he stood forlornly on the platform waving a large, white handkerchief after the gliding coaches until the dense plume of grey smoke from the engine petered out into a thin wisp of frail, diaphanous mist. Then he blew his nose hard, surreptitiously wiped his eyes and went back to Franz, Frau Krawinkle and the select company of Kant, Spinoza and Hegel.

CHAPTER II

In the late nineties and the early years of the twentieth century, there were no restrictions on the entry of immigrants into England. Britain opened wide her hospitable gates, and immigrants, mostly desperate, harassed Jews, poured in from Eastern Europe to supply the cheap labour power, the sweat to grease the wheels of industry in its fight against the increasing technical superiority of Germany. A steady flow of escaping humanity, like life convicts precariously on parole, trickled into England, amongst them Phineas and Shandel, journeying like the rest to London, the Canaan of the West.

They had gone from Vienna to Leipzig by train. On the journey they gorged themselves with Rappoport's chocolates until at Leipzig they were so sick, they could hardly stand. Food was terribly dear *en route* – even a glass of water at the German station cost them five pfennigs apiece. At Leipzig they entrained for Rotterdam via Halle, and at the Dutch port they boarded the mail boat *Hook Of Holland*. By this time they had only sufficient money left for a cup of coffee each. The boat sailed at midnight, and after a rough crossing the passengers landed at Harwich at seven in the morning. There, Phineas and Shandel, hungry and miserable, caught the boat train for the last lap of their journey to London. It was October 13th 1900, a date Phineas remembered for the rest of his life. Famished and bedraggled, he huddled beside Shandel in a corner of the coach and tried to sleep, but the roaring wheels jogged his nerves, beating an angry tattoo in his head. 'Thirteen! –Thirteen! October Thirteen!'

At midday, the train steamed slowly into the gloomy cavern of Liverpool Street station. Phineas and Shandel were amongst the last to step on the platform. The young couple looked about them with amazement, the rush and flurry, the babel of strange tongues and the Stygian darkness seeming more suited for a province of hell than an artery of the world's greatest city. Exhausted by the strain of the journey, they put their valises on the ground and sat on them while the rest of the passengers swirled past them and the platform slowly emptied. The guard, carrying a flickering lantern, his flag neatly rolled under his arm, chatted for a moment to the driver, then both of them walked off into the gloom with a clatter of heavy boots, without so much as one inquisitive glance at the weary travellers. The long black engine resting against the buffers, sweating like some coarse, gigantic monster from the underworld, seemed to grin at them malevolently, while the hoarse, melancholy whistling of incoming and departing trains added their dreary quota to the overpowering air of desolation. Shandel looked at Phineas and bit her lips to restrain the quivering flow of tears. They were penniless and completely alone in a strange country, understanding neither the customs nor the language of its inhabitants. Sitting glumly on their valises, they felt like a couple of stranded barnstormers, without even the salute of rotten cabbages to acknowledge their existence.

A porter trundling a loaded truck clattered down the platform. He slackened his gait for a moment as he approached the young couple, then walked right past them and disappeared. A few minutes later he returned, nonchalantly pulling the empty truck behind him. Halting before the immigrants, he stood over them with straddled feet, pushing his peaked cap to the back of his head.

'What's the matter?' he asked in fluent Yiddish. 'Why are you both seated on the ground? Has there been a death in the family, or are you observing the fast of Tisoo-Be-Ab?'

Phineas wearily regarded his interrogator. He was not in the least surprised to hear this smoke-begrimed individual in his shabby blue uniform address him in a familiar language. In his weakened condition he had no hold on reality; what was happening might be real or a nightmare. The porter might even, quite conceivably, change at any moment into his brother Samuel before his eyes.

'Well?' grinned the porter cheerily, with a flash of teeth comically white in his face of a Kentucky minstrel interlocutor. 'Well, brother, what are you sitting about for?'

'Because I can't stand,' replied Phineas dully. 'Could you, after you'd fasted for twenty-four hours?'

'Oh, it's like that, is it?' said the porter, serious at once. 'Isn't there someone coming to meet you?'

Phineas shook his head without replying.

'No money at all?'

'Not a copper,' said Phineas.

'Hmmm!' The porter scratched his head thoughtfully. 'At least, have you got some place to go to?' he asked.

Phineas took the precious envelope from his pocket and handed it to the porter, who glanced over it rapidly and stuck it away in his jacket.

'That's something, anyway,' he commented. 'Now you two orphans get up and come with me.'

The porter placed their valises on the truck and moved down the platform, Phineas and his wife following close behind. He led them past the barrier to the station buffet and, seating them at a table, placed their baggage on the floor beside them. Then he spoke some magical words to a high-busted blonde behind the bar, who nodded comprehendingly, glancing with large motherly eyes commiseratingly at the young couple. The parley concluded, the tall, blonde barmaid gave a decisive shake of the head and vigorously began to rub some dirty glasses. The porter came over to the emigrants.

'Just you two stay here till I come back,' he said.

He patted Phineas gently on the shoulder and, smiling reassuringly at Shandel, lit a short-stemmed clay pipe like a born Cockney. Then he stuck his hands in his pockets and clumped from the buffet, his head wreathed in a halo of grey smoke.

In a few moments, the blonde barmaid, who in her neat black dress appeared to the young couple like a smart society lady, placed before them two large mugs of coffee and a pile of sandwiches. Phineas looked at her gratefully, like a starving dog thrown the wing of a chicken.

'Danke schön, Fräulein,' he said in German.

The barmaid smiled and nodded regally. She understood that he was trying to thank her, although what he said sounded like some sort of Chinese. Shandel sat bolt upright, her hands resting before her on the table, looking nervously first at the sandwiches, then at the blonde angel. It seemed too good to be true. She stared piteously at the barmaid waiting for an unambiguous sign that all this food was for her and not at all a mistake. The barmaid bent down and gently caressed her hair.

'Go on. Drink it up, duckie,' she said encouragingly. 'Eat. Get some food in you. God knows you look as if you need it!'

In pantomime, she raised a glass to her lips and chewed vigorously, pointing to the coffee and the sandwiches. Shandel smiled gratefully; truly, this was manna from heaven! With a swish of stiff petticoats the barmaid walked off. Shandel passed a timorous hand across the table to feel her husband's warm grip. A current of rich, pulsating life seemed to course from his strong fingers into her veins, heating her blood like the action of a fine liqueur. She felt strong again and unafraid. Smiling gently like a radiant Madonna, she inclined her shapely head and began at last to eat.

An hour later the porter returned, followed by Shandel's Uncle Samuel, a raucous symphony in brown. He was a corpulent, chubby-faced man of about the average height but appeared much shorter because of his stoutness. He wore a brown bowler hat, a chequered brown tweed suit and brown snub-toed button boots with fawn cloth uppers. He recognised Shandel at once and greeted Phineas cordially. Dismissing the porter with a tip, and sufficient money to pay the bill, he picked up one valise and, followed by Phineas carrying the other, led the way out of the station, Shandel bringing up the rear.

It was still early in the afternoon, yet outside it was dark as night, the street being shrouded in a pall of fog, a phenomenon the young couple had not previously encountered. Visibility was limited to no more than six yards in any direction. The frustrated yellow flame of the gas lamps, miraculously suspended in mid-air, glimmered anaemically, and black muffled shadows shuffled past, like figures in a vapour bath filled with greyish-brown steam. Shandel's uncle hailed a hansom, and a strange horse-drawn conveyance pulled up at the kerb. It resembled a phaeton, except that the wheels were much larger, and the driver instead of sitting in the front of the coach, was perched aloft behind, in order, no doubt, that the foul breath from the horse's nostrils should blow without hindrance into the passengers' faces.

They climbed into the cab, and Shandel, filled with gloomy

forebodings at having thus stumbled into an Egyptian plague, clutched her husband's arm and huddled close to him. The driver made strange clicking sounds between his teeth, and the cab rolled off, sailing like Elijah and his chariot through the black clouds of heaven. Phineas, although outwardly calm, felt just as scared as Shandel, engulfed in this inexplicable darkness. London must be like no other place in the world; if this was their kind of weather, what sort of lives must these Londoners lead? What did they eat? How did they sleep? He felt lost, lost. They should have stayed in Austria. There at least the climate was comprehensible, the heavens were stable and not liable to descend suddenly in a tickling blackness in the middle of the day. He sat in silence, afraid to speak because the fog invaded his mouth and rasped at his throat. Even when he shut his lips tightly, his nostrils seemed choked with burning filth.

In twenty minutes, although to Phineas and his wife it seemed like so many hours, they reached their destination, a narrow street in Whitechapel banked on either side by small crooked houses that leered drunkenly over them like dirty hunchbacks. They alighted from the cab and, depositing their baggage on the pavement, listened uneasily to a terrific argument that immediately sprang up between Uncle Samuel and the suspended Jehu. There was no mistaking the subject of controversy, an argument sounded like an argument in any language, especially a dispute connected with money. Eventually the driver leaned downwards and accepted his payment with a surly string of guttural words. He straightened himself disgustedly, gave the crown of his beaver top hat a sharp pat, flicked his whip in the air and, producing the mysterious clicks without which apparently the horse would not start, moved off. The horse disappeared first, then the cab was swallowed into the fog, the driver wavered for a moment on his perch, looking like the unsteady shadow of a giant with a small head and a ludicrously enlarged behind, until he too vanished like a mad nightmare, only the sound of the horse's hooves and the grating of wheels showing that he still had a corporeal existence.

Their new home turned out to be a shabby three-storeyed house, the tallest building in the street. Rachel, a dark, buxom hook-nosed Jewess, fell on Shandel's neck as soon as she entered and shed copious tears of joy. There followed the usual interminable interrogation concerning relatives and friends left behind in the old country. Her inquisitiveness temporarily satisfied, Rachel led them to a room on the first floor, next to her own bedroom. It was obviously used for storing stock. Tall stacks of cardboard boxes and piles of new caps occupied the whole available space with the exception of a small area beneath a window overlooking the yard. Rachel apologised for having nothing better to offer, this being the one unoccupied room. The house contained six rooms in all, the two on the ground floor serving as kitchen and living quarters, two on the first floor for bedroom and stock, and the top two being given over to the manufacture of caps.

Uncle Samuel carried in a huge sack bursting with straw and laid it on the floor beneath the window. This was their bed. Thankful to find any sort of haven, the youthful wanderers laid themselves down wearily on the sack and, fully clothed as they were, immediately fell asleep.

Phineas woke soon after dawn. The sun shone brightly outside, no trace of the previous day's fog lingering in the keen air. Phineas felt refreshed, his confidence blossoming anew in the birth of a new day. Shandel lay beside him still sleeping peacefully, her hands clasping Phineas's arm pinioned protectingly round her waist. Phineas, afraid to free himself in case he wakened her, turned gently on his back and propped his other arm behind his neck, staring unblinkingly at the ceiling. Soon, heavy feet began to clump past the door and up the steps. A pressing iron banged in the room above and a machine started to whirr like a humming top. The iron thumped on monotonously, louder and louder, and several more machines started up singing like a chorus of drones, while the ceiling quivered sympathetically overhead, as if it too were a functioning part of the factory.

At last Shandel woke up with a smile as if she had been dreaming pleasant dreams. She kissed her husband and stretched herself luxuriously like a bride on a down-filled bed. Phineas rose to his feet and saluted the day with a tune on the fiddle, then they descended the rickety stairs, which were not wide enough to allow them to walk down abreast, and washed themselves beneath the tap in the yard. Brimful of optimism they breakfasted with

Rachel on eggs, bread and butter, coffee and questions, and at the conclusion of the meal sat back sated, eager to come to grips with London, no longer a dusky wilderness, but to them a magical garden, filled with the choicest fruits.

At one o'clock the workshop emptied and Uncle Samuel came down for his dinner. He washed his hands under the tap, and wiping his bald, greasy head with a dirty towel, loosened the top button of his trousers and pulled a chair to the table. He ate gluttonously, with terrific speed, and in ten minutes had completed his meal. He waited until Phineas had finished eating, then rose from his seat and called the young man up to the workshop.

The dividing wall between the two top rooms had been cut away, making one fairly commodious chamber; even so, it was ridiculously small adequately to accommodate its quota of eight workers excluding Uncle Samuel, the boss. Under one window overlooking the street was the boss's cutting table, and at right angles to the other stood a run of seven machines. The presser's table with its assortment of massive wooden blocks commanded the centre of the room, while in the farther corner was planted a small grooved bench for the female needle-hands.

Uncle Samuel balanced a portion of his behind on the corner of the cutting table, his short fat legs barely touching the floor, and faced Phineas. In the workshop, his undisputed kingdom, he dropped all his affability and the thin pretence of relationship. If Phineas wanted to stay he would have to earn his keep.

'Well, Phineas,' he said. 'You've had a long enough holiday. When are you going to start work?'

'I – I haven't had a chance to look for a job yet,' Phineas replied shamefacedly.

'Job!' snorted Uncle Samuel. 'Why, what can you do?'

'I am a musician,' said Phineas. 'After all, I used to earn a good living in Vienna, and in Kamenetz and Zvonitz as well.'

'Musician!' The fat man grunted disparagingly. 'That may be all right for Russia or Austria, but it won't get you anywhere in London. You've got a wife to keep now, my friend. Your best plan is to start at the machine,' he concluded pompously.

Phineas looked with a repellent fascination at the long row of machine tops glistening like black beetles with silver antennae.

Those inhuman little automata were waiting to ensnare him. His spirit faltered. The room appeared like a squalid jail, and the grinning machines like squat silent jailers. Uncle Samuel, his heavy-jowled judge, was casually condemning him to the sweatshop for life. He shuddered inwardly. Cursed be the day that had brought him to this cursed house! A black October Thirteen that would curl itself in a deep weal about his heart for the rest of his days.

Uncle Samuel's little brown eyes regarded Phineas shrewdly. He fathomed the dismay biting like a pecking bird at the young man's brain. Good! It was best that Phineas realised as soon as possible that in London, to eat, one had to work, and work hard. At home, in the small towns, these educated youngsters lived on the fat of the land. They did no manual labour, but spent the nights in study and the days wandering about, admiring the girls. This one had curves in front, that one curves behind. They played fiddles and wrote poems about birds and frogs, while the artisans slaved both day and night, and rarely had a chance to see either birds or frogs. More than once young students, still wet about the ears, had snubbed him as an unlettered ignoramus. They ranked in caste just below the wealthy merchants, while the workman was rated with the beggar in the social scale, and not always above the beggar either. In London the assessment was different. Skilled artisans were the gentlemen and the Talmudists had to drop their fancy airs and learn how to work. He would be revenged in a small way on Phineas for all the indignities he had suffered from students at home. 'I'll teach you what work is, my musician!' he reflected gloatingly. 'You'll fiddle with the machine till you won't know what any other music means!'

Phineas had no option but to begin as a learner at the machine. If the choice lay with him alone, he would have preferred to starve for a while until something better turned up, but he was no longer a free agent. Shandel must not starve. He was bound hand and foot – hand and foot!

The next morning he started at the machine. His teacher was a thin, freckled, red-haired young woman named Lena. She was thirty, but her physical development was that of a young girl of fifteen, only the dark rings under her eyes and the lines of care on her sharp, bony face betraying the load of years her undeveloped body had to carry. Lena was the one female machinist, the other five were pallid, stooping Jews. She seamed together cap linings all day and welcomed Phineas as a pupil, since she could, while teaching him, snatch an occasional few minutes from the endless grind.

Phineas proved an apt apprentice. Within a week Uncle Samuel transferred him from the linings to the caps proper. His new tutor was Benjamin, a short man with a twisted nose and black hair crinkled like a negro's. He had an enormous pale face, and wide, bent shoulders; stooping over the machine he gave the impression of a labouring Goliath, and the effect on a stranger when Benjamin rose was that of a startling optical illusion. The truncated giant was a gentle-mannered, soft-spoken, intelligent man, with always an undercurrent of bitterness in his conversation. He showed Phineas how to piece together the eight sections of the cap, and interwoven with the seams were his bitter, whispered words of warning. 'Escape, my young friend,' he kept dinning into his ears. 'Become a thief, a burglar, a cut-throat, but get out of the workshop. Escape while you're young, my friend.'

Phineas nodded; he meant to escape as soon as possible, but first, he intended to master the machine. He threw himself furiously into the distasteful labour. He went into the workshop at seven in the morning, half an hour before the rest of the staff arrived, and at ten when they left, he stayed behind. His fingers stiff from the unaccustomed straining, broad bands of pain constricting the small of his back, he stumbled downstairs to Shandel, always managing to put up a smiling front before he entered the room.

In a month he knew that he was proficient at his job. Already, he seamed caps fast enough by himself to feed three of the older machinists who did the more complicated work. For fourteen, fifteen hours a day he pedalled madly at the machine like a donkey harnessed to a crazy treadmill striving vainly for a juicy bunch of carrots. It was time, he decided, to ask for a rise. Uncle Samuel provided him with the leftovers from his table, and lodging, such as it was, and in addition allowed him two shillings a week for spending money. Phineas felt that was not enough. Trembling slightly in his nervousness he approached Uncle Samuel one night after the rest of the workers had gone home. The boss looked up interrogatively from the table. At once he sensed what was coming. He was only surprised that it had not happened before.

'Yes?' he said briskly.

Phineas coughed diffidently. 'I – I – think I am a worker now,' he muttered, turning red, the words stumbling thickly in his throat. '... I am quick... I want you to give me wages.'

'Hmmm!' Uncle Samuel scratched his head dubiously with the point of his scissors. '... Hmmm! Wages ... How much do you want?'

'... Well... I think I'm worth ten shillings a week.'

'What!' Uncle Samuel stared at him indignantly. 'Ten shillings a week, and board and lodging! Why, I don't earn that myself! Maybe *you'd* like to be boss, and change places with me?' he inquired sarcastically.

'I'm worth ten shillings,' repeated Phineas obstinately. 'And I can find somewhere else to live.'

Uncle Samuel considered the proposition for a moment. He appeared reluctant to concede such an exorbitant demand. After all, ten shillings was a lot of money to pay a beginner, but he was forced to admit to himself that Phineas was worth that much, and more; in reality he was pleased at striking such a hard bargain, but his visage betrayed only surly misgivings.

'Very well,' he said at last. 'You shall have your ten shillings. I'm only giving it to you because you're some sort of a relation. From next Monday, you start at ten shillings a week. But no slacking, Phineas, see you earn it!'

Shandel and Aunt Rachel went out hunting for lodgings. Eventually they discovered a narrow attic in Grove Street, a dirty little turning on the other side of Whitechapel, ten minutes' walk from the workshop. The tenant of the house, a cobbler, agreed to sublet the room for the peculiar rental of two-and-sevenpence a week; possibly he thought half a crown too little to ask, and three shillings too much. On the following Sunday Phineas piled his belongings on a barrow: two valises, an old iron bedstead and a verminous discoloured mattress lent indefinitely to Shandel by a warm-hearted neighbour. Phineas trundled his home to Grove Street, and, aided by the cobbler, lugged his furniture up the stairs into the attic. When the bedstead was set up and pushed against the wall, only a narrow corridor remained vacant, so that had the young couple possessed a table, there would have been no space to accommodate it.

When they wanted to eat, they balanced a baize-covered valise on two boxes and used another two boxes for chairs, but in spite of their cramped living quarters, Phineas and Shandel were happy. Every morning, after he had washed, said his prayers and breakfasted on weak tea and bread and margarine, Phineas played his violin before he went to work, keeping himself in practice against the day when he would earn his living by music once again. At night when he shuffled home wearily, his gait livened up at the corner of Grove Street, because he knew that a smiling Shandel would be leaning out of the tiny top window, waiting to greet him. Everything in the room was neat and clean, the bed tidied, and his supper, some bread and margarine and a penny-worth of chips, waiting for him on the valise. After supper Phineas played on his violin some of Velvel's music, and usually finished up with Tchaikovsky's 'Barcarolle', Shandel's favourite piece. During the recital his wife sat quietly on the edge of the bed, her hands folded modestly on her lap, and occasionally added her sweet soprano voice to the clear notes of the fiddle, blending her song to the instrument like the sound of a soft flute. Then they went to bed, and her love enfolded him, gripping him tightly like the closing petals of a slumbering flower.

Shandel soon discovered that she was pregnant. Her face was peaky from lack of adequate nourishment, but her belly was beginning to swell, and none of her clothes fitted her. She made some skilful insertions in her skirts and dresses, but the uppers of her high-laced boots were also beginning to divorce themselves from the soles, which were as thin as a cheap sheet of cardboard, and although she tried all manner of ingenious subterfuges the street damp seeped through uncompromisingly. At last she was forced to draw Phineas's attention to the alarming state of her wardrobe.

'Look here, Phineas,' she said one day. 'Don't you think my skirts are getting too short in front?'

Phineas looked up casually from his newspaper. 'No. I don't think they're so bad,' he said, returning to his reading.

Shandel sat on the edge of the bed and picked up her skirts a little higher.

'Do look,' she pleaded. 'I think they show too much of my legs.'

Phineas dropped his newspaper with an impatient sigh and glanced across at his wife. His eyes travelled down her legs and he saw with a shock the stockinged toes of her tiny feet wriggling like shy mice through the uppers of her boots. He sat up, appalled.

'Good God, Shandel!' he exclaimed. 'Your boots!'

Shandel nodded. 'It's about time you noticed them,' she replied. '... Well?'

'Well? What well?' he said. 'You'll have to get another pair of boots!'

'... Boots!' She smiled wistfully. 'With what?'

Phineas turned his head away in despair. She was right. They had barely enough for food. Boots meant an outlay of at least four or five shillings, and it was as much as he could do, with occasional fasts, to scrounge from his budget a surplus fourpence. No boots! In her condition, and in this damp, dangerous weather! Where was God to permit such a thing? He had sent down manna for the Hebrews in the wilderness, and opened them up a path in the Red Sea, and yet his sweet Shandel had to walk about without boots. 'Good God!' he prayed silently, fervently. 'If there is a God, show yet another miracle!' Perhaps Almighty Jehovah was listening. After all, he did not offer up an extravagant request; all he asked for was just a pair of boots.

The angel in charge of miracles must have been hovering about propitiously. He made a memorandum in his ledger – To P Kahn, one miracle – and flew over a couple of turnings into a tailor's work-shop where the presser, Schmiel Coleman, a tall, dark, taciturn man, was just finishing work. It was still early in the evening, being Sunday and a half-day, Schmiel's labours concluded at five-thirty. He drew on his overcoat, turned out the gas, said 'Goodnight' to the boss and descended from the workshop to the street.

Every night he went home through Grove Street, and every night stopped to listen approvingly to Phineas's nocturnes. The unseen violinist was obviously a capable musician, and tonight Schmiel had use for such a man. He mounted the stairs of the small house, following the sounds of the violin to the attic. Boots or no boots, Phineas had to play. When he was happy, joy was in his music, and when his heart wept, his fiddle cried with him.

Schmiel stopped outside the door and waited till the vibration of the sobbing strings died. Then he knocked gently.

Phineas put his instrument on the bed. 'Come in,' he said.

Schmiel opened the door and stepped in awkwardly. He had become after a fashion anglicised, although only five years separated him from the primitive life of a remote Russian hamlet. There, when a moujik or a Jew paid an unexpected call, he entered directly into the living-room and announced his presence by blowing his nose vigorously between his thumb and forefinger and skilfully depositing a splurge of mucus on the earthen floor. Schmiel closed the door quietly behind him and rubbed his chilled hands briskly together. Then, without troubling to remove his hat, he said: 'Good evening'.

'Good evening,' Phineas replied, wondering who the stranger might be. He was obviously a Jew, and middle-aged, but his face was entirely without expression. Such a Jew, thought Phineas in that brief hiatus, could very well be without a face, since apparently it served no useful purpose.

The visitor came to the point immediately, without any preliminary circumlocution. 'My name is Schmiel Coleman,' he said. 'I am a presser and I also play the clarinet. Every night I go through this street and hear you playing the violin. Sometimes I get a few musicians together to perform at weddings and simchas. Just for tonight I need a fiddler to play until twelve. Would you like the job?'

All this he rattled off in a voice as expressionless as his face. Phineas stared at him as though he could be none other than a manifestation of the archangel Gabriel himself. Half dazed, he dragged out a box from beneath the bed and begged the stranger to be seated. Schmiel shook his head.

'No. I must go now,' he said. 'Here's my address. Come round with your fiddle at eight o'clock.'

He turned towards the door, and as if reminding himself of something took his hand off the knob and faced them.

'As I'm already here,' he continued drily, 'I might as well give you a little advice. You should both take up the harp in your spare time, because it will probably come in handy shortly. From your faces you look as though neither of you is related to the Rothschilds, and in the other world I understand that all the musicians play on harps...Well, I'll see you at eight o'clock. Once again, goodnight!'

The young couple stared blankly at the door and heard Schmiel's heavy footsteps fade down the stairs, then they looked at each other dubiously, wondering whether their visitor was sane or just a stray madman. Phineas grinned at last, and, the tension broken, Shandel burst into a peal of laughter and flung her arms around his neck. He put his arms about her waist and, hoisting her off her feet, swung her boisterously around the constricted space. They were saved! Saved! The old God still lived!

At a quarter to eight Phineas arrived at Schmiel's house. The presser himself opened the door.

'Good!' he said. 'You're early.'

He ushered Phineas into the living-room and introduced him to Jacob, the cornet player, a stout, melancholy man seated on a shabby horsehair sofa. Now that the whole band was assembled, Schmiel decided on an impromptu rehearsal. Neither he nor Jacob could read music, and played entirely by ear, but fortunately Phineas knew all the tunes which were mainly traditional Jewish melodies and familiar Russian dances. An hour's rehearsal satisfied Schmiel's artistic scruples, and at nine o'clock the orchestra set out for the nuptial celebrations.

The guests were gathered in a large workshop temporarily emptied of tables and machines. Thirty people jostled together in a space that could comfortably hold no more than twelve. The bride, a young seamstress, had been given the freedom of the workshop for that evening by the boss, who, flushed and beaming, strolled patronisingly amongst his guests, while the bride's father, a meek little man, followed him about in fawning gratitude. The boss gave orders to the band, calling for polkas, waltzes, quadrilles, mazurkas, bulgars, controlling the tempo as if the band were turning out coats. When he shouted 'Faster!' Jacob's eyes almost popped out of his head with the concentrated strain of blowing. Rings of spectators gathered round serious-faced young couples dancing the kossatska. Hands clasped behind their backs they approached each other with short, mincing steps, danced round and round like courting cats, making advances, withdrawing coquettishly, then squatting in abandonment on their heels, wildly kicking alternate legs in the air, and the boss, the master of ceremonies, sticky with sweat, standing in the middle of the smoky room clapping his hands to the rhythm of the music, shouting 'Louder! Louder! Faster! Faster!'

Soon after twelve, when most of the guests retired, leaving the workshop to the bridal couple and their immediate family, the boss procured some chairs and a table, and the famished musicians seating themselves around it were served with wine and the remains of the wedding feast. After gorging themselves on cold fish and chicken, the boss paid off Schmiel, and the musicians departed. Beneath the light of a gas lamp in the street below, the cornet player and the violinist received their payment. Jacob's share was eight shillings, and Phineas got five. They shook hands and went their different ways, Phineas's colleagues, the cadaverous one and the stout one, vanishing into the early morning mist like unsmiling shadows. Walking seemed too earthy a mode of progression for Phineas, he felt light as a bird, graceful and buoyant. Hardly appearing to tread on hard pavements he flew home, clutching the silver tightly in his fist. Shandel, not yet asleep, was waiting up for him anxiously, lying quietly in bed.

'Well?' she asked as he entered.

Phineas nodded and took off his overcoat. He felt like a bridge builder at the conclusion of some prodigious feat of engineering. He tried to keep silent until he undressed, wanting to surprise her and delight her doubly by delaying the good news, but his enthusiasm bubbled over. He crossed to the bed and bending over her kissed her passionately till she breathlessly kicked up her legs beneath the counterpane in protest.

'Well? You haven't told me yet,' she said. She tried to speak sharply, but there was a laughing softness in her voice. '...You're not drunk, are you Phineas?'

'Drunk! Of course I'm drunk!' he whispered. 'Five shillings! Five shillings, Shandel. Think of it, I've earned your boots!'

CHAPTER III

Shandel, as the months wore on, leaned more and more on Phineas. She had no friends, nor did she desire them. Her moods had no independent existence; when Phineas was glad, she laughed, and when he was unhappy, she was miserable too. She even copied his grimaces, ate only when he ate, and when he did not eat, she refused to touch her food. Phineas was disturbed by the intensity of her devotion. He had other interests, the workshop, books, his music, but Shandel only lived when her husband was close to her.

In bed one night, she felt the child jerking in her belly. Reaching out for Phineas's hand she placed it gently over her stomach for a moment till the nervous pulsing of the embryo twitched the flesh below her husband's taut palm.

'Do you feel, Phineas?' she whispered.

'Yes. Yes, it's alive,' he breathed. Sharp, new emotions clouded his brain. He felt an immense access of tenderness towards his wife and the struggling mannikin in Shandel's body. A sense of awe and wonderment crept over him mixed with a tinge of anxiety at the rise of new responsibilities. He took his hand off her stomach and squeezed her arm gratefully. 'Alive! It's alive!'

'I'm glad,' she said simply. Caught up in the perennial miracle of life, the uneducated little milliner spoke with the words of a poet. 'I'm glad, Phineas. You are not only my husband, you are my lover and my child as well. I carry you about in my stomach. I won't be lonely any more. Even if you are somewhere else, I shall still feel you inside me.'

As Phineas grew more competent at the machine, egged on by Benjamin, he demanded increasing wages. Every two-shilling rise was dragged out of Uncle Samuel like meat from the paws of a hungry tiger, until, the Sunday before little Olga was born, his weekly wage with the latest increase reached the magnificent total of sixteen shillings. To celebrate the double event he moved into new quarters, on the second floor of a small house in the next turning. For four shillings a week he had one fairly large room which served as a bedchamber, and a small kitchen with a dirty chipped sink and running water, a rare luxury in those days. As a further mark of opulence he had discarded the valises and installed a table purchased second-hand on the Mile End Waste. Phineas now made a comfortable living, except that he had difficulty in obtaining sufficient food and paying the rent on Monday. As if that were not worry enough, Shandel demanded extra money every Thursday to buy, like other Jewesses, the plaited, poppy-seed besprinkled bread, and prepare the Sabbath dishes. Thursday he found the worst day of the week, a day that for poor Jews should be erased from the calendar. Phineas received his wages on Sunday and by Thursday his funds were at their lowest ebb. Every Thursday night, after listening to Shandel's plaintive requests for money, he would lie awake in bed for hours quarrelling with Moses in the darkness for commanding the Jews to remember the Seventh Day and keep it holy, and even in his dreams he had fierce arguments with the Lawgiver, who looked just like the rabbi of the local synagogue except that he was paler and greyer, and glowed with a luminous sanctity.

In the end, worn out by the Thursday complaint, he decided to become a Monday Jew. Sunday being his pay day, he resolved to observe the same night as the Sabbath Eve with all its attendant ritual and prayers, substituting only the word 'shanee' second, for 'shavee-ee' the seventh day, in the liturgy. Shandel, although she found it rather queer at first, adjusted herself to the new chronology. Phineas convinced her, not that she needed much convincing, that such a procedure under certain circumstances was within the rabbinical law. Phineas was an educated Talmudist; if Phineas said so, it must be right.

She went out to the market on Sunday afternoon and did her Saturday shopping. Being the eve of the Sabbath they had potatoes with their herring and bread and margarine, and occasionally fresh fruit. As they could not afford the large white wax candles, Shandel said the Sabbath prayer over two tiny Chanukah candles, one coloured red, the other perhaps green, stuck on two inverted egg cups. The tinted candles were used popularly in commemoration of a national holiday. When Judas Maccabaeus, one of the five sons of the priest Mattathias, had led the Jews to victory over the Syrian host of Antiochus, the everlasting flame before the ark of the Law in the Temple at Jerusalem had been left unattended, but for eight days the oil replenished itself and the flame still lived. To celebrate the miracle and the victory, the Hebrews burn every year gaily coloured candles in the menorah, the eight-branched candelabra, lighting one candle on the first day of the festival and adding one more each succeeding day until eight flickering arms testify to the greatness of Jehovah. Chanukah candles were sold cheaply in boxes, so Phineas and his wife celebrated the Sabbath, together with the second day of Chanukah, all the year round.

Phineas stayed with Uncle Samuel for two years, still working for sixteen shillings a week, a sum that in spite of his frequent solicitations remained as unalterable as the laws of the Medes and the Persians. When Olga was fifteen months old, Shandel became pregnant again. Phineas confided in Benjamin while Uncle Samuel was busy downstairs.

'My wife is going to have another baby,' he whispered. 'I can't make a living on sixteen shillings.'

Benjamin nodded without glancing up from his work. 'You are worth more, much more,' he replied. 'If I were you, I'd look for another job.'

'I'll ask him again tonight,' said Phineas. 'If he refuses, I'll have to take your advice.'

That evening, when the workshop emptied, Phineas stayed behind. As soon as he and Uncle Samuel were alone, he approached the boss and stood silently before the cutting table until Uncle Samuel looked up.

'... Shandel is going to have another baby,' Phineas said after an awkward pause.

'Well?' The boss grinned. 'I hope you're not blaming me!'

Phineas laughed sheepishly. 'I want another rise,' he said. 'I shall need the extra money.'

Uncle Samuel laid down his shears. 'I'm sorry,' he replied with an air of finality. 'I can't pay more. Sixteen shillings is all you're worth. Why, sixteen shillings is the equivalent of eight roubles, and in Russia, who earns eight roubles a week? A lawyer or a second-class government official! Because your wife's going to have another squawker, you find that's not sufficient. Well, that's not my fault. If you can't afford children,' he added sarcastically, 'you should leave Shandel alone!'

Phineas left the workshop, his face burning with resentment. Benjamin was waiting for him at the corner.

'Well?' he asked. 'Any luck?'

Phineas shook his head despondently.

'Look here,' said Benjamin. 'There's a firm in Edward Street – Birnbaum's. They're short of machinists, I know. Pop down there one day and see what you can do.'

On the following morning, Phineas arose earlier than usual. Neglecting his violin, he left the house soon after breakfast and walked to Edward Street, a narrow turning off the Minories, tenanted mainly by commercial houses. Birnbaum's factory was a drab three-storied building, the tiny windows of which were encrusted with layers of dirt that looked as though it had been left undisturbed for at least ten years. Outside the main entrance there was a large notice: CAP MACHINISTS WANTED, ONLY THOSE WITH OWN MACHINES NEED APPLY. Own machines – that was the snag! Dejectedly he walked back to work. It looked as though he were doomed to remain with Uncle Samuel for the rest of his life. During the dinner hour, Benjamin walked part of the way home with him.

'I've been to Birnbaum's,' said Phineas.

'Well?'

'It says, "Only those with own machines need apply".'

'That's all right,' said Benjamin reassuringly. 'Most of the big firms make that stipulation. You have to get the head, they supply the stand. You can pick up a second-hand machine almost any-where for ten bob.'

'Ten bob!' Phineas exclaimed. 'You might as well say ten pounds!'

Benjamin stroked his chin thoughtfully. 'Look here,' he said. 'There's a friend of mine in that business. Come round to his place with me on Sunday and we'll buy a machine. I'll lend you the money. Pay me back when you can.'

'Thanks,' said Phineas gratefully. 'But do you think I'll be suitable for Birnbaum's?' he asked anxiously. Living from hand to mouth, he could not afford to take chances. Even one week's speculative idleness was beyond the reach of his pocket.

'Don't worry,' said Benjamin. 'You'll do well enough. They make the same class of work as ours. In any case, you've got nothing to lose. You can earn sixteen shillings a week anywhere seaming linings.'

'And what about notice?' asked Phineas. 'Don't I have to give Uncle Samuel a week's notice?'

'Why should you?' replied Benjamin. 'The boss doesn't give any of us notice, we simply get the sack. Take my tip and say nothing to Uncle Samuel. Go to Birnbaum's on Monday morning and start work. If you're suitable, well and good; if not you can come back in a day or so and say you've been queer, and in the meantime you can be looking round for something else.' Benjamin's mouth drooped at the corners, his eyes clouded looking back on the thwarted hopes, the continuous misery of his life, and his face took on a bitterness to match his words as he continued. 'Uncle Samuel is like a leech. If you let him, he'll suck every drop of blood out of your body, I've had six years of him – and that's six years too much for any human being... If I knew who first invented caps,' he broke out with a whimsical ferocity, 'I'd pour filth all over his grave and curse him and his ancestors right back to Adam!'

Early next Monday morning, Phineas donned his phylacteries and wrapping his praying shawl round him prayed loud and fervently, enunciating every word clearly and unmistakably, unlike his usual matutinal procedure, which was to slur over the invocations at top speed. In medieval times his ancestors rent their garments, dressed in sackcloth and fasted when they craved a special boon from Jehovah, when they wanted him to spare a city, or rain down destruction on an enemy; in the same way Phineas set out for Birnbaum's without touching his breakfast, his clothes, the only garments he possessed, already rent from constant wear, and a disgrace to decent sackcloth, clutching the second-hand machine under his arm.

Mr Birnbaum himself interviewed Phineas. Although he had a manager and a staff of forty hands, he liked to engage or discharge each worker personally, keeping an intimate finger on the pulse of the factory. He was a slim, hawk-eyed active little man of middle age, with a large hooked nose and a sly peering expression. He asked Phineas where he had worked last, for how long, and wanted to know the class of trade to which he was accustomed. The particulars being satisfactory he engaged Phineas on a week's trial at twenty-five shillings.

He took Phineas up to the top floor and indicated a vacant machine stand. Then he introduced him to the manager, Mr Somper, a burly red-faced man, and left him to become acquainted with the details of the work. The first half-day Phineas had a little difficulty in adjusting himself. He had never worked in a large factory before. There were, apart from pressers and finishing hands, twelve machinists on his floor alone, more than the entire personnel of Uncle Samuel's workshop. Whenever he was in any doubt or difficulty with regard to the work, his immediate neighbours good-naturedly lent a hand. By the second day he was quite at home, on the best of terms with his neighbours and his work. He pedalled away feverishly, as if he were contesting a never-ending race against time. On one occasion he looked up to find Mr Birnbaum behind him. It was a habit of the boss's to appear silently and disconcertingly at unexpected times in different parts of the factory. He would pad about, soft-footed as a cat, and rise up like an apparition at the very elbows of the workers, his long nose thrust forward attentively, his keen eyes peering like X-rays for the slightest signs of slackness or bad workmanship. Mr Birnbaum watched Phineas in silence for a few minutes, then he smiled encouragingly, patted him on the shoulder and disappeared as abruptly as he had materialised. Phineas breathed a devout sigh of relief and continued his furious assault on the caps.

On the Wednesday evening when he returned home from work, he found a visitor awaiting him, none other than Uncle Samuel. His late employer rose to his feet as Phineas entered and treated him to an expansive smile, then he clasped his hand warmly, looking over him critically.

'I'm glad you're on your feet again,' he said. 'I've just heard that you've been ill.'

Phineas blushed. The lie was only too apparent, and he could see that Uncle Samuel had not swallowed the fabrication. Somehow he could not get over the feeling that he was still bound to his former employer. For the previous two days he had rehearsed over and over again the things he would say to Uncle Samuel. Although he had a withering, sarcastic speech all planned in his head, now, when that brown corpulence was poised like a chequered balloon in the room, he was reduced to an impotent, shamefaced stuttering, like the excuses of a criminal caught with his hand in somebody's pocket.

'I – I *have* been queer,' he faltered, 'but I'm all right now.'

'That's good!' said Uncle Samuel heartily. 'Now when are you coming back to work?'

'I'm sorry,' Phineas replied, 'but I've got another job.'

'Another job!' exclaimed Uncle Samuel. 'Why? Didn't I treat you well enough?' He seemed to swell with magnanimous benevolence as he continued. 'If it's just a matter of money, you know I'm not the sort of man to let a few shillings stand between me and a worker, especially a relation. Why do you have to work for someone else? Come back and I'll give you a pound a week!'

Phineas shook his head. 'That's not enough,' he said. I'm getting twenty-five shillings now.'

Uncle Samuel tilted his bowler hat back from his brow. 'Now let me warn you,' he said weightily. 'I'm a friend of yours. It makes no difference to me whether you come back or not, but the sort of job you've got is no good to you at all. You'll get twenty-five bob while the season lasts, but as soon as it gets slack, out you'll go. With me, you'll be getting a pound a week, but it will be regular, all the year round. There will be times when I won't be earning a penny myself, but you'll get your pound just the same. Now, are you coming back?'

'No,' said Phineas firmly. 'I'm satisfied where I am.'

'Right,' grunted Uncle Samuel with a surly twist of his mouth. 'Right! Whatever happens, you've only yourself to blame, but I'm not sorry for you, only for Shandel. After the way I've treated you, fed you, clothed you, housed you, taught you a trade and put you on your feet, you play me a dirty trick like this. Right! I won't forget! Just you try and get me to pick you out of the gutter again – that's all!'

Vastly indignant, the very air about him rippling with outraged righteousness, Uncle Samuel bounced out of the room slamming the door behind him with such force that the whole house seemed to rock, and the walls to quiver after he left.

Uncle Samuel's prognostications were not fulfilled. Birnbaum's always seemed to have plenty of work. Phineas was put on the piece-rate, and his wages averaged close on thirty shillings weekly. He was still unable to reconcile himself to the factory while his hopes of a musical career faded farther and farther in the background, although he still played regularly every morning and every evening. The factory seemed like an insatiable octopus, squeezing the marrow from his bones by degrees. The other workers were comparatively content. They had, since infancy, known no other life than the perpetual drudgery of the workshops, and apart from the higher wages, a thirteen-hour day was child's play compared with the diurnal amount of labour that had been extracted from them in Russia or Poland. Again, they found in England some degree of freedom. After the despotism of the Tsar, and the cast-iron fetters of the Polish Shliacta, the Western Isle was for them truly the home of the free and the land of the blest.

But for Phineas there was no freedom, either in the workshop or at home. He hated caps. He had been brought up to revere learning, and regarding culture as the ultimate aim of the full man, had laboriously schooled himself in the world of literature and music. It galled him to waste most of the day in the factory and to be unable to employ usefully his few hours of leisure at home. Shandel bore him a child every eighteen months; she now had a family of three, Olga and two boys, and monopolised his free time with the abundance of her love. When he tried to read a book she would brush it aside reproachfully. 'Look at me,' she would pout, 'not at the musty old book. I don't see you all day, and when you are at home for a few minutes, you bury yourself in a book. Look at me and the children. We are your books!'

Shandel's situation was tragic. Utterly friendless, and without mental diversions of any sort, she needed all of him that he could spare, but Phineas hungered for the more intellectual side of life. Secretly he put away a little money each week until he saved up enough to send for Copper Beard and his wife. Shandel's parents lived alone in Zvonitz, her two sisters having married and left the district. From their letters Phineas knew that they would not be averse to coming to London, and their presence in the city might save him. If Shandel had her parents close to her, he might be able to transfer some of her all-devouring love, and thus resume his acquaintance with Teitlebaum's friends the authors.

Berel, his magnificent copper beard now heavily streaked with grey, came to London with his right foot foremost. Practically as soon as he stepped off the boat he obtained a part-time situation at an East End synagogue, and started a small Hebrew class in his back room. Phineas's ruse succeeded. Shandel spent a good deal of her time with her parents, and the older children looked forward to such visits which meant toys and tit-bits that Phineas had never been able to afford.

When he came home from work in the evening and the children were asleep, he would sometimes urge Shandel to drop in at her parents', who lived only a few streets away. Shandel never required much persuasion, and after she was gone, Phineas would settle down contentedly to a few hours' solid reading. Only that occasional snatched pleasure, his music and the love of his wife and children made life at all bearable for Phineas. By the alchemy of the written word the encircling drabness was changed for a few hours into the richly woven tapestry of a more civilised existence, where men had minds and were allowed to use them, and talent was an asset instead of a shameful liability.

CHAPTER IV

Wages suddenly took a turn for the worse at Birnbaum's. A new contract had come in for fine worsted caps which required exceptionally skilled and careful handling, any alterations having to be made good in the operator's own time. The first week, Phineas's wages dropped by five shillings, and his pay docket was light by a similar amount on the following week. The Sunday after that, he brought home exactly a pound. Shandel turned the money over and over in her palm, and at last looked up at her husband.

'What can I do with that?' she demanded.

Phineas shrugged his shoulders despairingly. 'You'll have to manage somehow,' he replied.

How she could do it he had no idea, but manage she would by some miraculous means. He was determined, however, to get an increase of wages. All the machinists on his floor were grumbling, they were the luckless ones who had to work on the worsted caps. During the dinner hour next day they held an impromptu meeting, and Barnet, a tall, lean, lumbering man of sixty with hungry-looking, high cheekbones, the doyen of the machinists, was chosen to interview the boss. Barnet was closeted with Mr Birnbaum for half an hour, then he returned glumly to his machine. The rest of the workers had no need to inquire about what had happened, they could see only too clearly that their demands had been turned down. Barnet seated himself heavily on his stool and spread out his hands in a hopeless gesture.

'No use,' he said. 'Birnbaum says we'll have to carry on till the contract's finished.'

'That's what *he* says,' broke in Phineas. 'Haven't *we* got something to say about it too?'

'Well, say,' replied Barnet wearily. 'You can say your head off for all the good it will do.'

'That's just it!' said Phineas. 'Saying's not enough; we ought to go on strike!'

Snobby, a pale shifty-eyed man of about thirty-five, jumped excitedly to his feet. 'Strike! That's the idea!' he shouted. 'That'll bring Birnbaum to his senses!'

One by one the other machinists expressed themselves in complete favour of a strike. Only Barnet seemed dubious. His greater experience foresaw that such a partial strike was doomed to failure before it began. All the machinists were hot-headed and enthusiastic now, but of the eleven he knew that only five or six were entirely reliable. Six machinists could not carry on a successful strike in a factory where thirty were employed. If all the machinists were approached first for their support, then there might be sense in a stoppage, such a procedure at least held the germs of success. He tried to point this out to his comrades, but they refused to listen. A strike, at once, now, seemed a bold thrust at the employer, the heaviest weapon in their armoury, bound to bring success, and Barnet was no better than a scab, a blackleg, to talk about waiting till the rest of the machinists were consulted. The operators rose noisily from their stools and detached their machine heads from the stands. Barnet quietly followed suit. If they all stood together, he would not be the one to waver, no matter how hopeless the fight. Phineas clapped him heartily on the back.

'Bravo, Barnet!' he said. 'I knew you'd be with us.'

In a body, the twelve machinists descended the stairs. As they reached the bottom flight, the door of the office opened and the boss came out.

'What's this?' asked Mr Birnbaum. 'Why aren't you at your machines?'

'It's a strike,' said Phineas grimly.

'Oh is it!' replied Birnbaum with mocking gravity. His keen eyes singled out Snobby, a weak excitable character, and an inexpert craftsman. 'Are you on strike too, Snobby?' he asked sarcastically.

Snobby turned red and nodded, averting his watery little eyes.

'How long have you been working for me?' asked Mr Birnbaum.

'Six years,' said Snobby.

'How long did you work at your last job?'

'Eight months.'

'And now you're going on strike! If you leave this job it may be eight years before you get another like it. Don't be a fool, Snobby, get back to work.' His voice took on a threatening, imperious ring. 'That's enough of this nonsense! Get upstairs, Snobby. Back to work at once. Do you hear!'

Snobby turned as pale as the grey cotton he fed his machine. His enthusiasm was swept away in a sudden panic. His comrades stood around in a taut silence. If only someone would speak up to help him! – There was no one to lean upon, no one. This cold meeting with the boss was entirely different from what he had expected. Upstairs he had felt part of a corporate giant, inflamed by the warmth of his comrades; upstairs it had been all fire and victory, but here it was a cold douche and single combat in which all the advantage lay with his adversary. He could feel those keen, grey eyes boring relentlessly right through him, and he waited, keyed up and unnerved, for the next cruel thrust. Birnbaum read his mind like an expert psychologist.

'Upstairs!' came the sharp command, like the crack of a ring-master's whip.

Hypnotised, ashamed to look his comrades in the face, Snobby turned and walked slowly up the stairs. One by one Mr Birnbaum tackled the machinists. Unorganised, inexperienced, they allowed him to attack and detach the weakest-minded workers and send them upstairs without fighting to hold them back. Five workers were ordered to return, three more followed them unbidden, only four, Phineas, Barnet and two others remaining fast. Mr Birnbaum looked at the quartet coldly. The back of the strike was broken; these four could please themselves. Ostentatiously he turned his back on them without a word and closed the door of his office.

The four machinists walked to the nearest coffee shop to discuss the course of their future conduct. Over steaming mugs of tea they swore solidarity and eternal brotherhood, and fixing an appointment for the following morning, Joe and Solomon, the other strikers departed. Barnet walked part of the way home with Phineas. The younger man was still excited by the strike, and even now confident of its success, but Barnet, although he appeared placid enough, grew more and more discouraged as he walked along. They parted company at the bottom of Cannon Street Road, and Phineas went jauntily towards his house.

Barnet walked slowly homewards. The strike was over, he saw clearly enough. Joe and Solomon he gave another day at the most, then they would return to work, leaving him and Phineas out in the cold. Why should he sacrifice himself this way? he kept asking, and in the same mental breath answering: Principle! Principle! Yet where was the principle when his wife and five children would go hungry? To go back, he felt would be a shameful thing, yet the more he thought about it, the more it seemed clear that he had no option. He groaned aloud with the bitterness of his mental conflict. Ugh! When will we workers have some sense knocked into us! All the machinists at Birnbaum's had plenty to grouse about. Together, their collective grievances were formidable enough material for a successful strike, instead of which, a few hotheads had to split and dissipate their forces, putting the prospect of a victorious strike action back by months, maybe years.

He wavered for a moment by the corner of the street, and then started to walk back to the factory. Obsessed by his thoughts he zigzagged from side to side of the pavement like a drunken man. Phineas's voice kept calling him back, and his own conscience ceaselessly pricked him with 'Principle! Principle!' but stronger than either was the thought of his wife and five children, and only that, and the knowledge that it was useless carrying on the fight, directed his unsteady footsteps. Feeling the guilty numbness of one who has betrayed his best friend, he arrived at the factory. His boots seemed weighted with heavy sheets of hot metal, dragging him down painfully as he climbed the stairs to the top floor. Embarrassed, he walked to his place. Nobody looked up. There was only one vacant stool, Joe and Solomon were already back at work.

The next morning, Phineas waited at the appointed place. He waited for an hour and nobody came. Reflecting bitterly on the value of solidarity and eternal brotherhood, he drew in his belt a little tighter and prepared to add another fast to the four ritual ones of the year. Shandel and the children went every day to Berel's house. She was too proud to ask for help, but her mother saw that the children were hungry and fed them without asking any questions, although Miriam herself had little enough to spare.

Fortunately, Phineas found another job before the week was

out. His new employer, Eli Holzman, was not himself a finished craftsman but a lining machinist, who, coming into a fortune of several hundred pounds had used it as capital to start a workshop on his own account. Eli, a slim, bearded, good-natured Jew, was rarely in the workshop, staying there no more than two or three hours daily, the rest of the time he spent in the synagogue or travelling with samples to the City. Phineas, having somehow picked up a knowledge of cutting, was entrusted to prepare most of the work, and put in charge of the three machinists.

One day, Eli returned from the City in the highest of good spirits. He had landed an order of fifteen hundred dozen caps from a firm of shippers for the African market. He had contracted to produce them complete with his own materials and labour, for two shillings a dozen. Eli would not get paid until the whole contract was fulfilled, but the City firm had a high reputation and had promised him an advance of fifty pounds when half the order was completed. He immediately gave Phineas a rise of five shillings and engaged a female machinist to help with the linings. Phineas, earning thirty-five shillings a week, felt like a lucky prospector striking gold in the Klondike, although it was true that to make his wages he had to work on an average fourteen hours a day. That, however, was a minor detail; he had by this time been thoroughly broken in to the easy life of the cap trade. For a month the workshop turned out headgear for African potentates. Five hundred dozen caps were completed and sent to the City firm. They were blocked like sandwiches in batches of eight, instead of being pressed singly which was usual in the better-class trade. Each dozen was held fast by a string round the middle. No boxes were wasted on them; they were protected from dirt and dust by a wrapping of tissue paper.

In the City, Mr Stephenson, the exporter, greeted Eli cordially. He pulled out one cap at random from a bunch, and, examining it cursorily, threw it back on the pile. Good enough for Africa! He detailed a junior clerk to verify the amount of caps by counting the peaks and gave instructions for them to be shipped off immediately. Eli went down to the office with him and asked for a little money on account. Pleading the direst poverty, saying that he did not have enough money to pay the workers their wages, which was very nearly true, Eli wheedled out of Mr Stephenson a cheque for thirty pounds.

Seven weeks later the contract was almost completed and Eli was looking forward to another fat order. He was happy as a sandboy all day long. Sitting in his favourite position, perched on the corner of Phineas's cutting table, he swung his feet merrily in the air and cracked jokes with the workers by the hour. When he tired of the workshops he went to the synagogue and involved himself in endless Talmudic discussions. Confident that his little factory was in safe hands, he threw all care to the winds and enjoyed himself. He asked not more than this from life; he was not ambitious in the slightest. The Rothschilds could keep all their money and the worry it entailed. He, Eli Holzman, was ten times better off. Eli, the one-time lining machinist, was sitting on top of the world.

The last week of the contract, Phineas came in earlier than usual on Sunday morning, but, early as he was, Eli was before him. This meant something out of the ordinary was afoot, because Eli never appeared on Sundays before noon. Phineas looked at him in bewilderment. Eli had a wild look in his eyes, and wore a strange, haunted expression that had chased off the good-humoured grin from his face. He stamped up and down the workshop without a word, clutching a crackling sheet of white paper in his hand. At last he halted before Phineas and glared at him for a full half-minute before he spoke.

'Excuse me,' he said, in a mild, suave tone that was the exact antithesis of what the fierce expression on his face foreboded. 'Excuse me, Mr Kahn, but do you think you could remember the name of the ship that brought you over to England?'

Phineas was still more puzzled, but replied: 'Ship? Why, the *Hook Of Holland.*'

'*Hook Of Holland! Hook Of Holland!* Eli pounced on the name like a terrier fastening his teeth in the spine of a helpless rat. '*Hook Of Holland,* eh! ... Well, if the *Hook Of Holland* had struck a convenient rock in the North Sea and gone down with everyone on board, or better still, if only you had had the good fortune to be drowned on the way, then I might not have become a pauper once more.' He thrust the crackling white paper into Phineas's hand. 'Look, Mr Kahn. Look!'

It was a very brief note from Johannesburg that had been forwarded by Stephenson to Eli. As Phineas read it, Eli's agitation became clear, and Phineas himself blushed with shame and mortification.

He read:

Dear Sir,

We are forced to return the first consignment of your caps. It is quite impossible to wear them on the head, unless you provide clips with which to fasten them over the ears. As they are at present, they seem more suitable coverings for backsides, but as, even in Africa, the natives do not wear caps on their behinds, we are reluctantly compelled, in lieu of a cheque, to return your caps and to cancel our order for the remainder.

We are, yours faithfully,

J & M De Groot

So the cap artiste had to look round for another job. Shandel resumed her daily visits to her parents, while Phineas tramped the streets in search of work. As it happened, it was fairly busy in town, so within a week he had found another situation. Whether Phineas were employed or not, the gestative processes went on as usual. Regularly, every eighteen months, Shandel bore him a child, the latest addition to the family being a tiny, fair girl, Deborah. Phineas was now the father of two boys and two girls. He felt that a family of four was quite large enough and hoped devoutly that Shandel would now give childbearing a rest for a while.

His new boss was a broad, heavy, squat Jew named Mordecai. He had a thick, square black beard that had never been acquainted with either scissors or razor, a fat, Negroid nose, dark eyes under bushy brows and a huge bald head shadowed with a delicate tracery of veins. When he had one of his non-stop coughing fits, which in the winter was often, since he was afflicted by the terrible twins, asthma and bronchitis, the blue veins rode over his temples bulging in ugly knots that looked as if they must burst at any moment. After he ceased coughing and spluttering, he would become for half an hour so irascible that all the workers avoided him like a leper until his temper subsided into its usual bear-like gruffness.

Tied to the conventional centuries-old garb of his ancestors, he wore always, winter and summer, a long black alpaca coat reaching almost to his ankles that made him look like a particularly unprepossessing gnome.

Mordecai was a member of an ultra-orthodox sect, and most of his employees were pious middle-aged or elderly Jews. In the morning they donned their phylacteries and praying shawls in the workshop as soon as there was a minyan present of ten men, and Mordecai, with his full, rich bass, led the service. Then they commenced to labour, with only a short break for lunch until just before sundown, when work was suspended for afternoon and evening prayers. The wages were poor, and the work difficult, but with the exception of Phineas the workers preferred Mordecai with his punctilious observance of the religious rites to any other employer in London. True, they came to work a little earlier in the morning, and stayed a little later at night, but where, they asked, in the whole of this heathen land, was there such another Jewish boss?

Phineas, burdened with children, was forced by economic pressure to remain still a Monday Jew. On Sunday evening when he came home from the 'half-day' that finished at six-thirty, he found the Sabbath meal prepared, and waiting for him Shandel, radiant in a spotless white blouse, and the children, scrubbed clean, with shining faces. A bottle of cheap ceremonial wine glistened proudly on the table between the Chanukah candles and a stale plaited loaf. Phineas washed himself, donned his skullcap and sang in the bride of the Sabbath. Then he made the ritual prayer over a tiny glass of wine, sipped a drop, handed it to his wife and the older children and poured the remainder back into the bottle which was securely corked up and put away for the following week. After blessing the Sabbath bread, they began to eat. The children fed voraciously, this was their one real meal of the week, an event they looked forward to, from Sunday to Sunday. At the conclusion of the dinner, Shandel started to clear the table, while Phineas sat back in his chair and sang hymns to the Sabbath, substituting the second day for the seventh. At the top of his voice he sang: 'Kol makudish shanee kroue loi, Kol shoimer shanee kados mechulleh loi...' – 'Who observes the second day as the holy day of the week, the Lord will repay, according to his deeds...'

In the general festivity a knock on the door passed unnoticed. It opened quietly, and Myer, one of Phineas's workmates, entered. He had been passing by and had dropped in for a casual visit. His startled eyes took in the lighted candles and the Sabbath bread, and the chanted hymn came with the stark shock of blasphemy, strangely to his ears. Phineas turned and rose to his feet to welcome him, but Myer backed away in alarm and, turning tail at the door, vanished as if a battalion of devils were at his heels.

In the morning, when Phineas arrived at the workshop, the staff were seated silently on their stools like an accusing bench of grim magistrates. Mordecai stood in the centre of the room, and as Phineas entered, his rich voice rang out in greeting.

'Good morning, madman!'

Like a pre-rehearsed chorus the other Jews repeated the salutation, which was almost drowned by Mordecai in a violent spasm of coughing. When the attack subsided, Mordecai continued the heresy hunt. He spread his hands before him and chanted in a parody of the Sabbath hymn. 'Who observes the second day as the seventh ought to be, should be exterminated like a dirty flea.'

Mordecai, his face still purple from the previous coughing fit, gravely handed Phineas his machine, and observed in Hebrew with dry sarcasm: 'The Lord hath repaid you according to your deeds.' As Phineas still stood in bewilderment, rooted to the workshop floor, Mordecai supplemented the Hebrew with Yiddish that made his meaning perfectly clear. 'My good madman,' he said in a voice strangled by the strain of fighting the rasping cough that began to bubble in his throat, 'my good madman, kindly close the door on the other side of you!'

Phineas stumbled down the stairs to the street. He pulled the collar of his topcoat over his ears and hung his head, hiding his face. It seemed to him as if every other pedestrian knew of his disgrace and was slyly laughing at him. He walked home without dawdling, anxious to reach the sanctuary of his house. Quietly entering the bedroom he put the machine on a chair, and covering it with his overcoat, went into the kitchen.

Shandel was seated on a low stool before the fire, her knees spread out, her beautiful head bent in absorbed admiration of the tiny infant suckling at her breast. Olga stood in a corner holding an earnest discussion with a dirty rag doll, and Phillip and Stanley were seated at Shandel's feet, gazing with rapt attention at their baby sister. When Phineas entered, Phillip the elder boy jumped to his feet and clapped his hands with delight. Father was home! It was so rare for the children to see their father during the day; in the morning he went to work while they were still in bed, and in the evening when he returned they were fast asleep. Stanley, taking his cue from Phillip, toddled over to Phineas and clasped his chubby hands round his knees. He started to gabble incoherently in his excitement; Father at home meant all sorts of amusing games!

Shandel turned slowly and glanced at her husband. Her eyes widened and clouded with anxiety. Phineas averted his gaze and suddenly started to laugh. It all seemed so comic, tragic and yet comic with the bitterness of tears. Phineas the Scribe, the brilliant musician, Reb David-Moishe's messiah whose name would ring across the world, this was the same Phineas, the shabby cap-maker who had a wife and four children, but no job and not a shilling in his pocket. His wild laugh gathered momentum until he found himself shrieking hysterically. The children began to laugh too, and the insistent tugging at his trouser legs brought Phineas back to sanity with the realisation that the boys wanted to share the fun and were inviting him to play with them.

Although he was in no mood for such pranks, he could not disappoint the children. Why should they be downcast too, dear, innocent little souls, and walk about with long faces? Time enough for them to worry when they grew up; in the meantime their spirits were high, let them enjoy that infinitesimal bright facet of life that they knew. Face-upwards, he lay spread-eagled on the floor, and the children flung themselves over him like a litter of frisky kittens. At last, he rose, dusty and dishevelled, from the floor, and guiltily faced his wife. It was superfluous for him to tell her that he was again jobless. She was so much part of him that she understood the value of his every gesture, of every inflection of speech. She smiled wistfully and remarked in a tired, resigned voice in which there was still a hint of hope: 'Never mind, Phineas. You'll find a cure for this complaint as well.'

The next morning he was out early visiting all the most likely places, but returned home in the evening, morose and discouraged.

Expenses went on, his family had to live. Shandel would understand, but there was no arguing with children. They would not listen to reason, they simply opened up their mouths and howled. He must somehow stuff up their little stomachs with food whatever else happened. The second day he left the house at half-past six and returned at ten o'clock in the evening, empty-handed. Still no luck! It was beginning to prey on his mind. Another week of this and he would go stark raving mad. He buried his hot, aching head in Shandel's lap and cried like a baby. Although she felt like tears herself, she stroked his hair gently, and quietly soothed him with encouraging words. When Phineas felt bad she must be the strong one, if both cracked up together, then they were lost indeed. She whispered to him hopefully, riding over a dark, sickening turmoil in the pit of her stomach. Her tears could wait till tomorrow; tonight she must comfort Phineas, her oldest, her most helpless child.

On the third day Phineas found himself near the Minories. Passing Edward Street, he was impelled to enter the narrow turning overcome by a desire to look upon Birnbaum's once more, a fascination something akin to the attraction of a murderer for the scene of his crime. He crossed to the opposite pavement and walked past a bend that revealed across the road the dirty building standing in its nakedness like an ugly, unwashed tramp. Somebody was lounging in the doorway. Coming closer, Phineas noticed that it was Mr Birnbaum himself. It was too late to retrace his footsteps; hoping that Birnbaum would not see him, he half turned, hugging the dirty warehouses in an attempt to efface himself amongst the surrounding greyness. He was unsuccessful; the keen eyes of Mr Birnbaum had unerringly fastened on him. He heard a whistle behind him, and a shout – 'Hey, Phineas!'

Phineas stopped. He turned and waited on the kerb. Mr Birnbaum signalled an invitation. 'Here, Phineas. Come over. I want to talk to you.'

Phineas crossed the road and approached his former employer. Mr Birnbaum seemed jovial enough. Probably, he wanted to rub in a little sarcasm, but Phineas made a mental resolve to give him no sort of satisfaction.

'Working?' asked Mr Birnbaum.

'A little,' said Phineas. '... I'm on short time.'

'Don't lie!' replied Mr Birnbaum. 'You're not working any time at all. Come on – out with it. Have you got a job?'

Phineas shook his head shamefacedly. It seemed impossible to lie to Mr Birnbaum; very few things were hidden from the penetrating glance of his probing grey eyes. Mr Birnbaum laughed.

'Do you realise now what a fool you were to go on strike?' he said. 'How comes a Jew with a wife and little children to be a striker? Your own comrades, your blood brothers, who swore solidarity and the Lord knows what else, were back at work the same afternoon, while you were left like somebody's bastard on a strange doorstep in the street. Don't trust those ignorant hoodlums any more. You're a good mechanic, Phineas. I'm willing to forget what's happened. Come back and you can carry on as before. But whatever you do, my boy, no more of those striking tricks!'

Phineas rushed home for his machine, and the same afternoon started work. Apart from himself, only two of the four original strikers were left. Barnet had disappeared and his place was vacant. Joe and Solomon avoided Phineas awkwardly at first, conscious that they had let him down badly. Any reproaches that he might level at them they felt would be justified, and more, but as he never made any mention of their behaviour, they speedily became friends again, that black memory being relegated to the limbo of the past, and in their new relationship it was to all intents and purposes as if the strike had never occurred.

Barnet had gone to pieces in the last few months. He had had two bouts of acute bronchitis. He was still ill in bed at home, and the doctor had prescribed for him a selection of coloured bottles, and warned him that to resume work too early would mean a recurrence of the trouble. Barnet ignored the doctor and refused to touch the multi-coloured medicines. What he really needed, and what he couldn't get, were plenty of food and rest and fresh air and, best of all, a long sea cruise round the world, but he could afford those luxuries as little as he could afford to stay in bed. The only rest he would get would be in his grave, and his only cruise would be to the next world. So Barnet lay chafing in bed, eager to return to the front line, eager to grapple again with life, the more so since he realised that his hold on it was slipping away, surely and steadily. Gaunt and emaciated, he returned to work. For a week his spirit battled hardily, but he was only the shell of a man and had drawn on the last reserves of his physical resistance. On Friday, at four o'clock his machine stopped. His grey head slumped on the stand and slowly his long body slipped from the stool to the floor. With the large-hearted compassion of the very poor, the factory spontaneously started a collection for the widow, and Mr Birnbaum, shamed by the generosity of his employees, reluctantly contributed five pounds.

As soon as little Deborah was able to control the movements of her tiny limbs and could toddle around, Israel was born. It seemed to Shandel that she was doomed to remain a perpetual milch cow for as long as her reproductive organs functioned. His neighbours and workmates, when they congratulated Phineas, knowing his circumstances, repeated to a man the old Jewish saw that every newly born infant brought with it a run of good fortune. Phineas thanked them, reflecting dubiously that hitherto the advent of each little bawler had only added to his debts and responsibilities. Israel was no exception. A fortnight after the baby's ceremonial entry into the priestly caste of Phineas and his ancestors, the finances of the cap machinist received a staggering blow. At a time when Birnbaum's was the one busy factory in London, it went up in flames overnight and was razed to the ground.

Arriving at Edward Street a few minutes later than usual one Thursday morning, Israel having kept him up with an attack of colic in the small hours, Phineas found a crowd of dispossessed workers and sightseers on one side of the narrow turning, and on the other, the smouldering ruins of a gutted factory. His heart gave a leap of dismay. Somewhere in that charred, tangled mass was his machine, his livelihood. His workmates stood around with grey faces, silently regarding the remains of the holocaust, bitter emotions swamping their minds. All were concerned by the loss of their machines, but the shock of the blow had numbed them, and their dark passions slumbered below the surface, awaiting the tiniest spark to fan them stridently vocal.

On the opposite side of the road, close to the ruined building by virtue of ownership and superior social status, stood a little group consisting of Mr Birnbaum, Mr Somper the manager and the two foremen. As soon as Phineas joined the crowd of workers, their discomfort seemed to crystallise. Phineas was known as a fire-brand, the leader of the first abortive strike, and they looked to him to do something for them. Ugly murmurs ran round the mob of machinists. With the quick thrust of innuendo the blame for the fire was fixed on the boss. Nobody had definite proof, but one machinist, staying later than usual the night before to alter some caps, had been pressed by Mr Somper to go home, the manager waiving, with hitherto unsuspected magnanimity, his claims upon the operator's time. Other workers too had noticed suspicious things during the course of the day, like the accumulation of rags and waste in the basement, but whatever emerged were only whispers, surmises, with nothing actually concrete. Phineas, chosen unanimously as spokesman, was sent over to negotiate with Mr Birnbaum. He crossed the road, and at his approach the manager and the foremen closed round the boss like a body-guard. Phineas halted on the pavement, and Mr Birnbaum pushing his protectors aside, confronted him questioningly.

'It's a black day, Mr Birnbaum,' said Phineas sombrely.

The boss nodded. 'Black indeed, for all of us.'

'Everything we possess has gone up in flames... Our machines... Everything!'

'True,' said Mr Birnbaum. 'Everything I had, my stock, my factory, my whole life's work wiped out completely.'

Phineas smiled wryly. 'Well, what are you going to do about it?' he demanded.

'Do?' said Mr Birnbaum. 'What can I do? Take all that you and the others have lost, and multiply it by ten, and you'll have some idea of what this has cost me. Really, I'm worse off than any of you!'

'Maybe,' replied Phineas sarcastically, 'but your family won't go hungry next week – they'll have enough to eat, and won't be in any danger of finding themselves without a place to sleep in either. Without our machines we can't earn food. You must do something for us!'

Mr Birnbaum stroked his chin thoughtfully, his bright eyes peering uncomfortably right through Phineas.

'It's hard, hard,' he admitted. 'I'll tell you what I'll do. It will practically ruin me, but I'll show you I've also got a heart, although I am a boss. I'll give you all a week's wages!'

'That's very good of you, Mr Birnbaum,' broke in the manager enthusiastically. He turned patronisingly to the machinist. 'There, do you hear that, Phineas? A week's wages! Not many bosses would be so generous. After that, Mr Birnbaum is a jewel, a diamond! Go over and tell the men.'

'Wait a minute, wait a minute,' said Phineas. 'Not so fast, Mr Somper. What about our machines?'

'Machines!' Mr Somper burst into a loud guffaw. 'Be satisfied with what you're getting. Machines! What next? What do you think Mr Birnbaum is, the Jewish Board of Guardians?'

'Never mind about that,' insisted Phineas in a hard, dry voice. 'The men want their machines!'

The manager, his florid complexion darkening viciously, seemed about to embark on an angry tirade when Mr Birnbaum's hand fell restrainingly on his arm.

'*They* want?' he said soothingly. 'You mean *you* want. Personally I like you, Phineas. You shall have your machine.'

'But the others, Mr Birnbaum,' Phineas pleaded, 'they are all as badly off as I am.'

'I'm sorry,' said the boss firmly, 'but I am not a millionaire; a week's wages is the best I can do.'

He turned away as if the interview had terminated. Phineas was desperate, his blood seemed to congeal in thick icy clots. The boss, who would profit enormously by the fire, was magnanimously offering a gift of a whole week's wages, when the machinists had already worked off three and a half days. A sudden fury shot through him, heating his blood with passion, until it seemed to rush in a hot frenzy through his veins. He could hear the hungry cries of his own children, multiplied by fifty, a hundred; a multitude of innocent sufferers being starved to make a rich man richer. The insurance company would handsomely compensate Birnbaum for the loss of his plant, and he wanted to make a profit on the workers' private property as well.

'No, Mr Birnbaum,' he said firmly. 'That's not good enough!'

The boss turned towards Phineas, and his sparse eyebrows arched quizzically... 'No? What are you going to do about it?'

'We'll stop the insurance money,' Phineas blurted out wildly.

'What?' asked Mr Birnbaum, in an ominously quiet tone.

Phineas was flustered, but divorced from the control of his reason, he had shot an arrow in the dark, and through his excitement he became aware of the effect it had had on the boss, who blanched as if stung by a sudden electric shock. The machinist permitted a sarcastic knowledgeable grin to play across his face, although his heart was thumping almost audibly, wondering how Birnbaum's shrewdness would counter this unexpected thrust.

'What – what exactly do you mean?' repeated the boss, his grey eyes drilling with an almost physical intensity through the machinist's skull.

'... Well... the insurance company might like to know what we know,' said Phineas.

The boss averted his eyes and looked at the manager, as if his subordinate's bungling was responsible for this new situation. Mr Somper fingered the coarse bristles on his square aggressive chin and glanced repeatedly at Phineas, wondering how much he really knew. Personally, he felt like kicking the dirty blackmailer into the gutter. Let him do his worst! It was only his word against theirs, and who would trust the testimony of this ragged tramp against the honour of two such eminently respectable Jews as himself and Mr Birnbaum? However, it was not his funeral. He would take his cue from the boss. If the boss said 'Clear that rubbish out of the way' he would do it with pleasure, and with such thoroughness that Phineas would have difficulty in sitting for a week. If not, he would be as sweet as sugar and even offer Phineas a cigar – one of the boss's. Mr Birnbaum, whose brain all the while was functioning with express speed, testing every alibi and examining every available loophole, decided to come to terms. He was a businessman, not a gambler. A few hundred pounds would not make all that much difference, and, in any case, the insurance company would foot the bill, although he had expected to pocket that extra money as well. Right – a week's wages and new machines. Better to write that off as a loss than to have insurance detectives nosing about the place and forfeiting the lot. Yes. It was better to come to some sort of an arrangement.

'Right,' he said sourly, with evident reluctance. 'It will practically break me, but the men will have a week's wages and new machines. Satisfied – you bloodsucker?'

'Certainly, Mr Birnbaum,' replied Phineas mildly. 'Now you're behaving like a gentleman!'

He turned, anxious to place the result of the parley before his comrades, but Mr Somper's beefy hand grabbed his arm.

'Just a minute, Phineas,' he said. '*You* don't expect to get a new machine, do you? I have seen better machines than yours thrown out of dustbins. And if I recollect rightly, the stand belonged to us.'

'Oh, no, Mr Somper,' Phineas lied unblushingly, a pained look on his face. 'It was a new machine, and a new stand. Why, I only bought the head the other week.'

'Hmmm,' growled the manager. 'Sure it didn't have twenty-two-carat gold fittings?'

'Quite sure,' said Phineas gravely. 'How could I afford golden fittings?'

'That's enough cross chat,' interrupted the boss snappishly. 'Go over and tell that bunch of thieves what I've just told you – and remember, Phineas, when the factory is rebuilt don't trouble to come round and ask for a job!'

'Thanks – I won't,' said Phineas. 'You've got my address. I'll wait until you write!'

CHAPTER V

The new machine was a godsend to Shandel. All day long she was busy seaming shirts cut down from Phineas's garments for the boys, and little dresses for the girls. Phineas, after a great deal of cogitation, decided to branch out on his own account. He dinned a new slogan into his consciousness. 'No more slaving for bosses!' With the new machine as capital he would manufacture caps for himself. Berel, by virtue of his semi-official position at the synagogue, which was the clearing house for all the gossip of the neighbourhood, found him a new domicile in Chicksand Street, a tiny thoroughfare close to where Shandel's parents resided. It was a dilapidated two-story house, comprising four rooms and a basement which had been originally a coal cellar and lumber depository. The rent of the whole house was twelve shillings a week. Phineas found two families, almost as poor as he was, to tenant the four upper rooms, and he himself occupied the basement-cum-cellar. His tenants paid him thirteen shillings between them, so that Phineas lived rent free and was still a shilling to the good. Managing somehow to put off the landlord, Phineas with the first week's rent bought three second-hand cap blocks, a pair of shears, a small pressing iron and some remnants of material, and started to make a few sample caps. His workshop was the rear end of the cellar which, formerly quite a commodious chamber, had been cut in two by the erection of a thin plaster partition in the centre. His machine and cutting table occupied a section of this space, the remainder serving as kitchen, parlour, reception room and dining-room. The other side of the partition was the bedroom; in all it was a highly desirable residence not very much worse than the first mud hut of the Kahns in Zvonitz.

The samples completed, Phineas commenced to hawk them about the City. Soon, he discovered that it was as difficult to obtain orders as it had been to sell outright his labour power. As a last resort, he tried Stephenson, who paid the very worst prices, and exported the lowest grade of caps. He bearded the tall, fresh-complexioned Englishman in his office, and without disclosing that he was the original creator of backside caps, put his samples on the table before him. Mr Stephenson was a blunt man of few words. He picked up one cap and turned it over in his hands.

'How much?' he said.

'One-and-nine a dozen,' replied Phineas, cutting his profits as fine as he dared.

Mr Stephenson shook his head and returned to the file of papers he was perusing.

'Too dear!' he said without looking up.

'How much can you pay?' asked Phineas desperately.

Stephenson laid his papers aside. 'One-and-tuppence,' he replied. 'They're for export to the Hottentots. It doesn't matter if all the pieces aren't of the same colour, or the same material, and it doesn't matter if they can only be worn once, so long as they *can* be worn once. If they fit the head, that's all that counts.'

Phineas blushed, this seemed to him like a direct reference to Eli's contract, but he speedily dismissed the thought, for Stephenson could not possibly connect him with that masterpiece of the cap-maker's art. The exporter watched him closely.

'Well?' he said. 'Come on, I haven't much time. If you can do it for the price, I can promise you fifty dozen a week.'

Fifty dozen! Phineas decided to fulfil the order. Somehow he would have to make it pay.

'...Yes... I'll do it,' he replied.

'Good!' said Mr Stephenson. 'I'll expect the first lot at the end of the week. Fifty dozen. If they're any good you'll get a repeat. All big sizes. Those niggers have heads like footballs.'

He returned to his file, and after a while looked up, surprised to find Phineas still in the office.

'You... you see, Mr Stephenson,' Phineas stammered, 'I haven't any money. If you could advance me a couple of pounds I could go ahead with the work.'

'Hmmm! ...Advance you the money! How do I know you won't run off to Poland, or Palestine, or wherever it is you come from?'

'I've got a wife and five children,' said Phineas. 'I can't run far with two pounds.'

Mr Stephenson clicked open the lid of a big gold hunter.

'Where do you live?' he asked. 'Far from here?'

Phineas gave the exporter his address, and Mr Stephenson, noting it in a little black diary, tucked the book away in a capacious waistcoat pocket. Tapping the pocket with two slender fingers of a well-tended hand he leaned back in his chair.

'Right,' he said. 'It's two o'clock. I'll be there in an hour.'

On the stroke of three a smart carriage rolled down Chicksand Street, and with a brisk tattoo of hooves the horse drew up outside Phineas's house. Mr Stephenson, a picture of sartorial magnificence, stepped down and with the knob of his gold-mounted cane lifted and released smartly the knocker on the dilapidated door. Phineas, who, waiting in the passage, had spied the visitor through the keyhole, allowed a decent interval to elapse before he answered the knock. Striking a match to show the visitor down the stairs, for even in broad daylight the entrance to the cellar was as gloomy as a subterranean cavern, Phineas led the way to his workshop. One tiny window refracted the watery sunshine from the cluttered yard which, overshadowed by the opposite houses, was a jumble of boxes, tin cans and broken chairs. An incredibly small segment of blue sky was visible, a patch no bigger than a man's fist. Mr Stephenson looked about him with scarcely concealed disgust. It reeked with the sour stench of overcrowded humans. The exporter's nostrils dilated and his broad nose crinkled with distaste. He had been in more salubrious pigsties. Taking out an embroidered cambric handkerchief, he applied it with a discomfiting flourish to his nose. The strange nausea of claustrophobia overtook him till he felt the panic of a suffocated prisoner. His glance took in the machine and the blocks on the table; it seemed a bona fide workshop. That was good enough; it would be worth two pounds just to escape from this stinking little hell.

'You really mean to say you live here?' he asked incredulously.

'Yes,' said Phineas, 'I live here, and my wife and five children.'

'Hmm!' grunted the exporter. 'Let's get out of this, anyway. We can talk business upstairs in the passage.'

Obtaining first a receipt, he handed Phineas two golden sovereigns and hurriedly left the house. In his carriage he breathed a sigh of relief. It seemed hardly conceivable that human beings could live in such filth. It did not occur to him that precisely because of the poverty of the dozens of Phineases that fed his warehouse he was able to maintain a town house and a country residence, and keep his daughter at an expensive finishing school. His skin seemed to be covered with creeping vermin. He felt unclean, contaminated, the aroma of the dark airless cellar still seemed to envelop him like a corporeal cloak. He could not return to business like this; nearing the warehouse he gave his coachman orders to drive straight on to Charing Cross. Only a Turkish bath could cleanse his pores of this crawling virus. He would sweat out the outlandish pestilence, and a good rubdown by the masseur would restore his good humour and his customary feeling of healthy cleanliness.

Phineas went out the same afternoon and brought home two sacks of assorted woollen cuttings and half a bagful of crumpled pieces of lining. Shandel smoothed out the linings with a warm iron, while her husband chalked out and cut the material to fit the pattern of the caps. In the same cap one-eighth of the crown would be of black velour, while the section next to it was of grey flannel neatly wedded to blue serge, vicuna or Harris tweed, whichever came soonest out of the sack. The two elder children were pressed into service. Olga had a tiny pair of scissors with which she trimmed jagged edges, while Phillip made himself generally useful, and Shandel did the finishing, sewing the buttons on the completed caps. At the end of the week Phineas produced the fifty dozen. Stephenson paid him the balance due for his labour, and after the exporter had deducted five per cent for cash the cap manufacturer was left with a net profit of thirty shillings.

One advantage he had gained by becoming his own boss was that he could start work as early as he pleased and finish as late as he chose, and Phineas made full use of these opportunities to produce his quota of caps. To earn thirty shillings he had to start work at six in the morning and slog away till past eleven at night. Shandel helped, the two children helped, and yet fifty dozen seemed the peak of human endeavour. The three babies were still mainly concerned with food and toys, or he might with their assistance have earned yet another two or three shillings a week. One day of relaxation he had, Saturday. He would go for a walk with his wife along the Whitechapel Road, but she dragged him home quickly, shamed by the shabbiness of their garments in contrast with the flashy costumes of the more affluent promenaders, and jealous of the masculine appraisement she saw in his eyes for good-looking women, although the attraction he felt for them was the animal connoisseur's admiration for the beautiful lines of a healthy beast. In the cellar Shandel had no competition, she had her husband all to herself. Fortunately, Phineas possessed an iron physique. A less hardy man cloistered in that constricted space would have had grass growing over him long since. He grew paler and thinner, but still worked like a pair of yoked oxen.

The days shortened, the autumn darkened into winter, spring budded greenly on all the world, neglecting only the twisted wood and tin entrails of the festering jungle in Phineas's backyard. The summer came and brought with it the seasonal plague of bugs. They oozed out of the walls like drips of dark sweat on the grimy brow of an exhausted man, the bedclothes swarmed with greasy little pests and the pillows and sheets were stained with the blood squashed out of them by the restless fingers of the unfortunate cellar dwellers, fruitlessly squirming in their efforts to obtain a little sleep. In desperation they discarded the beds and slept on the floor, with but slight alleviation of their discomfort. Only Phineas slept well. Worn out by his daily labours, he was almost asleep before he undressed. Stephenson was a guaranteed cure for insomnia; when Phineas slept only an earthquake could wake him.

During the summer days, Phineas was swept by a wave of nostalgia. At home in summer, he had roamed the woods and swum in the rivers, and lazed for hours on his back in grassy fields; here he was tied to the machine and cutting table, and even when their hold loosened, no less binding were the chains of his wife and children. He went to the synagogue very rarely, but seeing in it a chance of escape, he joined the congregation of the 'Bnai Poltusk'. Early on Saturday morning, he took his praying shawl under his arm, ostensibly for a visit to the synagogue, and instead walked to Victoria Park and there flung himself on the grass and breathed into his shrivelled lungs the life-giving air. In the stuffy synagogue the brethren of Poltusk would be swaying ecstatically over the nineteenth chapter of the Book of Numbers.

And the Lord spake unto Moses and unto Aaron, saying,

This is the ordinance of the law which the Lord hath commanded, saying, Speak unto the children of Israel, that they bring thee a red heifer without spot, wherein is no blemish, and upon which never came yoke:

And ye shall give her unto Eleazar the priest, that he may bring her forth without the camp, and one shall slay her before his face:

And Eleazar the priest shall take of her blood with his finger, and sprinkle of her blood directly before the tabernacle of the congregation seven times:

And one shall burn the heifer in his sight; her skin and her flesh, and her blood, with her dung, shall he burn:

And the priest shall take cedar wood and hyssop, and scarlet, and cast it into the midst of the burning of the heifer.

Then the priest shall wash his clothes, and he shall bathe his flesh in water, and afterward he shall come into the camp, and the priest shall be unclean until the even...

A gentle wind played on Phineas's forehead and blew the thick hair over his eyes. He breathed a sigh of contentment. Let the Bnai Poltusk worry about a red heifer without spot or blemish. He had enough of his own impeccable red heifers at night. The air from the surrounding trees was more aromatic than either cedar wood or hyssop. He flung out his arms, pressing down into the springy turf, and the sun beat down on his ashen face. Mother Earth! – Father Sun! He felt like a pagan worshipper of the elements; every Saturday morning he was free for a few hours; free from the cellar, free from the cares of wife and children, in close communion with nature, a child himself again and not one of the drabbest, most heavily beshackled slaves of the ghetto.

With the passing of summer, and the voracious interlopers, the beds were set up again. Israel was a troublesome child. He ate all day long and cried half the night. His cot was close to Phineas's bed, and when the cap-maker retired to sleep he hung out one naked leg, resting it on the cot. When Israel cried, Shandel would nudge her husband, and by a complicated subconscious reflex action, Phineas, still asleep, would automatically rock the cradle with his foot. At nine o'clock Phineas played his slumber songs, Tchaikovsky's 'Barcarolle' and Mozart's 'Wiegenlied', and the children one by one fell off to sleep. Shandel, tired out by a heavy day's washing and mending, yawned and slowly undressed herself in the dark, while Phineas went back to the workshop for his last nocturnal spell of labour in preparation for the hungry hands of the new day.

Looking reflectively out of the window on the dark sky, a cloud slid away from the face of the moon, and the queen of the night in all her glory revealed herself to the weary labourer. She seemed to wink mischievously at him with her dazzling brightness. 'Put away your work, Phineas,' she seemed to say. 'You are free now, what are you slaving for? Put away your tools and enjoy yourself. Go to bed! Go to bed!'

Such an invitation could not be disregarded. Phineas yawned and rubbed his eyes. It would be just one solitary lapse. After all, why shouldn't he go to bed for once at a respectable hour like normal people? He looked up again at the moon and this time she nodded definitely. That settled it – let the Hottentots wait! He turned out the gas jet, felt his way into the bedroom, undressed like a fledgling tasting forbidden delights and sticking out his baby-comforter settled down luxuriously to sleep.

He walked in his dreams down leafy lanes, and fished in cool waters, bowing to plaudits in crowded concert halls that miraculously superimposed their urban structures over bucolic delights, and throughout the peaceful glimpses of what had passed, and what had never been, the round moon winked solemnly, saying: 'I told you so, Phineas. I told you so!' He saw himself observing the Sabbath again on Saturday like other Jews. Large white wax candles held firmly in candlesticks of pure silver most elaborately carved, burned brightly on the table covered by an embroidered cloth of dazzling whiteness. Shandel was not there, he found nothing strange in that; perhaps she was on a visit to that same mysterious moon, but she had laid the table with the daintiest, most appetising dishes. Two chairs were drawn up to the feast. On one side of the table were a bottle of expensive wine, plates heaped with hors-d'oeuvres, caviar and salmon and a golden-brown roasted duckling, and on the other side a glass of water and a swollen herring. Phineas looked up questioningly at the moon. 'Go on, Phineas, eat, it's for you. All for you!' the celestial luminary assured him. Phineas put on his skullcap and intoned a grace of such sweetness that word for word, phrase for phrase and note for note it was an exact replica of the recorded song of a world-famous cantor. Just as he was about to sit down, the door opened and his first boss, Uncle Samuel, bounced in. Rudely he pushed Phineas away from the repast.

'Over there, you greenhorn!' he said roughly, indicating the opposite side of the table. 'That's yours, the herring. If you find it too salted, drink plenty of water. Hurry up and eat, you've got to get back to work!'

Tilting his bowler hat to the back of his head, he unfastened the top button of his trousers with the same familiar gestures and dug his fork through the belly of the duckling. This was too much for Phineas. He gazed upwards, but the moon had disappeared. A gust of passion blew over him till he shook like a pegged shirt in the wind. No! This was too much! He pounced on Uncle Samuel and with Herculean strength carried him effortlessly to the door and with a well-placed lunge kicked him up the stairs. Uncle Samuel soared like a blown-out bag in the sharp breath of a winter blizzard, his fat face opened into an enormous mouth and he howled with terror, his panic-stricken bass jumping whole octaves, passing higher and higher into an infantile treble as he flew.

Phineas felt Shandel's elbow nudging him violently. He kicked out but his toes met with no solid resistance, and Uncle Samuel's childish screams still rent the air. Shandel's voice broke through his dreams.

'Wake up, Phineas, for God's sake!'

He opened his eyes and saw the cot lying like an abandoned perambulator on its side, and Israel, his crust of bread clutched tightly in a podgy fist, sprawled protestingly on the floor. He picked up the child, who was more frightened than hurt and, pacifying him, placed him gently in his cot. When Israel went off to sleep again he climbed wearily into bed. Even the moon played jokes on him. He was finished with the lies of bright moonlight for ever. No more would he allow himself to be fooled by the seductive wiles of that distant enchantress.

Phineas, experimenting constantly with his work, evolved a system of subdivision of labour that lightened his task and allowed him to produce more caps. He was like an ingenious one-man band, performing with equal dexterity on the machine, with a pressing iron and the shears. Shandel helped with the finishing, so to maintain the balance of labour, Phineas performed all the more menial tasks of the house. He scrubbed the floors for her, cleaned the children when they dirtied their clothes, collected and emptied the rubbish, and in between his labours managed to find time to coach Olga, evolving into a brilliant little scholar, at her homework. He was determined to rescue his children from the ignominy and the living death of the workshop. He did not want his children to augment the ranks of those tens of thousands of pallid, crooked little Jews who performed prodigies of labour, and yet were unable to stretch their wages comfortably over the week. So long as he had an atom of strength left, he would slave to educate them up to a more respected sphere of life. In London the children had opportunities that were unknown in Russia. There were scholarships and grants that made higher education a royal petal-strewn road compared with the 'numerus clausus' articles of the Tsarist universities and gymnasia that effectively blocked every path of progress for those aspiring young Jews who did not have the backing of enormous inherited wealth behind them.

Phineas belonged to a Passover Club, run by a neighbour in the same street. Starting at Passover he paid a shilling a week into the club, which shared out the accumulated money to its members at the end of the year. It was also useful in that it loaned out to the members their own money in between times and charged them a substantial interest, but Phineas did not mind the interest so long as he could obtain the loan of a few pounds in an emergency. Besides which, he much preferred to owe the club money than have it indebted to him, since more than one local Passover Club had been involuntarily wound up by the treasurer's absconding to America with the funds. One of the usual emergencies occurred, forcing Phineas to obtain the loan of three pounds, when Michael was born, not quite two years after Israel. He was a frail child, much below the normal weight, so that his circumcision had to be postponed for several weeks until he put on sufficient flesh to enable him to undergo the operation with safety. Michael was the first product of the cellar, and it looked in his early post-natal days very much as though the airless, damp underground chamber would prove too much for his wheezy little lungs. However, the baby came of tough stock and managed precariously to survive. He was born late in the evening of a summer's day, delivered by the midwife who had attended Shandel at her previous confinements, and the following morning the invalid sat up in bed, her back propped up by high pillows, sewing buttons on the crowns of the caps. Her face was bloodless, the skin almost transparent. Her long fair hair was piled in layers on top of her head like a cottage loaf, her blue eyes seemed larger than usual and her small, straight nose with the sensitive nostrils more firmly chiselled. She seemed too slender and girl-like to be the mother of six children, too delicate to be at the same time both housewife and needle-hand; it appeared almost impossible to attribute to this frail, beautiful flower the miracles of labour she performed every working day.

Michael being the most delicate of the children, Shandel lavished on him especial care. Every day, every month that passed without some serious illness laying him low left her feeling unutterably relieved. She felt that this last blossoming bud held on to life by a thread more tenuous than any of her other children, and as she watched him grow, she seemed to sense something tragic, unhappy and frustrated about him, and she tried with all her motherly care to shield him from she knew not what. Often she found herself crying over the hoarsely squawking bundle of bones, but why she cried, she was unable to say.

By some mysterious quirk of nature, Felix, next in the Kahn succession, born eighteen months after Michael, was a lusty roaring rogue, a Pantagruel from birth. Phineas regarded his rapidly filling quiver and thought ruefully that procreation was the only function he seemed able to perform with complete success. If only someone recognised his abilities and gave him a job making babies! But after Felix he seemed to dry up as if the marrow had been squeezed from his bones. The cellar was at last claiming its victim. He developed a bad cough and one evening had an alarming haemorrhage of the throat. At the London Hospital the physician gave him some medicine and prescribed good food, plenty of fresh air and best of all a sea voyage if that were possible. Like his former comrade, Barnet, Phineas contemptuously discarded the medicine and the advice, until a second haemorrhage laid him low. This time Shandel wrote to some relatives in America explaining the situation, and some months later a steamship ticket arrived from New York.

At first Phineas refused to leave his family, but Shandel was adamant. She preferred a live husband, even if he were in New York, to a dead one in London. Phineas lay awake whole nights pondering the problem in his head while his wife lay beside him silently weeping. There appeared to him no hope left at all in London; perhaps the New World would set him on his feet again. His whole mind seemed in those sleepless nights to be alive, a complete entity, utterly divorced from his body.

His last evening at home he lay close to Shandel. Neither spoke, but she clasped him tightly as if she would never let him go, and spasmodic sobs ceaselessly racked her taut slender frame. A revolution seemed to stir violently in his head. The shapeless blob of grey matter split up into sharply defined components, each with a curious little body like a microscopic worm, two legs, hands and a disproportionately large head set with clever eyes. The turmoil resolved itself into a hotly debated meeting. A chairman was appointed and called the grotesques to order, tapping repeatedly with his mallet on a solid block before him until the banging re-echoed through Phineas's body like a sounding board.

'Brother Malachi has the floor,' said the chairman.

Malachi cleared his throat importantly. 'I think we do right to take our body across the Atlantic,' he began. 'There seems to be no opportunity for it here. Our Talmud teaches us "Meshanah Mokoim, Meshanah Mozel", who alters his domicile changes his luck, therefore I propose that we go to America.'

A clangour of applause greeted him, but a tiny figure with bright, shining eyes rose resolutely to address the meeting. 'Mr Chairman and brothers,' he said. 'I am against the project. Think how much trouble, think how many sorrows and stomach aches our body has endured before he reached his present position, before he married and brought up seven such marvellous children. True they are nine bodies, but they are linked together in one soul.

154

If our body breaks away and journeys to the other side of the world, will he know any happiness without them, or they without him?'

A roar of dissent cut him short, and Baltavnik, the slick-tongued grotesque took the floor. Baltavnik was the foolhardy one, the weaver of fantastic dreams; Baltavnik wanted to see America.

'Our body will be faithful,' urged Baltavnik. 'We know our Phineas. He will go into a new land and find some means of rescuing his wife and children. Besides, think what adventures we will have in the Golden Land. America, brothers! I vote America! America!'

With shrill huzzas the assembly was carried with him, and the meeting slowly melted again into a sprawly clot of porous grey matter. Phineas exhausted by the mental turmoil fell asleep. Early in the morning he rose and strapped his valise. Tearfully he embraced his wife, caressing her with quivering tenderness and kissed each of the children as they slept. Then like a thief, shamefully, with bowed head, he stole away from Chicksand Street.

It was October 13th 1911. On exactly the same day eleven years ago he had arrived in England. 'Meshanah Mokoim, Meshanah Mozel.' Now he was changing his domicile again. Dismissing the thought of his wife and the seven beautiful children that weighed like a heavy stone on his consciousness, he set his face to the brightness of a new day. Perhaps his luck *would* change. Phineas, tearing himself away from his family, felt like a leaky boat cut adrift from an ocean liner, but he had his ticket and he was on his way. It was too late to turn back. He hoped and prayed devoutly that his long journey would be crowned with some measure of success.

CHAPTER VI

In little less than a week the White Star liner *St Paul*, one of four maritime quadruplets each named after an American city, reached and passed the Statue of Liberty in New York harbour. The ship was packed from bow to stern with emigrants, mostly Polish, German and Russian Jews. The first-class passengers, merchants and tourists disembarked immediately and were courteously attended to by the customs officers, but the motley throng of emigrants, excited by their first glimpses of the towering man-made cliffs of New York, were herded unceremoniously into ferry boats and shipped across to Ellis Island to undergo the preliminary physical and financial inquisitions.

Disembarking on the island, Phineas followed a queue into an enormous building. At the entrance to a long corridor they stripped to the waist, and clutching their trousers tightly to conceal their nakedness, filed past a line of six doctors, stern-looking men with square American chins, dressed in long white coats, all without exception wearing horn-rimmed spectacles like Chinese mandarins. The doctors were spaced unevenly along the corridor, three on either side. Doctor number one caught Phineas by the head and peering through his hair hunted for traces of lice. A peremptory tap on the back made him move on and number two pulled open his eyelids and shining an ophthalmoscope on the corneas searched for traces of trachoma, cataract or glaucoma. The third, equipped with a stethoscope, asked him to draw his breath and say 'ah', to inhale and exhale. Number four slapped his chest and back, number five examined his muscles and number six made him drop his trousers ignominiously, squeezed his privates and asked him to cough.

Having successfully run the gauntlet of the six Chinese torturers, Phineas dressed himself and walked up a wide flight of stairs into an enormous hall crowded with people who clustered round small tables which were dotted about the floor. Behind the tables sat uniformed officials busily interrogating the variegated stream of immigrants. Phineas awaited his turn and at last reached the examiner. He was a thickset man with a mop of unruly hair, a strong face and wide-set, humorous eyes. He looked at Phineas as if trying to determine his nationality, then addressed him in a deep, pleasant voice that seemed a natural concomitant of his personality.

'Haben sie Geld zu ziegen?' he asked in German.

Phineas smiled. 'English, please sir,' he said. 'I understand very well.'

The official nodded good-humouredly. 'Splendid! Have you any money, young man? Can you produce twenty-five dollars?'

Phineas shook his head. If he had possessed the equivalent of twenty-five dollars wild horses would not have dragged him away from Chicksand Street and the bosom of his family. But he could not tell that to this American, he had somehow to justify his presence. He decided to brazen it out. At the worst they could only send him back, and he half hoped that that would happen because he missed more and more every hour Shandel's comforting body and the happy babel of his children's voices.

'Your honour,' he said gravely, as if he were addressing an ermined judge, 'there is no question of money. In London I couldn't pick it up anywhere, but maybe in America, if you'll let me in, I'll be more fortunate. I have no money, but I have something much better.' With a flourish he drew out a photograph of himself and his family and handed it over to the official, who looked at the glossy postcard in amazement. 'May I present to you my wife and seven children?' he continued. 'You see what I have produced in eleven years, and in such a foggy town as London. I am only thirty-six, you must remember, and it's quite probable if I bring my wife over, that by the time I'm sixty I'll have another dozen or so. Then I'll be the father of twenty children, and supposing fifteen of them marry and have a couple of pairs of twins apiece, which is quite within the bounds of possibility since twins run in my wife's family, in twenty-five years I will have produced about a hundred American citizens, and by the time my grandchildren get going, I will have populated a small-sized city.'

The official guffawed. He held the postcard in the air, helpless with laughter. Staggering from his chair he went round to his colleagues, showing them the photograph and reproducing Phineas's story with his own embellishments. He left a trail of hearty laughter behind him, and to Phineas's amazement he saw dollar bills changing hands as if the official were making a collection. Soon his burly interrogator returned, his face red from the strain of continuous laughter, one hand holding his side, the other clutching a bunch of crisp, green dollars. He stuffed the money into Phineas's pocket.

'There's your twenty-five dollars,' he said. 'With your cheek you deserve to become at least a millionaire!' He stamped the immigrant's landing permit and handed it over with a bow. 'Go ahead, brother!' was his valedictory salute. 'Enter into the Golden Land!'

He collapsed on to his chair and exploded into a fresh cascade of merriment. Phineas walked towards the exit, the heavenly gate to New York, as if he were treading on clouds, followed by nudges, the craning of heads, whispers and the cackle of laughter.

His first act, even before he tried to locate his new home, was to telegraph the entire sum to his wife with a message of hope and greeting. Then, when the money was well and truly on its way, he asked a messenger boy to direct him to Brooklyn.

Baile, Shandel's relative, was married to a cobbler named Smulevitch. They lived with their young children, two boys and a girl, on the ground floor of a tenement house close to the Bowery, in three small rooms, one of which was the cobbler's workshop and sitting-room, the other two being used as bedrooms. When Phineas saw the poverty of his hosts he was unable to understand where Baile had raised the funds to send him a ticket, but the stumpy, red-headed, homely woman explained that his landsleit, his fellow townsmen from Zvonitz and Kamenetz, of whom there were a considerable number in New York, had subscribed to bring him over. Surprise followed surprise when Phineas learned that the prime mover in his transplantation was none other than his old army comrade Mendel Weisman, now domiciled in New York and doing well as a furrier.

Phineas went to see Mendel at once. The timid recruit was now a paunchy, substantial citizen. After a rapturous reunion, they supplied each other with breathless biographical details. Mendel too had seven children, but unlike his former comrade, he could well afford to keep them. The shy, nervous Mendel with seven kids! Phineas thought that it must be some sort of contagious disease. A man had only to rub shoulders with him to become as fruitful as an amative stallion. Mendel immediately got on the phone and, communicating with the landsleit, arranged for them to meet at his house. Then he shook hands with Phineas and escorted him to the door, and when the immigrant left he was richer by ten dollars, all of which he immediately sent home.

In the evening, nine men answered the call. The self-appointed committee filled Mendel's drawing-room, lolling about in arm-chairs, drinking endless cups of Russian tea and nibbling at macaroons supplied by Mendel's wife and a young servant girl. Phineas sat in a corner trying to efface himself while the committee discussed what was to be done for him. These solid, respectable citizens he had once looked down on as ignorant, unkempt small-town louts. Now one was a realtor, another had a Singer sewing-machine agency; they were grocers, butchers, pants manufacturers; and Phineas the celebrated scribe had to come to them cap in hand. Years earlier, Phineas would have starved sooner than be dependent on such assistance, but his experience in the London slums had taught him to respect the topsy-turvy system of values whereby the go-getter, the money-bag squatter, ruled the roost, and good taste, intelligence and education counted for less than nothing.

'I have a suggestion,' said Mr Kritz, the realtor, importantly, in his high-pitched soprano. 'As our Phineas is a cap-maker, I propose we find him a job in a cap factory.'

'Good! Good! Good idea!' assented the butchers and the grocers.

'One moment,' interposed the pants manufacturer, Hymie, a pale, stooping Jew with a crystal-clear pendant perpetually glistening at the tip of his long nose, an adornment he had never managed to divest himself of from childhood. 'One moment. This isn't Europe. Here, an operator has got to be a union man and to belong to the union costs twenty-five dollars.'

'Well, we can easily raise that,' said the soprano. 'I'll start off with five.'

'Hold on – hold on!' cried Mendel. 'Don't be in such a hurry, brothers. He's just run away from one cellar, and you want to stick him in another. No! That won't do. My suggestion is to make a businessman of him.'

'Yes, but what business?' asked the realtor, slightly piqued at being ejected from the pedestal of patron saint.

'What's the difference?' replied Mendel. 'Let him go about the streets. New York will soon teach him what to do.'

After a short discussion Mendel's proposal was carried, and like most Jewish conferences, the meeting was adjourned for a fortnight. In the meantime Phineas had to live, and he could not forget that at home his wife and seven children had to live too. On the following day, Smulevitch gave him to understand politely, but firmly, that he really ought to find more comfortable lodgings. Phineas packed his valise and moved a few blocks away into a small apartment house run by a woman from Kamenetz, Mrs Kramer, whom Smulevitch had recommended. She was a widow, a tall, healthy-looking Amazon, and she agreed to let Phineas a small box room at a rental of three dollars a month, the three dollars to be paid in advance. After Phineas had explained his position, being a warm-hearted woman and a landsfrau at that, she was content with his promise to pay at the end of the month, and she even lent him a dollar when she found that he was completely destitute, tossing him the idea of starting a newspaper round with the money.

The same afternoon Phineas went to East Broadway to the offices of the Jewish daily *Warheit*. He invested the dollar in a hundred and forty copies of the newspaper and ran down the sidewalks of Esther Street, Essex Street and Delancey selling his wares at a cent apiece. As soon as he sold out his papers, he returned to the office for a fresh supply, and by the evening had earned eighty cents. The next morning he was out early and by nightfall had realised a net profit of one dollar, and on the days following he managed to make on an average a dollar a day. He sent home whatever he earned, allowing himself only a few cents for cigarettes and other necessities. Food he obtained from his landsleit. He became a confirmed dropper-in, dropping in at one place for breakfast, at another for dinner, at a third for supper, and occasionally skipping a meal or two or, when his luck was out, all three.

A week of newspaper selling was enough for Phineas. He went to Mendel and begged his friend to give him a job in his workshop. Mendel demurred at first, but agreed eventually, and Phineas started the next morning at the machine. He was one of twenty machinists, and being unacquainted with fur, was put on to seaming linings for the ties, at which job he was more than merely competent. The hours, from eight till six, with an hour off for lunch, were gentlemanly compared with the labour day in London, but the work extracted from the men in nine hours was at least equivalent to thirteen or fourteen at home. Every section of the work was finely subdivided, and each machinist was kept with his nose continually to the grindstone without being allowed to chat to his neighbours or even find a mournful anodyne in song. At the sound of the least sustained whispering, the forelady, an angular hatchet-faced woman of middle age, would move amongst the delinquents, her lips pursed in a long-drawn, sibilant 'Shush-Shush!'

At the end of the second day, Phineas was more than fed up, and on the morning of the third was three-parts disposed not to return to what seemed to him the most degrading form of penal servitude. A blizzard came to his rescue, piling up snow in the streets to a height Phineas had not seen since Russia. A fine rain had fallen earlier and frozen overnight, and to the top of that glacial surface a monstrous white counterpane relentlessly attached itself. With the contrariness of blizzards, the snow had settled most deeply in huge drifts between the tramlines, so that the trolley cars were unable to move and the roads were completely impassable.

Mrs Kramer had been up hours before him and had already hewn a path from the porch to the pavement, but Phineas did not appreciate her foresight when he slid like an expert skier down all the steps and narrowly avoided breaking his neck. The municipal buildings were plastered with posters calling for volunteers to assist in clearing the snow. The authorities supplied all the necessary implements and in addition were offering a wage of a dollar and a quarter a day. This seemed to Phineas an occupation infinitely preferable to sweating like a deaf mute at the machine, so he lined up in the queue of down-and-outs waiting for the chance to wield a pick and shovel.

At the end of the fourth day Phineas collected five dollars and found himself a white man, over twenty-one, and free again. He sent home four dollars and retained a dollar for himself in case of emergencies. His landsleit were by this time thoroughly sick of his dropping-in habits, which in any case could not continue *ad infinitum*, so he was confronted with a new problem, that of how and where to eat. He had chummed up with a lanky Jewish hobo named Joe who had worked side by side with him clearing the snow-drifts, and Joe, an old American of ten years standing, promised to procure for him choice meals at three cents a time. Joe had evolved a technique whereby for the price of a mug of beer he could obtain a substantial meal from the free-lunch counters.

Working Joe's system, Phineas went with his friend to a saloon in Delancey Street. Pushing open the swinging half-doors that left a gap of several feet above and below the portal, they sat down on the long bench that ran parallel to the bar and ordered two beers. Phineas's eyes almost popped out of his head as he saw the tasty row of viands set out in plates along the length of the counter. Joe paid six cents to the burly Irish landlord and started to sip his drink. Casually he reached over to a chunk of bread, and spearing a piece of fried liver, thoughtfully began to eat. Phineas followed his example. Hail Columbia, Land of the free! As soon as the landlord's back was turned they helped themselves to another portion of liver and more bread, and by way of a change tried some herring and a little cheese. By the time their mugs were empty, several correspondingly large plates were similarly picked clean. Their nakedness seemed too blatant, so brushing the crumbs from their jackets, Phineas and his friend left the saloon with an access of new confidence and the high spirits that only a square meal could provide.

Phineas had, apart from the army and the Viennese interludes, drunk perhaps two pints of beer previously in the whole of his life, now he was a regular visitor to the Delancey Street saloon, and every day cheerfully paid his three cents for alcoholic refresh-ment. At last, the landlord's suspicions were aroused. Phineas and his friend usually chose times when the saloon was crowded, but on one occasion, for no accountable reason, the room emptied and very few customers remained seated round the bar. The landlord slid over two beers, and propping his hairy, freckled forearms on the counter, faced them belligerently. Joe took a tiny sip of beer and commenced a rambling semi-detached conversation with his companion on the political situation. Phineas nodded politely, occasionally whispering a few monosyllables, his eyes wandering frequently to the plate of crisp, golden-brown liver, a delicacy of which he was inordinately fond. The landlord listened silently, his beefy face set with the same stern expression. Phineas decided to chance a piece of liver. He picked up a chunk of bread and chewing nonchalantly reached over for the tasty dish. Before his hand could grasp the fork, the plate was whisked away and the landlord, holding the liver in the air with one hand, rubbed his napkin over the empty space on the counter with the other. Phineas drank some more beer, then when he thought the landlord's attention was diverted, he tentatively pushed his hand in the direction of the cheese. The landlord, however, had observed this strategy from the corner of his eye. He served a customer quickly, and before Phineas's hand quite reached its objective, the cheese described an arc in the air and the landlord was vigorously polishing the counter. Ostentatiously he placed the cheese on a shelf behind him and leaned towards the two interlopers. His face was flushed with anger, his tiny, deep-set, almost colourless eyes flashing maliciously. He extended a massive, freckled arm and shook a podgy finger threateningly under Phineas's nose.

'See here, you two sheenies,' he growled angrily, addressing himself to both, 'are you trying to ruin me, or what? Now beat it, quick!'

Phineas tried to gulp down the remainder of his beer, but his presence stank in the landlord's nostrils. Phineas was not moving fast enough for him. He whistled peremptorily to the bouncer, 'Hey Phil!' but the friends, glancing just once at the battered features of the advancing thug, decided to forego their drinks in a hurry and shot through the doors like a couple of pellets ejected from a sling.

The landsleit had met again in the meantime, only six of the original nine committee men being present, the soprano, the machine agent and the pants manufacturer having some more important business, a bridge party, on hand, and after a convivial evening with plenty of talk, smoking and drinking, had adjourned the meeting once more until the following week. Meanwhile the end of the month drew on and Mrs Kramer was expecting her four dollars. Phineas did not want to sponge on Mendel again, because he had earlier in the week borrowed five dollars from him to send to Shandel, and if he had to do any more borrowing the following week, he wanted that to be for his family as well.

Seeing that apparently there was no other solution to the problem of the four dollars, Phineas went mad. Long past midnight, when all the other lodgers were asleep, Phineas resuscitated his violin which ever since his arrival in America had lain neglected in his valise, and started to play some gypsy dances. Soon the whole apartment house resounded with irritable knocks, and after about an hour's wild fiddling the sleepy voice of Mrs Kramer, full and rich like her luxuriant body, reached him from the staircase. 'Hey there! Shut up, will you!' He played a screechy finale, then put his instrument away.

At six the following morning, when Mrs Kramer went to the boiler in the basement with a pile of dirty washing, she found Phineas dancing to greet her, gesticulating like a madman. She dropped the linen on the floor in alarm, and Phineas, seizing her round the waist, started to propel her to the tune of a polka. She pushed him off indignantly, but Phineas smiled sweetly at her and began to recite, in sonorous Russian sing-song, flowery verses from Pushkin with a wealth of endearing gesture. This was too much for Mrs Kramer. She ran to the door and bawled loudly for help, but Phineas, having no desire to appear before a lunacy board, slipped past her and ran into the street.

When he returned late in the evening, he found his strapped valise resting on the porch. He guessed that Mrs Kramer's eye was peering through the keyhole to see that nobody ran off with it. Desperately he started pounding on the knocker.

'Let me in! Let me in!' he yelled.

Mrs Kramer's heavy body gave a scared jump behind the door. In a voice breathless with agitation she answered him.

'No! Go away! Go away!'

'But I've nowhere to sleep,' shouted Phineas. 'Let me in, *dear* Mrs Kramer!'

'If I let you in, *I'll* have nowhere to sleep,' she retorted. 'Out of my house, madman! The fiddle he plays all night, and Pushkin he sings to me six o'clock in the morning!'

There could be, of course, no clearer proof of madness. Complimenting himself on his histrionic ability, Phineas picked up his valise, and after a last abortive attempt to gain access to the house, walked slowly down the steps. He went to a neighbouring doss-house and, booking a bed for a nickel, slept with his valise propped up behind his pillow in case any of his rascally looking neighbours took a fancy to it.

In the morning he left his baggage at a railway cloakroom and went to meet Joe in Central Park. His lean friend was disgruntled at the prospect of another job. Joe very rarely worked, and then only in winter. He usually bummed his way from town to town during the summer, on foot and in freight cars, until he reached the southern climes, where a hobo could still sleep at ease in the sun; but an accident had laid him up, and he had been forced to winter in New York. Work he regarded as a disgraceful function for a healthy man with the full use of his limbs, and he was never quite reconciled to it. Pulling his threadbare overcoat about his ears he shivered and thought of California. If that lorry hadn't put him in hospital with several fractured ribs, he would not have been reduced to the ignominy of work. Sweat, and make somebody else rich? No sense in that. Work was the last resource of halfwits, and he, Joe, in full possession of his faculties, was about to accept a job as sandwich-board man. He almost apologised as he told Phineas of some vacancies tipped him by a friend, and was half inclined to give such distasteful activity the cold shoulder, but Phineas grabbed him by the arm, and in spite of his protestations marched him off to the depot.

A new corset was appearing on the market, and a long line of sandwich-board men were heralding the product to an indifferent public. Phineas had a shapeless old dowager with sprawling breasts perched on his shoulders, and Joe, behind him, was more fortunate in supporting a beautiful brunette with a figure like an hour glass, 'before and after'. Strangely enough the advertisements attracted only the attention of men, very young boys and old dodderers whose senile minds should have been years removed from such foolishness, the women for whom the display was really intended glancing away in embarrassment. Phineas grew tired of seeing the same grinning beauty on the man in front of him bobbing up and down like a salacious chorus girl, and the old dowager that squatted astride him grew every minute heavier and heavier, until at the end of the day he could almost believe that like her living counterpart she weighed all of fifteen stone.

When he parked the boards at last and received his pay, his shoulders were so stiff that it pained him to stretch his limbs. Hours after he had finished work it still seemed to him that he was supporting a rigid framework, and he had to touch his shoulders to convince himself that his muscles were not constricted by the ridiculous harness of the corset advertisement. On the second day, ambling at a leisurely pace in the gutter watching the shabby, downtrodden heels of the preceding beast of burden, he heard a shout of 'Phineas! Phineas!' He looked up and saw Mendel beckoning to him from the pavement.

Phineas turned red and shook his head. 'Sorry, I can't stop,' he said. 'I have to keep moving.'

'Come and see me tonight, then,' yelled Mendel. 'Don't forget.'

Phineas answered him with a tired wave of the hand and continued his monotonous progression. In the evening, he called at his friend's house. Mendel was walking up and down agitatedly in his parlour. Phineas stepped inside the room and waited silently. At last Mendel stopped before the immigrant and shook his head in disgust.

'A sandwich-board man!' he uttered, distressed by the mere mention of the name. 'Pfui, Phineas! That is not for such as you?'

'Maybe not,' said Phineas. 'But what can I do? I am still waiting for the landsleit. By the time they decide how to help me, all they'll have to do will be to provide my funeral expenses.'

'See here, Phineas,' said Mendel, dismissing the sarcasm. 'A friend of mine has a wholesale dry-goods store. I'll take you there tomorrow morning and try to fix you up a job as a pedlar. That will have to do until something better comes along.'

The following morning Mendel took Phineas to his friend Jake Schulman of Schulman's Inc. Recommended by Mendel as a trustworthy person, Phineas got the job. It was that of a low-grade commission agent canvassing for custom for Mr Schulman's wares.

One of the warehousemen bundled up a selection of goods in a waterproof wrapper around which were strapped two belts with loops that allowed the package to be slipped over the shoulders. The procedure was simple. All Phineas had to do was go round the tenement houses and those private residences that did not have 'No Beggars – No Hawkers' affixed to the door, and display his wares.

The first dozen doors that he tried opened two inches, and irate housewives glared at him; some shut the door immediately, but the more considerate ones snapped 'No thanks!' before even Phineas had a chance to say 'Good morning'. At the next apartment the door opened wide enough for him to wedge his boot against the doorpost.

'Bedspreads? Coitans? Towels? Linens?' he rattled off eagerly.

The woman shook her head. 'No thanks,' she said.

'Cotton sheets? Handkerchiefs?'

'No thanks,' she repeated with acerbity. 'Now will you take your foot away, you little kike, or shall I call a cop?'

One in every twenty was a customer. Then Phineas unfolded his wrapper and displayed his goods. The woman picked out what she wanted, or if he did not have the article she required, he made a note of the order which would have to be sent on. He entered the purchase on a card which he handed to the client, and made a similar entry into his own account book. At the end of the day he returned to the depot and received twenty-five per cent commission on his bookings, the collection of payments being an entirely distinct branch of the business. The paucity of commission on his first two days' trading was so discouraging that he thought of allowing peddling to go the way of fur-machining and sandwich boards, then he remembered his landsleit. This time they would have to help him. He ferreted them out one by one and begged them to assist him by buying Schulman's goods.

For several months he played on the sympathies of the landsleit until they had so many bedspreads and towels that they could have opened up in the dry-goods business on their own account. It was a fatiguing occupation. The best customers amongst his townsmen were the poorest ones, and they usually lived five or six floors up, so Phineas tramped up and down stairs all day long in the effort to keep going a home four thousand miles away.

Around March, when the landsleit were so saturated with Schulman Inc. bargains that they became completely deaf when Phineas called, Mendel had another idea. Passover was approaching, and matzos, the unleavened cakes of the ancient ceremonial, would be in demand, so he suggested that Phineas start a round as agent for a matzo firm. Again the landsleit suffered. Phineas touted for orders and delivered the matzos himself on a pushcart until Passover arrived, and with it Phineas's occupation disappeared once more.

Passover he spent at Mendel's house, worrying about what was happening at home. Shandel sent him regularly cheerful letters, but she barely managed to exist on her husband's remittances. More than once she had sat with her children in a freezing cellar when the mail was late, in total darkness, short even of a penny for the gas but too proud to ask strangers for assistance. Phineas sensed that things were not going too well and redoubled his efforts to find a permanent situation and thus a means of bringing over his sorely tried wife and all his children.

He discovered that one of his very old friends had married into a well-to-do family and was practising as a doctor in Philadelphia. Young Berel Zelefsky had sung tenor in the choir of the synagogue at Kamenetz; in America he was known as Dr Saul. Dr Saul had the reputation of being a very generous man, which Phineas could well believe, since Berel had been one of the gentlest and most honourable boys in the choir and, apart from old Nachum, his best friend in Kamenetz. Phineas decided to put all his eggs in one basket and leave for Philadelphia. He had been in New York for six months and was still exactly the same pauper that he had been when he arrived, with no apparent hope of improving his material position. Mendel was the soul of goodness and would not let him fall entirely, but he could not continue sponging on his friend. Sooner than carry on in that fashion, he would write off America as a failure and return home to pick up the threads of his old life.

Obtaining Dr Saul's address from a relative, he wound up his life in New York, paid Mrs Kramer, astonished at this further manifestation of insanity, her four dollars, and took the train to Philadelphia. Dr Saul lived and had his surgery in a big brownstone house in the centre of the city. Phineas, depositing his valise on the porch, tugged the bell at the entrance to the doctor's private residence and waited. Soon a dark, stout, good-looking woman dressed in a neat gingham frock opened the door. She glanced over Phineas as if trying to discover signs of his ailment.

'What do you want?' she asked sympathetically.

'I would like to see Dr Saul,' replied Phineas with his best Anglo-American accent.

'I am sorry,' said the woman, 'the doctor is at the clinic. Are you a patient?' she inquired with a pleasant smile.

Phineas shook his head. 'No. Not yet. I have private business with the doctor. Very urgent business.'

'Well, you'd best leave your card,' said the woman. 'He'll be back in an hour.'

Phineas extracted a crumpled envelope from his breast pocket, and on it wrote rapidly a message in Yiddish: 'Berel – Your wealthy friend has come to visit you. Phineas.' He handed the note to the woman, apologised for troubling her and walked away.

An hour later he returned and rang the bell again. The same woman opened the door and smiled welcomingly as if he were expected.

'This way, please,' she said.

She led him through a long corridor and up a flight of stairs into the waiting-room that opened into the surgery. The woman disappeared and Phineas took a seat and glanced over some magazines lying on the table. A few minutes later the surgery door opened silently and Dr Saul, a short, spare man, stood in the doorway, intently regarding his visitor. The doctor was prematurely bald and wore rimless pince-nez attached by a length of black braid to his starched white coat. He had high cheekbones and narrow slanting eyes that gave his features a Mongolian cast, and to complete the racial illusion a long, thin, black moustache straggled over his upper lips and drooped down the corners of his mouth. He stood quietly in the doorway, unwilling to disturb Phineas, his needle-sharp dark eyes taking in every detail of his friend's appearance. At last Phineas looked up. With a glad cry he dropped the magazine and rushed towards the doctor who moved quickly in his direction with wide-open arms. They embraced warmly in the centre of the room, then Dr Saul pushed Phineas away, and looked him over again critically at arm's length, a suspicious moistness clouding his eyes.

'Phineas!' he exclaimed with bantering roughness. 'May the cholera take you! What the devil are you doing here?'

'It's a long story,' said Phineas, 'but I'll make it short and sweet. I couldn't earn a living in London so I came to America. I have been in New York for six months and made in that time about a hundred and fifty dollars. Thirty dollars I kept for myself, and a hundred and twenty I sent home to my family. Since my arrival in America I have become a man of many trades, the best of which is civil engineering, wherein I walk about surveying the city and see that the New York streets are kept free from snow.'

Berel laughed. 'I can see what sort of civil engineer you are by your clothes and your face. Now come into the surgery.'

'Why?' asked Phineas. 'I'm not ill.'

'Don't argue!' said Dr Saul sternly. 'Come into the surgery.'

When the surgery door closed behind them, Dr Saul took a sterilised instrument and poking it into his friend's mouth looked down Phineas's throat. Then he put a stethoscope to his heart and lungs. Replacing the instrument on the table he shook his head gravely.

'Hmmm – I thought my diagnosis was correct,' he smiled disarmingly. 'I'm going to prescribe a long schnapps, chopped liver, lokshen soup and roast chicken. Do you think you could manage it?'

'Could I!' said Phineas enthusiastically.

Arms linked round each other's shoulders they left the surgery and descended the stairs. Phineas caught a fleeting glimpse of the stout woman disappearing into a room below.

'Nice-looking servant you've got,' he said.

Berel laughed heartily. 'Thanks for the compliment. That's not a servant, that's my wife. It's the servant's day off.'

Phineas blushed. His friend was indeed fortunate to have married a woman with looks and money as well. He had been dreading the meeting with Berel's wife, imagining that she must be a harridan on the wrong side of forty. He was glad for his friend's sake. Berel deserved all the luck in the world. The doctor's wife made him comfortable at once and was genuinely pleased to have him in her house. She seated him at the table in the dining-room and plied him in spite of mock protestations with food and wine, until he was so blown out that if he swallowed another mouthful he felt he must burst.

When he was sated, Dr Saul produced cigars, and comfortably seated in an armchair Phineas told his story at length. When he had concluded, the doctor's wife was weeping unrestrainedly, softly blowing her nose in her handkerchief. The warmth of her maternal instinct, so far denied fruition in babies of her own, went out to the seven hungry children left behind in that distant foggy land. She insisted that Phineas must stay as a guest in her house until Dr Saul found something for him to do. The doctor was an untiring benefactor like Rappoport of his Vienna days. Within a fortnight he had located a delicatessen shop, a paying concern, the owner of which wanted to emigrate farther West and was willing to sell. Dr Saul was prepared to advance the money for the purchase of the shop. He bought tickets for Shandel and the children, and Phineas sent them off at once enclosed in a six-page letter, one long paean lauding the virtues of the angelic Dr Saul.

Before the property deal was completed, a letter came from Shandel that blasted all Phineas's hopes. A few weeks previously, on April 15th, the *Titanic* had fouled an iceberg on her maiden voyage and gone down with an appalling loss of life. Shandel had read and re-read the details of the disaster and swore that whatever happened she would not entrust her brood to the mercy of the angry waves of the Atlantic. The more she thought of the journey across that boundless ocean, the more terrified she became. She had nightmares in which hissing seas swirled about her, and she saw her little ones floating off out of her reach, becoming engulfed beneath rearing crests of speckled foam. Numbed by the terror of hysteria she wrote to Phineas imploring him to return home, saying that if he did not come soon he would no longer have a wife to return to. He *must* come home! Even if they showered on her handfuls of diamonds, she would not, could not, because of the children, brave the ocean crossing.

Again, just when Phineas's star was brightest, it hurtled from the sky like a flaming meteor into the stillness and darkness of everlasting night. He wandered about like a moody ghost for several days, seemingly cut off from life, and at last made preparations for his departure. Two days before he left, he was sipping a lemon tea in a little Jewish restaurant, trying to collect his scattered thoughts and focus them on the forthcoming journey and the trials and tribulations that lay beyond, when a hearty slap on the back jerked him into pained recognition of his surroundings. A tall, swarthy man stood over him, Rubin, one of his landsleit, who in New York lived on his wits. Rubin was always floating fantastic schemes. He always seemed to be on the verge of making a fortune, but it never quite came off. A cheerful Micawber-like personality, he drifted from one project to another, a showman one week, a drummer the next, the third hawking inventions, only waiting for some shrewd financier to take up the biggest money-maker ever. Rubin sat down opposite Phineas and ordered a lemon tea. With incorrigible good humour he slapped the table with the palm of his hand and announced: 'You're just the man I want to see!'

'Me?' said Phineas. 'You want to see me?'

'Sure!' replied Rubin. 'Are you working?'

Phineas shook his head.

'Good!' exclaimed Rubin rubbing his hands cheerfully.

'What's so good about that?' inquired Phineas.

'I'll tell you what's good about it,' said Rubin. 'You don't have to worry any more. You're a made man!'

He picked up a receptacle shaped rather like a violin case and placed it on the table. He opened the case and extracted a small camera, a tripod and a square tin tank. He leaned confidentially across the table, and like a purveyor of precious stones, poised the camera under Phineas's nose.

'You see this little machine,' he whispered. 'It's one of the greatest inventions of the age. It takes photographs and develops them in five minutes. You can go about the streets and pleasure resorts and they'll be fighting to have their pictures taken, and it is so simple that a child can work it.' He put his hand in his pocket and drew out a pile of tintypes and passed them over to Phineas. 'Taken with this identical camera. Good eh? ... Good! It's marvellous!' He continued enthusiastically without waiting for a reply. 'And it's yours for ten dollars!'

Rubin's enthusiasm seeped through Phineas. It seemed

legitimate enough. They finished their lemon teas and walked back to Dr Saul. The doctor examined the camera sceptically and Rubin tried it out before his eyes. He photographed Dr Saul, his wife and Phineas in a group, and although the reproduction was slightly bleared, owing to the poor light Rubin explained, all three were portrayed recognisably. It worked! The experiment was a success.

Phineas bought the camera, that is to say he bought it, but did not pay for it. Dr Saul guaranteed that the ten dollars would be forthcoming when required and Phineas promised to send the money from England as soon as the camera was a working proposition. He set out on his long journey, sorry to bid farewell for ever to Dr Saul and his wife, but glad to be on his way home to Shandel and the children, returning not empty-handed but with a heaven-sent contraption that would put him on his feet once more and prevent those eight long-suffering stomachs from ever going hungry again.

CHAPTER VII

Back in Chicksand Street, Phineas was garlanded with greetings like a conquering hero. At his homecoming he embraced his wife and every one of his children separately, held the infants up in the air and admired their youthful charms which, in spite of their tattered garments, radiated from them like warmth from a hidden sun. He looked at his treasures, altered surprisingly in his seven months of absence, and wondered how he had managed to steel his heart to stay away from them even for so comparatively short a period. Never again would he be separated from his family, no matter what the temptation; wherever he went they would all have to go with him.

Like a conjurer extracting rabbits from a hat, he produced the camera, the touchstone of their salvation. He photographed the family in a group, then each member individually. He photographed old Copper Beard and Miriam, and his neighbours all gratis. The first pictures bore traces of amateur handling, the figures being swathed in a greyish mist, but in a day or two he discovered the trick of precise exposure and development. Now he was all set for his new career, but simultaneously with his perfection of the process his plates gave out and the quick-developing solution dwindled into a few weak drops at the bottom of the tank. He went round to every photographer and chemist in the district trying to replenish his apparatus, but nobody could match up the exact size and composition of the plates, or had any idea of the ingredients of the solution. To import these necessities from America would be too expensive, so after a week of fruitless endeavour Phineas reluctantly discarded his photographic career and sold the camera for the best offer – three-and-sixpence.

America had taught him one thing, that in a big city it was possible to earn a living by means other than the continuous drudgery of a subterranean workshop, that his head was as competent a procurer of the necessities of life as the unimaginative manipulation of his ten overworked fingers. He went round to general dealers and rag merchants and purchased whatever was going cheap, and heaping the remnants of cloth, silk or shirting upon a barrow, took his sorry stock out to the street markets and sold it at any price that showed a margin of profit. He managed to earn four or five shillings a day, and Shandel helped him nobly in eking out his resources. For the best part of the week they were vegetarians, subsisting on a diet of fruit, bread and margarine, only tasting fish or meat on Friday and Saturday. Very often the children had nothing to eat between a scanty dinner and a scantier supper, so the elder ones followed Deborah, who was something of a madcap in organising searches amongst the dustbins for fruit or scraps of unpalatable food thrown away by their more fortunate neighbours.

On one occasion Phineas, having sold the best part of his stock in the morning, trundled the remainder on a barrow to a market in Bermondsey early in the afternoon. He stood for several hours in the gutter while women came over and rummaged amongst the pieces, and finding nothing to suit them went off. Next to Phineas was an old man with a pile of straw hats. He saw the women cluster around Phineas and go off empty-handed. True, they bought nothing, but they did approach close to Phineas's barrow, which was more appreciation than they extended to his hats, and showed that his neighbour's stock had a potential sales value. Towards the end of the day, neither had made a start and stood by their bedraggled stock commiserating with each other.

'I'll tell you what,' said the old man. 'Let's change our stuff. Maybe we'll have some luck.'

Phineas had no objection, since the value of their combined merchandise could be no more than a shilling or two, and placing a straw hat at a rakish angle on his head he transferred his pieces to the old man's stall. At nightfall neither had broken the ice, so the old man took home his pieces and Phineas, still crowned by his jaunty headgear, trundled home the hats. He sold three or four, the cream of his stock, in the days that followed for a penny apiece, and the rest he distributed between his children and the ragamuffins of the street. For a week Chicksand Street was peopled by diminutive dudes in straw hats that fell over their ears. When the novelty wore off, the boaters became footballs and were kicked around in exciting variations of soccer that littered the gutters with dirty patches of straw.

Then Phineas bought an immense quantity of buttons for eight shillings. He took a barrow-load to the market, not a quarter of his total stock, and selling an insignificant number brought home five shillings. The next day he made three shillings, the day following the same again, but the inroad this made upon his stock was like a bucket of water lifted from the sea. In a week he had taken more than twice their original purchase price and still there seemed an endless number. Phineas computed that by selling them all he would make a profit of about ten thousand per cent, the only apparent snag being that that process would take about thirty years to complete. The buttons littered the cellar and proved such an unremitting nuisance about the house that a fortnight later Shandel put her foot down firmly, and after an unsuccessful attempt by Phineas to sell them in bulk, the buttons went the way of the straw hats.

Meanwhile, Phineas got deeper and deeper in debt to the landlord. His two tenants paid him regularly, but he used the money in his business ventures, and when there was a shortage of food, his children came first. The agent who collected the rent threatened him unavailingly until at last Mr Davis the landlord came down personally to interview the black sheep. Mr Davis was a tall, broad, red-faced Jew resembling a country farmer who in bulk could make two of Phineas. He knocked peremptorily on the door, and, being admitted by one of the tenants, went straight down to Phineas's living quarters.

Phineas answered the staccato rap, and Mr Davis, clutching an officious-looking ledger under his arm, came into the kitchen. The landlord had come at an opportune moment, Shandel and the children were visiting Copper Beard, so he could talk freely and to the point. He seated himself on a rickety chair, placed his hat upon the table and opened the ledger. He ran a stiff red finger down a column of arrears and totted up the number of missed payments. At last he looked up.

'Mr Kahn,' he said sternly. 'Do you know that you owe me nine weeks' rent?'

'Nine weeks?' asked Phineas with a deprecatory gesture. 'I thought it was ten.'

'Correct,' assented the landlord. 'With this week it will be ten, but I have no intention of allowing you to stay and make up round numbers. I know you're a poor man and that you've got a lot of kids – so I won't be hard on you. But I want you to do me a favour in return.'

'If it's only within my power,' said Phineas.

'It's within your power all right,' replied the landlord. He closed the ledger with a snap. 'The biggest favour you can do me is to clear out. Right away!'

'But, Mr Davis,' protested Phineas. 'Give me a little time and I'll try to pay back the arrears; otherwise, I can't pay anything at all.'

'Suits me,' said Mr Davis. 'I'm not asking you for any money. I just want you to move.'

He rose to his feet, bowing his head to avoid scraping the ceiling, and moved to the door. Phineas ran after him and appealingly caught his arm.

'Where shall I move?' he asked earnestly, almost tearfully. 'How can I move? I haven't a penny in the world!'

The landlord stopped. 'How you move and where you move, are no concern of mine,' he snapped. He glanced round the room and his gaze shifted uneasily, evidences of the direst poverty shouting at him from every corner. The glance proved his undoing, the hard lines round his mouth softened. He could not further submerge a drowning man. Irresolutely he fumbled in his pockets and drew out a golden sovereign. He pressed it into Phineas's hand. 'There you are,' he growled to cover his embarrassment. 'Take it. It's your luck that I'm a blasted fool!' The door closed behind the landlord and immediately opened again. Mr Davis stuck in his bowler hat. 'Now see you do move!' he said severely and vanished.

Two days later Phineas found a huge room in Lordship Square, an aristocratically named quadrant of houses with nothing even remotely aristocratic about them. By an ingenious system of drapings suspended across the room from rods attached to the top of the walls, half of the chamber was converted at night into sleeping quarters and sub-divided into three compartments in one of which Phineas and his wife slept, the other two being shared between the boys and girls. By day the drapings were drawn flush against the walls and the room became workshop, nursery, lounge and refectory. Phineas had by this time become an old-clothes dealer. He went round the streets with a pushcart on certain days collecting discarded and unwanted garments. At home they were sorted out. Shandel confiscated the more presentable clothes, washed them, darned them and added them to her wardrobe. Skirts and dresses she took for herself, and shirts she made up for the children, or when there was a dearth of shirts she altered blouses to fit them, and the remainder Phineas took to the markets. Never since birth had the luckless little Kahns had the good fortune to wear new clothes; everything came to them cut down or second-hand.

Two events enlivened their first year at Lordship Square. Shandel, refreshed by the brief hiatus of seven months' continence, immediately conceived and bore a little girl in less than a year after Phineas's return from America. She was a pretty, rounded dumpling, with cheeks the colour of red fruit. They named her Rose, but her puffed cheeks blossomed like ripe oranges, pomerantzen, so they called her affectionately Pompele, and Pompele she remained until she was old enough to reclaim her christening name. The other triumph was Olga's winning of a county scholarship, thereby becoming entitled to a free place in a secondary school, together with a small monetary grant. Phineas began to see the fruition of his sacrifices. Most of his neighbours withdrew their children from school at the age of fourteen whatever their scholastic promise, needing the few shillings they would earn in the workshops to supplement the family income, but Phineas decided that Olga must continue her education, even if he had to support her until she was twenty-one, or older.

With each succeeding child, the problem of feeding them adequately grew more and more difficult. Shandel went to the market late in the evening and bought provisions that the earlier shoppers had rejected. The fish was not so good, the meat was not so fresh. The best portions went by right to the children, and Shandel and her husband had to content themselves with food that was not really fit for any human consumption. Phineas's skin erupted in painful boils so that he had the greatest difficulty in going about his business. One afternoon it got so bad that he laid himself in bed with his face to the wall to try and snatch a little sleep and relief from the pain. Shandel was out with the younger children but would be back in time for tea, and the older ones were still at school. Olga and Phillip came home together, bursting into the room with the bright babble of early spring. The girl flung her books in the corner; they were enclosed not in a satchel but in an old Gladstone bag such as doctors carry. Phineas had picked it up in the street green with age and mildew, and after a day's soaking under the tap, had passed it on to Olga. They quietened down as they saw Phineas, apparently asleep on the bed, and walked about on tiptoe, both of them ravenously hungry. Phillip saw a hunk of bread on the table, and picking it up longingly was about to fasten his sharp young teeth into it when Olga took it out of his hands.

'Leave it alone,' she said. 'There's nothing for tomorrow.'

Phineas heard and groaned with anguish. Mentally and physically he was beset on all sides. It seemed to him that he was embogged in a slimy black swamp, his struggles only sinking him deeper and deeper into the mire without the slightest possibility of his ever being able to extricate himself.

Each year, during the winter months, a soup kitchen was opened in the East End for the relief of the Jewish poor. A kindly neighbour, a regular customer at the kitchen, showed Phineas the ropes. He accompanied him to the soup kitchen and took him into a tiny waiting-room. Phineas tapped at a small frosted glass window at the farther end of the room. After an interval of a few moments it slid open and a middle-aged woman neatly dressed in an expensive navy frock inquired his business. Phineas told her that he had come for relief, and his face and his personal appearance showed only too clearly that he was not lying. He filled in the blank spaces on a printed questionnaire and the lady told him to return two days later. When he called, a man answered his timid tap, and on discovering Phineas's name, gave him a huge black enamel pot with instructions to call at the side entrance for soup and bread. On the pot, stencilled across its circumference, were bold white letters, 'SOUP KITCHEN, SOUP KITCHEN', so that carried uncovered in the street, nobody could be under any misapprehension that its possessor was not the recipient of charity. Phineas took the pot to the cook, who filled it with a steaming brew from an enormous tub and handed him a quartern loaf. That was the portion. A loaf to every pot, and no more than one pot per applicant.

At the corner of the next turning the gutters were greasy with stew that had been shot down the drain. The steaming mixture was like a lucky dip. The cook ladled out a saucepanful, whatever came into the ladle went into the pot. The cook's arm went up and down the regulation number of times, never once more or less. Sometimes a lump of meat was amongst the stew and then the lucky ones kept the meat and threw away the soup, for in any case it was worth their while to go to the kitchen just for a quartern of bread per day. Phineas never threw his stew away, no matter how thin or how tasteless. It was life, nourishment for his children, but unfortunately it was not enough. He found out when the personnel behind the frosted glass was changed, and a few weeks later he presented himself as Jacob String, a man with six children, and giving an address at the house of another obliging neighbour in case the investigator called, received a second pot and a second quartern of bread. When the children came home from school every afternoon, Phillip and Stanley, who fortunately did not resemble each other, were deputed to bring home the rations, Phillip representing Phineas and the younger boy the corporeal embodiment of the mythical Jacob String.

At Passover, each pot-holder belonging to the paupers' club received a hundredweight of potatoes, twenty pounds of matzos and a parcel of groceries sufficient to last over the holidays, and the soup kitchen closed down until the following September. Phineas's family, enjoying the additional bounty of Jacob String, lived like fighting cocks for a few days until the store of food gave out and they lapsed back into their usual state of chronic malnutrition.

Phineas and his family were a constant source of annoyance to the people who lived in the rooms above. Phineas always played his fiddle as soon as the children were on their feet in the morning. Playing his instrument toned him up for the day; it was as much a part of his matutinal ritual as the donning of phylacteries and the intonation of the morning prayers. In the evening, when the family was assembled after supper, he played again, and the children danced and sang, yelling and stamping with carefree abandon. The neighbours upstairs complained, and Phineas promised to abate the nuisance, but after several days, when night fell and the fiddle was still, the children begged him to play for them, and he had not the heart to ignore their ingenuous pleadings.

The cantankerous old couple in the rooms above were furious. They had never had children of their own and could not imagine the delight Phineas felt in the wild stampeding of his hilarious flock. The old grouch thumped heavily on the floor with his walking stick, but Phineas only played louder, and the yells of the delighted children penetrated with maddening clarity into the ageing eardrums. The next day the old man went to the Public Health authorities and lodged a complaint. On the same afternoon an inspector called. He was horrified to learn that ten people actually resided in the one room, had all their meals there and slept there too. Definitely it was overcrowded to the detriment of the occupants' health. He gave Phineas twenty-four-hours' notice. He must vacate the room or proceedings would be taken.

Faced with this ultimatum, Phineas almost went off his head with worry. Late in the evening, he hung round the corner of the street lying in wait for Ma Kaminsky, the landlady. She was a spare, grey-haired elderly woman with a keen, sharply chiselled youthful face, always shabbily dressed in a faded blue coat, a string market bag permanently suspended from her arm as if it had been grafted on to it. She owned all the houses in Lordship Square and much of the surrounding property, but to look at her, one unacquainted with her idiosyncrasies would have imagined, and with justification, that she was the wife or widow of some struggling little tailor. Her tenants called her the 'Barefoot Lady' behind her back and Ma Kaminsky to her face, but the landlady had no objection to whatever they called her, so long as they paid the rent regularly on Monday morning.

At last, when Phineas had given up all hope of seeing her that evening, her lean familiar figure rounded the corner, the string bag swinging before her in the breeze. Phineas ran to accost her in case she should manage somehow to escape him, and breathlessly told her his story. She listened to Phineas in silence, then shook her head regretfully.

'I am sorry,' she said. 'If the Public Health say you must go, you've got to go, that's all.'

'But haven't you got a little house somewhere I can rent?' he begged. 'I don't care where it is, or what it's like.'

Again Ma Kaminsky shook her head. 'I haven't a house to let anywhere... Wait a minute,' she went on. 'I'm lying. There *is* a little house to let – but it's in Sammagnus Hill.'

She watched Phineas keenly to see the effect this pronouncement would have on him. Phineas's jaw dropped disconcertingly. Although she owned the whole street Ma Kaminsky could never pronounce its name. She meant St Magnus Hill, a crooked little turning in Wapping that sloped down to the docks. Phineas shook his head dubiously, he had said any place, but he had not dreamed of St Magnus Hill. Not for nothing had the house stayed empty for years. It was likely to remain so indefinitely. All the most lurid characters of the waterfront lived there. Habitual criminals, pickpockets and mobsters, the few respectable inhabitants going about in terror of their lives. Policemen rarely ventured down St Magnus Hill after dark, and then always in couples, and only the sharp tongue and intrepid bravery of Ma Kaminsky enabled her to collect the rent and take it away in safety after two successive agents in less than that number of months had been refused payment, beaten up and robbed of the money they had already collected. The old lady was a shrewd businesswoman. She realised that a tenant like Phineas would be an asset to the property. If he stepped in where angels feared to tread, and survived, there was a possibility when other houses fell vacant that profiting by Phineas's example she could let them to honest hard-working citizens. She decided to tempt Phineas.

'I'll tell you what,' she said. 'If you take the house in Sammagnus Hill you can live there the first month rent free. There are four rooms and a scullery. Just what you could do with, and the rent is only ten shillings a week. I'll even do it up for you from top to bottom, providing you promise to stay... Well?'

Phineas was full of misgivings. It hardly seemed right to subject his family to the dangers of living in St Magnus Hill, but it was possible that those dangers were exaggerated, and that peaceful citizens could live there without fear of incurring bodily violence. Robbery he was not afraid of, since he had nothing any self-respecting criminal would steal, and if there were any injuries to be sustained they would most probably fall on him, so that was all right. But the most tempting and tantalising inducement was a month's free lodging. Throwing all hesitation to the wind Phineas decided to accept the landlady's offer. A month was four weeks, and in that time anything could happen. He might transact a lucky stroke of business and pick up enough money to move to a healthier neighbourhood, or the denizens of the Hill might take a liking to him and refrain from molesting him. In any case the financial risk lay with Ma Kaminsky. If he found it impossible to live there, he could always move before the month was up.

The next morning Phineas's furniture van, a wheelbarrow, was loaded with his possessions and in three journeys his whole home was transferred to St Magnus Hill. Olga stood guard in Lordship Square while her parents' chattels were being removed from the room, and Phillip was watchman at St Magnus Hill. The three journeys, including loading and unloading, were accomplished in as many hours. Phineas returned his furniture van to the stable – there was no charge for its use since he hired it by the week – and went back to his new home. The rooms were small, dirty from long neglect, but structurally in sound condition and, above all, habitable. To Phineas, after his apartments in Grove Street and Chicksand Street, it seemed like a suite in The Ritz. The whole family set to with a will, and by evening everything was in ship-shape order and the house in St Magnus Hill rose again from the dead, resurrected like a putrescent corpse miraculously garbed with living flesh.

The first day everything passed off peacefully. Phineas went about his business and nobody molested him. The children played about in the gutters chumming up with other youngsters and enjoying themselves like old friends in the most natural manner in the world. Phineas began to think that the street's reputation was a malignant slander, until the following day the real face of

St Magnus Hill asserted itself with all the sudden violence and terror of a tropical storm. He sat on the threshold of his house sorting out the old clothes by daylight, the tattered garments heaped in a pile about the doorstep, when he heard Stanley set up a tearful wail. Phineas looked up and saw that the children were involved in some dispute. A boy several years Stanley's senior had forcibly confiscated his son's marbles and Stanley not unnaturally objected to this mode of highway robbery. The incident did not merit Phineas's intervention. Poor as he was, he could always afford to spare an occasional farthing for marbles; it would teach Stanley to play with boys of his own age against whom he could always hold his own, but not satisfied with this primitive form of capitalism the aggressor grabbed Stanley's arm and twisted it behind his back until he was almost hysterical with pain. Phineas jumped up, ran over to the red-headed, freckled pirate and releasing his son soundly boxed the older boy's ears. Now it was the red-head's turn to cry. He rubbed two grimy knuckles in his eyes and between his tears uttered the most lurid threats couched in the complicated adult vocabulary of an irate bargee.

Later in the day the threats materialised. Phineas, from his vantage point on the doorstep, saw the redhead emerge from a house at the bottom of the street accompanied by a tall shaggy man in corduroys who rolled slightly as he walked, like a sailor used to the undulating rhythm of the decks of a ship. Harrigan had been a seaman once, but that was a good many years ago, now he spent his time loafing about the docks in the intervals between inhabiting other docks and jails. Phineas, scenting trouble, rose to his feet and with his boot pushed the old clothes into the room behind. As he had half expected, the truculent couple halted before him. The shaggy man was also red-headed, an enlarged and much uglier replica of his son. He stuck two thick thumbs in his belt and spitting a blob of tobacco-stained juice on the pavement faced Phineas, his legs like twin-grooved brown pillars spread wide apart as if to give a firm purchase to his unsteady feet.

'Naow, wots this 'ere? You bin knockin' my kid abaout?' he growled.

'I'm sorry, mister,' Phineas replied apologetically. 'You've made a mistake. I didn't knock anyone about.'

'This *is* the bloke, ain't it?' the redhead senior demanded, turning to his son.

'Course it's 'im,' assented young Harrigan. 'That's the one 'oo done it.'

Phineas tried to explain what had occurred, but with a lightning and utterly unexpected movement one brawny hand detached itself from the leather belt and, shooting out, the thick fingers grabbed the collar of Phineas's shirt. The sinewy fist tautened, puckering the garment tightly round Phineas's throat, and dragging him half-choked by the savage grip down from the step, Harrigan shook him like a rat. A sour stench of stale beer and chewed plug wafted sickeningly over Phineas as Harrigan thrust his face close to him.

'I'll give yer touch my Freddie!' he snarled.

Harrigan loosened his fingers and like a trick of legerdemain a large bone-handled clasp knife appeared naked in his hand. Phineas retreated in horror up the doorstep while the seaman becoming even more enraged by his passive attitude followed after him, his little eyes inflamed by a deep yellow tinge.

'I'll cut yer gizzard aout, I will. Touch my Freddie, would yer!' he roared.

The knife winked dully in the air. Fascinated, Phineas watched it, and with his hands groped behind him for some means of defence. His grasp fell on a lump of wood from the yard that the children had propped against the door. His actions outpacing the conscious promptings of his brain, he swung round the block of wood and brought it down with a soft thud on Harrigan's skull. The knife fell to the ground with a clatter, and its owner dropped to his knees and slowly rolled into the gutter. Phineas watched in a horrified, hypnotised silence as Harrigan picked himself up, blood streaming down his face and over his clothes. He looked at Phineas unsteadily like a dumb animal wondering why it has been thrashed, and wiping his face with alternate sleeves staggered down the street, his head bowed like a drunken man.

It had all happened with such speed that only two or three neighbours had been attracted into the street. It was a tame little affair and over too quickly. To these cynical residents of the Hill used to gang fights, flying beer bottles and murderous razor attacks, this little skirmish was hardly worth bothering about. The street became deserted again and Phineas went back into his house. That portion of the block of wood that had made contact with Harrigan's head was speckled with glistening oleaginous clots of blood clustering round the projecting points of several rusty nails. Phineas shuddered and threw away his weapon. A blow like the one he had delivered could kill a man, but Harrigan did not look the sort to be killed so easily. Phineas was not so fortunate. Harrigan would live to plague him again, and this time a lump of wood might not be so fortuitously placed. He bolted the front door and the back door and for two days Phineas did not venture into the street, but when he did at last emerge St Magnus Hill regarded him with new respect. Even Harrigan, when he passed Phineas the day following his hibernation, the seaman to all appearances none the worse for his injury, nodded affably and crossing the road shook him warmly by the hand. He took a fistful of marbles out of his pocket where apparently they had been resting for days and gave them to Phineas.

''Ere, take these fer yer kid,' he said, his ugly face lighting up with a shamefaced grin. 'I didn't 'arf give my Freddie a tousing. Jest tell me if 'e starts them tricks again!'

Harrigan walked off as if the pavements below him lifted regularly to the swell of a sea. Phineas stared after him. Like a young fox-hunter, blooded at his first kill, he had been initiated by the rough-and-tumble sportsmen into the select society of St Magnus Hill.

CHAPTER VIII

In August of the following year, the perpetually smouldering volcano of the Balkans burst into the eruption that precipitated the long-awaited European conflagration. In an excess of patriotism St Magnus Hill was denuded of half its male population. Some reservists were recalled to the colours, and others, convinced that the victorious termination of the conflict was only a matter of weeks, or at most months, joined up for the duration. Harrigan was welcomed into the merchant marine, and in a burst of glory sailed away to an unknown destination from which he was destined never to return. Phineas kept his head. He had had enough of soldiering in the Russian army. He had no particular quarrel with the Germans, and, besides, he was busy fighting a daily battle of his own, in which he and hunger were the chief protagonists.

The air raids burst over a defenceless London and created a panic amongst the civilian population. It was especially bad along the waterfront, for the shattering din of the bombs was augmented by the angry roar of the adjacent battery of anti-aircraft guns at Tower Hill. When the maroons sounded the alarm, Shandel went into hysterics. She was not afraid for herself, but was terrified of any accident that might befall her children. Gathering her brood about her skirts like a frightened hen, she rushed off to one of the wool warehouses or to Tilbury Docks, to take shelter in the underground caverns used for storing merchandise. Phineas brought up the rear, loath to leave the excitement behind. It never occurred to him that a bomb might fall on his house and demolish it like a plaster cast with everything it contained. If Shandel had not dragged him with her, he would have thoughtlessly exposed himself on the streets, gazing at the darting beams of light flashing across the sky, oblivious to explosions and flying shrapnel, waiting only for an enemy aeroplane to come down in flames before his eyes.

After the raids, when the 'all-clear' bugles sounded and policemen rode about on bicycles with the reassuring placards on their backs, the family streamed back to St Magnus Hill. Shandel was always pale and taut, her features finely drawn, her heart playing all sorts of funny little tricks, beating steadily, subsiding to the barest perceptible flutter, pulsing like an overwound alarm clock and jumping alarmingly from side to side. The boys would linger in the street digging up lumps of still-warm shrapnel embedded in the road and, carrying them home in triumph, would swap them next day in school for other much-prized mementoes.

One moonlit night, the maroons set up their blustering reverberations. Shandel jumped out of bed, but before she could rouse the children her heart seemed to tear apart and she fell back breathless on to the pillows. She recovered quickly, but was still so weak that she could scarcely stand. She begged Phineas to take the children under cover and leave her there alone, but Phineas, since he could not carry her, decided that they would all stay at home together. The three consecutive explosions giving the third and last warning of the approach of enemy aircraft died away and there was a strained silence broken only by a distant cry in the street. The family huddled together in the kitchen and waited. Soon the guns started their ear-splitting racket and above the noise of firing soared an insistent wasp-like buzz punctuated by the flat detonations of high-explosive bombs. The windows were crisscrossed with searchlights manifesting themselves abruptly like flashes of lightning, and the frail walls of the house shook as if a major battle were in progress at its very door. Phineas took down his violin and began to play light-heartedly. Soon the younger children, to whom, having no inkling of death or disfigurement, the war was no more than an exciting game, started to sing and dance, and their gaiety communicating itself to the others, the whole family joined in the merriment, everybody with the exception of the terror-stricken Shandel nursing little Pompele in her arms, becoming utterly unconscious of the grim duel outside in the skies. Shandel bent over the baby, obsessed by the thought that if a bomb fell on the house her body would amply serve as protection for the peacefully slumbering infant. Phineas played on until the younger children fell asleep again, and the buzz of the nocturnal marauders faded with the sharp challenge of their adversaries into the weird breathless silence of the night.

After that, they never left St Magnus Hill to take shelter in the modern catacombs. The neighbours thought them irresponsibly foolhardy, until one night Mrs Harrigan, superstitious like most Irishwomen, came knocking at the door with Freddie asking for shelter when the staccato barking of the guns was already shooting disturbing ripples of sound through the long-suffering atmosphere. She had overslept the last warning, and in this wild pandemonium no power on earth could keep her in her house. Devout Catholic as she was, she believed the legend that all Jews were lucky, although to any intelligent observer Phineas's life more than disproved that myth. She was certain that Phineas and his house and his belongings were under the divine protection of the Jewish God, for otherwise would they not run like the rest to the docks or the wool warehouses?

Inside the house she was amicably received, Phineas and his wife showing no curiosity or resentment at her intrusion. Freddie produced some books that Phillip became interested in immediately and Mrs Harrigan at once fell into a conversation about children with Shandel. Then Phineas played his violin and she listened with absorbed delight. Thereafter Mrs Harrigan was a constant visitor during air raids, and after a time brought other neighbours with her. They brought with them their own provisions, and sometimes even bottles of beer, the nights of terror having been dissolved for them by the grace of Jehovah and under his protection lifted into convivial gatherings of the elect. Shandel served tea, and Phineas, adaptable as ever, played jigs and folk songs of the expatriated Irish Catholics. While the heavens resounded with the combined fury of a dozen thunderstorms, St Magnus Hill rang to the strains of 'The Wearing Of The Green'. Phineas was now a fully fledged Irish minstrel, and the little Jewish children joined willingly in the choruses of the comic songs, trilled endlessly by Maggie Harrigan. She stood in the centre of the room and sang in a well-meaning soprano, her thick arms bare to the elbow, conducting Phineas and her auditors. Her fat, pudgy face with the tilted little nose always reminded Phineas of the publican in Delancey Street. No doubt that worthy gentleman too had an enormous repertoire of those jiggery ditties. If ever he went back to New York, he could, except for his face, easily pose as a son of Old Erin. All he would have to do would be to stand akimbo like Maggie Harrigan and sing in the same brogue and the same rich inflexions:

> Are you the O'Reilly as owns this 'otel?
> Are you the O'Reilly they talks of so well?
> If you're the O'Reilly they talks of so 'ighly
> Gorblimey O'Reilly you are lookin' well...!

... Begorrah, landlord, how's that? Can I have a little more herring, and some cheese and some liver? – Sure! Sure, Phineas O'Kahn. We Irish must stick together. Are the Irish worse than the Jews...?

At other times, the guests to be doubly safe felt the need for the solace of their own religions. The Christies, Moores, the Smiths and Harrigans joined in soulful appeals to their respective deities. From the Jewish house, above the sullen roar of gunfire, rose the strains of the fiddle accompanying Ave Marias and plaintive hymns to the eternal mystery of three in one and one in three:

> Jesus Lord, I beg for mercy,
> Let me not implore in vain,
> All my sins I now regret them,
> Never will I sin again...

In this way the raids passed over St Magnus Hill, Phineas learning of the habits of the Irish, and in return making the Jew comprehensible to them. When Phineas played, not a thought of danger entered into any of their heads, although the walls of the house were so thin that any respectably sized chunk of shrapnel striking it with sufficient velocity would have flattened it like the blow of an angry crocodile's tail falling on some puny insect.

Late in 1915 Shandel bore another child. The war showed no signs of coming to a successful conclusion, neither did Phineas's material position in any way improve; on the contrary, the price of clothes and foodstuffs had rocketed to the sky, and he had to struggle harder than ever to make ends meet. Under these circumstances, infant number nine was not even a mixed blessing. The grandfather clock, a recent acquisition exchanged for old clothes, croaked wheezily on the kitchen wall while Phineas, seated anxiously at the table, waited for news of the confinement. The midwife was in the bedroom with Shandel. Her labour cries rose like the squeals of a wounded animal, regularly, at shorter and shorter intervals as the pain constricted her stomach like an iron ring and pounded at the base of her spine. Like most orthodox Jews in times of stress since days immemorial, Phineas sought relief in the Book of Psalms. He opened the volume at random and his glance fell on the third verse of the 127th Psalm:

Lo, sons are a heritage of the Lord; and the fruit of the womb is his reward.

As arrows are in the hand of a mighty man; so are the sons of the youth.

Happy is the man that hath his quiver full of them; they shall not be ashamed, but they shall speak with the enemies in the gate.

Opposite was the English version, mistranslated. 'Children' had been set down for the Hebrew 'bnai', sons. *Traditore, traduttore.* Of what use were girls to speak with the enemies in the gate? This was his ninth child. His quiver was certainly full but he was far from being happy. It would be a boy, he was sure of that from the unequivocal augury of the oracle of the Psalms. The tormented labour cries of his wife quietened down and were succeeded by a series of low, strenuous grunts. In a burst of energy the grandfather clock that sounded only at haphazard hours, and then never in any calculable relation to the time indicated by the hands on the dial, chimed forth twenty-six peals, the resonant strokes echoing through the house. Shandel was silent, then after a lusty slapping, the first thin howl from the baby's lungs announced the advent of yet another little Kahn to St Magnus Hill. The door of the kitchen opened and the midwife, a gigantic, untidy woman, like a walking bundle of rags, entered, red from her exertions, several wisps of grey hair straggling over her moist brow.

'Mazel tov!' she said with a smile and a commendatory nod of the head. 'It's a boy!'

The new arrival was the tiniest of Phineas's children. At birth he weighed only three and a quarter pounds, and as in the case of Michael his circumcision had to be postponed for several weeks. Then again a new problem arose, to find the wherewithal for the circumcision, for no mohel would perform such a delicate surgical operation gratis. Phineas went to the Jewish Board of Guardians and explained the position. They agreed readily to undertake the responsibility of fulfilling the covenant of Abraham. It cost Phineas a great deal of mental anguish to sell his son's birthright to the Board. The most honourable office a male Jew could perform was to keep faith with the ancient troth in the person of his son by being responsible for the child's circumcision. It was the very first commandment of Jehovah to Abraham when the idol-breaker was ninety and nine:

> This is my covenant, which ye shall keep, between me and you and thy seed after thee; Every man-child amongst you shall be circumcised.

Only the poorest and most destitute Jews asked aid from the Board on such occasions. The mohel, a qualified doctor, as distinct from the usual clerical practitioners who officiated at circumcisions as a side-line from slaughtering chickens and bullocks, came down on the appointed day, accompanied by two substantial citizens from the Board, the godfathers, who brought with them a bottle of wine and a large cake. One godfather held the infant on a white cushion while the mohel intoned the ritual prayers. He dipped a finger in a glass of wine and rolled it in the infant's mouth to quieten his yells. Then with deft fingers he skilfully performed the operation. The child, named Joseph after a maternal uncle, howled piteously until the doctor deadened his pain with a few more drops of wine. Shandel pressed her fingertips in her ears to shut out the agonising screams. She felt a physical torment as though lumps were being cut from her own body, as if she were bleeding unrestrainedly. Although she had witnessed this ceremony five times previously, on each occasion it came with the same stark, almost unbearable shock. The godfathers presented Phineas with a golden sovereign and departed with the doctor. As soon as they had gone Joseph started howling afresh. Shandel doped him with minute doses of liquid aniseed until he fell off into a fitful sleep. The next day the doctor called to redress the bandages and by the following morning the little Jew was gurgling as happily as if the mantle of original sin had not descended on his tiny shoulders.

The father of nine children cudgelled his brains, both by day and far into the night to find a solution to the evermore pressing problem of how adequately to feed his family. Whichever way he turned he seemed confronted by a blank wall liberally surmounted by chunks of broken bottles in case he ventured to climb over. The war in France was absorbing more and more men and the government clamoured for volunteers. Clearer and clearer the conviction grew in Phineas that the only way open to him was to join the army. Then at least his wife would have a liberal allowance for herself and the children, and for the duration of the war a sufficiency of clothes and enough to eat. If he were killed that would be unfortunate for him, but Shandel would receive a handsome pension. The conclusion was forced irresistibly upon him, that as a worker and as a businessman he was a failure. As a soldier he would be an asset to the government and his family, and in the event of the worst occurring he would be worth more to Shandel dead than alive.

Without mentioning a word to his wife he trudged to Whitehall and after a cursory preliminary investigation appeared before a staff officer. The major, a handsome bronzed man with a fair close-clipped moustache, looked him over critically.

'... Yes... Yes... You look fit enough,' he said. 'What's your nationality, now?'

'Russian,' replied Phineas.

'... Ah, Russian. That's good. We could do with a bit more of the Russian Steamroller... You're married, aren't you?'

'Yes, sir,' Phineas replied.

'Any children?'

'Nine.'

'How many?'

'Nine,' repeated Phineas.

'Phew!' The officer whistled and tapped the butt of his pencil on the desk. He made some rapid calculations on the margin of a printed sheet, and looked up fingering the short hairs of his bristly moustache... 'I'm sorry,' he said. 'You'll be too expensive a soldier. To pay your family the full allowance we'd have to make you a general at least – and we're not short of generals at the moment.'

'So... So, you don't want me?' said Phineas, with an air of bewilderment.

'We do, old chap, we do,' replied the major. 'But you must understand that the government could get six soldiers for what you'd cost. I'm afraid we'll have to grant you exemption, seeing that you're engaged on work of National Importance.'

Phineas was nonplussed. This was a new name for old clothes... 'National Importance?'

The officer grinned. 'Why, to be sure! A man with nine kids. I should say so! Go home and make another half a dozen, Mr Kahn. That's work of real National Importance!'

Crestfallen, the rejected recruit returned home. His journey had been in vain, even a government crying out for soldiers had turned him down. He was of no value to anybody, not useful even as cannon fodder. He was without any tangible assets, weighed down by ten heavy liabilities; financially, morally and spiritually he seemed to all eternity bankrupt.

The man in the gutter has at least one consolation, he knows he can fall no lower. That philosophy would have served Phineas too, but the ever-present reproach of his wife and nine children denied him that cynical satisfaction. The gutter might be the best place for him but it was not good enough for them, he would not have another peaceful moment until he found a means of extricating his family from the morass. Their plight spurred him continually to fresh endeavours. At night before retiring he looked at them sleeping peacefully in their beds. Olga and Deborah together, and Pompele, her rosy cheeks blooming as if her lungs were fed with sweet country air, lying placidly beside them in her tiny cot. The five elder boys slept in another room. Phillip, Stanley and the brawny Felix in one bed, Michael and Israel, the inseparables, in another, each one of them adopting in sleep a characteristic pose. Michael lay flat on his back, his frail body tense even in slumber, while Israel was curled protectingly beside him, one hand thrown over the younger boy's body. After his nightly visits a fresh fit of depression would fall on Phineas to round off the day. His thoughts seemed to goad him bitterly...What have you done? ...What have you done? ...What are you going to do? ... Like an endless roundelay they jabbed unmercifully at his brain as he lay in bed worrying about the next day, until sleep closed his eyelids and his subconscious mind carried on the tireless refrain asking, and asking, while another part of his head seemed to be bursting with specious arguments endeavouring to find an answer.

At that time, the district around St George's adjacent to the docks was the centre of the rag-cuttings trade, which was a flourishing industry during the war owing to the scarcity of raw-wool supplies. Phineas, passing Fogelman's warehouse every day, saw tons of cuttings coming in, and huge bales of sorted rags being loaded on to the enormous trailer lorries for the North Country mills. Leaving his empty barrow outside one afternoon, he went into the dusty building and asked for Mr Fogelman. After waiting for about a quarter of an hour a small pale Jew, with a pointed little black beard, wearing a dirty drill smock, came up to him. The pupils of his eyes were dark, almost black, and his gaze had an uncanny sharpness. Phineas felt uncomfortable before him, as though the rents in his clothes had suddenly become larger, and his shameful poverty more apparent.

'Yes?' asked the little man abruptly.

'Are you Mr Fogelman?' said Phineas.

'I'm Mr Fogelman,' he assented. 'What do you want?'

'You buy woollen rags?'

The little Jew waved his hand at the mounds of cuttings strewn over the floor. 'Does it look like it?' he inquired. 'Or maybe you think it's all a blind and I've got a counterfeit plant at the back?'

Phineas laughed sheepishly. 'I hope you don't mind me troubling you,' he said. 'My name is Kahn. I deal in old clothes, but I've got a big family and I can't make a living. I thought if I went in for rags, you might give me a chance.'

'I give everybody a chance,' said Fogelman. 'Go round to the tailors and buy the sweepings. I'll pay you sixpence a pound for whatever you get, providing it's not all paper and string. Now you must excuse me, Mr Kahn, I have some work to see to.'

Borrowing some sacks from Mr Fogelman, Phineas put them

on the empty barrow and trundled it round the tailors' workshops. Wherever he saw a bill in a front window calling for machinists or felling hands, he knocked at the door and asked to see the boss. He had to turn down several lots of rags, either because there was too large an amount to clear or the price asked was beyond the limit of his meagre capital. Eventually he bought a sackful of sweepings for ten shillings and took it round to Fogelman's. Mr Fogelman slit open the sack and extracted bunches of crumpled brown paper, pieces of canvas, string and some woollen cuttings. He weighed the sack and offered Phineas twelve shillings for its contents. After a little argument he went up to fifteen shillings and the deal was concluded. Phineas put the money in his pocket and went home, having profitably embarked on his career as a ragsman.

Every day, with the exception of the Sabbath, Phineas had a parcel or two for Mr Fogelman, and his daily earnings averaged about ten shillings. He bought the sweepings from the tailors, squeezed them tightly into sacks and took them straight to the warehouse. The prices fluctuated from day to day, rising higher and higher as supplies of raw wool became more difficult to obtain. A fellow ragsman, Lazarus, with whom he had become acquainted at Fogelman's, waylaid him one afternoon as he was leaving the warehouse. Lazarus bore the reputation of being an exceptionally keen businessman. A tall, stooping Jew with a long, tangled beard and fierce eyebrows, he was, in spite of his unprepossessing appearance, a kind-hearted man, and seeing how Phineas was struggling, he decided to take him under his wing, actuated by sincere fellow feeling, since he himself had a large family of his own.

'You know rags are going up?' said Lazarus, his shaggy eyebrows jutting out belligerently.

'I know,' replied Phineas. '... Well?'

'Well, why do you take all your stuff straight to Fogelman?' he asked, laying a huge leathery hand on Phineas's arm. 'Don't you think he's got enough money?'

'Where else shall I take them?' said Phineas. 'Everybody seems to go to Fogelman, even ragsmen in a bigger way than ever I can hope to be.'

'True enough,' replied Lazarus. 'But they sort the stuff out first. You sell your rags like sausages, you don't care what you put inside. You give Fogelman some stuff that he can't give away for a farthing, mixed up with cuttings that he sells for one and six a pound. Now when you buy your next lot of rags, come round to my workshop and I'll show you how to sort them out.'

The same day, Phineas brought two sacks of rags to Lazarus's workshop. His mentor emptied them on to an oblong wire-gauze sieve arrangement and sorted them out for him, showing Phineas how to distinguish pure wool from cotton and cotton-and-wool mixtures, giving each pile of cuttings its distinctive name. When he had separated the wheat from the chaff, he weighed up the selected bundles and computed that at the current market prices the rags would fetch thirty shillings, nearly double what Fogelman would otherwise have paid.

When Phineas took the rags to the warehouse, Mr Fogelman looked them over quizzically and smiled as Phineas told him exactly what he had brought. He threw the sacks on to a huge scale, weighed them up and gave Phineas almost the precise sum that Lazarus had calculated.

'There you are,' he said. 'It didn't take you long to learn the trade. Now that you've become a real ragsman and know all the tricks, I'll have to watch you on the weight.'

Phineas soon converted his kitchen into a workshop. He brought the rags home, and his wife and the older children gave a hand in sorting them out. They sang cheerily as they bent over the sieve, evolving a rhythmic antiphonal chant as they flung the rags on to their allotted piles. A chorus of several voices chanted in perfect time – 'Canvas – Dyes – Light Coarse – Mungo. Canvas – Dyes – Light Coarse – Mungo.' His earning capacities were increasing, but Phineas still found it a difficult struggle to live with any degree of comfort at all. As his earnings rose, the cost of living rose much higher, white bread was at a premium, and the price of meat, sugar, fruit, potatoes and other vegetables put them up into the luxury class.

When he attained the position of having more than just a few shillings with which to speculate, Phineas over-reached himself. He bought a load of cuttings from another ragsman for four pounds, the whole of his available capital, but as he sorted them out, he realised to his horror that there was such a surprisingly large proportion of cotton mixtures that he would be exceedingly fortunate if he could sell them all and not lose more than a pound. A pound, one quarter of his working capital, and that not entirely his own, was in danger of vanishing for ever if he could not find some means of disposing of the rags at cost. Feverishly he worked half the night and cunningly stuffed them into several huge sacks, making in each sack an outer kernel of the best Mungo wool, a thin bottom layer and another of the same material on top, the rest of the space being crammed with cotton mixtures. With a great deal of trepidation he took them to Fogelman, and saying that he had no time to sort them, asked him to quote a price for the lot. Mr Fogelman took a handful of rags from the top, slit open one side, and took another handful at random from the bottom. He offered Phineas four pounds, about half the value of the load if the samples he had extracted were any criterion, and to his surprise, after a little while, Phineas accepted. Fogelman smiled into his little black beard. Phineas was nowhere near a real ragsman yet!

For the next fortnight Phineas stayed away from Fogelman's, doing his business with smaller ragsmen, buying from one and selling to another. At last he decided to return to the warehouse. Fogelman had shifted by this time so many tons of rags that it was quite possible that his small delivery had been passed over and sorted without any comment. He hoped sincerely that that was the case. He had had no intention of cheating Mr Fogelman, and if the warehouseman had been an impoverished individual, he would have never attempted to do so, but Fogelman had for months, when he was new to the trade, paid him a fraction of what his goods were worth, so this was merely recovering part of what was rightfully due to him, and, in any case, the stuff had been bought in bulk, it was a legitimate business transaction. If Fogelman, on the other hand, felt badly about it, he could at the worst simply show him the door, and even that would not be so terrible since there were other ragsmen in London. Only the other day he had been recommended to a firm in a Thames-side wharf. However, he determined to beard Fogelman; at least he would know where he stood.

He trundled his barrow into the warehouse yard and waited for the proprietor. Mr Fogelman saw him enter, but purposely kept him waiting, busying himself with other tasks. At last he came over to Phineas and halted before him, his arms akimbo on his hips, his short legs wide apart. The dark eyes scintillating like black sapphires travelled slowly over Phineas from head to foot until the culprit blushed with embarrassment, fearing what this inspection betokened. Suddenly Mr Fogelman shot out his hand.

'Shake!' he said. 'Kahn, if you can cheat Morry Fogelman you deserve a couple of medals! You're the only man in London who's ever done so. Shake hands. You're a champion, a molodetz!'

Phineas clasped his hand a little guiltily and told Fogelman what had forced him to do it. The warehouseman waved his apologies aside, it had served him right for being too greedy, but with a smile like a sarcastic challenge, he assured Phineas that he would be unable to trick him again.

'Well, that's all over,' he said, brisk and businesslike once more. 'What have you got for me now?'

Phineas threw his load at Fogelman's feet. The warehouseman slashed the sacks in the unlikeliest places, examining each of them minutely. At last, satisfied that the rags tallied with Phineas's description, he shifted them over to the scales to be weighed. After he had paid Phineas he took out a choice cigar and thrust it into his pocket. Patting him benevolently on the back, he sent him into the street.

'Now don't try those games any more, Kahn,' he shouted jovially after him. 'They don't work twice. Not with me, at any rate!'

Business improved rapidly, the price of rags rose higher and higher. To cope with his increasing trade Phineas moved into a house in St George's Street. The ground floor consisted of a large workroom leading into a tiny kitchen, and upstairs were four bedrooms, since Phineas had neither use nor furniture for a parlour. Beneath were commodious cellars, which unfortunately were valueless because of continual damp and seasonal floods. Six girls worked for him sorting the rags, Nellie Christie and Alice Moore from St Magnus Hill, and four other young women from Wapping, all descended from exported Irishmen.

Fogelman was making a fortune. He could not supply sufficient rags to cope with the demand from the mills. Even the smaller ragsmen were showing some degree of affluence. Lazarus had shaved off his beard, his enormous eyebrows more thickly menacing by contrast, and ran a private car and a Ford for business purposes. Only Phineas remained comparatively poor. He could not drive or browbeat his girls. He allowed them decent intervals for lunch, and supplied them all with tea at five o'clock, and could very rarely resist when they begged him for a tune on the fiddle. In the middle of a busy day the mad Kahn workshop would drop everything and start dancing jigs, or Nellie Christie would sing accompanied by Phineas and the chorus of sorters.

Old Mrs Riley
Said: 'Look 'ere, Mary Jane,
'Oo was the feller you was walkin' with down the lane?
Long, wiry whiskers was 'angin' from 'is chin.'
''Twas only Paddy McGinty's goat,' she answered with a grin.
She went away
From the village in disgrace;
She came back with paint an' powder on 'er face;
Rings on 'er finger, she wore a sable coat;
You bet yer life she didn't get that
From Paddy McGinty's goat...

Shandel's health was another source of anxiety for Phineas. She had repeated heart attacks recurring at more and more frequent intervals, until she walked about half dazed, in a constant state of terror feeling that she only held on to life by a wavering line as frail as a spider's web, that could at any moment be swept into the darkness by a sudden breath of wind. She was afraid to stay in the house alone, and even if Phineas had a business appointment, she would not let him go unless one of the older children could stop at home with her. Now for the first time since his arrival in England, Phineas was earning real money, but it was swallowed up in doctor's bills, and poured down Shandel's throat in an endless stream of patent foods. Whatever was recommended to him he bought in the endeavour to cure his wife, but nothing availed her. When the attacks came on, suddenly, without any warning symptoms, her face blanched, while her heart fluttered like a bird imprisoned in a cage no larger than the span of its wings, and she felt that surely this agony must be her last.

Phineas and the older girls took all the arduous labour of the house off her hands. On Saturday morning, he put a sack round his waist and scrubbed the floors, while Olga, but recently matriculated, prepared dinner for the family. After the meal, Phineas donned a white apron and washed up the crocks, making the kitchen tidy, spotless and neat once again. He cleaned floors and washed dishes on his free day and thought of the cruel fortune that had dogged him since he had set foot in England. It was a tiny little land, a step almost in any direction brought one to the ocean, and yet, during the whole of their eighteen years in London they had never once had a holiday by the sea. For sixteen years they had been unable to raise the fares, and now that money was a secondary consideration, Shandel's heart could not stand the strain of a long journey.

In 1918 David was born, and just before and immediately after her confinement Shandel felt fit and well, and could almost imagine that she had conquered her ailment. Her flow of milk dried up, and one of Phineas's girls who a year previously had left the workshop to get married and had recently become the mother of a plump little girl, volunteered to suckle the infant. David grew fat on the rich milk of his foster mother, and Shandel became almost her old self again, until a few months later she experienced once more the horrible pain of a heart attack with its aftermath of nagging fear and almost unbearable uncertainty.

Again Phineas went to doctors, until one, more conscientious than the rest, gave him a letter for Victoria Park Chest Hospital. On Saturday afternoons, when the more fortunate Jews could parade with their wives up and down the broad pavement of Whitechapel, displaying their jewels and their smart clothes, Phineas had to travel by tram and bus to the hospital, and spend most of the afternoon there.

The children helped nobly. Olga, while she was preparing for college, and even later, when she was an undergraduate at the university, came home after lectures and washed the baby's napkins and mended the children's clothes. Deborah's job was to look after the youngsters and keep them in order, her assistant being Phillip, the eldest son. Olga, Phillip and Deborah were brilliant musicians, they had an instinctive grasp of phrasing and sang tunes from Mozart, Wagner, Bach and Beethoven with equal facility; a flat note was to them on a par with an obscene jest, and like a curiously large proportion of musicians they showed a remarkable aptitude for mathematics. Phillip and Deborah were following in Olga's footsteps, having both won Council scholarships, but Stanley, Deborah's immediate senior, had fallen by the scholastic wayside. Phineas always expected his children to come to the top of their respective forms. When Deborah brought home a report at the end of one term showing that she had come second, he said 'What's this?' and refused to talk to her for the rest of the day. She cried half the night, and was moody in the morning until Phineas's smile showed that she had been forgiven.

Deborah was a very sensitive child. She was small, but beautifully built, and Shandel delighted to put her in short tightly fitting gym slips that showed off her shapely legs and her blossoming figure. In the street, she was a madcap, refusing to play with other girls, but joining in games of cricket, football and leapfrog with the boys. She knew that Shandel was seriously ill, and her imagination frightened her with pictures of sudden death coming to her mother while she was far away. She was the first out of school in the afternoon, and the first to board the tram for home. She half ran down Cannon Street Road until she reached the top of her turning, and only when she saw that there was no tell-tale crowd round the door did she relax the tension of her nerves and walk quietly down the street.

After a bout of pleurisy, Shandel's ankles swelled to twice their normal size, and coupled with the awkwardness of an unsteady heart, she now had the additional disability of being unable to walk without serious discomfort and pain. She still attended the hospital every Saturday afternoon and received a supply of medicine for the whole week. One Saturday, Phineas had the opportunity he had long sought, of speaking privately to the head physician. The doctor was a tall, grey-haired gentleman with a pleasant, sympathetic face. He bent his handsome head down towards Phineas as the ragsman timorously buttonholed him.

'Please, tell me the truth, doctor,' begged Phineas. 'How is my wife getting on?'

The doctor tugged gently at the lapel of his white coat and seemed to have some difficulty in answering him. 'Hmmm!' he said at last. '... She is getting along as well as can be expected.'

'Is there any hope of a cure?' asked Phineas.

The doctor shook his head. 'I'm afraid not.' He looked at Phineas keenly. 'Do you still insist on hearing the truth?'

Phineas nodded. Through hot, parched lips he whispered, 'Yes, doctor. Please tell me everything.'

'Well, to be blunt with you, my friend, nothing that I or anyone else can do will help your wife. Your trouble in coming here is for nothing. Your wife is liable to die at any moment. The slightest attack can finish her off. She has been carrying about this incipient disease inside her ever since she contracted typhoid as a girl. While she was able to bear children, her life was still tolerably safe, but at this period, when the feminine organs undergo a radical change, the heart is very delicate in the healthiest of women, and in the case of your wife it is tantamount to a sentence of death. It is now just a matter of time, it may be a month, or it may take a year, but she cannot last more than a twelvemonth at the longest.'

He patted Phineas gently on the shoulder as if to mitigate the pain of the blow, and walked away. Phineas, in a daze, looked after the doctor, then as the full shock burst upon him that his wife and companion was irrevocably doomed, he broke into a torrent of tears. Seating himself on a chair to steady his nerves, he hurriedly wiped his eyes and composed himself to meet Shandel.

Her attacks became more and more frequent. When her heart strained like a leashed animal, and she gritted her teeth under the searing agony, he carried her wasted form in his arms and blew his living breath into her mouth. He walked about the room agitatedly holding her before him like a sacrifice, then laid her gently in her bed. Her face was pinched and blue against the virgin whiteness of the pillows, and her mouth twitched under the intolerable pain. Phineas was goaded almost beyond control by the spectacle of her suffering. The frail body of his wife had to bear the full brunt of that agony, and he could not help in the least, could not take on himself the slightest portion of her pain. He dropped on his knees beside the bed, flushed and heart-sore from the mental strain, and despairingly placed his head beneath her feet.

'Tread on me! Hit me... Bite lumps out of me, Shandel,' he pleaded hysterically. 'Perhaps it will ease your torture.'

When the seizure passed over, she became normal again for a little while, but she kept Phineas close at hand in case of any emergency. He had to leave the house to buy and sell his goods, but he cut down the periods of his absence to an absolute minimum, afraid to leave her for a second longer than was necessary. Apart from business calls, the only time he was away from her for any protracted period was when he scoured the market at Petticoat Lane for fresh eggs, butter and cream that were unobtainable in St George's. Coming back from one of his shopping expeditions, he had a presentiment that Shandel was in danger. He hurried almost to a run, his heart beating an alarming tattoo against his ribs. From the top of the street he saw a throng of people pressed against the walls of his house, and as he ran homewards, neighbours detached themselves from the crowd and rushed to meet him.

'Hurry! Hurry! Mr Kahn,' they shouted breathlessly. 'Your wife is dying!'

He brushed his way impatiently through the excited spectators, gathered like a mob at a hanging scenting the smell of blood, and ran up to the bedroom. Shandel was lying in bed, pale as a ghost, her breast heaving convulsively as if her heart were trying to force its way outside her body. On the floor near the bed was a bucket half-filled with blood. Phineas thought this was the end, but the local medico reassured him. Death did not come so easily. She had a long time to linger yet.

After the haemorrhage, Shandel changed completely. Her flesh turned ash colour, and her eyes, abnormally enlarged, stared out of her face feverishly. Her nose and her fingers seemed to grow longer, her lips thinner and bluish in colour. She became very irritable and nervous, flaring up at the least provocation. Phineas dared not look out of the window alone, for to her warped mind it seemed that he was admiring the healthy, full-blooded women who walked about the streets erect with the pride of life. Thoughts of death and disease monopolised her brain. In the middle of an ordinary conversation she would branch off into gruesome details of deformity and mutilation, describing the ravages of cancer or leprosy, telling of breasts cut off, of noses and fingertips rotting away, until the very hair on Phineas's head pricked with horror.

In the autumn she grew thin as a rake. Ugly veins like thick blue cords stood out on her neck, and her legs swelled again to a hideous size. She was unable to budge from the house or to perform even the lightest domestic tasks. Gradually, as if sensing her approaching dissolution and becoming reconciled to it, she grew calmer, and regained her old sweet temper. A smile was rarely absent from her lips, and she fondled the children with the most delicate tenderness, especially the three-year-old David. She knew she would never see him grow up, and in the darkness of the night, when she thought of him, the hot tears coursed unrestrainedly down her wasted cheeks.

When Olga graduated from the university, a Bachelor of Science with first-class honours in mathematics, Shandel seeped in gratification distilled like the quintessence of joy.

A fortnight later, she felt that death was very close at hand. On the Friday, shuffling like a cripple, she accompanied Olga to the public baths, and when she came back, she embraced Phineas joyfully.

'Phineas,' she said tenderly, looking at him with large, loving eyes. 'It seems to me, Phineas, as if we've just stepped down from the canopy.'

Phineas swallowed a huge lump, and his eyes clouded with tears. Her skin seemed as waxy and transparent as that of a person already dead. Under his eyes she was fading from the world of living people.

On the Saturday night, she lay in bed, still and silent as a shadow. Only the doctor and Phineas were present in the room, the children waiting anxiously in the passage. Phineas bent over his wife. She was motionless except for a barely perceptible tremor in her throat. In the arms of death she was as beautiful as ever she had appeared in life. Her nose was straight and finely chiselled, her lips set in a graceful line. Only her forehead seemed wider and more prominent, dominating her face with its noble expanse. It was smooth and unwrinkled like that of a young girl, and on it was a moist sprinkling of cold dew. Phineas bent lower and kissed her wet brow. Her lips moved, but she made no sound. Her eyes sought Phineas, and he understood what she meant. Rising from the bed, stooped like a man shouldering an overbearing weight of sorrow, he walked slowly to a corner of the room and picked up his violin.

Outside in the passage, Olga heard the sweet searing notes of Tchaikovsky's 'Barcarolle'. She stiffened, and silent sobs rippled through her frame. She understood that this was a farewell to life. Phineas was playing her mother to everlasting sleep with that old, familiar lullaby. She shepherded the children into another room and waited. Soon Phineas came in, bent like an old man, his face pale as ashes. Olga flung her arms around his neck and sobbed bitterly on his shoulder. Gently, like a somnambulist seeing things in a dream, he pushed her away and sank down in an inert heap on the sofa. He stared straight before him, then his face contorted into an unnatural grimace. His mouth opened and he set up a piercing howl like the whine of a sick dog. Then for the first time he saw his ten orphaned children, and the tears swept over him afresh in a hot blinding flood. Olga sat down beside him, and the rest of the children gathered round in a pyramid of sorrow on the floor, and eleven stricken voices wept in unison for the mother who was dead.

BOOK III

THE CHILDREN GROW UP

CHAPTER I

After the funeral, Phineas took stock of his position. He was still comparatively young, only forty-six, yet he was a widower with ten children dependent upon him, from Olga the college graduate who had just passed her twentieth birthday, down to David the youngest, who was only three. The post-war slump had hit him badly. Fortunes had toppled to the ground. Rags that had brought two shillings a pound during the war could not fetch sixpence, and prices fell week by week. Lazarus had been forced to sell his house and his car and was back where he had been before the war, trundling a barrow in the gutter. Only Fogelman withstood the debacle. At the first whisper of a slump he sold the whole of his enormous stock, railway arches packed with hundreds of tons of rags, closed his warehouse and entrenched in an impregnable financial position sat back and waited for prices to rise again.

Phineas reluctantly sacked his staff, half of whom had already left, tired of being paid for doing nothing and seeing that they were an intolerable strain on their employer's resources. For a month Phineas allowed his beard to grow and walked about in a daze, paying no attention to his work and hardly noticing whether he ate or slept. He became a prey to moody fits and sat in the kitchen silent for hours, staring unblinkingly at the walls. The slightest scuffle would disturb him and make him concentrate his attention on the door. It still seemed incredible that Shandel was dead; at any moment the door must open, and Shandel would walk in with her bright smile, and enfold him in her warm embrace. But the door never opened unless to admit one of the children. Shandel was dead, dead, a cipher to all eternity.

At the end of the month of rigorous mourning, Phineas shaved off his beard and pulled himself together. For the first time he noticed how the house had assumed an emaciated appearance like a once-ripe field devoured by an army of locusts, and how the children were walking about lean and shifty-looking like unhappy outcasts of the street. The strange devastated vision of the house and its inhabitants was a bitter shock to Phineas, who had emerged from one nightmare only to discover another bad dream in reality. The neighbours did their best to help him. They organised a door-to-door collection and brought him in eleven pounds, the fruit of their endeavours. An investigator from the Jewish Board of Guardians called and suggested that Phineas should send the younger children to an orphanage as there was no competent female to look after them. Phineas turned down the proposal indignantly, he would not be separated from any of his children, not for so short a period as a week, or even a day, and as for a competent female, either Olga or Deborah would have to relinquish her scholastic career and act as foster mother. The investigator was sympathetic and agreed to the shelving of the suggestion. He went through the rooms, and appalled by the dilapidated condition of the furniture told Phineas before he left that he would recommend the Board to supply some household necessities, notably new beds and mattresses to replace the old, verminous ones which would not look respectable even on a junk heap. Several weeks later the beds arrived together with an unsolicited gift of twenty pounds from the Board.

Olga had just obtained a situation as pupil teacher at a secondary school, so on Deborah fell the task of mothering the shattered family and bringing the run of life back to normal again. At the age of fifteen, the most promising pupil of her class, she left her studies and voluntarily gave herself over to the domination of pots and pans. It was not an entirely new experience for her, since during the last two years of her mother's life she had shared most of the household drudgery with Olga. Two weeks after her withdrawal from school, a grey-haired gentleman from the Council Education Committee came down to interview Phineas. He seated himself on a rickety chair in the kitchen and placed an imposing-looking brown leather portfolio on the table.

'Mr Kahn,' he said, 'I have come here to talk to you about Deborah.'

'Well?' asked Phineas.

'We are interested in your daughter,' said the stranger. 'She is a brilliant scholar. We need her brains.'

Phineas glanced about the kitchen and waved an arm at the younger children playing on the floor.

'*They* need her too,' he replied.

'Surely you can get a woman in to do the cooking and house-work?' urged the stranger. 'Why, I daresay we might even be prepared to help you by making you an allowance for a housekeeper. It really is a pity, Mr Kahn, to throw away the brilliant prospects of your daughter.'

Again Phineas waved an eloquent arm towards the children. 'True, true,' he admitted. 'It is a very great pity, but I have a still greater pity for them, the motherless ones. They need a mother, and only one of my daughters can take their mother's place. I would sooner cut off my right hand than harm Deborah in any way, but she is only one child, and I have ten – I am very sorry, sir, it was kind of you to come and see me, but there is no longer any question of Deborah's career, it has already been chosen for her.'

The stranger shook his head gravely and rose to his feet taking the portfolio from the table. Phineas courteously escorted him, stumbling over hillocks of unsorted rags, to the door. The visitor's face wore a bewildered air. He had never come across such a case before. It was wrong to take the child from her books, yet at the same time Phineas's arguments held a sober challenge. He wondered what he himself would have done in a like situation, then dismissed the thought from his mind; such poverty was too abject to contemplate. He shook Phineas's hand warmly and raised his hat.

'Well, think it over, Mr Kahn,' he said. 'If you change your mind, perhaps we can come to some arrangement.'

He turned away, and his trim, erect figure sailed down the street with a precise, delicate gait, a spectacle as incongruous in this backwater of the slums as a millionaire's yacht moored to wharf-side coal barges. Phineas stared after him. With the stranger was passing the cherished goal of education, one of his most constant dreams for Deborah; Olga was well on the road, with Phillip advancing rapidly. Now circumstances had forced his second daughter, the most brilliant of all his children, to stop her progress to the light and become part of the kitchen, an uncreative but necessary item, like the gas stove or the sink.

Deborah had no intention of being conquered by the culinary despotism of the kitchen. She seemed to enjoy cooking meals and looking after the children, but at the same time she insisted that she must be free every evening and during certain hours of the day to utilise those periods for whatever took her fancy.

Now that Olga was earning money and contributed her entire salary towards the upkeep of the house, Phineas, no longer dragged down by the unremunerative burden of a fully staffed workshop, was able from his earnings to give Deborah sufficient money to purchase ample provisions for each day. She disbursed her allowance economically, buying the very best food at the keenest prices, and the money she saved she hoarded away until she put by enough to obtain every other week a good seat at the Albert Hall or the Queen's Hall to hear a famous orchestra or a great virtuoso. She was not conscious of doing anything underhand in scraping off odd pennies and hiding them away. Five shillings was an exorbitant amount of money to pay for a seat at a concert, and Phineas would have been appalled at such extravagance had he known, but she had given up a career to become cook and housemaid, and she felt that in return those stolen pleasures were no more than she deserved.

Under the capable hands of Deborah the entire household was reorganised. A char came in twice a week to do the rough work, the scrubbing and window cleaning, and the girl managed to perform efficiently the rest of the chores herself. She learned to cook to perfection, even making individual dishes for such children as had particular preferences, or were finicky about food. Michael was her especial care; the colossal Felix, his immediate junior, ate whatever was set before him with gusto, and grew taller and broader day by day, overshadowing Michael, who had to be coaxed to his food. Deborah cudgelled her brains to devise for the boy appetising dishes, and cajoled him into eating plenty of butter and cream, but he remained lean and taut as though perpetually half starved. Although he appeared to the casual eyes of strangers a normal, fairly healthy youth, Deborah felt the same uncanny, unexplainable desire that had obsessed her mother to protect him and shield him, as if he were a precious, but very sickly plant under the care of a conscientious husbandman.

Olga obtained a permanency at a suburban secondary school for girls in one of the outskirts of London, and the journeys from and to St George's being too strenuous to undertake in one day, she moved into lodgings near the school. Soon after, Phillip graduated with a mathematical degree and found a position at a boy's college in Hertfordshire. He bought a second-hand motor bike that chugged along in noisy, smoky bursts of speed, travelling not as though propelled by a normal petrol engine, but as if its pistons were governed anarchistically by a number of rockets exploding in series within the cylinders. On his snorting, detonating iron horse, coated like it with a layer of grey dust and mud, he arrived home every Saturday afternoon and stayed over Sunday. On the Monday, refreshed by Deborah's rich food and the unvaryingly warm homeliness of his family and the neighbours, he started off at five in the morning, long before the rest of the household was awake, in order to reach the school in time for morning lessons. In two hours he travelled from one social extreme almost to the other, from one little world to another, poles apart. In St George's, his neighbours and friends were on the borderline of destitution, living in slums as bad as any in London, and from this milieu he bucked and throttled across miles of open green country to the well-ordered, secure little microcosm of a boys' college where the pupils were well bathed and well fed, and exhibited none of the distressing symptoms of poverty that he had come to regard as inseparable from St George's, and which, before he had passed into a secondary school, knowing nothing better, he had looked upon as the norm of life. Fortunately for his own peace of mind Phillip was an extremely adaptable young man. In St George's he forgot the college, and at the college St George's did not exist. He was popular with the boys and his seniors on the staff, a perfect representative of the solid, sedate, comfortable burgess class.

At the age of eighteen, Deborah was as experienced domestically as any mother of a large family, yet she still looked surprisingly youthful and even younger than her years. Now that Phillip and Olga had left the house, she urged Phineas to take advantage of their absence and turn the top front room into a sort of parlour, or sitting-room. The children were growing up, the girls would need a room to which they could invite their male friends, and where the boys could take visitors. The status of the family was rising, the eldest children were educational successes and some of the younger ones showed signs of development in the same direction. It would be too much to ask of them to invite their school or college acquaintances home and then expect them to huddle in the kitchen, or sit on the rags in the workshop. Phillip and Olga between them purchased a hide suite comprising a large couch and two comfortable armchairs, and Phineas bought four high-backed chairs upholstered to match the suite and a squat oak table with solid ornately carved ball-and-claw legs to decorate the centre of the room. The walls were camouflaged with a brown wallpaper overrun with brilliant red pagodas, and to complete the opulent design an upright piano was obtained on the hire-purchase system. The entire Kahn family threw themselves upon the instrument like a pack of neglected waifs on a feast. They all strummed tunes on it, from Olga, playing, during her rare visits, snatches of the first Brandenburg Concerto by ear, down to the six-year-old David, fascinatedly picking out, at meal times and other oddly inappropriate hours, the resonant bass notes with one finger.

Phineas, who had picked up some knowledge of the instrument in his Vienna interlude, taught Deborah the elementary fingering, and a *Smallwood's Pianoforte Tutor* completed her musical education. In two months, by dint of diligent practice, she was able to play not too complicated melodies, and to accompany Phineas in duets. Yielding to the importunities of neighbours with a little money to spare and little darlings of daughters, Deborah consented to give lessons at ninepence an hour. Fortified by the technical equipment of two volumes of Smallwood and her own unlimited cheek she taught the daughters of two publicans and nine other children from the neighbourhood how to sit at the piano. Fortunately, the only musical inclinations her pupils possessed were securely locked in the bosoms of their mothers. None of the eleven ever caught up close enough to Deborah to disclose her pedagogic limitations, but long before they had even mastered the first volume of the celebrated Smallwood, they retired with unashamed gladness to their dolls and fairy tales and left the field to other tyros.

Almost every evening the Kahns would have impromptu concerts in the parlour, and in a pre-wireless era entertained the neighbours with instrumental duets and popular songs that percolated through the open windows with such rhythmic invitation that half the street joined in. Saturday night was gala night, for then Phillip was at home, and the house rang with lusty voices yelling choruses from the students' songbook. Often, as he played the cheery accompaniments, Phineas's eyes would suddenly grow moist with tears. The room was blossoming with glad-eyed youth like a riot of sweetly scented flowers in a garden, yet the one who should have been bathing most deeply in their fragrance was dead and cold, buried beneath the rough dark earth, miles, miles away. If only Shandel were here! They had gone through so many rough times together, shared so much misery and deprivation, and now that for a little time at least fortune was smiling on them once more, the partner of his sorrows, the mother of his children, was not by his side to garner the rich harvest of the years. There was a bitter ache in his heart that made the laughter and song almost unbearable, but he laughed with his children, sang with them, and tortured himself with thoughts of his wife.

Only Deborah, the one most closely attuned to him, observed the change, and would shyly seek an opportunity to press his arm in silent sympathy. Again his chin would tilt to the ceiling like a challenge to Fate, and he would try to enter with the youngsters into the joyous abandonment of song, but for the rest of the evening a sombre refrain stalked with a wide, dignified beat through the happy jingles, a mournful insistent bass plucking at low strings inside his head. Shandel! ... Shandel! ... If only Shandel were here!

CHAPTER II

At mid-term a large grey touring car drew up outside Phineas's house in St George's. The bareheaded young man at the wheel looked at the ramshackle building.

'This it?' he said.

Olga seated at his side, nodded, for the first time a little ashamed of the scrofulous exterior of her father's domicile.

'This is it, Ben,' she admitted.

The driver of the automobile swung open the door and stepped on to the pavement. He was a tall, heavily built, attractive young man of about thirty. His hair was auburn like his sleek moustache, and his round face rosy and shining like the features of a young boy. His clothes were well tailored but hung slackly about his body with the artistic figure suggesting looseness that only expert craftsmanship can convey. An unlit, long-stemmed pipe, the charred edges of the brown bowl coated with traces of grey ash, was gripped between his strong, white teeth, and a huge striped muffler was wound round his throat, one end dropping almost to the fly of his trousers, the other making a splash of colour down the back of his grey tweed jacket. His appearance gave the impression of a professional man, a doctor or a barrister in mufti. He looked as though he went to church regularly on Sunday morning and played golf every Sunday afternoon. Ben Hammerton, however, had never played golf in his life, and, like most Jews, had never attended a church service. So far from being a doctor or a barrister, he was merely a tradesman, but a successful one, the owner of two flourishing gown shops, and even the swashbuckling collegian note of the scarf was false, since his scholastic achievements had never carried him farther than the fifth standard of his elementary school.

Ben skirted the bonnet of the car and courteously opened the door for Olga. She gave him her hand and stepped down into the road. Her escort pushed both doors to vigorously, one after the other, and they closed with a sharp, satisfying snap. Together, the couple stood on the pavement, Ben towering head and shoulders above Olga. She did not look her twenty-seven years; like all the Kahns, the tribulations of those early days had not prematurely aged her features; on the contrary, it was hard to imagine this slim, pretty blonde a week older than twenty. Ben eyed her with undisguised admiration, then drew himself up and squared his shoulders with masculine swagger.

'Do I look respectable?' he asked.

Olga laughed. She surveyed him critically. He shouted *Gaudeamus Igitur* more successfully even than her brother Phillip, the genuine college graduate, who also liked to dress that way. She herself tried hard not to appear like a schoolmistress, so perhaps it was natural in some people to seek relief from the ties of their occupations in fancy clothes. She did not dress her hair in a tight bun, had never worn spectacles and severe dark clothes were anathema to her. If it was right for her to dress like a typist or a shop assistant, then Ben was entitled if he chose to bluff the world with his student disguise.

'You'll do,' she said with a little nod. 'Only don't be shocked by my father. I can promise you that *he* won't look at all respectable.'

'That's all right,' he replied reassuringly. 'You don't have to worry, Olga. Any father of yours is good enough for me.'

Olga laughed and rapped smartly on the door. She had never remembered it being adorned at any time by a knocker. Phineas had found it knockerless when he had moved in from St Magnus Hill, and after so many years, knockerless it still remained. The girl's sharp ears detected footsteps muffled by the carpet of rags coming closer, and before Ben realised that the summons was being answered, the latch clicked and Phineas himself stood framed in the doorway. Troubled latterly by his eyes, overstrained from too much reading, he wore large tortoiseshell glasses, and an old tweed cap covered his rapidly dwindling crop of greying hair. A thick brown hand-knitted cardigan sheathed his torso, and two pockets, stuffed like a schoolboy's with odds and ends of rubbish, sagged over dirty grey flannel trousers. A pair of cracked black patent-leather shoes completed his normal working garb, unchangeable during the whole week except for clean shirts and an entirely new wardrobe for Saturday. Phineas's face broke into a broad smile at the sight of Olga. He threw his library book on a low, narrow ledge that jutted out from the workshop wall, and impulsively embraced his daughter, kissing her effusively on both cheeks. Then he stepped back half a pace, gazing at her affectionately.

'Really!' he said. 'Is this beauty my little Olga? Come in – come in. It is an honour to welcome such a krasavitza to St George's.'

Olga blushed with pleasure tinged slightly with embarrassment at her father's ebullience.

'Don't be silly, Dad,' she replied, and with a delightfully awkward smile she introduced her companion. 'This is Ben Hammerton.'

Phineas shook the young man's hand.

'Any friend of my children's,' he said warmly, 'is always welcome in my house.'

Apologising for the littered state of the workshop, as though it were more tidy at any other time, he led the way to the kitchen and invited his guests to be seated. Ben took a chair at one end of the table, while Phineas seated himself between the young couple. Olga was evidently ill at ease, her hands fidgeting nervously with the tablecloth, but Ben sat back with an assured tolerant air, sucking at his empty pipe, he had not troubled to remove his muffler, the insignia of higher education remaining coiled round his neck like a preposterously reticulated python. Phineas glancing from one to the other sensed immediately the purpose of their visit. He rose to his feet.

'Come, let us go upstairs into the parlour,' he said. 'It is much more comfortable there.'

'It's quite all right, Dad,' Olga answered. 'We shan't be staying long. We just happened to be passing this way, and... and... well, I just wanted you to meet my friend,' she concluded lamely.

'Friend! Is that all?' broke in the irrepressible Ben jovially. He turned to Phineas. 'With your permission, Mr Kahn,' he said, 'I hope to be more than just a friend of Olga's.'

'Something more?' said Phineas. 'What more can there be? When you grow as old as I am, young man, you will realise that in the whole world there is nothing more precious than a friend. However, while we become a little better acquainted, perhaps I can make you both a cup of tea.'

Laughingly, the young couple declined the invitation; Phineas seated himself again, and they dropped awkwardly into desultory snatches of small talk. Ben was not averse from talking about himself, or his shops, or the latest styles of ladies' garments, but the more he talked, the less his real personality revealed itself. All the while, Phineas was trying to take the measure of this young man who had invaded his household, but was rebuffed constantly by Ben's assured aloofness. There was no warmth in the words that came from him in crisp, flat, monotones; from whatever angle Phineas probed, he could find no fundamental likeness to himself or any sympathetic strains, nothing embryonic even to play on and develop at a later stage. It was as though Ben's mind and his own were functioning on different planes without a single fusing point of communion. Superficial facts about the young man emerged: he had been left a little money by an aunt and had built up a successful business by his own efforts, that he had no parents and lived with another aunt, but Phineas was not greatly interested in those details. The real Ben, like a volatile blob of mercury, seemed to slip from under his fingers defying all his attempts to pin him down. All this searching of course presupposed another Ben, for Phineas simply could not accept him as the smooth husk of a man that his conversation revealed. It hardly seemed possible for an intelligent young woman like Olga to be attracted by mere superficial gloss. Perhaps, however, this silent arrogance was a defence mechanism, put on like a cloak to shield his essential shyness from the rough contact of strangers; perhaps Ben would be more at ease by himself, and more communicative without Olga.

Phineas resolved to see Ben again, alone, before he made up his mind about him. He would go to a great deal of trouble over a suitor, a tentative one even, for Olga's hand. Olga, after all, was old enough to be able to decide for herself, and in the long run she probably would, even in the face of any opposition on Phineas's part, but she had had very little experience of men, and might perhaps ask his advice. In that event he had to be prepared to produce at the right moment a clearly formulated judgement. Olga was his eldest child, a brilliant young woman who would be an adornment to the home of any man, but Phineas felt that it was up to him to help her to find the man really worthy of her. Strange that he had so rarely thought of Olga this way before. She was twenty-seven; other girls of her age had been married for years, even had almost grown-up families, but he had always regarded Olga as wrapped up in her career, and although Ben sat boldly materialised before his eyes, this whole episode had a vaguely unreal tang.

At length, Olga rose to go. Phineas escorted the young couple through the workshop to the street, and kissed his daughter warmly as she took her leave on the pavement. Ben ran solicitously to the offside of the car and opening the door helped Olga in and made her comfortable. Then he started up the engine, and as soon as it commenced to boil with a regular chug, made for his seat. Before he could get in the car, Phineas called him over.

'Young man, would you care to drop over and visit me one evening, alone?' he said. 'I would like to have a chat with you.'

'Why, certainly, Mr Kahn,' Ben replied. 'It will be a pleasure. Tomorrow night do?'

Phineas nodded. 'Tomorrow night.'

Ben took his place in the car. 'OK,' he shouted with a wave of his arm. 'Cheerio!'

He bent over the gears, pulled a lever, straightened himself in his seat, and the car moved off. Accelerating, Ben looked back again and, bumping with the jaded springs of the upholstery, smiled a triumphant smile, like a victorious mechanical centaur. Phineas stood on the pavement waving his arm till the car vanished in the direction of Tower Hill. Caught up in the strong current of the broadening stream of life, he felt profoundly uneasy. New vistas were opening up before him, new responsibilities. His children would get married. They too would have children. Almost before he looked round he would be a grandfather! And if Shandel were here she would be a grandmother. It would have suited so well her natural dignity. Everything had suited her, from the fine clothes she had worn in their brief period of affluence in Vienna to the second-hand rags of St Magnus Hill. Ach! What was the good of bringing that up again? Life pulsed onwards, forwards, never backwards. What did he expect to be all his days, a young musician, a stallion newly mated? His hair was falling out, his eyes were beginning to play him tricks, the fingers that once had pressed so firmly and lightly over the strings of the violin were becoming shaky and uncertain. Each phase of life brought with it its own responsibilities: youth had its troubles and compensatory happiness, the prime meant more than just the zenith of physical vigour and late middle age was not entirely a season of deadness and the blunting of sharp sensory joys. Rather it held the mellow softness of the golden early autumn, the russet shades without extremes of dazzling brilliance or stark, uncompromising greys. He had known enough sorrow; each phase of his existence had been over-balanced by a double measure of tribulation. Now in the autumn perhaps he would find peace. The hardy plants were flowering prolifically, the children were growing up with a vengeance! Phineas smiled and unconsciously took off his spectacles and polished the lenses with his handkerchief. That aspect of maturity appealed to him. Soon, very soon, it seemed that he would be garlanded with the fullness of life – Phineas a grandfather!

CHAPTER III

Next night, Ben came again. Still hatless, his auburn hair neatly parted, he wore a tightly fitting black jacket and waistcoat, striped trousers, dazzling black shoes and spotless white spats. Chameleon-like his outward personality changed with his clothes. To Phineas he looked like a successful stockbroker, or the manager of an important bank; at least, so the ragsman imagined they must look, since in real life he had never had the opportunity to come in contact with either.

Deborah was in the kitchen. With feminine curiosity she had stayed at home to get an intimate close-up of her sister's fiancé. She had already sent the younger children to bed, and the older ones had been peremptorily dismissed from the house with instructions to return not earlier than eleven. Phineas introduced Ben to his daughter, then ushered him upstairs into the parlour. The young man carefully chose the most comfortable chair, and hitching up his sharply creased trousers, sat down. He extracted his pipe and filled it with a coarse light-brown tobacco from a crocodile-leather pouch.

'Mind if I smoke?' he said.

Phineas shook his head. 'By all means do,' he replied. 'I am a smoker myself.'

'Sorry I can't offer you any cigarettes,' said Ben. He held out his pouch invitingly. 'But you can help yourself to tobacco if you've got a pipe. Good stuff this. Virginia. I have it specially blended for me. Costs one-and-nine an ounce.'

Phineas waved him off with a smile, and Ben complacently completed the ritual of filling his pipe. Two matches burned out before he got it to draw properly, then he sat back contentedly folding his arms across his chest, puffing a soft cloud of blue aromatic smoke into the air. They were a queerly assorted couple, the old man's clothes hardly good enough for a scarecrow, his companion's a sartorial picture that on the line in the Royal

Academy would have silenced the censorious shafts even of the critical *Tailor & Cutter*. Ben seemed thoroughly at home, a little superior to his surroundings but oblivious of them; Phineas, on the other hand, appearing ill at ease, as though he were a stranger in his own house. It irritated him that Ben could make him feel so uncomfortable. A suitor coming to ask a man for his daughter's hand had no right to be so cocksure. Ben's attitude was the tolerant pose of the gracious conqueror, unbending slightly, conscious that his presence was merely a matter of formality. This whole meeting seemed to bore him, seemed so unnecessary, as if, the girl being as good as his, he had only to humour the old buffer for a while.

'Young man,' said Phineas breaking the awkward silence, 'I suppose you've got some idea of why I asked you to come?'

Ben smiled. 'Well, not exactly,' he replied. 'But I think I could give a pretty good guess. About Olga?'

Phineas nodded. 'Yes. I want to know just how things stand between her and you. Don't think me inquisitive, but I am her father, and perhaps a little old-fashioned, so you will excuse me for asking questions that may be a little personal… You are very fond of Olga?'

'I am,' said Ben, for the first time a hint of softness creeping into his voice. 'I think she's a wonderful girl, Mr Kahn. So clever. So talented.'

'I'm glad you appreciate that,' Phineas replied, warming a little at his evident enthusiasm. 'Such a young woman deserves the very best from life. These are hard times, I know, but can you afford to keep a wife in comfort?'

'One wife!' Ben laughed good-humouredly. 'I can afford to keep six! My shops are doing very well, Mr Kahn, so well that I am thinking of opening up another very shortly.'

'Hmmm!' Phineas stroked his chin. What he had to say now might not be so pleasant, but he had in all fairness to say it. 'You know, of course, that Olga has no money?'

'Of course I know!' said Ben forcefully. He sat up. Now was the time to sweep away every obstacle, to show his overwhelming hand and get the thing over, settled once and for all. He spoke very deliberately, waving his pipe before him to emphasise his words. 'Money doesn't matter, Mr Kahn. I have more than enough for the two of us. Of course, she'll have to give up her schooling and help me with the shops. After all, what can she earn as a teacher? Six, seven pounds a week? Why, with her brains and appearance she'll be worth twice that much to me in business!'

Phineas nodded comprehendingly. Ben's words shot a little chill through him, but he still maintained his pleasant composure, his face did not betray by the slightest muscular quiver the flare of indignation that the young man's proprietary claim had aroused. There was a gentle tap at the door and Deborah entered carrying a tray on which were two cups of coffee and some biscuits. She placed the tray on the table and stood irresolutely for a moment in the centre of the room.

'... Coffee?' she said lamely.

'Oh – I'll have a cup. Thanks very much indeed,' Ben replied off-handedly.

The girl blushed. Perhaps the young man had not meant to be rude, but he had not even troubled to look properly at her. She had put on her smartest frock in honour of her sister's fiancé and here she was being snubbed as though she were a housemaid. She excused herself hurriedly and ran down the stairs, her face burning with resentment. She felt that she was not going to like Ben very much.

Upstairs Ben sipped his coffee slowly, and thoughtfully nibbled at a biscuit.

'Hmmm!' he muttered approvingly. 'These are nice. Home-made?'

Phineas nodded. 'Yes. Deborah made them. She's a good cook, like Olga.'

Ben's face erupted into a superior smile. 'My wife won't have to cook,' he said. 'I wouldn't allow Olga to waste herself in the kitchen. Cooks can be hired cheaply enough, but young women like her are hard to find.'

'That's true,' Phineas admitted. 'But what are your plans, supposing you and Olga get married, what do you intend to do with her?'

'*Do*?' said Ben. 'Why, I believe I've already told you. I'm going to open up another shop, a really smart place this time, in the West End – and I'll put Olga in sole charge!'

Excited by his words, his eyes sparkled. Business, or talk about business had the same effect on him as hashish on a drug addict: it titillated his senses, enlarging and heightening his prevailing mood to a disproportionate pitch. Now, drunk like a prophet on a vision, he saw in himself another Gordon Selfridge, with Olga as a very efficient private secretary. He placed his coffee on the table, stretched his legs and settled back luxuriously. One hand cocked itself grandiosely in the armhole of his waistcoat, the other grasping his pipe like a lethal weapon stabbing at the air.

'Yes,' he repeated masterfully, 'Olga will be in sole charge. That will give her a real opportunity to show what she can do. She won't have to mess about any more with a lot of sloppy schoolgirls!'

'Tell me,' interposed Phineas gently. 'Have you already spoken to Olga about these things? ... I mean about your shops, and giving up school?'

'No, not yet,' Ben replied. 'I've just hinted at something of the sort. I want to surprise her when I've got everything settled.'

'I think she'll be surprised all right,' said Phineas sarcastically, then as an uncertain look came into Ben's eyes he hastened to change the subject. It was a shame to disturb the mirror-like brightness of his entranced state by little darts of unrest. Ben was in the mood that a psychologist might pray for. His conscious mind being entirely wrapped up in a single subject, his replies to other questions would be free from repressive inhibitions. Now Ben was at his mercy, securely pinned down, ready for dissection and examination.

'Have you read anything interesting lately?' Phineas remarked with apparent irrelevance.

'Read?' Ben looked uncomfortable for a moment, then the enchantment recaptured him. 'No,' he replied. 'To tell you the truth, Mr Kahn, I haven't had much time in the past few years. In fact, all I do is just to glance through the morning and evening papers, and I read the *Draper's Record* once a week to see if anyone I know has gone broke.'

He laughed. Other people kept on going broke. He had the contempt of the strong, thoughtless man for the weak and inefficient. Phineas smiled too; not for nothing had his prospective son-in-law learned how to read.

'I suppose you haven't much time for music, or the theatre, either?'

'Oh no. I wouldn't say that,' Ben replied. 'I see quite a few shows. This last Drury Lane musical comedy that's just come off, for example. I saw that four times, once with Olga, although she didn't seem to like it very much. Yes, I'm very fond of musical plays, but I appreciate good stuff as well. I like to hear a nice waltz selection, operettas and pieces like *Poet And Peasant* and *In A Persian Market*.

He relit his pipe and brushed some ashes from the impeccable stiffness of his trousers. He was showing himself as a broad-minded man well-acquainted with the world, tied to business, yet finding time for the higher things of life. He felt that he was acquitting himself admirably.

During the course of the haphazard, and apparently futile time-stretching conversation, Phineas prodded in the most inaccessible parts of Ben's mind. Gently and considerately he put the young man through a sort of third degree, but he did it with such flattering expertness that the only sensation Ben experienced was one of soothing self-satisfaction. Phineas, at the end of the revealing interview, preceded the young man down the stairs to the workshop, and guided him over the rags to the door. He opened it, and bowed to his visitor with exaggerated deference, but Ben in his chronically puffed-up state took the salutation as a discerning tribute to the excellent impression he had created.

Phineas went back to the kitchen. It was empty. Deborah, annoyed at Ben's neglect, had left the house and gone to visit a friend. Phineas switched on the light and walked over to the mantelpiece. Just above it, in the centre of the wall, hung a framed enlargement of his favourite portrait of Shandel. Always, when he was alone, Phineas held silent communion with her likeness. It was as though her personality had survived death to live again in the dead picture. Her face was wreathed in a misty softness, her lips smiling, that well-remembered smile. Phineas rested his elbows on the mantelpiece and looked at her. 'We did not struggle and starve to educate Olga for this,' he thought; 'to throw her away on an ignoramus like Ben, even though he does happen to have money.' If she married him, she would have her own house and a car and servants; she would be comfortably off, by their standards of living, almost rich, but wealth was not what they had fought for. Olga deserved something better... 'What do *you* think, Shandel?' He almost said this aloud, and ever so gently she seemed to shake her head in reply.

The following Sunday Olga came round alone. She sat in the kitchen with the rest of the family, but answered all their sallies with a preoccupied air. After a little time she excused herself and went upstairs to the parlour. Phineas heard her playing softly Mozart's slumber song, 'Schlafe Mein Prinzchen, Schlaf Ein'. He understood that she wanted to talk to him privately, so warning Deborah not to allow anyone to intrude, he went upstairs. He sat on the armchair so that she appeared in profile before him. The girl quickly gave up her pretence of playing. She half turned on the piano stool in his direction, one finger still touching the notes, her head lowered shyly towards the keys.

'Well, Dad?' she murmured, almost to herself.

'Well?'

'Ben was round to see you, wasn't he?'

'Yes. We had quite a long chat together.'

The girl fidgeted, scarcely able to conceal her impatience.

'... Well?'

Phineas leaned forward gravely. 'I'll let you into a secret,' he said with mock gravity, 'I suppose you'll have to know. He wants to marry you.'

Olga sat up with a nervous laugh, and her stiffened finger rippled over a string of treble notes.

'Thanks for the information, Dad. As it happens, I've known that for quite a time. What I do want to know is what you think of him.'

'Olga,' Phineas's face was grave, and his voice, the bantering note completely gone, deadly serious. 'Tell me, does that really matter to you? Do you really want to know?'

The girl nodded her head slowly.

'Yes.'

'Do you love him, Olga?'

'... I... I think so.'

'Really love him? The way your mother and I loved when we

were young? Nothing else mattered. The rest of the world could die, but if we were together we would have been happy. Do you too feel that oneness, that completeness?'

Olga hesitated for a moment. She seemed unable to make up her mind.

'Do you?' Phineas pressed.

She shook her head at last.

'No.'

'Then you don't really love him, you can't,' he said.

The girl remained silent. Phineas harried her unmercifully. It hurt him to be cruel, but her well-being was so important to him that he could forgive himself for inflicting temporary wounds knowing that in the long run he would be justified. He allowed her no escape, no side alley of excuse. Bluntly he posed the question before her in a form that permitted of no equivocal reply. Either she answered 'yes', or whatever else she said meant 'no'.

'Do you really love him? Tell me straight out,' he demanded again.

Olga threw up her hands in a little gesture of puzzlement.

'... I... I don't know,' she faltered.

Phineas saw clearly that her defences were tottering.

'Now I want you to listen to me,' he said. 'You don't *have* to take my advice, but you must listen. Ben is a very nice chap, he would be an ideal husband – but for someone else. He's got a different mentality from yours, a totally different outlook on life. What really surprises me is that you haven't noticed it yourself, but that's probably because you haven't had much experience of men. To my knowledge, Ben is the first one you've taken at all seriously. You've been out together, and had amusing times, but you mustn't forget that a man may be an enjoyable companion for three hours every other night, but not for twenty-four hours every single day. Tell me, have you ever been to a good concert together? To a decent play?'

Regretfully, Olga shook her head. It was the truth, but how and when did her father manage to discover it all?

'Imagine,' Phineas continued, 'a whole lifetime spent like that. You'll have to give up teaching, that will be the first thing, then by day you'll be a glorified shop assistant, and at night the companion of a tired businessman, all your entertainment on the level of the cinema or the cheap music hall. No. You don't realise what you are letting yourself in for. Think it over. Take a holiday, a long one. You need it. See new people, new ways of life, then if you still feel you must have Ben, marry him, he'll always be here, but for heaven's sake, give yourself a chance to look round first!'

In the days that followed, the more Olga thought about what her father had said, the more she realised his wisdom. It was true that between her and Ben there was a vast incompatibility that only the blindness of love could bridge or conceal, and now that it had been plainly pointed out to her, the gulf was clearly visible. Perhaps she had been too hasty. She hinted as much to Phineas, who started to pull the necessary strings. It was his idea that she should go abroad for several months. He was in constant touch with his relatives in Russia, who would be only too glad to be visited by any one of Phineas's family. The sole expense would be the passage money, and Olga could quite easily manage that and some extra clothes from her savings.

She obtained two months' leave from school, and early in the autumn parted from Phineas at Dover to catch the Ostend boat. From Ostend she travelled overland to Berlin, and there entrained for Warsaw. Her passport and visa were perfectly in order, but travelling on from Warsaw, as she neared the Russian frontier, arrogant young Polish officers smartly dressed in dark-blue uniforms with long, peaked caps, were constantly boarding the trains to examine the papers of the various passengers, and each time the officers passed through they made Olga feel uncomfortable, as though they might discover something incriminating in her documents, and prevent her from proceeding farther.

There were five others in Olga's compartment, four stout men and one middle-aged woman, all of them dressed like members of the merchant class. They all seemed very friendly, and one of the men who happened to be a Jew translated her requests to the porter and the other passengers. Olga was more than glad that she still remembered her Yiddish; that Jewish Esperanto could carry her all over the globe and make her understood wherever members of her race were scattered.

At last the train reached the Russian border. Those passengers desirous of crossing the frontier went into a ramshackle wooden customs house with their luggage. Then they waited for a little time on a narrow decrepit platform until their train steamed in. The Russian train ran on a wider gauge, and although it was not as new as the Polish one, it seemed much more comfortable. Ledges jutted out from the sides of the compartment and Olga, hiring through her Jewish cicerone a rouble's worth of bedclothes, retired to sleep on the ledge. With a great deal of preliminary squeaking the train began to move. Olga, exhausted by the journey, was almost dozing off when she gazed across sheepishly at the opposite bunk. One of the men who had travelled across Poland with her was looking out of the window and unashamedly weeping. His face had worn a strained expression during the whole of the Polish journey, and like her, he had seemed vaguely uncomfortable whenever the officers had gone through the train, glancing repeatedly over his shoulder like a man with a nervous affliction. Now he was crying, but although he wept, he seemed at ease, as though his tears were tears of deliverance. Olga watched him wearily till her eyelids became glued together in sleep, and the Russian versts sped unconsciously behind her, the train roaring forward on its journey to Moscow.

A telegram had preceded her, but when the train steamed into the Briansk station it was five hours late. The Briansk was a massive building in the modern style, the walls faced with mottled marble, the benches and platforms newly constructed. Only the station was new and up to date; the same peasants that she had seen at every wayside stop were sprawled all over the place with their ugly bundles, sleeping on the floor or huddled on the benches. They looked like passive, lifeless bundles of clothes themselves, as though they could sit in this fashion without complaining for hours or days, or even weeks if necessary.

To her surprise her cousin Ruth was waiting for her. Ruth was a Russian and used to the chaotic railroad system. To arrive five hours late was a normal occurrence, two hours was merely unusual, but for a train to be on time would have been a miracle. However, Ruth had braved a miracle and waited for five hours. Several months older than Olga's father, suckled on the same milk that had saved Phineas from joining the heavenly throng of his predecessors, she was a tall, stout woman, looking older than her uncle and foster brother by a good many years. Her hair was snow-white, and lines of care furrowed her face. She had lived through war, revolution, counter-revolution and famine, and each of those events had etched a tell-tale seam on her features, while in her large, dark eyes was mirrored the suffering of them all. Her generation had borne the brunt of those turbulent years. Before the war, she herself had been hunted from town to town because her husband was a notorious and active Social Democrat, during the war she had been persecuted by the Germans in Kiev because she was Russian, and after the war by the White Russians because she was Jewish. Then their cause had triumphed, but in the triumph she had lost her husband, and in the famine two of her children.

Like a tractor tearing its way over stubborn fields Ruth pushed through the crowd of broad-shouldered peasants who at the arrival of the train stood gaping open-mouthed, or sat up irresolutely scratching their heads, and set a direct course for Olga. There was no mistaking Phineas's daughter; she was the image of her mother, and yet she had a great deal of her father about her too.

Beside Ruth, Olga, a grown woman herself, looked like a school-girl. Her cousin's huge breasts swelled from under her coat like ripe melons, and her stomach was distended like that of most women past middle age who have borne many children. Ruth gathered her in her arms and clasped her tearfully to her bosom. It seemed foolhardy to Ruth's compassionate motherliness for one so young and frail to have undertaken alone the risks of such a strenuous journey. For this woman, who, dressed as the wife of a peasant, had without thought of danger smuggled herself behind the counter-revolutionary lines with a message concealed between her toes, the very idea of Olga's unchaperoned jaunt across the continent roused a shudder.

'Die Anglechanka', the little English girl, as Olga became christened affectionately, was an enormous success in Moscow. Her clothes were admired and coveted, especially her shiny rubber Wellington boots, a novelty in Russia, and another rarity, her artificial silk stockings. Olga dispensed her garments with a prodigal generosity. She had six pairs of silk stockings, and of these four went to female relatives. Her spare slips and knickers went the same way, and the gratitude of the recipients of these tawdry trifles that were common necessities to every English working girl and could be picked up at the most ill-stocked of London drapers was more than ample compensation for such insignificant gifts, especially when in London they could be so easily and inexpensively replaced. She was borne around Moscow in triumph, the homes of all her relatives were thrown wide open to her, and everyone begged for the privilege of entertaining Die Anglechanka.

A week of Moscow was enough for Olga. Here, the old guard of her relatives was entrenched. They were all charming and the soul of hospitality, but Olga yearned for young people of her own age. Her opportunity to escape came when Ruth's eldest daughter, Brucha, who, with her husband Lonya, an aeronautical engineer, lived in Kiev, sent an urgent letter demanding that Die Anglechanka visit her.

Ruth read the letter to Olga, and asked her half wistfully, knowing what her reply would be, whether she wanted to go.

Two days later Brucha met her at the railway station in Kiev. She was about two years older than Die Anglechanka, dark, with her black hair combed tightly back from her forehead and coiled behind her small, shapely ears. To Olga's surprise she welcomed her in delightfully broken English. Brucha was learning the language, but her attempts at explaining herself were so grotesque that, baulked by Olga's laughter at the incomprehensibly knotted barrage of words in which her attempts became involved, she relapsed into homely, understandable Yiddish.

Brucha shared with her husband one enormous room in a large house off the Kreschatik, the main thoroughfare of the city. Before the revolution it had been the home of a bachelor, a wealthy merchant; now, a dozen families were domiciled there. Each family had its separate room, but all did their cooking in a large kitchen on a huge stove. Fortunately, not all of them ate at home at the same time. The men were mainly employed in the factories with their wives, and had most of their meals at the works' canteens or the clubs. Olga did not quite see how such a system could work satisfactorily, but in practice Brucha assured her that there was not the slightest unpleasantness.

In the centre of the room there was a large grand piano, and opposite, against the wall, on a sort of tripod, a polished brass samovar. There were a few chairs, a table, a double bed and, fitting into an alcove in the corner, a divan. One wall was lined with books, and the floor on that side was littered with more books, square sheets of cardboard, blue prints, rulers, compasses and other instruments. Lonya himself was a tall, good-looking man of about thirty-five, with a square, dimpled chin, a straight broad nose, wide-set grey eyes and a sparse crop of sandy hair, very thin on top and greying at the sides. He gravely shook Olga's hand, asked her a few questions that newly acquainted relatives usually ask, then inquired about the political situation in England. His questions were brisk and sharp with intelligence, his grey eyes watching her keenly, until Olga blushed, being forced at last to admit that he was far better acquainted with the trend of English politics than she was herself. Lonya shook his head in mild reproof and went over to the divan at Brucha's suggestion to fix up a curtain across the alcove to ensure more privacy for Olga. He himself hardly considered such bourgeois prejudices worth pandering to; privacy was the prerogative of every individual, but those who really desired it could be solitary in the midst of a roomful of people. In his private life, he himself hardly noticed where he ate, slept or what the people with him were doing, and he saw no reason for others bothering about what he did before them, provided of course that he did not annoy or interfere with them in any way. Such an act would be a heinous crime, anti-social and worthy of punishment; as far as Lonya was concerned Die Anglechanka could walk about naked during the whole of her stay, and as for her being ashamed to undress in the same room, why, such inhibitions seemed laughable in these days.

Brucha's room was filled every evening with young people. They were young in years, all of Olga's age or younger, but even the most youthful of them seemed strangely matured, like middle-aged men and women, a heritage from the rigours of revolution and civil war. The samovar worked overtime, the guests consuming count-less cups of weak Russian tea. Brucha was fond of playing dance tunes, and to wind up a strenuous night of excitable conversational bouts that started off in casual thrust and parry and ended up usually in a verbal battle royal, she would play the latest jazz hits, tunes that had been forgotten two years ago in London. Olga introduced them to the 'Black Bottom'. At once they were attracted to the rhythm, and in spite of her protestations, Die Anglechanka was appointed tutor. Brucha sat at the piano vamping the tune, and Olga showed them the steps, vamping the words!

> Black Bottom – You've got 'em,
> You've got 'em – The Black Bottom,
> Cha – cha – cha
> Cha – cha – cha – cha – cha – cha...'

The same serious politicians that half an hour previously had been excitedly discussing the successes of the New Economic Policy, stamped about the room, jerking their hips in a clumsy imitation of Olga. Only one young man sat in a corner, aloof from the rhythmic orgy. A dark, vivacious girl, with her hair cut short like a boy's, pulled him from his seat and forced him to partner her. His six-feet-two of slender, stooped manhood leaned grotesquely over her as he awkwardly clasped her waist and tried to master the intricacies of this new jazz step. His heavy shoes slithered unconvincingly over the floor, pressing on the girl's toes until the dance on her part became a series of unsuccessful attempts to avoid his feet. At last, she pushed the tall young man away and limped to the divan. The others were still dancing, and Brucha still pounding away at the 'Black Bottom'. Deserted, the young man mopped his brow in relief. Olga standing next to him was so tickled by his expression of deliverance that she burst into an uncontrollable chuckle. He looked at her, clicked his heels in military fashion and bowed.

'My name is Boris Edelman,' he said with a smile. 'I am sorry. I am not good at your English dances.'

'To tell you the truth, neither am I,' Olga replied. 'I don't think it's so important, anyhow.'

His handsome face broke into a broader smile. 'I am glad you think that way,' he said. 'To my mind, the piano could be much better occupied.'

'You play?' she asked.

'After a style.'

'Will you play for me then?' she said.

'With pleasure, tovarish,' he replied, 'but not here, amongst all these people. Some other time, only for you, and Brucha and Lonya.'

'It's a promise,' she said. 'I'll hold you to it.'

'I'll see that you do!' His dark eyes twinkled. 'But tell me your name. I can't very well call you Die Anglechanka to your face.'

'Olga,' she said, unaccountably experiencing a sudden sense of shyness.

'Mine is Boris. Oh, I've already told you that. Boris Edelman, Borya to my friends. *You* will call me Borya, won't you?'

She looked at him. Without appearing in the least affected he had a shock of dark hair that he wore overlong, and which he was constantly smoothing back from his forehead. His complexion was sallow and his cheeks drawn in like one who has suffered from mental strain, or for long periods not had enough to eat, but his large brown eyes with their laughing clearness gave his face a cheerful expression. His suit, a new one, was badly creased, not so much from careless wear as from the inherent shoddiness of the material, a synthetic worsted with a prominent herringbone stripe, made in Germany from wood pulp. Olga imagined how Ben would have shuddered and sniffed in disdain at the mere sight of such a suit. Had anyone had the temerity to offer him payment simply to wear it he would have shied like a frightened horse. Borya's clothes, however, did not interest Olga. She only saw his face, and heard his soft, eager voice, and noted his long, sensitive hands.

Of course he wanted to show her the city. All her relatives and friends had offered themselves as guides, but Olga had declined gently in favour of Brucha or Lonya. With Borya, however, she had a feeling that Kiev would seem different. Every moment that passed with the tall, stooping young Russian close to her seemed inexplicably to charge her with a mounting excitement. When the party broke up, she had promised to go out with him on the following day.

Brucha and Lonya approved of her cicerone. They were both extremely fond of Boris, so they delivered their charge into his hands when he called the next day, together with a long duet of instructions, as though he were a new nurse taking out for the first time the heir of the ducal house. Boris hired a droshky, and driving slowly to take in the full quaintness of the old city, they clattered over the cobblestones of the narrow streets, the isvostchik avoiding with consummate ease and a steady flow of muttered profanity the numerous potholes on the steep hillocks. Every other building seemed to be a church, most of them now sequestrated by the Soviet authorities for use as workers' clubs or anti-religious museums. From the Byzantine grandeur of St Sophia's Cathedral they drove to the underground eleventh-century monastery of Pechersky Lavra, a decade and a half earlier, the most holy spot of the holiest city in Russia. There they dismissed the droshky and purchasing long, slender wax candles from an old man at the door, followed him through a chapel and down a long flight of stone steps to the now uninhabited subterranean homes of the former monks. By the unsteady yellow light of the flickering candles they saw lines of old coffins resting in niches in the walls hewn out of solid rock, the last mortal remains of seers and saints, to the superstitious wonder-working even in death and decay. Some of the coffins had been opened by the government, revealing eerie mummified fragments, disproving the carefully fostered peasant belief that the holy ones remained miraculously preserved during the centuries, and showing convincingly that the saints had also been merely flesh, and now were only dry bones and dust.

Olga was thankful to reach the fresh air again. They were on top of a bluff overlooking the Dnieper. Below, Kiev and its environs spread before them like a vast oil painting, a maze of golden spires and cupolas, a city of churches like an enormous Kremlin. Boris waved his arm like an art patron showing off his choicest treasures. Kiev still remained Kiev, beautiful and fascinating as ever. Made capital of the Ukrainian Democratic Republic by the Rada in October 1917, recaptured by the Soviet forces in January 1918, only to be taken once more by the Rada, aided by the Germans, in the following March. In February 1919 again incorporated into the Union of Soviet Socialist Republics until raped in August by Denikin and the pogromchik Petlura, when the hilly streets were cascades of Jewish blood. Bolshevik again in September, then overrun by the scoundrelly hetman and an army of Poles until the Soviet power was firmly and finally re-established in

June 1920. All the horror and carnage that had defiled the fair city had only caused temporary scars which, healing in less than a decade, had left Kiev still serene and radiant in her centuries-old beauty. Boris swelled with pride as he pointed out the various landmarks of his birthplace and noted how Olga's lips parted in wonder at the sight of that glistening diorama.

'Beautiful! ... Beautiful!' she breathed.

Boris nodded. 'Not for nothing do we rave about it. Do you know what we Russians say?

> '"Kto iv-Kieve nye bevall
> Tot krassote nye vedall."'

He translated:

> '"Who in Kiev never has been
> Peerless beauty never has seen."'

Olga shook her head dreamily. She could hardly bear to part from such a vision of beauty; she could well understand being in love with such a city. They made their way down the hill and ate at a little restaurant, then walked slowly homewards. Before they reached the Kreschatik, Boris stopped outside a modest-looking three-storeyed house.

'I live here,' he said simply. 'Will you come in?'

She followed him up a flight of stairs to the top floor. Boris opened the door of his room and, when she entered, closed the door behind her. It was a fair-sized room. A large, low divan stood in one corner, and in the centre were a table and two easy chairs. Hugging one wall was an upright Bechstein piano, badly chipped and in want of a coat of varnish, and against the other a huge writing-desk, covered with books. On a shelf above the desk a long rack was suspended which accommodated a number of test tubes and small retorts, and by its side rose three more formidable pillars of books. Without an invitation, as though Boris spoke to her without words, Olga sank into one of the chairs, and the young man seated himself at the piano.

'Chopin?' he said.

She nodded with an expectant smile. Nocturne and nocturne trickled from under his fingers like a single stream of sparkling crystal water, and the moon rose high and bright above the tapering gilded fingers thrusting greedily towards the clouds, and the soft, seraphic curves of the enchanted cupolas of the ravishing city of Kiev, the holy mother of ancient Russia...

Two weeks later, Phineas heard from Olga, the longest letter he had had from her since her departure. It ran:

Dear Father,

What I am going to write may come as a surprise to you, but somehow I don't think it will. I have decided to stay in Russia. I met in Kiev, Boris Edelman, a friend of Brucha's, and he has asked me to marry him, and I have said 'yes'. I am sure this time. Now I know what you meant. He is an agronomist, a scientific research worker on agricultural problems, but he also plays the piano. If you knew him, you would love him too. He has the soul of a musician. When we talk music his eyes light up, and his face shines, and his fingers itch for the keyboard of a piano. He plays Chopin beautifully, understands him better than any pianist I have ever heard, better even, and I know this is blasphemy, than dear old Pachmann himself. So you see, I must stay.

He lives in one room, and when we are married I suppose I shall have to get a job, for here in Russia everyone is expected to work. To tell you the truth, living in one room and doing my cooking on a communal stove holds no terrors for me. I went through worse just before mother died. This will only be temporary, however; new buildings are going up every day that will solve the housing problem, but houses and furniture and decorations have never meant a great deal to me. I suppose I am like you, a bit of a nomad. Anyway, I will be happier in a cellar or a garret with Borya in Russia than with Ben in some spick, suburban bungalow equipped with running water, H&C, and every modern convenience.

Borya is very busy on experiments, studying the various grades of wheat, their diseases and how to raise a hardy hybrid strain that will flourish in the rigours of a less temperate climate. The government has decided on the foundation of another Jewish settlement in Biro-Bijan, near the borders of Manchuria. It is a fertile district with an equable climate, rich in minerals and untapped oil resources, and as soon as enough Jews settle there it will become an autonomous Jewish Republic. It will be a great thing for our people. Yiddish will become the official language, and all immigrants who settle there will be expected to know both how to read and write it, apart from Russian. Borya and I are polishing up our Yiddish, and he is teaching me how to write. Borya says this Biro-Bijan will go a long way towards liquidating the Jewish problem in the Soviet Union and elsewhere. He wants to go to Biro-Bijan. They will need him there, and I expect that I will find something to occupy me too.

Apart from you and Deborah and the rest of the family, England seems so remote, so far away and unfamiliar, as if I had only known it through a cursory visit. I feel at home here, I love it. Kiev is so warm and full of life. It is not one-eighth the size of London, the buses are shabby, the trams old, dilapidated and overcrowded, and the sanitary arrangements are nothing like what they should be, but I love the city and its people, and I feel like one of them.

In a year or maybe two, if Borya gets a long vacation we will come to London to see you, but I will write often, and often, and I want you to write to me. Give them all at home my love. I can't help crying a little, but I am happy. I want you to believe me, Father. It's true that sometimes, although I never hinted as much, I used to regard you as fossilised and out of touch with contemporary life, but I apologise now for those things I often wanted to, but didn't say. I want to thank you because you were cleverer than I, much cleverer, although you didn't go to a high school or university, and I am glad I was sensible enough to take your advice. Think of me, Father, and whenever Boris plays those pieces you love so much, I will think of you and the others.

Thank you again, and with all my love – Goodbye!

Phineas's eyes dimmed behind his glasses as he read the letter and his hands trembled a little. Almost, he missed the tiny postscript, just two words:

PS Tell Ben.

CHAPTER V

Olga's settling in Russia was the prelude to a further exodus from St George's. Phillip sat for an examination for a post in a Mancunian high school, and, passing with honours, backed by the enthusiastic recommendation of his former headmaster, he took up the position in Manchester. Within three months he met a girl there, married her and settled down comfortably in one of the smarter suburbs. Stanley was the next to wed. He ran a flourishing little business in a London market selling silk and woollen piece goods. One of Deborah's friends, a tall, blonde, intelligent young woman, attracted him as soon as she began to visit the house, and in a short while Deborah lost an acquaintance only to be tied more firmly to a sister-in-law. Israel was in an accountant's office, and being already on more than friendly terms with one of his female colleagues it seemed as though this diffident, very fair, typically Nordic-looking Israelite would be next in the running for the matrimonial stakes.

Phineas was satisfied with the way things were going. One after another his children were feeling their strength and leaving the squalor of St George's to hew their own paths through life, starting not under the heavy handicaps that had burdened his adult struggle, but aided by every advantage that education could give. Deborah he was not worried about; she had her sister's looks, plus her own sparkling brilliance, and Rose, the youngest daughter, was showing a natural aptitude for the piano, and was still rosy and plump like a well-turned dumpling. Joseph had just left school, helped Stanley in his business, and was allowed by his elder brother ample leisure to study art at the polytechnic, while David, the youngest, was earmarked for medicine. Ever since he was old enough to take an interest in such things, he had played the violin and wanted to be a doctor. Phineas encouraged him, although he knew that a medical degree was a long and costly process, and, in a rational view, immeasurably beyond his resources. But he was determined, if David's ability only equalled his ambition, to allow no barrier to impede his son's progress, even if he impoverished himself beyond reclamation by so doing.

Felix and Michael were a puzzle. They grew up unlike any of his other children. They were the tallest, both nearly six feet, but whereas Michael was slender, Felix had the physique of a heavyweight boxer. Apart from an inherited love of music, Felix had no interests outside physical fitness. His bedroom was piled with heaps of health-and-strength magazines. By day he held a minor clerical position, and at night attended classes at a South London institute to qualify as a physical training instructor. He shared a room with Michael and Israel, and Michael often twitted him, when he stood admiring himself before the mirror stripped to the waist and flexing his biceps, with sarcastic intimations that an extraordinary increase was clearly visible in the circumference of his arms. Felix took his remarks good-humouredly, he respected and looked up to Michael, although his elder brother had no desire whatsoever to attain big muscles. Michael played tennis moderately well, swam and walked at weekends in the country, but he always had an unnaturally high colour and an occasional harsh cough that disturbed Phineas. Time and again, after a more than usually sustained bout of coughing, Michael was forced by his father to accompany him to a doctor, but the local medicos could never discover anything organically wrong with him.

Michael took his BSc degree with honours and embarked upon a career of chemical research. Paint, synthetic resins and varnishes interested him, and a few months after qualifying he obtained a position as assistant chemist in a paint factory. He had been warned by his father, who wanted him to take up teaching, that the practical manufacture of paint was a trade only for the robust, that the mixing and inhaling of poisonous chemicals was not beneficial for the soundest of constitutions; but Michael laughed at such scaremongering talk. In any case, he had not a great deal of choice in the matter. The field for qualified men in every profession was narrowing month by month. College graduates were ten a penny. Paint was a growing industry that could absorb many trained men from the schools and universities. Teaching, the only other profession he could tolerate, was overcrowded; so when the vacancy at the paint factory occurred, he took it up enthusiastically. He was twenty-two, and considered that he had been a burden too long on his father. He realised what a struggle Phineas had to maintain his family, and felt that it was up to him to earn some money, so that if he did live at home he could pay his way and recoup his father for the expense of his education.

He threw himself enthusiastically into his work. His firm was experimenting with a new type of cellulose lacquer, and he found the practical application of his training vastly more exciting than the theoretical routine of the university laboratory. The works were on the outskirts of London. To get there on time he had to be up before seven and travel across London for an hour by bus and train. Usually, apart from the newspaper, he took with him a book of poems, or a volume of Shakespeare, but he only read in the morning, at night he sat back exhausted in the railway coach, his energy flayed, left behind in the factory laboratory. The colour drained from his cheeks, only a slight smear glowing dully just below his eyes. His good-humoured sarcasm took on a bitter tang, he became irritable in the evenings. Eight weeks at the factory changed him from a lovable young man to a morose grumbler. Phineas watched the metamorphosis anxiously. Michael was heading for a nervous breakdown. Soon, the old man felt, he would be forced to clap on the brakes.

Michael and Felix arrived home from work at about the same time and usually had dinner together. Deborah had gone out, but she had left a hot meal for them on the stove. Phineas was sitting in the corner reading when Felix came in. The young man washed himself at the sink and twiddled the wireless set till a powerful blast of dance music came through. Then he seated himself at the table and Phineas set his meal before him, preparing a plate for Michael who was due at any moment. When the chemist arrived, he dropped wearily on to his chair and gave the curtest of greetings. He toyed with his food, then pushed the plate away. It was useless trying to eat, he had no appetite.

'What's the matter?' said Felix. 'Why don't you have your grub?'

'How can I,' replied Michael irritably, 'with all this noise in the room? *Must* you have the wireless on? Or if you must, can't you play something quiet? There's a Beethoven quartet on the National. Let's have that instead of this rubbish.'

'No fear!' said Felix obstinately. 'There's a time for Bach and a time for Beethoven.'

Michael rose angrily. 'There's a time for dance music too!' he said. He walked over to the set, switched it off and sat down again. 'I've been on my feet all day, rushing to work in buses and trains, then travelling home again on more buses and more trains, with all that infernal banging and whistling going on all round me, and now that I'm home, I want a little peace and quietness!'

'You mustn't forget that you're not the only one at home,' Felix remonstrated. 'And not the only one that goes to work, either. Don't think that because you're a university man with a BSc and have got a classy job and earn good money that you're boss in this house. I've got as much right to play the wireless as you, or anyone else.'

'Nobody's denying that,' said Michael. 'But there's all day to play it in, and all night. I'm going for a walk soon, then you can have as much music as you like.'

'As it happens,' Felix replied, 'I'm going out too, and I want to listen to dance music now.'

He leaned back, balancing on two legs of his chair, and switched on the set. A blare of jazz shot out. Michael's eyes flashed. He pushed his chair back, rose abruptly to his feet and left the kitchen. His footsteps faded up the stairs and the door of the parlour slammed. Phineas had been quietly seated in the corner, apparently immersed in his book, but he had taken in every detail of the quarrel, and had it shown signs of developing into something more serious, he would not have been slow to intervene. He put his book on the table and, carefully removing his glasses, polished them slowly with his handkerchief.

'Aren't you ashamed of yourself?' he said to Felix, without even looking at him.

'Ashamed? Why? ... I'm not a bit ashamed!' said Felix defiantly. 'And I'd do it again! Since Michael's got a job he's become too high and mighty. He wants taking down a peg or two.'

Phineas replaced his glasses as Felix lowered his head before him and fidgeted with his fork. He was softening. Phineas could see that the boy was already repentant in spite of his uncompromising tone.

'Now don't be silly, Felix,' he said quietly. 'Use your eyes, and your head too. Can't you see that Michael's been living on his nerves for the past few months? His head is working all the time, he never gives it a rest. You're his brother, and more than anyone else you should understand. You have no nerves because you're fit, you're a healthy animal, but Michael hasn't a tenth of your stamina. The work and the travel and the noise knock him up. Why can't you try to understand that? People should go a little out of their way to be considerate, should try and put themselves in the other's position. Life would be so much easier for everyone if only human beings could be a little more tolerant.' He went over and patted Felix on the shoulder. 'Now, stop behaving like a sulky schoolgirl and go up and apologise.'

Felix stood up. His eyes were large and bright, and there was more than a hint of moisture in them, as though he could barely refrain from tears.

'I... I'm sorry, Dad,' he faltered. 'I'll go up... I think you're right.'

Before he could reach the door, it opened, and a contrite Michael entered. His face wore a foolish twisted grin as though he were ashamed of himself. Impulsively he stuck out his hand and his brother grasped it firmly.

'... I'm awfully sorry, Felix,' he said.

'Rot!' Felix replied '*You've* nothing to be sorry about. I behaved like a ruffian, Michael. I apologise.'

Michael shook his head. 'No. It was all my fault. I'm so strung up. Working too hard.' He smiled wryly. 'A bit of a change for me, I suppose. But really, that journey does take it out of me. At the end of a day I'm not really responsible for the things I say or do.'

Immediately, the health-and-strength crusader flared forth in Felix. Half his life he spent in convincing people that they were ill, and explaining why they were ill, and what they ought to do about it. He had one panacea for every disease, intensive physical exercise. For years he had been urging Michael to go in for Swedish Drill, but his brother had always laughed at him. Now he would show Michael that really he was not so clever. He put one arm round his brother's shoulder and led him firmly to the mirror.

'Look!' he commanded.

Michael saw before him a strange, small face, hardly recognisable as his own. The brow was wide and very white, the blue eyes too large and staring, the pale cheeks drawn together as though all his teeth had been extracted, a slightly protruding underlip and a chin tapering almost to a point. His ears stuck out prominently, like an elephant's flaps, he thought, and the nose was too long and too thin, and the nostrils too wide. No, it was not a very prepossessing picture.

'Well, do you like it?' said Felix.

Michael shook his head. 'No,' he replied. 'But you can hardly blame me for my face.'

'But there's nothing wrong with your face!' said Felix. 'It's your general health. You know why you look so bad? It's simply because you're out of condition. Because your bloodstream is sluggish and doesn't circulate properly. I know I'm not brilliant, but I'll give you a tip. Take up physical training. It'll make a man of you. Give you back your appetite. Fill your face up, put some flesh on you and some real colour in your cheeks. Join a good class. You can break your journey two nights a week at Oxford Circus and go to the Regent Poly. Give it a trial and I guarantee that in a month you won't recognise yourself!'

Michael was intelligent enough to see the wisdom of Felix's argument. The very next night he joined the polytechnic. Under his brother's guidance he bought a singlet, jock strap, shorts and rubber plimsolls, and the following Monday enrolled in the beginners' class. He undressed himself in the locker room that reeked with the dry smell of mingled masculine sweat and hot rubber, and put on his kit, then he went into the large hall to await instruction. Large, bronzed young men were lying on their backs on rough mats in odd corners, kicking up their legs and going through complicated manoeuvres with their limbs, while others were running round the hall moving with a beautiful rhythmic swing, their muscular legs and arms placed with smooth meticulous precision like highly lubricated pistons, each pace covering the same span exactly as its predecessor and the one that followed, each arc of the elbows curving mechanically like an exquisitely adjusted pendulum. A peremptory whistle sounded and the floor was cleared. The class of about thirty formed up, and at the word of command ran round the room at a slow jog-trot. Just when Michael felt that his heart had swollen to the size of his chest and would most certainly burst, the whistle sounded again and they formed up in two long lines. The instructor, a small, spare, grey-haired man in a white sweater and flannel trousers, climbed on a table and the class spread out in open formation.

The exercises commenced. Hands on hips, heels raise, knees bend, knees raise, heels lower...With legs wide astride, arms bend! ... Head bending and chest lifting. Head on neck roll! ... One position succeeded another with bewildering rapidity and without a breathing space: at one moment he squatted on his heels with his hands clasped round his knees bending his head forward to touch his toes; and a few minutes later his palms were resting on the floor while he lay full length, and keeping his legs taut tried to arch his back in the position illustrated by the lithe rubber-bodied little man on the table. The assistant instructor went round showing the novices the correct postures, and Michael had constant need of his guiding hands. He had never imagined physical exercise to be so complicated, or that such apparently easy postures were so strenuous to retain. Almost it was too much for him; he had thought that three-quarters of an hour would be far too short a period to have any effect on his stamina, but here he was finding fifteen minutes too much. His body rested on his hands, and sweat trickled from his forehead down his nose and dripped in warm blobs on the wooden floor. His arms were aching. He glanced round to see if anybody else was in like difficulties, but the rest of the class seemed as though they could hold their positions comfortably for another hour at least. His glance caught the eyes of his opposite number, propped up and also perspiring freely, a pace away from him. He was a thin sallow young man of about twenty-five with a tiny imperial, who looked like a foreign student, French or Italian. With his hair disarranged and a crystal of sweat trembling on the tip of his glossy little beard, as Michael looked more closely at him, he recognised that here was another distressed one and an even more ludicrous spectacle.

The bearded young man shook his head and grinned wryly. He dropped with an exhausted grunt on his elbows and rested his chin on his forearms.

'No use,' he said, 'it's getting too tough. I think I'll drop out.'

Michael slumped on his belly. He had been wanting to do that for what seemed an age. Shakily he picked himself up and followed his neighbour to the side of the hall, away from the ranks of the shiny gymnasts. He was glad that he had not been the only one to throw in the towel. They stood on the side-lines together fascinated by the easy rhythmic swing of dozens of shining limbs, then, just before the exercises concluded they made their way to the showers to escape the rush of sticky athletes. They lathered themselves thoroughly under the tepid spray, then washing off the soap beneath a powerful hissing rain of ice-cold water walked to the locker room and dressed. Fully clothed, Michael felt remarkably fit, and so far from being fatigued, extraordinarily energetic. A soothing warmness ran through his blood; he seemed to have had grafted on to him in that brief period a new perception and appreciation of his body. Only his limbs ached a little from the unaccustomed exercising.

'How do you feel now?' he asked his companion.

'Fine!' the other replied. 'And you?'

'First class! I feel as though I could do the exercises all over again without any trouble.'

'So do I,' said the bearded young man enthusiastically. 'Remarkable! Remarkable! I'm really looking forward to Wednesday already.'

They boarded the same bus home. Michael's companion turned out unromantically to be neither French nor Italian, but like himself, an ordinary Jew from Whitechapel. His name was Leon Altman, he worked on a Jewish journal and did some translating from Hebrew and Yiddish in his spare time. He was self-educated. At fourteen he had left school and gone into a tailor's workshop, but he had studied in the evenings and eventually broken into journalism. He told Michael about his ambition one day to get a post on a big national daily. He felt that sometime in the future he would arrive in Fleet Street. All his life he had worked consciously or subconsciously towards that end, and he seemed very confident that somehow he would attain his ambition. Michael listened with interest while his companion in warm, excited language, gesticulating like a deaf-and-dumb linguist, spread his career before him and his hopes for the future. Michael talked sparingly about himself. For one thing, Leon hardly gave him a chance, and for another, there was so little to tell, just the normal gradation by means of scholarships from elementary school to secondary school and thence to university, a common enough process in the East End. Leon, however, had done something different and, so it appeared to Michael, infinitely more difficult. To jump from a workshop to the offices of a highly reputable journal seemed a vastly more commendable feat than his own smooth progression from classroom to laboratory. He encouraged Leon in his recital, and before either of them realised it they were already at the Aldgate terminus. By this time Michael had developed a very real liking for his companion. They got off the bus together, Leon still talking, and Michael felt it would be a pity to break off such an interesting, even if so one-sided, a conversation.

'Why not walk home with me?' he said. 'I would like you to meet my father. You two should get on well together; he's also a bit of an Hebraist.'

Leon fell in immediately with the suggestion. He had very few friends in the neighbourhood, and he felt a strange sort of attraction towards Michael. The chemist lived just a few minutes' walk from his house, yet to his knowledge he had never seen him before in his life. The district resembled a teeming ant heap, and, crowded as it was, only part of an immeasurably vaster colony of scurrying, indistinguishable insects. People could be brought up, live and die in adjacent streets, yet never at any time come into personal contact nor feel any desire for each other's company. He hoped Michael would not disappoint him, and that this encounter would not follow the path of so many of his tentative friendships that had been struck up so promisingly only to wither away stalely in disillusionment.

The little kitchen in St George's was crowded when Michael and Leon arrived. Most of the family were seated about the table with Phineas. Deborah was clearing away cups and plates, and a mound of crockery was piled in the sink waiting to be washed up. It was an unsightly jumble, but Deborah refused to do any more work that evening, and had delegated that task to Rose. Michael introduced the visitor, presenting last of all Deborah with scarcely concealed pride and deference, as though she were the showpiece of the household. None loved her and respected her more than he, for she had been his mother for almost as long as he could remember. When she flared up occasionally in a fit of tantrums, only he and Phineas made allowances for her shrill screams, knowing that she had to let off steam sometimes as a compensation for the unnatural strain of bringing up a large, and partly adult family. He was gratified to note the look of admiration on Leon's face as he introduced his sister. Deborah sent Felix up to the parlour for an extra chair, and the husky giant ran up without a word of protest, like a small boy terrorised by a spell-binding ogress.

Leon dropped in naturally with the trend of conversation. It was as though he had been there many times before and knew each of the Kahns one by one, while they on their part drew him in amongst themselves, a trait that made all their visitors, even complete strangers like Leon, comfortable immediately. A hush fell over the kitchen while Felix began to manipulate the wireless, looking impatiently at his wristwatch. At last the sound of an orchestra tuning up came over. Faces lit up. Felix had tuned in to a foreign music festival. Bruno Walter was about to conduct the Fifth Symphony of Beethoven. Soon the first notes of the symphony came through. The Kahns listened at first in silence, then one by one began to hum until finally they accompanied the third movement in unison. Deborah conducted, her baton a long breadknife, while the rest of the Kahns added their vocal obligati in tonic solfa...

> Me-me-me-me, Me-me-me-me
> Me-me-me-me, Sol-fa-me-ra...

An imperceptible sliding into a higher key, then the phrase repeated:

> Me-me-me-me, Me-me-me-me
> Me-me-me-me, Sol-fa-me-ra
> Me-doh, Me-ray-doh-te...

They were note perfect, a gift fostered by Phineas and developed in them before they could speak properly. It was a novel spectacle, the father and eight children singing Beethoven in chorus, in perfect time and tune, swaying ecstatically with the music. For the first time Leon felt a little out of it. He liked Beethoven, but lacked his hosts' uncanny gift of entering into the heart of the music, and translating the orchestral into vocal notation. He seemed to be missing some exquisite enjoyment. The young man watched Deborah's face and saw her joyous expression heightened and transmogrified by some inner spiritual disturbance. He felt that all these people had stolen a march on him.

After the symphony, Stanley left and Leon entered into a Talmudic discussion with Phineas. He spoke to the old man, but most of the time his eyes followed the bird-like movements of Deborah as she bustled about the room. For some mysterious reason she had decided to do the washing-up after all, and only Michael, intercepting various side-glances, had any inkling of why she had suddenly made up her mind to stay, while Rose thankfully accepted her freedom and vanished. From the Talmud the conversation drifted to the giants of Jewish literature, but not even the delightful drolleries of Shalom Aleichem, that Phineas quoted *ex tempore,* could quite monopolise Leon's attention.

At last it was past midnight and time to go. Never had time seemed to fly so fast for Leon. He made his excuses, and with obvious reluctance left the house, Michael volunteering to accompany him part of the way. The two young men walked for a little way in silence, until eventually Leon spoke.

'If you've no objection,' he said, 'I'd like to visit your house again one day. Your father seems to know all there is about Yiddish literature. That's my hobby. I would very much like to talk to him again.'

'Would you?' said Michael blandly. A dry, humorous grin played about his mouth. 'It isn't by any chance my sister, and not my father you're interested in?' he inquired.

Leon blushed. '... Well...'

'That's all right!' said Michael jovially, still in the same bantering tone. 'You don't have to excuse yourself, you're old enough. Really, she's a very charming girl, but I'm warning you, I'll be sorry for the man she marries. Before he knows what he's about, she'll make him as mad and irresponsible as she is.'

'I haven't said anything yet about marrying,' Leon replied, 'but now you've brought it up I don't think I'd mind taking a chance.'

'Neither would a good many other young men who hang about the house,' said Michael. 'She's got about twelve on a string, but God help the one she takes a fancy to!'

Leon grinned. 'God helps those...'

'Help yourself by all means,' said Michael. 'Only don't say I didn't warn you. The Kahns are a mad lot. They're teachers, doctors, chemists, artists, musicians, and there's even one embryonic all-in wrestler amongst them, my brother Felix. They never keep appointments, have no sense of time or orderliness and are liable to go off the deep end at a moment's notice, or more frequently, without even a moment's notice, and Deborah is the worst of the lot. Now, if you still want to come round, you're welcome.'

'Well, I'm sorry to disappoint you,' said Leon, 'I will.'

CHAPTER VI

Leon became a frequent visitor at St George's, and, strangely enough, every Monday and Wednesday when he returned from the poly with Michael, Deborah was at home too. The lean, dark-bearded young man was very popular with Phineas because of his Hebrew erudition, and evidently found favour in Deborah's eyes as well, although probably for quite a different reason. She sobered down remarkably. No longer did she return from a play, a concert or a ramble at one o'clock in the morning with an escort of half a dozen young men serenading her on the pavement, and she cut down ruthlessly the number of visits from her male friends. Those that insisted on coming to see her, she put to igno-minious tasks, like helping her fry the weekly fish ration, nearly two stone of plaice, or washing up mountains of crockery, and when such ruses were unsuccessful, she was not at home when they called. Soon it became evident that her choice had fallen on Leon, and like a modern conflict between two nations, when war rages without an open declaration on either side, it was tacitly understood that they were engaged.

Their wedding was a hilariously jolly affair. It was celebrated in St George's and attended by the entire Kahn family and Leon's parents and sister, his only relatives in London. Michael drew the bridegroom aside just as the young couple were about to leave for the honeymoon. His face was flushed with excitement.

'I think, Leon,' he said, 'the whole family owes you a vote of thanks for rescuing us from Deborah. At the same time, allow me to offer you my condolences.'

'Thanks,' Leon replied. 'I'll probably need them for the next fortnight in Paris.'

'Well, enjoy yourself,' said Michael. He grew even redder and his voice turned suddenly very serious and trembled a little with emotion. 'Look after her. *Bon voyage*, old man!'

They returned from Paris with a load of gifts and one-andtenpence in cash, all that was left of the fifty pounds they had collected as wedding presents, and settled down in a newly decorated flat near St George's. Deborah had decided to live there so that she could still keep a maternal eye on her old home. She proved to be an expert housekeeper and a remarkably good cook. Occasionally, she set before Leon a meal sufficient for six, and poured into his soup enough salt for ten, and sometimes also there descended on his one head a tornado of shrieks that previously had been shared amongst a whole family, a hangover from her previous mental state. Leon, however, discounted the value of her tantrums, and as the attacks passed off as speedily as they overcame her, the young couple managed to live together without any serious quarrels. He realised her value, and knowing his own shortcomings understood how fortunate he was in having her to share his life. She had gained her cooking experience on other stomachs, and budgeting for ten had made her exceptionally keen in buying for two, while added to that was a high degree of intelligence and her elder sister's looks plus a better-moulded, more feminine figure, which delighted Leon, who had all the normal man's admiration for soft, delightfully rounded curves.

Rose took over the reins of government at St George's. A bronze medallist of the Royal Academy, she still practised on the piano for several hours daily although she no longer desired to take up music as a career. Phineas had intended to employ a housekeeper, but Rose, feeling that she was only competent at the piano, and had never been in any danger of developing into a virtuoso, decided that staying at home was the more interesting occupation. Things were fairly easy for her. A char came in several times a week and the boys had had all the rebellion knocked out of them by years of Deborah's vociferous agitation. She was also free during the afternoon and almost every evening, and never did any cooking on Saturday or Sunday, another direct benefit of her elder sister's propaganda.

One evening, a friend of Rose's came to visit her for the first time. She was a shorthand typist employed by a City firm, and had become acquainted with Rose during her schooldays in the reference library where they had done their homework together in the evenings. Bertha, shining like the sparkle of an exquisite jewel, entered the drab kitchen. Rose herself was very attractive, but her fresh prettiness paled before the dazzling beauty of her friend. Bertha was about nineteen, of medium height and slim build, dressed in a neat businesslike navy-blue silk frock, well worn, but scrupulously clean. Her long, lustrous black hair was gathered in a tight knot on the nape of her shapely neck, a glowing background for the perfect oval of her face. Her skin was pale as alabaster, her nose delicately aquiline and her full red lips soft and sensuous, but her large black eyes were the most striking feature of that over-whelmingly beautiful face. She seemed unconscious of the stir her beauty caused wherever she went, and although as a child she had been drawn several times by a well-known etcher, and her portrait hung in the Royal Academy, she remained as natural and unaffected as she had been when, as a young girl, a talented Chelsea artist strolling aimlessly down the East End had discovered her playing in the gutter, and captivated by her beauty had followed her home and persuaded a reluctant mother to allow the child to sit for him.

She had come to arrange a game of tennis with Rose. Phineas greeted her warmly. She smiled at him, and as the lambent flame of those dark eyes burned before him like two vast flickering wells of oil, a sudden faintness came over him. For a moment her features wavered before him, he closed his eyes and when he opened them again the beautiful face still smiled at him, the red lips parted as though to ask a question. He apologised for his behaviour. Something had come over him but it had passed, and what it was he could not explain. He was himself once more, polite and charming as ever.

The street door slammed. With a cheerful whistle Michael entered. He threw his hat on the ledge and his newspaper on a chair, and then he saw Bertha. He stood stock still, staring at her. She looked up at him, her lips parted again showing her dazzling white teeth. He turned red and was about to say something, but Rose, sensing that he would blurt out some incomprehensible farrago of nonsense, stepped in.

'This is Bertha, a friend of mine,' she said. 'We used to do our homework together. My brother Michael.'

'Pleased to meet you,' said Michael.

Bertha smiled and withdrew her eyes. Michael walked to the

sink and started to wash. He felt as though he were burning, the cold water ran over his hands but he did not feel its soothing caress; he seemed to be on fire. He wiped his hands mechanically and sat at the table.

'Make me a cup of tea, please,' he said.

He noticed that his voice shook a little and that he was trembling. He tried not to look at Bertha but his eyes covertly stole in her direction. She was surely an apparition, something unreal conjured up by a grinning sorcerer. But she *was* real. She was smiling and talking although his blurred senses could not gather what she was saying. Across his mind swept the glorious revealing lines of Shakespeare's star-crossed lovers:

> O, she doth teach the torches to burn bright!
> Her beauty hangs upon the cheek of night
> Like a rich jewel in an Ethiop's ear:
> Beauty too rich for use, for earth too dear!
> So shows a snowy dove trooping with crows,
> As yonder lady o'er her fellows shows.

After a while he recovered himself sufficiently to join in the conversation. All his remarks were addressed to his father or his sister, but somehow he felt that Bertha understood that he was talking to her alone. When she left, her tennis engagement with Rose had become a mixed foursome, Michael promising to bring along a friend to partner his sister.

Bertha played tennis extremely well. Her graceful figure flitted about the court with the easy-footed sureness of a trained athlete, and aided by Michael, who hovered constantly near the net, they succeeded in trouncing their opponents. They came back to St George's for tea, having enjoyed themselves so much that the game became the prelude to a series of bi-weekly visits that continued while the fine weather lasted.

Michael became more and more deeply enamoured of Bertha. She coloured his whole world, and soon he was meeting her practically every night. He cut down his visits to the poly to one a week, and even that seemed too much when it deprived him of the warm, intoxicating glow of Bertha's company. Dressing himself in the locker room, he appeared wrapped in thought. Leon regarded him curiously, having noted the change that had come over him in the past few weeks. From Deborah he understood that Michael was sweet on a girl, but he saw no reason why such an ordinary phenomenon should change a highly intelligent young man into a mooning Trappist, with a fixed, semi-imbecile grin.

'Snap out of it, Michael,' he said.

'Eh?' said Michael.

'Pull yourself together, old chap. She's not the only girl in the world, and you're not the only man.'

Michael shook his head. 'I won't be coming to gym on Wednesday,' he replied irrelevantly.

Leon burst into a loud guffaw. 'I've seen some chaps in love,' he said, 'but when you get these fits, you take the cake! You're absolutely hopeless. You don't seem to understand now when people talk to you. What is she, this charmer of yours, a combination of Helen of Troy, Venus and Mona Lisa?'

Michael smiled sheepishly. 'It's true,' he admitted, 'I am in love. But you should see her, Leon. She has the whitest skin, the darkest eyes and is the most good-natured person I have ever met in my life. I can't explain her to you; I'm not a poet, I haven't the words, but Shakespeare must have known someone like her, with that miracle of a complexion, when he wrote:

> "... She never told her love
> But let concealment, like a worm i' the bud,
> Feed on her damask cheek..."

Damask! That's the word to describe her skin, and it fits hers like a glove!'

'You've got it bad!' replied Leon cynically. 'But you're not very apposite in your choice of illustrations. You're not suggesting that your love like Viola in the context "sits like patience on a monument", because you're sitting here like a castrated chorus boy, are you? Or that she "mopes with a green and yellow melancholy"? Personally, I should imagine that her damask cheeks are more the result of a physiological rather than a psychological disorder. The odds are, you'll find out yourself when you know her more intimately, that her poetic pallor is most probably due to constipation.'

Michael flushed as though he had been slapped in the face. His eyes glinted dangerously and he braced himself as though about to strike his friend, but calmed down and tried ineffectually to smile. Leon's words had seemed at first like blasphemy, but he understood now, in colder blood, that his brother-in-law was merely trying to jolt him from his bemused preoccupation. Leon had succeeded, but his words left a nasty taint in the air that could not be easily dispelled, although, thinking it over, he could see that he had been badly in need of Leon's crude corrective.

Leon himself seemed a little taken aback by Michael's crest-fallen air. The disease had caught on pretty seriously for such flippancy to affect him so severely. After all, he, Leon, had been in love himself, was still in love, but so far as he could remember had never ceased at any time to behave like a normal, rational individual. The sensitive equilibrium of Michael's mental poise had been disturbed; this infatuation might only be temporary, but even so, Leon felt that it was his duty as a relative and a friend to help to balance the tilted scales. He suggested that they walk as far as the Bank, and Michael readily agreed. Leon got him to talk about Bertha, and the chemist was surprised at the sympathetic reception accorded his recital. He had been afraid to unburden himself at first lest Leon should scoff, but the journalist encouraged him to speak, his cursory remarks skilfully directing Michael's thoughts into the most revealing channels.

At the end of the monologue, Leon began gently to administer his anti-toxin. Delicately he tried to implant the seeds of a rational outlook in his friend. Michael was placing Bertha on a too ludicrously high pedestal, a perch far too precarious for any mortal to maintain with any degree of safety. He had got to realise that in spite of her beauty and charm she was a normal young woman of flesh and blood, and not a confection of fruits and spice and all things nice. There was a danger too that if he invested her with solely a spiritual glamour the fleshy reality would be too grave a disillusionment. He was sure that Bertha, although he had never met her, had no desire to be regarded in that light, and that Michael on his part would not want to make the mistake with her that Swift had made with his Celia and fret his soul because her bowels functioned regularly.

The West End and City streets flowed under the bridge of their words like a swiftly moving river. The night was mild and the luminous star-sprinkled sky a rich, dark blue. They reached the Bank without experiencing the slightest fatigue; a clean, fresh gust of invigoration blew through them, generated by the mental tonic of their conversation. The night air smelled too good to be confined beneath the roof of a bus, so they decided to walk the rest of the distance. The glowing sky and the shimmering stars seemed to induce confidences, seemed after a while as they walked in silence to turn their thoughts in on themselves.

'Strange,' said Leon, 'how life catches us up and swings us along with it. We can't directly mould life, we can only mould ourselves and be prepared for what is to happen. What then happens to us is not fortuitous, since we have prepared for it, consciously or unconsciously. Thus life moulds us, we react according to our circumstances and environment, and in our turn we react on life. Four years ago I was a tailor. Four years ago I had no idea I would be wearing a beard and working on a journal – if only a small Jewish one – but really, the metamorphosis was not so strange, since subconsciously I had been preparing all my life for that moment, and when the chance came I took it. Four years ago you were little more than a schoolboy, now you are a qualified chemist and in love with a beautiful woman. We carry within us the seeds of our own future development or decay. Who can say where the next four years will bring us? What will happen to me? What will be happening to you...?'

Michael paced beside him in silence. His small head was turned towards the stars. The image of Bertha flashed again across his mind and he smiled. His future was bound up with hers just as surely as those planets were bound to the sky. His eyes rested on a bright star on the edge of the heavens. It seemed to grow more luminous, then all of a sudden it shot below the rooftops carrying with it a tail of white light. He shuddered involuntarily, and when he spoke at last, his voice seemed tinny and unreal.

'I wouldn't like to think,' he replied slowly. 'I don't want to know... The present is good enough for me.'

CHAPTER VII

Michael flung himself into his work with redoubled zest and enthusiasm. He felt that he was only living half a life. As soon as he earned more money he would marry Bertha and move out of the district, away from St George's, away from the East End, to some quiet suburb where in the evenings they could be together, just the two of them, living solely for themselves. Again the taut emaciated mask disfigured his face, and irritableness crept over him once more. He came home from work in the evening and nibbled at his food, silent. When he spoke, he was sarcastic. Phineas watched him anxiously, growing more and more perturbed at these now familiar symptoms. He sensed that somehow, soon, Michael would erupt, but what form the explosion would take he could not yet fathom.

For the past few days Michael had been trying to get closer to his father. Phineas could see that something was on his mind and tried diplomatically, whenever his son approached him, to give him an opening to relieve his mental strain. At last, Michael broke the ice. He waited one night until they were alone together in the kitchen, and rapped distractedly on the table before he could begin to talk.

'Dad,' he said, 'I want to ask your advice.'

Phineas put down his book. 'Ask away,' he replied. 'I only hope I shall be able to help you.'

'... I – I'm going to get married,' said Michael abruptly.

Phineas removed his glasses and slowly polished them, breathing on the lenses with irritating deliberation.

'... Well?' said Michael.

Phineas shrugged his shoulders. 'I don't know what to say,' he replied. 'You said you wanted advice. Good. I am prepared to give it you. Then you say you are getting married. Very well, but you are telling me, not asking me. When do you intend to get married? This year, next year, or perhaps you are already married?'

'Of course I'm not,' said Michael. 'You know that. But I'm going to get married as soon as possible.'

'Why? What's the hurry?'

Michael rose to his feet and paced about the room. He felt hemmed in here, suffocated, but how could he explain all that without hurting his father? He felt that every moment he lived at home was robbing him, and Bertha no less, of their heritage of full life. His own plight was of secondary importance, primarily he thought only of her. Her parents were poor, desperately so, having to support a family of five, and most of her earnings went towards the upkeep of the house. She had to be at work by eight-thirty in the morning, and often walked to and from the City to save the fare. For lunch she had the usual synthetic meal of the underpaid typist, thin, genteel sandwiches and coffee. That was no life for a girl like Bertha. She deserved the best the world could give. He felt that if people really understood what she was they would carry her about on their hands and tend her like a living goddess. But if nobody else appreciated her, he would. He would take her out of the musty office and the slum, and so long as he could provide for her she should be surrounded with love and beauty and tenderness. Couldn't his father see that? That it was absolutely necessary for him to do it? Was he blind, too, like the rest of the world? And he asked what was the hurry! He wanted to know why! The question goaded Michael into a fury, all his distaste for his surroundings welled up in a furious froth of words.

'Why? I'll tell you why!' he blurted. 'Because I'm fed up with this dump! In the summer it's lousy with vermin, and in the winter we have to have buckets in the bedrooms to catch the rain. I don't see why *I* have to live like that. I'm earning a decent wage. I want a room of my own, clean surroundings, decent furniture and a bath that I can use every day if I choose. Those are the things I want and those are the things I'll get when I'm married. Now do you know why?'

'Sit down,' said Phineas soothingly.

Michael glanced at him quickly, but Phineas did not appear to be at all angry. He himself felt a little shaky, he had never spoken to Phineas this way before. He sat down opposite his father, his sensitive nostrils quivering with agitation. Phineas seemed strangely calm, but if Michael imagined that the old man had been deceived by his vehement denunciation he was mistaken.

'Now suppose we talk this over quietly,' said Phineas. 'As man to man. For twenty-odd years you have been living this way; in fact, St George's is a paradise compared to what you have known, but in the last few months you have developed a violent distaste towards the house. Now it's not the house that's at fault, although God knows it's bad enough, it's simply that you want to break away and live your own life. You want to get married.'

'What's wrong with that?' interjected Michael. 'I'm old enough. How old were you when you married mother?'

'Not much younger than you are,' said Phineas. 'But that's not the point. There are other objections in your case. When I got married I was a husky soldier. I could eat two pounds of bread and a pound of meat at a meal and still be hungry. I had no ailments and my nerves were steady as a rock, while you...' He hesitated and his face clouded. What he had to say now was painful but it was being forced out. 'Well, to be truthful, I don't think you're in a fit condition.'

Michael's head reared like an angry charger. 'Not fit? What do you mean?'

'I don't think you're strong enough,' said Phineas.

Michael laughed derisively. 'Strong! I'm strong as a bullock!' he replied.

'You may imagine so,' said Phineas. 'But you are my son, I know you better. Your love for Bertha is eating you up, consuming your vitality. If it is having this effect on you now, what will it be like when you are married? Don't think I can't appreciate the fact that a man of your age feels the need for a woman. I am a broad-minded person, London is full of women, but you don't have to marry them all. I know how hard it is to want a woman and to be without one. When your mother died I was still young, in the prime of life, but I have never touched another woman all those years – and I am still alive. So it *can* be done. Somehow you should be able to adjust yourself – how, is your own problem, and you'll have to find your own solution, but my advice to you is to wait a couple of years, build up and conserve your strength. Bertha won't run away if she really loves you, then, when your position is a little more secure, get married.'

Michael was silent for a while. His father did not seem to understand the true urgency of the problem. Women did not worry him at all, he was interested only in one woman, and even in that woman not in the fashion that Phineas imagined. Bertha was not going to be broken on the rack of slum existence for a moment longer than he could help. She loved poetry, and under his guidance was learning to appreciate the best in literature and good music. He refused to allow much longer the sap to be sucked from her by the vampire of economic thraldom, and the flowering of that rare soul to be vitiated by nagging poverty. He knew that he was selfish in desiring only for her a means of escape from the shackles that fastened relentlessly round most of his friends and acquaintances, and even his own family, but he had made up his mind to rescue her, and he would allow nothing to stand in his way.

'I'm sorry, Father,' he said. 'I can't wait. As soon as I see my way clear, we'll be married.' He stretched his hand across the table and placed his warm palm over his father's fist. 'Don't be angry, Dad,' he said appealingly.

'I'm not angry,' Phineas replied. A heavy weariness descended upon him. He had tried his utmost and had failed. All he could do now was to acknowledge defeat gracefully. 'I wish you luck, my son,' he said, 'with all my heart. Get married if you've decided on it. If you'll invite me to the wedding, I'll go; if not, I'll stay at home. But remember, I wish you all the good fortune in the world!'

CHAPTER VIII

The advertisement in a paint-trade journal of a small firm special-ising in the manufacture of cellulose lacquers caught Michael's eye. They were applying for a chemist with practical experience. It seemed just the right job for him, precisely the opening he was looking for. The year of probation at his first job had just ended and his progress had been satisfactory, but he had not yet signed the new agreement for the renewal of his employment. He wrote for an interview and was engaged on a six-monthly contract, at a salary nearly two pounds a week higher than his previous employers had offered. His new situation was advantageous too, in that the works were in the heart of London and he would no longer have to face the fatiguing morning and evening journeys.

He began to prepare for his wedding. He bought a new outfit for himself and Bertha, and gave thirty pounds to the son of a neighbour, a cabinet-maker with whom, as a boy, he had been friendly at the elementary school, to buy the specially dried wood for his furniture. The cabinet-maker had begged Michael to give him the job. He was working short time and could make the furniture at home, in the afternoons and evenings. The specimens of his work were evidences of his expert craftsmanship, and the price quoted a good deal below the terms that could have been obtained elsewhere. Even then, Michael would not have bothered, had he not decided that the cabinet-maker was more in need of the money than an established firm, and moreover there was the sentimental bond of a schoolboy friendship.

Preparations for his marriage and his home were well advanced when, a month before the termination of his contract, he was informed that it would not be renewed. It was a shock, but he was not unduly despondent, feeling sure that he would quickly obtain another post. His wedding plans continued unaltered until there came a fresh bombshell; his friend the cabinet-maker disappeared, and with him, Michael's thirty pounds. The chemist was urged to put the police on his trail, and in his first burst of anger was almost inclined to do so, but after an interview with the boy's tearful mother whose intense poverty was only too apparent, he calmed down and took his loss resignedly. After all, worse things could happen. 'I suppose he must have needed the money badly to do a thing like that to *me*,' he said.

Weeks of unemployment followed. He wrote sheaves of applications and had interview after interview, but the jobs that previously had appeared so plentiful now suddenly vanished from existence. Reluctantly he postponed his wedding, but each obstacle that arose only kindled in him a fiercer determination to get married at the first opportunity.

Weeks passed into months, but Michael still remained jobless. He grew thinner and his harsh, dry cough grew more and more in evidence. Phineas begged him to go to a doctor, but Michael was unapproachable, he flared up violently at any such suggestion and became so touchy that he misconstrued the least well-meaning gesture as a scarcely veiled insult. It hurt him terribly to walk idly about the streets and remain a charity guest at home, although all the family treated him with the greatest consideration and tried their very best to make things pleasant for him. One evening when he was seated morosely at home, Stanley dropped in, ostensibly to visit his father. He knew how things were with Michael and privately had talked the situation over with Phineas. They were both afraid that the chemist in his desperation might do something foolish, although Phineas was quite prepared to support him for as long as he remained unemployed, and Stanley begged repeatedly to be allowed to advance the money to send him away to the country for a couple of months to regain his health and drive the morbid nervousness from his system. It would have been useless, however, to broach the subject of a holiday with Michael, since every mouthful he ate he regarded as placing him under a deeper and almost unbearable obligation.

Stanley was always sprucely attired. His red face was rugged with masculine strength, his whole appearance breathing confidence and success. He looked the high-pressure salesman he was, the very antithesis to the pallid Michael. He could sell anything, he boasted, but as he looked at the weedy dispirited looseness of his brother's body, elongated like a listless tapeworm, he had the uneasy feeling that here was a Lazarus that none of his vital breath could resurrect, that here was a subject too cynical to respond to any of his naive blandishments. However, he had come here for a set purpose. He tried to be jovial; his technique rarely failed.

'How're you keeping, Michael?' he inquired cheerfully.

'So, so,' said Michael. 'As well as can be expected.'

'Cheer up! There's no need to worry. So long as you're alive and kicking, you can always get a job.'

Michael essayed a faint smile. 'I hope so,' he said wearily.

'And even if you don't go back to paint, there are other things you can do.'

Michael looked up. His brother became painfully aware of the drawn haggard lines of his face and the grotesque exaggeration of his prominent ears.

'Such as?'

'Well…' said Stanley. 'There's my business, for example. I need someone to help me.'

'Oh?'

Michael's voice was curiously hushed, but Stanley plunged in blindly with his proposal; he had somehow to get it off his chest.

'It's not hard work,' he said. 'I'd give you three pounds a week – and – and…' He broke off abruptly, noticing the effect his words were having on Michael, whose face was reddening with suppressed indignation, his nostrils twitching like an excited greyhound. 'And – and of course, it would only be temporary,' he added hurriedly, 'until you get another job.'

Michael rose to his feet, his face flaming. 'Is that why I won scholarships?' he snapped. 'Is that why I studied nights and fought my way through college and university, to learn how to sell dress-lengths to stout old ladies? No!' He drew himself up proudly. 'I am a chemist, even if I am unemployed at the moment. Thank you very much for your offer, Stanley, but I don't have to accept while I still have a few pounds left.'

He snatched his hat from the ledge and walked out of the kitchen without another word. Stanley looked at his father with a crest-fallen air. He felt that his tactlessness was somehow to blame, but

Phineas shook his head and gestured with a despairing sweep of his hands. Stanley had done his best. God alone knew where this pride and obstinacy would lead his son.

The next morning, Michael dressed himself in his smartest suit and went out early. He told nobody where he was going, merely saying that he would be back in time for dinner. At midnight he had not returned. Phineas sat with a grey face in the kitchen. Soon the boys came in and they waited up with him. Knowing Michael's state of mind, they were worried by his inexplicable absence, hardly daring to speculate on what might have happened to him. At last, at half-past twelve, they heard the welcome sound of his key turning in the lock. An oppressive load seemed to drop from them as they heard a cheerful whistle approach the kitchen door. He was whistling! A sign that he was pleased about something. Whistling, when Phineas had almost become inured to the prospect of never hearing him whistle again.

Michael burst into the kitchen and cheerily flung his hat in the air. In his excitement it did not seem strange that they were all up and dressed at this hour of the morning. Intoxicated by the glow of high spirits it did not even occur to him that they had all been anxiously awaiting his arrival.

'I've got it!' he shouted joyously. 'I've got the job!'

Immediately they overwhelmed him with congratulations. He had read of a job going in Slatford, a small seaside town eighty miles from London, near Blatchley. For once he decided not to write for an interview, but to chance a direct, personal application. He had been fortunate enough to see the proprietor, and producing his testimonials, all couched in the highest terms of praise, had pressed his claims with the urgency of desperation. He was only waiting now for postal confirmation of the verbal agreement. As soon as the contract arrived, he would start for Slatford, and work. Work! Blessed word. Blessed state. Green oasis of hope in a desert of parched dreams.

At the end of the week the contract came, and Michael decided to place all his eggs in one basket. He felt that for him it was now or never. He ran around making arrangements for his wedding, and on the hire-purchase system bought new furniture. He moved temporarily into lodgings in Slatford, and Bertha came down for the weekend to help him hunt for a house. At the end of the second day they found a small, newly built five-roomed house to let near the seafront that seemed to fulfil their requirements. Michael immediately christened it 'Sheba' after Bertha's Hebrew name, 'Sheba Brucha', seventh blessing, and the girl went back to London to arrange the last details of the wedding. Several weeks later, Michael came to town on Sunday morning, and in the evening returned to Slatford with his bride.

The small town was asleep when the young couple descended from the last London train and left the station to walk to their new home. An immense stillness seemed to surround them. Michael dropped the bags he was carrying and handed a small electric torch to his wife. The road was still unmade, only rudimentary pavements skirting the detached houses as a sort of concession to good taste, the roadway itself a squelchy bog of mud and hard stones, the only light occasional glimmers from the far-flung houses. This was a short cut, he explained. She had never seen this part of the town at night, by day it had seemed quite pretty, now it was inhospitable, even hostile, and cold and dark, swept by sharp winds from an angry sea. To Bertha, born and brought up in a London slum, this quietness, the sense of vastness and the chilly wind sweeping from the coast, all seemed immeasurably exaggerated. She had been one of a fairly large family, always she had lived with people around her, at home and in the streets. Lights never seemed to go out in the East End, life never seemed to stop. Here one could commit murder, or scream oneself blue in the face only to an accompaniment of shrilly cawing seagulls. And supposing there was an accident? Supposing someone were ill? She clasped Michael's arm tightly and, projecting a thin beam of light before her, they made their way gingerly across the embryonic pavement to 'Sheba', the last of those distant spaced houses, the house of the seventh blessing.

The interior of the house was spotlessly clean. Michael had prepared for her coming, but the rooms still had an aloof air; they had not yet been broken in to people, had not yet drawn from a succession of previous inhabitants a domestic atmosphere. The gas and electric light had been laid on in her absence, and there was some food in the larder, but Bertha was not hungry; she wanted to go straight to bed. They unpacked their intimate belongings in the hall and walked upstairs. Michael undressed first and stretched himself full length in the bed. His own bed, his own house – it was a wonderful feeling – and opposite him, brushing her long black hair by the window was Bertha, his own wife, like the Lorelei looking over the Rhine, combing her shining tresses. How Leon would laugh if he ever mentioned this to him! The little beard would shake like those funny automatically nodding dolls in the Christmas shop windows. 'Extremely appropriate,' Michael could hear him saying. 'Die schönste Jungfrau reverses the process by henna-ing her peroxide aureole, and having caught her sailor, scours the water for fresh customers. Michael! Michael! Haven't I always warned you of the dangers of aping a classical education? Shakespeare and Goethe are first-class mental pabula, but a chemist should always be chary of mixing them in his private life... Michael! Michael!'

It was not an echo of his thoughts, Bertha was calling him from the window. He sat up.

'Are you calling me, dear?' he said.

She nodded, automatically twisting upwards the ends of her hair with the brush. There was such a world of blackness outside, she wanted to cry, as though the darkness were pressing in on her, trying to overwhelm her. Courageously she forced back her tears.

'What is it?' he asked.

'I... I'm a little frightened, Michael,' she said.

'Nonsense, dear! There's nothing to be frightened about,' he answered.

He threw the bedclothes back and walked over to her. Soothingly he placed one arm around her waist and pressed his lips in the perfumed softness of her hair. Outside it was so dark, only a solitary star gleamed far overhead; no wonder she felt strange, but it was nothing, it would pass, in a day or two she would be laughing at herself and, like him, looking confidently towards the future. Caressing her gently he led her to the bed. Under the counterpane they both lay silently, taut, listening, but nothing disturbed the stillness except the distant low grumbling of the sea. She began to cry softly. He put his arms around her and gradually, worn out by the strain of the day, her tears ceased and the regular breathing of sleep lifted her bosom in a gentle swell. Only then did he disengage his arms, and lying on his side to face her, gently stroked her hair with the tips of his fingers. He looked at her till his eyelids drooped and his eyes began to smart, then with a sigh of contentment he dropped off into a dreamless sleep.

CHAPTER IX

For several weeks their life passed tranquilly, and wrapped in each other they were ideally happy. Michael left for work at half-past eight in the morning and returned at half-past six. They walked along the deserted seafront every night, and Michael's face acquired a reddish tan, but his cough still troubled him, especially in the early hours of the morning. Bertha had very little to do in the house; so little, in fact, that her enforced idleness during the day began to pall on her after a while. She had no friends in the town, and no desire to cultivate the acquaintance of her nearest neighbours, middle-aged people with grown-up families. Perhaps in the summer, when visitors began to arrive, things would be livelier, but now in the early autumn everything seemed to be dead. There were two libraries in town, one municipally owned, the other a private concern, but both were equally bad in the uninspired mediocrity of their choice of books. A repertory company visited Slatford every year, but their season had just finished and the town hall was given over to weekly revivals of trashy Edwardian musical comedies.

Michael too began to feel lonely at times. The wireless set was always working, but he grew tired of tinned music, and longed for the cheery intimacy of a concert hall. That was one good point about London; wherever you lived, you could always go to the West End when you felt like it and hear a symphony orchestra, or go to a decent play, and even if you wanted to stay at home the libraries offered a vast selection of the latest literature. He even began to miss his family and his few friends, although he hesitated to admit as much to Bertha. Above all he began to miss Jews. He had imagined that he was thoroughly anglicised, but only now that he was separated from them did he realise how strong a hold his people had on him. He had never been religious, had rarely attended the synagogue, but his early environment had so seeped into his subconsciousness that he longed for the sight of a swarthy hook-nosed face, and the loud unabashed sound of a fruity Jewish voice.

A visit to Blatchley, to attend the complaint of a customer, brought his Jewishness more closely home to him. His features were not conspicuously Hebraic, but as he passed the local synagogue the beadle, a tiny dark man with a grizzled black beard, recognised him immediately as a co-religionist and pulled him up.

'Shalom aleichem,' he said. 'Peace be with you, my friend. You are a Jew?'

Michael nodded and returned the greeting, his face unaccountably flushed with pleasure.

'We are one man short for the minyan,' said the beadle. 'Will you come inside for morning prayers?'

'I – I'm sorry,' Michael replied, 'but I have a business appointment.'

The beadle gathered him in with a proprietary gesture, as though his answer had been in the affirmative.

'Business can wait for a few minutes,' he said, shepherding him into the synagogue. 'God comes first.'

Michael was in no particular hurry, so he went inside. The service was familiar, and although he did not understand one word of the sonorous Hebrew, the liturgy made him feel at peace with himself and contented. He had never envisaged a time during adult life when he would enter a synagogue and like it; previously he had only attended once a year, and then only under compulsion from Phineas, who liked on the day of the Black Fast to have all his sons around him. When he left the synagogue the effect of the heady drug of religion vanished, but he was not sorry that the beadle had intimidated him into entering; it had been a tonic to him to see nine other Jews gathered together in one place, if only for the worship of their own particular God.

Returning from his appointment, he passed a little Hebrew general store. Packages of matzos, unleavened cakes, were displayed in the window, and when he entered to purchase some delicacies as a surprise for Bertha, he discovered that the feast of Passover was only a week distant. Again a fit of nostalgia overwhelmed him, only it was not a vague sort of longing, but this time sharply particularised. One week to Passover, the first Passover he had not spent at home. He could see the table with its snowy festival cloth laden with food, the shiny silver candlesticks and the goblets of sparkling red wine. Phineas at the head, smiling on his children gathered round in force together with relatives by marriage, even the door left open for any homeless Jew to enter and take his place at the table. The ancient ritual followed exactly as prescribed, the Hebrew set to old folk tunes, and the long, rhymed parable chanted near the conclusion, 'Chad Gadyoh', with all the family shouting at the top of their voices:

> One kid, One kid...
> Which my father bought for two zuzim;
> One kid, One kid
> And there came a cat, and devoured the kid
> Which my father bought for two zuzim;
> One kid, One kid...
> And the Holy One, blessed be he
> Killed the angel of death
> That killed the slaughterer
> Who slaughtered the ox
> Which drank the water that extinguished the fire
> Which burned the stick that beat the dog
> Which bit the cat that devoured the kid
> Which my father bought for two zuzim;
> One kid, One kid...

He came back to Slatford in the evening with several mysterious packages under his arm. Bertha looked at him with astonishment as he carefully sorted out the parcels.

'What on earth have you got there?' she said.

'Matzos!' he replied triumphantly. 'Matzos, and wine and bitter herbs. The feast of Passover begins on Tuesday. We're going to celebrate!'

The following Tuesday Bertha was busy until the evening. She had prepared an enormous meal like her mother used to do at home, sliced the horseradish tops, bitter as the cruel days in bondage, and mixed the confection of nuts, apples and wine, another reminder of the days when the Jews had toiled for Pharaoh in Egypt making bricks from lime, straw and mortar. When Michael came home from work, the table was tastefully laid and three tall candles burned brightly in silver candlesticks, a wedding present from Phineas, on the mantelpiece. Michael washed himself, shaved carefully and put on his best suit and a black satin skullcap he had picked up in Blatchley. It had not been easy for him to decide on the skullcap; the cynical grin of Leon was ever present in his mind when he handled it, but he dismissed the picture of his brother-in-law, whose mordant wit would have run riot at the spectacle of the scoffing prodigal's return to the fold. He clapped the skullcap more firmly on his head; might as well look the part too, he thought defiantly.

He sat down opposite Bertha, both of them reclining against large cushions according to the custom to show that they were free from bondage and could eat at leisure. Michael made the prayer over the glass of wine; the feast of Passover had begun. There seemed to him something apposite about the whole cere- mony, about the unleavened cakes and the symbolism of the bitter herbs. But were they really free? Were they really out of Egypt? Wasn't that a metaphor too? What was Egypt, and where was Egypt?

They drank the sanctified wine, leaning to the left side as they did so, according to the Law. Then they washed their hands. After the ceremonial ablution Michael dipped a sprig of parsley in salt water and handed a piece to Bertha. Then, having eaten the parsley, Michael broke the first unleavened cake and filled the wine glass for the second time.

'Now,' said Michael, 'the youngest son should put four conun- drums to the master of the house, but as we haven't any youngest son, and aren't likely to have any this side of Jerusalem, you'll have to undertake the catechism.'

He passed the prayer book across the table and Bertha read from it in English:

Wherefore is this night distinguished from all other nights? Any other night we may eat either leavened or unleavened bread, but on this night, only unleavened bread; any other night we may eat any species of herbs, but this night only bitter herbs; any other night we do not dip even once, but on this night twice; on all other nights we eat and drink either sitting or leaning, but on this night, why do we all lean?

She handed back the book and Michael responded:

Because we were slaves unto Pharaoh in Egypt, and the eternal God brought us forth from thence with a mighty hand and an outstretched arm; and if the Most Holy had not delivered our ancestors from Egypt, we, and our children, and our children's children had still continued in bondage to the Pharaohs. Therefore it is incumbent upon us to discourse of the departure from Egypt, and all who do so are to be praised.

They went right through the service before they began to eat, relishing every detail of the annually repeated story, and finished up with a banging of knives and forks, hilariously forgetting themselves in a lusty rendering of 'Chad Gad-yoh-oh-oh-oh, Chad Gadyoh'. Then they filled themselves with so much food that reclining was no longer optional, but a necessity for them if they were to digest the meal in comfort, and they drank so much wine that they staggered to bed at last, giggling foolishly, both of them slightly tipsy, but radiantly happy, feeling that even if they woke up with headaches in the morning, the celebration of this strange Passover would have been well worth while.

Several weeks later, a letter came from Leon announcing that he would visit them at the following weekend. He had just completed a Hebrew translation and wanted to revise the proofs in Slatford, away from the hurly-burly of the East End. They wrote back that they would be glad to have him. They had often written to him and Deborah begging them to come down for a few days, but somehow they had never found the time, or the weather had been too uninviting for the seaside. Deborah had recently given birth to her first child, so naturally a visit from her was out of the question at the moment.

Leon came down by the late train on Friday night. Michael met him at the station, and in spite of Leon's protests took charge of his portable typewriter. They set off at a brisk walk until they reached the gloomy, still uncompleted road that led to Michael's house. Michael slackened his gait and Leon followed half a pace behind, his hesitating footsteps guided by the light from Michael's torch.

'Well, how d'you like it here?' he said.

'Not too bad, really,' Michael replied. 'We're very comfortable and I've got a good job. The only drawback is the social life, or rather, the lack of it.'

'None of the chosen people knocking about?'

'Not so far as I know,' said Michael. 'There are a few retired majors and colonels, and an ex-director of the Bank of England, but none of those seems to be an Israelite. There is one Jewish-looking gentleman floating around, but he happens to be a high church dignitary, so we can count him out too, though in Germany I doubt whether he would be able to slip through the Aryan paragraph.'

'So!' said Leon. 'No more Jews. Then for once I am a person of importance, a worker of miracles. I come to Slatford and overnight the Jewish population rises by fifty per cent!'

They reached 'Sheba' without any mishaps, the uppers of their shoes plastered with mud from the potholes in the glorified cart track that was still boggy underfoot from the recent rains. Bertha was waiting up for them and had a hot supper ready. She had grown a little stouter, her white skin had a faint tan, and the slightest touch of red coloured her cheeks. After supper they all went to bed, Michael appearing so tired that his eyes closed, and his head seemed to nod several times as they climbed the stairs.

Leon found it difficult to sleep. He was covered by two thick blankets, yet he felt cold. His mind was as alert as though the day were just beginning; either it was the invigorating seaside air, or the strangeness of a new bed. He got up and put his overcoat on top of the blankets. He felt a little warmer after a while, and gradually he dozed off. He was a heavy sleeper, but he found himself wide awake on several occasions, disturbed by a peculiar noise like the loud, hoarse rasping of an angry frog. He listened intently, the noise always dying away before he had full control of his faculties, but on the third occasion he discovered that it was a harsh, dry cough, and came from the direction of Michael's bedroom. Profoundly uneasy, he dropped off to sleep again. Something was very wrong with Michael's health. He determined to seek an early opportunity to bring up the matter with his friend.

The opportunity arose sooner than he anticipated. Leon had come down early, intending to start work immediately after breakfast. Bertha was brewing some coffee, but there was no sign of Michael.

'Isn't Michael up yet?' Leon inquired.

Bertha nodded. 'He's *up*, but it always takes some time before he's ready to come down.'

A fit of coughing echoed through the house. Leon looked at Bertha and noticed how she paled, suddenly ceased her activity and stood perfectly still, clutching her bosom in distress as though the cough were racking her own chest.

'Is he always like this?' said Leon. 'I heard him hacking away half the night.'

'Not always,' said Bertha, 'but far too often. And he perspires terribly, the bedclothes get soaked through night after night. I wish I knew what to do about it.'

'What to do about it!' Leon echoed. 'Why, if anything else isn't obvious, that is. He should go to a doctor.'

Bertha sighed. 'That isn't so easy with Michael. He seems afraid of medical men. I've forced him to go once or twice, but I don't believe he tells the doctor all the symptoms. "Only an affection of the throat," he says, and each time he comes home with pastilles and creosote lozenges, but the coughing goes on just the same.' She turned her large, troubled eyes on the journalist. 'I wish you'd talk to him, Leon,' she said. 'Perhaps he'll listen to you.'

Leon walked up the stairs and rapped smartly on the bedroom door.

'Come in,' said a weary voice.

Leon entered and saw his brother-in-law, dressed only in trousers and a vest, resting on the edge of the bed like a somnolent half-animated question mark, his head leaning forward on his chest, his body a concave arch, and his legs dangling dispiritedly over the carpet. His skin was a ghastly green, lending his face a peculiar mottled colour, and after the strain of coughing his breath came in short, sharp gasps. Leon was shocked at his drooping slackness. Michael did not appear to be the same person who not so long ago had been able to throw his supple, responsive body about in the gymnasium.

'What's wrong, Michael?' he asked concernedly.

'Nothing much... Why?'

'Your cough,' said Leon. 'It sounds terrible!'

'It's just a bark,' Michael replied, waving his hand deprecatorily as though to minimise its seriousness. 'It only *sounds* bad. Smoking too much, I suppose. I'll have to cut it down.'

'Have you been to a doctor?' said Leon.

'Yes. A couple of times. They give me...'

'Yes, I know,' interposed Leon sharply. 'Creosote lozenges. Now why don't you stop acting the idiot and have yourself thoroughly examined. After all, you're not playing fair. You've got Bertha to consider as well.'

Michael was silent for a moment, then he rose to his feet. 'Perhaps I *am* considering her,' he remarked cryptically. 'No, Leon, I know my body better than you do. There's nothing terribly wrong with me. I promise you I'll go to a doctor, but I know what he'll tell me beforehand... I've been working too hard, that's half the trouble. A fortnight's rest and I'll be OK again.' He picked up his towel and patting Leon reassuringly on the shoulder, moved towards the door. 'Now I'd better be moving or I'll be late for work.'

When he returned to 'Sheba' in the afternoon, Michael seemed much more like his normal self. He went for a long walk with Bertha after lunch, and was flushed and in high spirits when he came back for tea. That night and the following night Leon slept peacefully without being disturbed, and when he left for London by the early train on Monday, his literary task completed, he had almost deluded himself that his fears for Michael's health were groundless.

CHAPTER X

Michael's firm was doing very well. It had recently, thanks to the chemist's tireless experiments, perfected a new process of manufacturing paint that cut down the expense of production without in any way altering the quality of the goods. It decided to branch out and invade the London market. A factory was bought on the borders of Essex, and Michael moved to London to take charge of the technical staff. He worked harder than ever, and, not content with his research in the factory, rigged up a small laboratory at home and experimented in his leisure hours. He visited Phineas infrequently, coming to St George's about once a fortnight, and then not staying longer than an hour. He usually came with Bertha in the evening and talked always of general matters, avoiding Phineas's attempts to ensnare him into a conversation about himself. He knew that he did not look very robust and that he could not conceal for much longer the state of his health from his father, but the very mention of his personal condition set Michael off at a tangent, fobbing the discussion with forced trivialities. He was under no disillusion as to Phineas's concern about his physical state, the troubled sadness that haunted his father's eyes during his brief visits was sufficient indication. He was terribly run down. He knew he must pull himself together and have a thorough overhauling. But not yet; there were some pressing debts to pay off, and he had to consolidate his position in the factory, to render himself indispensable, then, and only then, would he be able to afford the luxury of medical treatment.

Early in October the family gathered in Edmonton Cemetery to witness the consecration of the tombstone of old Copper Beard's wife who had died the year before. Berel, the glory of his copper beard transmuted by the years into the delicate, silken sheen of silver, stood by the head of the tombstone with a clergyman and some friends. Opposite him were grouped Leon, Deborah and Rose. The masculine members of the Kahn family stood a little distance away, gravely watching the ceremony. Being members of the highest Israelitic caste they were expressly forbidden, by the biblical injunction of the twenty-first chapter of Leviticus, to approach closer than four ells from the grave of a person not of their direct blood, in order that their spotless priesthood should remain untainted by death.

Michael was in the centre of the group, surrounded by his father and brothers, plainly ill at ease. He wore a large slouch hat, the brim pulled well down over his eyes to conceal as much of his face as possible, but in spite of his attempts at subterfuge, his ghastly appearance was only too obvious. Although the day was sunny, his cheeks were pinched and his lips swollen and blue as though distorted by intense cold, his long thin nose and huge pale ears projecting like a macabre disguise from his tiny face. Michael wriggled like a captive worm trying to avoid Phineas's eyes, but wherever he looked, he met the no less horrified stares of his brothers.

After the ceremony, they all went along to hold a memorial service at Shandel's grave. Phineas went first, leading Berel by the arm, the rest of the family following slowly behind. The old man walked with unsteady footsteps, halting every few paces to wipe his eyes and sigh heartbrokenly, but in spite of his grief, he still maintained his dignified, patriarchal air. At last they reached Shandel's last resting place. A path overgrown with weeds, so narrow that they could only pass down it in single file, led between the serried tombstones to her grave. They grouped themselves round it, and Berel in a quavering voice, hoarse with the agony of a two-fold bereavement, began the memorial service. Michael stood at the head of the tombstone, leaning wearily on it, his thin fingers lovingly caressing the inanimate marble. He kept his head well down, unwilling to aggravate the prevailing despondent mood by the spectacle of his ravaged face. The old man's voice broke off in a thin wail like the whinnying of a distressed filly; he could scarcely find the strength to complete the last prayer. One by one they bade farewell to Shandel, until only Deborah lingered behind. She had one last rite to perform, to take with her one last memento of this visit to her mother. She stooped down over the grave and, plucking a small handful of the long wild grass that grew over it, pressed it for a moment to her lips then tucked it in the pocket of her costume. Then she followed behind Phineas, the last of that mournful line.

To Phineas the sight of Michael on that day hurt him like a knife in his ribs twisted slowly by a sadistic torturer. He refused to remain silent any longer. Michael would have to be saved before it was too late – unless – and the thought tantalised his grief-stricken mind with an overwhelmingly certain foreboding – unless it were not too late already. He sent for Stanley, Deborah and Leon, and the next day the whole family sat in conclave. Michael would have to be saved even if they had to kidnap him and drag him to a specialist by force!

They were all gathered silently in the kitchen. Phineas had not given any indication of why he had sent for them, but they knew it was about Michael. Even if he had not asked them to come, they would have all been drawn there just the same, on the same errand. For a long time nobody spoke, they were all busy with their own thoughts of Michael. Stanley fidgeted nervously on his chair. At last he jumped up as though the seat were burning and paced distractedly about the room.

'What are we going to do?' said Deborah at last.

'Do?' said Stanley fiercely, halting in his nervous peregrination. 'Do? He's got to go to a doctor. I'll take him to a specialist even if I have to drag him by the scruff of his neck. We've got to find out what's the matter with him!'

'We don't need a doctor,' interposed Phineas in a strange, flat voice. 'I am a good enough doctor for that. He is terribly ill. How ill he is, none of you really know, he doesn't even know himself. Only I know, and the knowledge is bitter. Bitter as gall...'

Phineas leaned his elbows on the table and cupped his chin between his hands. There was no mistaking the symptoms written on Michael's face and on his wasted body. He knew what it was, but he hesitated to say the word, as though on the saying rested all his son's hope of life. He wished he could not say it, but the dread syllables were bubbling on his lips, and he had to say it although he felt that in uttering it Michael's days were doomed.

'It's con – consumption!' he blurted out at last.

Deborah felt as if an icy grip had fastened round her throat.

She leaned forward tremulously, her face all at once haggard, although the revelation had not been entirely unexpected.

'Are... are you sure?' she faltered.

Phineas nodded, his head shaking slowly like a suddenly shell-shocked soldier. 'I wish I were not so sure,' he said.

Stanley flung himself back on his seat. 'Well, it's no use sitting here and groaning.' The words rushed out of him in a scarcely controllable torrent. 'We've got to do something, and do it quick! He's got to stop work, that's the first thing. Then we'll send him somewhere to recuperate. There's a place called Papworth I've heard about. Or to Bournemouth. Or Italy, or the South of France, or – or – or –'

His voice rose hysterically till it cracked under the impact of a surge of tears. He covered his face with his hands and wept unrestrainedly. With the exception of Leon, who stood by the window alone, they were all crying.

'What's the good of it all?' cried Stanley between his tears. 'I've got a business and a nice house and a car, but what's the good of it all? I'd give them up tomorrow, everything, the whole lot, if only Michael could get well again!'

CHAPTER XI

Phineas had not been the only one suddenly stirred to action by his son's dreadful appearance. Returning home from the visit to the cemetery on Sunday, Michael dropped into his favourite arm-chair, as though exhausted by a hard day's work. Bertha made him a cup of tea and sat opposite him, waiting quietly until he finished. He placed the empty cup on the corner of the hearth and sat up, attempting to look cheerful, but Bertha faced him sternly, uncompromisingly. She had come to the end of her patience, she would not be put off any longer.

'You are going to a doctor!' she said.

'Yes... But...' he attempted half-heartedly.

'I'm not listening to any more excuses,' she said firmly. 'You are going to a doctor. Not tonight, or tomorrow, but now. Now!'

He rose shakily to his feet. 'Must it be now, this very minute?' he said with a sheepish smile. He tried to temporise. 'Can't we leave it for a day or so? You know I've got some important work to do. It's nearly finished. Really, you can't expect me to leave it now.'

He looked at her hopefully, but no answering smile relieved her features. It was the first time he had ever seen her in such an unyielding mood. Her face seemed to harden and the colour rose to her cheeks.

'I *do* expect you to leave your work,' she said. 'Unless you want to leave me. Let's not delude ourselves any longer, Michael. You're seriously ill. You know I love you, and if you love me you'll do your best to get well for my sake. We're practically out of debt now, we ought to start leading a normal life. I want to have a baby. For the past few months you've been burning like a furnace at night, but we haven't been together, not since we came back to London. What sort of life is it for me? I'm a wife, but I haven't got a husband; I'm only twenty-two, not ninety – but even that doesn't worry me so much; if necessary I'd stay away from you for a year, so long as I knew you were getting better. You're killing yourself. I won't stand it any longer, do you hear me? I want a husband, not a corpse!'

Michael flinched before her impassioned outburst. He stood with his head lowered like a repentant dunce. He knew how right she was, but Bertha, as soon as she saw the pathetic, thrashed schoolboy expression creep over his face, thawed immediately. She bit her lips, and felt she could beat herself for having been so cruel. She went over to him and caught his arm affectionately, all softness once again.

'Don't be angry, dear,' she said.

Michael drew himself up and looked down on her proudly. He knew what mental torture she must have undergone before she could bring herself to erupt so bitterly. The least he could do would be to listen to her. He kissed her gently on the forehead, and moving away from her, reached for his hat.

'I'm going to the doctor,' he announced.

She hastily brushed away her tears.

'Wait a minute, Michael,' she said, 'I'm coming with you.'

The nearest surgery was in the next street. They waited for a moment in a tiny off-room, equipped with the minimum of cheap, varnished oak furniture. The doctor, a tall, well-built man of early middle age, ushered them into a bright, clean surgery, and sat down opposite them, his keen grey eyes behind large tortoiseshell spectacles travelling penetratingly over Michael's face. He took some particulars of the patient's age and profession, jotting the details down on a pad, then leaned back, pressing the palms of the delicate white hands before him in an attitude of prayer, his fingertips gently clapping together like a diminuendo of applause.

'Now, what can I do for you?' he asked, addressing Michael directly.

Bertha answered for him. 'I want you to give my husband a thorough examination,' she said.

'Hmmm!' said the doctor. 'You'd better strip to the waist.'

When Bertha saw Michael's torso in all its frail nakedness, like the body of a starved boy of sixteen, she could hardly repress a shudder. The shoulders were rounded, the chest sunken and his ribs stuck out like the hoops on a barrel. The doctor bulked over him, his broad shoulders making Michael appear even more tragically thin and bloodless. He prodded the chemist's body with his fingers, the stethoscope travelling down the nape of the neck, across the back, over the heart, pausing for Michael to breathe deeply, again and again, then busily jumping over the pale flesh once more like a skilful boxer feinting for an opening and pouncing unerringly on his opponent's weakest spots.

At length the doctor put aside the stethoscope and examined Michael's throat. Then he told him to dress. He sat back in his chair, his fingers rapping gently on the desk, waiting for Michael to replace his garments.

'There's an irritation in your throat,' he said when Michael was seated again. 'Do you cough much?'

'Not a great deal,' Michael replied.

'Pardon me, doctor,' Bertha interposed hurriedly. This was what she had been afraid of. 'He does cough, very badly indeed, especially in the early morning.'

The doctor nodded gravely. This time he addressed himself to Bertha; he could see that he would get the truth more easily from her.

'Perspire much?'

'Terribly,' she said. 'The sheets are wet through, night after night.'

The doctor turned to Michael.

'Young man,' he said, 'you're in pretty bad shape. There's no use trying to conceal it, and if you do you're only fooling yourself. You're a chemist, an intelligent man, surely you can see that it's not to your advantage to try to pull the wool over my eyes. After all, I want to help you. We doctors are not such a terrible lot, and medical science isn't still in the Dark Ages. We don't use magical potions and philtres, and tap veins at the slightest provocation. We believe that the greatest recuperative powers lie in the body itself, and we try to guide the patient on the lines where he can make most use of those wonderful gifts of nature. We believe in plenty of rest and air, and food to multiply the red corpuscles of the blood that are mainly responsible for animal metabolism. The mechanism of your body is badly run down, but if you are prepared to co-operate with me, we will do our best to tune it up again. Now, if it's understood that there's no need for antagonism, and that my services are placed in your best interests, will you answer my questions and do as I tell you?'

Michael nodded a little shamefacedly. This obscure suburban practitioner seemed something of a psychologist as well. He was glad he had come here. The doctor had explained things so simply, his professional manner and attitude to medicine were so unlike what he had expected, that he felt a sudden access of confidence and relief.

'Go ahead, doctor,' he said with a smile. 'As my wife is my witness, I swear to tell the truth, and nothing but the truth.'

'Good! Now what hospitals have you been attending?'

'Hospitals?' Michael sat up, the expression of surprise on his face too obviously genuine. 'Why, I've never been in a hospital in my life, except when I scalded my hand once as a kid. As a matter of fact, I'm still at work.'

'Very well,' said the doctor, 'then you must stop work.' He raised his hand authoritatively as he saw Michael's lips part in an unuttered protest. 'You should have stopped work weeks ago. How long do you think one can keep flogging an exhausted horse? Or to return to our imagery, what's the use of pouring more petrol into an engine whose cylinders are clogged with filth? The wise motorist decarbonises, he even gives a thing of steel and nuts and bolts a rest, and your body is a far more delicate machine than ever man can invent, and yet you refuse to allow it to strengthen and renew itself. You must stop work immediately if there is to be the slightest hope of a cure.'

'All right, doctor.' The words were wrung from him reluctantly. 'As you say. I won't go to work tomorrow.'

'Excellent! Have you any parents, Mr Kahn?'

'Only a father. My mother died fourteen years ago.'

The doctor pricked up his ears. Was a hereditary taint about to emerge? This was an advanced TB case, not a shadow of doubt about that, even though he had not tested the sputum; in all probability the susceptibility to the disease has been handed on by the mother.

'Of what did she die, may I ask?' he continued.

'The death certificate said heart disease,' Michael replied, 'but really it should have read birth uncontrol.'

'Birth – what? What does that mean?'

'It means lack of knowledge of birth control. My mother had ten children at eighteen-monthly intervals when my father's wages were not sufficient at any time to support even one in comfort. She suffered from an overworked womb more than from an overworked heart, that's why I say the death certificate was at fault.'

The doctor smiled at Michael's sardonic jest. His patient was a peculiar young man joking in this fashion about death certificates when, if this examination were any portent, he was not so far from one himself.

'And the rest of the family?' he inquired. 'All fit and well?'

Michael nodded. 'In perfect health,' he said.

The doctor wrote rapidly on a sheet of headed notepaper, which he placed in an envelope. He addressed it and handed the missive to Michael.

'I am sending you to a specialist at Victoria Park Chest Hospital,' he said, 'for an X-ray. You will go there tomorrow morning, and when you return, I want you to go to bed and rest, and above all, don't worry. I shall get in touch with you as soon as the result of the X-ray is known.'

The next morning Michael went to the hospital. When he returned home he undressed without demur and got into bed. It seemed as if an enormous burden had dropped from his shoulders. There was no longer any need for him to ape a healthy man; it was all so simple now where previously everything had appeared so complicated. He was ill, and he would stay in bed till he got better, and he didn't mind now who knew about it.

As soon as the news got round, his family came to visit him. He seemed actually cheerful as he lay in bed, and this time, his cheerfulness was no dissimulation. He agreed readily to Stanley's proposals for sending him away; now that there was no necessity to conceal the fact that he really was ill, he wanted to get well again as quickly as possible.

Deborah had already been to visit him on Monday, but on the Wednesday she came again with Leon. Michael was lying back in bed, his long thin arms stretched over the counterpane, his tiny face resting in profile on the pillow. He turned his head slowly as he heard them come in, and the colour of his flushed cheeks seemed to heighten with pleasure. He held up a limp hand and Leon grasped it, but not too tightly; he felt that a hearty grip would crumple that bony, fleshless talon like a brittle piece of chalk.

'Hello, Leon!' Michael said in a thin, hoarse voice. 'Take a seat, old chap. You too, Deborah.'

'No thanks,' said Deborah. 'I want to speak to Bertha. I'd sooner leave you two boys together for a while. I'm sure you've lots to talk about.'

She followed Bertha into the kitchen. She could not look at her brother's wasted features without wanting to cry. In the kitchen Bertha turned, and the two women stood face to face, and suddenly, drawn together by a deep stress of emotion, they intertwined their arms round each other's bodies and began simultaneously to weep.

In Michael's room, Leon sat before the invalid, hardly knowing what to say. A steam train puffed by in the distance and Michael slowly turned his head in the direction of the sound.

'Marvellous how soothing trains can be,' he said. 'As they rush by, they seem the embodiment of strength and life, as if they are bound up with the rhythm of existence.' He stretched his arms with a luxuriant gesture. 'Strange how clear my mind is, and how my body wants to rest. It seems to be trying to make up now for lost time. Do you know that in the past few days I've had my only real sleep for months! Bertha tells me I used to toss about at night and match dozens of shades, and order loads of Vandyke brown and linseed oil and whiting. Now I don't care a damn about work and I can sleep. I shut my eyes and magically my body floats off. Sleep! – What an exquisite luxury. Perhaps the nearest approach to the quintessence of life – death.'

'Don't let's talk about death,' said Leon. 'It gives me the willies. Death doesn't strike me as the quintessence of anything. It's just death, the negation of life, and personally I want to live.'

'So do I,' Michael whispered softly, a peculiar look dimming the sharpness of his keen blue eyes. 'There is so much to live for. I don't want to die. I am not going to die. There are so many things to do that I haven't done, so many things to experience that I haven't experienced. I want to hear Toscanini conduct the allegretto of Beethoven's Seventh Symphony in person, I want to hear again the juicy crunch of pruning shears cutting through thick, wet grass. To read the books I've been promising myself for years to read, to buy the records I've wanted for ages to buy. To have a long holiday in the country, to walk about all night and see the mist rising over the downs at dawn. To see Bertha fondling a baby that belongs to me, and hear it say "Dada" like yours does to you...'

His whispering became scarcely audible, then ceased entirely. He lay quietly, exhausted by his words, his chest heaving painfully, the distant look still in the large, sunken eyes into which had crept the faintest tinge of moisture. Leon sat watching over him till he saw the heavy-veined lids close in sleep, then he silently tiptoed from the room.

His wife and Bertha were talking softly in the kitchen as he entered. They looked up as he came into the room.

'Asleep?' said Bertha.

He nodded. 'Sound as a baby.'

'He sleeps all day now,' she said.

'That's good, surely, isn't it?'

She shrugged her shoulders. 'I don't know. I hope so.'

'Well, he'll be all right soon,' said Leon. 'Stanley's found out all about a place in Bournemouth. We'll get him there as soon as possible.'

Bertha sat down on a kitchen chair and dabbed at her eyes with a handkerchief. For the first time, Leon noticed how wretched she looked. Her face was a sickly white, and an ugly-looking boil was festering on her right eyelid. Obviously she was run down too; it would not be such a bad idea to send them away together.

'I... I'm afraid Bournemouth is out of the question,' she faltered.

'Why?' asked Leon.

'Because he's in no condition to be moved. He's got to go under hospital treatment first.'

'Which hospital?' asked Deborah. 'Victoria Park?'

Bertha shook her head.

'Brompton?' hazarded Leon.

Again Bertha shook her head. She lifted up her face and her eyes stared at them like two deep, flaring black pits. 'I've been to the doctor this afternoon,' she said. 'They won't accept such advanced cases either in Victoria Park or at Brompton. The specialist wrote that he had been behaving like an ostrich for too long...'

A little squeal of pain escaped from Deborah. 'Go on,' she begged, fighting with her breath for every word. 'W – what happened about the X-ray?'

'They found cavities at the apexes of both lungs, and a tubercular ulcer in the throat. Tomorrow, or the day after, they're taking him into the local Memorial Hospital...' Her voice dropped almost to a whisper, and the flickering flame in her eyes died down, leaving them burned-out caverns of blackness. She could not cry any more, all her tears seemed to have been squeezed out. She was suffering, she thought recklessly, let them all suffer too. Why should only Michael choke his life out? Oh she was mad! Mad to think like this. Wasn't one Kahn a sufficient sacrifice to the juggernaut of pain? Poor Deborah. Poor Deborah... 'Once he's in,' she said dully, 'God knows if we'll ever see Michael alive again!'

CHAPTER XII

While he was in hospital, Michael's firm allowed him half pay. They sent Bertha a cheque for a month's salary in advance, expressing the hope that he would soon be back at work again. Bertha moved out of her flat, and storing the furniture in the commodious basement of Stanley's house, went back to the East End to live with her mother. She went to see Michael every day, but there was no apparent change in his health. He lay listless, and apparently indifferent to his critical situation, on a balcony outside the ward. When his family visited him, he appeared cheerful and never complained of any pain, but he grew visibly frailer each time they saw him. The doctor assured them on each occasion that there was a slight improvement in his condition, but that he was still too ill to be moved. Bertha provided him with books. He read intermittently most of the day, and when not reading, he watched the antics of the tiny patients in the children's ward opposite. He had no idea how long he would lie like this, so he urged Bertha to find a temporary part-time job to occupy her mind. Reluctantly, she agreed, with the mental proviso that she would not accept anything that would interfere with her daily visits.

He had been in hospital for a fortnight, and the house surgeon had left after a pleasant chat about books, when Bertha entered. She had her knitting with her and she sat down on a chair by his side and began to unroll a ball of wool. Michael looked at her, she was still as beautiful as ever, but the deep mauve shadows under her eyes betrayed the strain of her waking hours, and her troubled, sleepless nights. She began to knit. She had no need to talk, her presence was sufficient comfort to the invalid, and she felt somehow that she could express herself more fully by silence.

Michael's thin hand reached over the side of the bed and closed over her white arm. She stopped the busy click of her needles and looked up inquiringly.

'I want to ask you something,' he said.

She placed her knitting on the bed.

'Ask away, dear,' she replied.

He looked at her steadily. 'Do you think I'm going to die?' he said.

She hesitated for an almost imperceptible fraction of time. 'Nonsense, Michael!' she answered with a nervous laugh. 'Whatever makes you talk like that?'

His large, clear eyes held hers unflinchingly. 'You know I'm very ill,' he said gravely.

She nodded without replying. This was the first indication he had given that he realised the gravity of his condition. If he understood, there would be no purpose served by false optimism.

'They're doing their best for me here,' he said. 'They've started to give me gold injections. They're pouring liquid gold into my veins. That's the last resort, the last hope, but it's no good, I'm all up... I feel I'm going to die.'

She began to cry softly. He patted her smooth white arm.

'Don't cry for me,' he said. 'I want you to enjoy life. That's what you were born for... You remember the clown's song from *Twelfth Night*? We saw it twice, once at the Old Vic and again at Sadler's Wells... Do you remember...?

> '"Come away, come away, death,
>   And in sad cypress let me be laid;
>   Fly away, fly away breath;
>   I am slain by a fair cruel maid.
>   My shroud of white, stuck all with yew,
>   O prepare it;
>   My part of death, no one so true did share it.
>   Not a flower, not a flower sweet,
>   On my black coffin let there be strewn;
>   Not a friend, not a friend greet
>   My poor corpse, where my bones shall be thrown.
>   A thousand, thousand sighs to save,
>   Lay me, O, where
>   Sad true lover never find my grave,
>   To weep there..."'

His soft, hoarse voice died down to the faintest whisper. He turned his head away. 'Don't weep for me,' he said, and by his facial contortions she saw that he was fighting against tears.

Bravely, she dried her eyes and leaned over him.

'Michael!' she whispered softly.

He turned with an effort to face her and smiled tenderly in her eyes. He was not afraid of death, he was resigned to it, but to the thought of losing Bertha he could never be resigned.

'I won't weep for you,' she said, 'neither need you cry for me. When you die, I shall die.'

He struggled up to a sitting position. What new madness was this?

'Don't be childish, dear!' he whispered urgently, the words struggling out of him with difficulty. 'There's no call for heroics. That attitude is so old-fashioned, so antiquated. You have no right to die. On the contrary, you have everything to live for!'

'Everything!' she replied bitterly. 'Everything except you. Don't you understand that you are everything? I can't live without you, and I won't. Do you think that after that new world of books and poetry and music we opened up together, I'm going back to the old, drab, dreary existence? No! When you die, I shall die,' she repeated dully. 'We shall die together, you and I.'

Michael dug his fingers in his ears and threw his head about as though he were in mortal torment. 'Stop! Stop!' he croaked, every word an agony tearing through his larynx. 'I forbid you to talk like that!'

Gently she drew his hands down and leaned over him, the inspired flame in her eyes shining like the mad light of a lunatic or a prophet.

'We shall die together, dear,' she whispered. 'In death as in life. They will bury us together, and we shall lie side by side in peace, and the flowers will grow over us, and the winds will blow over us, and the sun and the sky will be always overhead. No more worry. No more agonising coughing at night for you, no more anxiety for me, only peace, everlasting, eternal peace, and you and I secure in the heart of it...'

When she left, Michael lay tranquilly, bathed in deep contentment. He had no idea what she intended to do, but whatever she decided on would be right, and a merciful release for them both. Almost he gloated over the thought, and seemed to swell with god-like power. He could snap his fingers at these scurrying, healthy animals that cluttered the surface of the earth; he ranged above them like a supernatural being sneering at their rudimentary attempts at living. He had discovered at last the secret of life, eternal, unhurrying, untoiling life. He felt like chuckling out loud. Death! Death! Where is thy sting? Grave, where is thy victory...?

On the Sunday, Deborah tossed about all night. Leon could not sleep. He spoke to her several times but she did not answer. She awoke in the morning earlier than usual. Leon was already up. He went into the kitchen to make some tea. When he came back, he noticed that she was deathly pale, rings of dark flesh pouched beneath her eyes.

'What's wrong?' said Leon gently. 'You gave me the hell of a night. Nightmares?'

She shook her head. 'No. I have been dreaming of Michael. I dreamt that he was dead.' She shuddered. '... I dreamed that he was dead.'

Leon set the tray before her. 'Have your tea,' he said reassuringly. 'Bad news travels fast, too fast. You would have known before now if anything was wrong. You'll see,' he added cheerfully, 'Michael will fool them all, and live to be a hundred.'

Again Deborah shook her head.

'I know he is going to die,' she said. '... I can feel it.' A flood of tears swept over her and she reached a shaking hand to her husband for comfort. '... I am sure he is going to die.'

Phineas had also been pacing about the house since the early hours. That queer Kahn premonition ran like a forked wave from the ether between him and Deborah; both had received at the same time the uncanny warning of doom. At nine o'clock the telephone bell summoned him. It was the message he had been waiting for, an urgent call from the hospital. He flung on his jacket and rushed from the house.

Leon was just about to leave for the office when Phineas, distraught and haggard, startled him by a loud banging at the door. He let the old man in. He had no need to ask the reason for this impetuous invasion. Phineas flung himself on the couch and buried his face in his hands.

'Michael! Michael!' he moaned.

He jumped up again, the tears streaming down his face. 'I've got to get to the hospital! The phone, the phone – where's the phone?'

He tore the receiver off the hook. 'Hello, operator... Get me the taxi-rank... Hurry!' he panted.

He looked round at Deborah sobbing heartbrokenly in Leon's arms and pressed his free hand to his head.

'Hello!' Phineas gasped in a hoarse, strangled tone.

'Taxi? ... Come round at once to forty Abbey... Abbey...' His voice choked with sobs, his bloodshot eyes glared impotently at the telephone.

Leon came over and took the receiver out of his hands.

'Hello! ... Taxi-rank? ... Good. Send a cab round at once to number four Abbey Road. Four, not forty. And hurry, it's urgent. A matter of life and death...'

The taxi arrived in a couple of minutes. Leon left his portfolio in the kitchen and got into the cab with Phineas. Deborah had a child to look after, and Phineas, half out of his mind with grief, was in no condition to go to the hospital alone. He would ring up later to the office and explain.

'Where to?' said the cabby.

'The hospital, the hospital... Memorial Hospital, East Ham,' Phineas cried impatiently, as if the driver should have known.

The taxi started off. Phineas huddled in the corner talking hysterically to himself.

'How about Bertha?' said Leon. 'We ought to pick her up. She's not on the phone so she can't know yet. Where does her mother live?'

Phineas whispered the address and Leon gave fresh instructions to the driver. Fortunately it was on the way, there was no need to turn back. Leon jumped out of the cab as it slowed down outside a dilapidated old house and ran up the steps, knocking hurriedly on the door. A young girl opened it, the cast of her features pro-claiming unmistakably her close relationship to Michael's wife.

'Bertha in?' said Leon.

The girl shook her head. 'She left about half an hour ago.'

'Where's she gone? Can you tell me? It's important!'

'I... I believe she's gone to the Labour Exchange at Poplar,' the girl faltered. 'What's it about? Michael?'

Leon nodded without replying, and ran down the steps.

'Labour Exchange, Poplar,' he flung at the driver. 'Know it?'

'Yes.'

'Women's department. Hurry!'

When they arrived at the Labour Exchange, Leon walked up the stairs past groups of giggling girls to the waiting-room. His eyes travelled sharply over the women seated on chairs and standing by the counter. At last he saw her, sitting in the front row of applicants, reading a book. He pushed his way over to her, ignoring the curious glances and shrill, uncomplimentary comments on his strange appearance and the rudeness of his progress. He had too much urgent business on hand to feel even slightly uncomfortable. He tapped her gently on the shoulder. She glanced up, and as she saw him, the book dropped from her hands and a startled look came over her face. She jumped to her feet without a word and followed him, her large black handbag clutched tightly under her arm.

'How is he?' she asked tremulously as they ran down the stairs. 'He... he isn't dead yet?'

Leon shook his head. 'No. Not yet. But he must be pretty bad. They rang the old man up round about nine o'clock.'

Bertha glanced at her wristwatch. It was just five-and-twenty to ten. She climbed into the cab in the farther corner from Phineas, and Leon sat between them. The taxi started off. Bertha looked out of the window, at the backward rushing houses and the strangely normal people walking about the streets, going to work, coming from work, husbands returning to wives, wives returning to husbands... Husbands... The full implication of the swiftly moving cab struck her with the dreadful realisation that she was rushing to meet death's implacable advance on Michael. And suddenly the taxi was not travelling fast enough. Her lips moved in silent prayer. If only they found him alive, if only they were not too late! A wild sob from the corner shook her from her preoccupation. Phineas had lost control again, and was shouting his son's name as though the continued iteration of 'Michael, Michael' had the magical power of an incantation and could retard the enveloping wings of the hovering dark angel. His hysteria communicated itself to Bertha and she burst into an uncontrollable fit of sobbing. The driver glanced back through the glass partition and bent over his gears. The speedometer shot up as he urged the cab forward. Leon was jogged up and down between them, glancing concernedly from one to the other. This hysterical journey had taken on the thick, gloomy quality of a nightmare ride; he put one arm round Bertha and drew her protectingly against his shoulder, and with his free hand he patted Phineas's knee restrainingly...

When they arrived at the hospital Michael was still alive, but sinking fast. He had been moved in from the balcony, and they heard the querulous babbling of his delirium from the other end of the ward. They hurried to his bedside and the cold canvas screen closed round them, cutting them off, isolating this stagnant pool of death from the warm, flowing life of the ward. His eyes were closed, and his tiny head, with the sharp chin tilted upwards, seemed too pathetically small to be supported by such huge pillows. His face was luminously bright, shining with high mixed colours like the testing mess on an artist's palette, and his forehead glistened ominously with the last travail-sweat of life. Bertha dropped on her knees at the head of the bed, and leaning over him, called his name.

'... Michael! Michael dear,' she cried urgently. 'Speak to me, Michael!'

A smile of ineffable tenderness wedded to almost unbearable pain suffused his features. His eyes were still closed, but his lips moved in coherent speech. In a thin, hoarse, high-pitched voice, words issued from him, each word an agony, each word a victory over the tortured body, the grotesquely enlarged Adam's apple moving painfully up and down in the effort to drag those mountainous words through the narrow, constricting channel of his throat.

'Bertha... Bertha... Are you here?' he gasped. 'I... I am glad.'

She rested her head on the pillow, her smooth pale cheeks beside his tiny, ravaged face. Her hand caressed gently a long thin arm, while Phineas, on the other side of the bed, almost overcome by emotion, babbled his son's name to a Michael completely impervious to everything in the world but the sense of Bertha's presence.

The excruciatingly ecstatic smile lingered on his face. 'I... I am glad... Glad,' he repeated.

Bertha's tears ran over his features like a refreshing sprinkle of rain. With an effort, he tried to clear his brain. He became conscious of his father's rough hand resting on his arm, and Phineas's voice entreating his recognition.

'Look after her, Dad,' he said. 'Look after her... H – have you any money, Bertha?' he gasped painfully. 'E – enough to get on with?'

'Don't worry about money, Michael dear,' she replied. 'I'm all right. Don't worry about me, dear.'

Leon stood at the foot of the bed. He began to feel uncomfortable. He felt that he had no right to be present at such an awesome, intimate leave-taking. The journalist in him wanted to stay and mentally register each word, each emotion, and if Michael had been a total stranger he would have stayed from a macabre professional curiosity. Had he been someone of his own blood, it would have been his duty to be present at the moment of the last, hideous death rattle, yet Michael was somehow too near to him, and, at the same time, not near enough. He felt that he was an intruder at a sacred rite privy only to these three.

Silently, he left the ward, Phineas and Bertha, submerged in their sorrow, scarcely conscious that he had gone away. He walked rapidly to the high street, trying deliberately to keep his mind from the tragedy, and ordered coffee and toast in a teashop, but when they arrived he pushed both away, untasted. Crossing the road he bought a bottle of smelling salts and returned to the hospital. He found Bertha pacing agitatedly about the corridor. She stopped hesitantly, seeming to have come to some decision.

'The sister of a friend of mine is married to a Harley Street specialist,' she said eagerly. 'Could I ring him up and ask him to come?'

'There's nothing to prevent you,' Leon replied, 'but it can't make any difference. From what the doctor says, it's a matter of minutes rather than hours before...'

She nodded. Her face fell. 'I suppose so,' she whispered gloomily.

Suddenly she seemed to stiffen with resolution, as though faced with the certainty of Michael's death she had steeled her mind to resign herself to the inevitable. She signalled to a passing nurse.

'My husband would like a drink,' she said. 'Could you make him some warm milk, please?'

'Certainly dear,' the nurse replied.

She disappeared into the kitchen, and Bertha resumed her monotonous peregrination, except that now she did not walk so fast or so aimlessly, placing each step with care as though thinking over some difficult, but not imponderable problem. The nurse came out holding a white enamel cup with a long spout, and passed down the ward. Bertha watched her till she disappeared behind the screen, then she turned to Leon.

'I wish you'd call his father out for a few minutes,' she pleaded, 'I'm afraid he might be upsetting Michael and I would like to talk to him alone.'

Leon walked on tiptoe through the ward, running the gauntlet of the curious faces propped up in various attitudes on the beds that ranged on either side. It seemed to take an unconscionable time for him to reach the screen. From the corner of his eye he saw a man stroking his chin and winking to a neighbour as though to indicate that such an adornment as a beard was a ridiculous affectation in one so young. How could people think of such things when a man was dying in the corner? He himself should have been ashamed to allow these little personal vanities to occupy his mind, but the sense of ridicule persisted until he reached Michael's bedside. He saw the milk untasted on the locker and heard Phineas whispering softly to his son, soothingly like a mother getting a tired baby off to sleep. He tapped him gently on the shoulder and Phineas looked up.

'Come out for a few minutes,' said Leon.

Without asking for an explanation Phineas rose wearily and followed Leon down the ward, passing Bertha, who had started for the bedside as soon as she saw them coming towards her. It was Phineas's turn now to pace about anxiously as Bertha had done before.

'How is he?' asked Leon. 'Can he speak?'

Phineas collected his thoughts with an effort. 'Yes,' he said. 'He's been talking to me about everyone except himself. About you and Deborah and Rose and the boys. He keeps telling me to look after David, not to let him work too hard, to see that he goes out a lot in the fresh air and the sun... Just like Michael... Fresh air and sunshine. He understands now, but what's the good? ... There won't be any more fresh air and sunshine for him.'

He sat down on a chair and gazed despondently on the floor, his body sprawled inertly like a flapping ventriloquist's dummy. He seemed utterly broken up, and in the brief space of a morning, ten years older. Leon did not have the heart to talk to him. Whatever he said would only aggravate his distress. He felt an overwhelming desire to get out into the fresh air and sun himself, as if the mention of those two had suddenly made him realise how precious were the things to which in normal life one paid little or no attention.

'I'm going out for a smoke,' he said.

He passed down the corridor and stopped at the hall porter's desk. The uniformed man looked up.

'I'm from Kahn, Ward A,' said Leon. 'Will you give me a call in case I'm wanted? I'll be walking about outside.'

The courtyard was quiet, clean looking and fringed with grass. From the distance came the swish of the overhead wires of the tramcars and the faint yells of children playing in the streets. The sky was almost cloudless and the sun shone with the intensity of an early-summer's day. Inside, Michael was saying farewell to all that. He would die, and the sky would still be blue, and the sun would still scatter over the world its mellow warmth, and green sprigs would pry through the earth, and life would go on in the same old way. He filled his lungs deeply with the air that seemed sweeter and more exhilarating than ever he had known it before, and instantly felt ashamed, as if he had no right to be so ostentatious about the possession of healthy lungs. An aeroplane, high up, like a tiny insect, winged its way slowly overhead. People joy-riding in the skies. The parks were full, the streets later on would be crowded. Yesterday it had rained, and in the country it would smell like paradise. A perfect day. One could not wish for better. Perfect, but no Michael. No Michael...

Phineas, alone in the corridor, sat up, looking about him in

298

bewilderment, as though he had no knowledge of how he came to be there. What was he doing outside the ward? He should be at Michael's bedside. He rose to his feet, then he remembered that Bertha was with his son. He sat down again, then jumped up instantly. Something would not let him rest. He looked round for Leon, but his son-in-law was nowhere in sight. Everybody seemed to have disappeared, the nurses, the doctors, everybody except those strangely cheerful-looking invalids in their beds. He tried to resume his cloistered walk but his movements seemed to make him more agitated, working him up to a crescendo of anxiety. He moved towards the ward and stared in the direction of the screen. It seemed quiet, too quiet. Had Michael died and nobody called him? He dismissed the thought, yet there was something uncanny and death-like about the rigid lines of the screen. Impelled by a strange premonition like the feeling that had obsessed him earlier in the morning, he moved towards Michael's bed. Peering round the side of the screen, he saw that Bertha held the invalid's cup to Michael's lips and that he was slowly swallowing the milk in painful gulps. Phineas moved the screen aside and stood at the head of the bed. As soon as Bertha saw him, she snatched the cup from Michael and, draining the rest of the liquid, flung the cup on the floor.

Defiantly she faced the old man. 'I am poisoned!' she said wildly. 'Poisoned!'

Phineas stared at her in astonishment. He could not understand what she meant. Surely she did not imagine that drinking from the same cup as Michael would be fatal, that the germs could be so deadly and instantaneously transferable with immediate effect? As he watched, she flung herself on the right side of the bed and put her arms round her husband's neck.

'Michael, darling,' she whispered, 'I am coming with you. You won't be lonely, Michael dear.'

Still dazed, unable fully to comprehend the drift of her actions Phineas poked his head round the side of the screen.

'Nurse! Nurse! Hurry!' he called urgently.

He returned to the bedside and a moment later a tall, blonde, young nurse appeared. She went over to Bertha and tapped her gently on the shoulder.

'Please get off the bed, will you? There's a dear,' she said.

Bertha only clasped her husband more tightly, ignoring the nurse's appeal.

'It's all right, darling. I am coming with you,' she repeated to Michael, as though to reassure him endlessly. 'I am coming with you.'

The nurse picked up the cup from the floor and noted a white powder deposit at the bottom. At once, a suspicion of the truth shot across her mind.

'What have you been doing?' she said severely.

'I have taken a dose of sodium arsenic,' Bertha replied calmly in a cold, impersonal tone without even troubling to look up, like one passing the most casual of comments.

'Me too,' said Michael weakly. 'I have taken some as well.'

The nurse helped Bertha off the bed and sat her on a chair. The young wife was deathly pale, and the long black hair had come loose and hung down her back and about her shoulders in lank, untidy strands. She lowered her head over her bosom, her mouth half open, as though she were about to retch.

'How long will it be before the end?' she asked in a flat weary voice.

The nurse pushed the screen back and rushed into the ward. 'Doctor! Doctor!' Phineas could hear her shouting. He walked over to Bertha and held her face up to him in his two hands.

'What have you done, child?' he said sombrely. 'Isn't one sacrifice enough? How dare you take life! Does it belong to you? ... God gave life and only He can take it away. If only for as little as a minute you had no right to interfere with God's work.'

She twisted her face away and shook her head despairingly. 'How can you still talk about God and Life?' she said with a bitter note in her low voice. 'My life is my own and I can do what I like with it. They robbed Michael, so I can rob myself. With Michael dead there is no life, no justice. There is no God left in the world!'

The porter motioned to Leon as he passed by the door.

'Kahn,' he said, 'you're wanted in the ward.'

Leon threw his cigarette away. He jumped up the steps of the lobby and rushed down the corridor. So it had happened at last. ... Oh, they told me Heraclitus, they told me you were dead. They gave me bitter news to hear, and bitter tears to shed... Michael dead! Even now, it seemed unbelievable. He hurried down the ward and found a tragic little group behind the screen. Bertha was not there, but that somehow did not seem strange, and Michael was propped up in bed, supported by pillows, his eyes wide open, apparently in full possession of his faculties. Leon was surprised to see him sitting up, he seemed to be more vigorous now than at any time since they had arrived that morning. The journalist caught his eye and smiled, but Michael looked right through him, as though he were occupied with far more important problems than the mere recognition of a friend's smile. He was fighting for his life, perhaps there was an excuse for him. Phineas stood on his right and on the other side the doctor leaned over him with a stomach pump. The tall, blonde nurse stood at the foot of the bed, gravely watching the operation. Phineas seemed to sway on his feet as though he were going to faint, and Leon, remembering his smelling salts took out the bottle and held it towards the old man. Before it could reach him, the nurse moved over to Leon and clutched his arm tightly.

'What's that you've got there?' she demanded.

Leon showed her the bottle. 'Smelling salts. Why?'

The nurse patted her chest in relief. 'I was afraid it might be poison. They've all been poisoning themselves around here. Why, the very sight of a bottle makes me jump!'

'Poisoning?' said Leon incredulously.

'Yes. The young woman took poison and gave him some too.'

'When did this happen?'

'Just now. That's why we called you in, to see if you knew anything about it.'

'Good heavens!' said Leon. 'Why should *I* know anything about it?' He pulled the cork from the bottle and held it under the nurse's nose. 'Smell! That's not poison, is it?'

The nurse shook her head and Leon proffered the bottle again to Phineas. He glanced down at the smelling salts and pushed Leon's arm away.

'I don't need it, thanks,' he said wearily. 'I have gone through enough sorrow in my life. I can stand this as well.'

Phineas turned back to Michael. The incredibly shrunken face of his son, highly coloured, with the unnaturally large protruding ears, rested on the pillows. He was gasping from the strain of his sufferings, and his nostrils were quivering agitatedly. His large eyes stared out wildly from his face, to Phineas they looked like the eyes of a wounded stag at bay, surrounded by a mob of howling dogs and huntsmen intent on a kill. Oh why had Bertha done this insane thing? Michael had been slipping out of life in a half-daze, only half conscious of his sufferings, but the poison had purged his mind and left it free to experience the whole gamut of the last agony.

Michael twisted his head in an effort to find some relief from the pain. The doctor bent over him again with the stomach pump. Michael gazed at him almost with hatred. Why didn't they leave him alone? ...Why did they keep on torturing him? ...Why, why didn't they let him die in peace? ... He pushed the doctor's hand away.

'Don't force the pump down my throat again,' he begged. 'I can't stand the retching. I haven't the strength... All the poison's come up. I didn't take very much... Sodium arsenic is not very soluble in milk...'

His Adam's apple moved convulsively and the sweat stood out on his forehead as though freshly generated by this strenuous physical tussle with death. A terrible, constricting pain ran through his groins and commenced to burn like a slow fire in the pit of his stomach. He almost welcomed this new agony, it meant that the poison was taking effect. He had taken enough sodium arsenic to kill a dozen men, it should not be very long now. First he would lose the use of his legs and his arms, then the lower part of his body would be numb. Then hearing, sight and smell would vanish. Then the overstrained heart would burst...Then oblivion... Then Bertha...

Leon could not help thinking of her. Michael was finished; it was obvious that he was in his last death throes and that the oxygen apparatus could not prolong his life much longer. His heart went out in pity for the young wife, so gentle, so ravishingly beautiful. He guessed the torments she must have gone through before she had lost her head in this futile, melodramatic gesture. It would be dangerous to let her out of the hospital now; this action had betrayed the unhinged state of her mind. It was quite on the cards that the moment she was out of observation she would stick her head in the gas oven, or do something equally foolish.

'How is the young woman?' he asked the nurse.

'Pretty bad,' she said.

'Bad!' It came as a shock to Leon. 'Is it really as serious as all that?'

'I'm afraid so,' said the nurse. 'She's in that little off-room outside the ward. She refuses to swallow the stomach pump. Perhaps you can cajole her into doing so.'

Leon hurriedly left the bed and rushed through the ward. The tragedy had taken a turn that hardly anyone could have foreseen. He found her sitting on a chair, her head drooping over her chest, wrapped in a voluminous pink dressing-gown. A nurse bent over her and was urging her to swallow the pump, but obstinately, Bertha shook her head.

'I can't,' she repeated dispiritedly, 'I can't.'

'Hello, Bertha!' said Leon, trying to appear cheerful.

She looked up. 'How's Michael?'

Leon shook his head gravely. 'Cheer up,' he said. 'It's you we've got to look after now.' He took the pump from the nurse. 'Now be a good girl, Bertha,' he urged, 'swallow this. That'll bring all the rubbish up. There's a dear!'

She pushed his hand away. 'What's the use?' she said with a sad little gesture. 'I don't want to live any more... I don't want to live.'

She half rose and leaned over the bath, and retched violently into it, but all that came up was a slight mixture of sputum and a greenish bile-like liquid. A porter entered with a wheeled basket chair, and, helping Bertha into it, trundled it out of the room in the direction of the women's ward. Leon looked at the nurse. What was he expected to do now?

'You're a relative, aren't you?' she said.

'Yes,' Leon replied.

'Then you'd better help me go over her belongings,' said the nurse.

There was nothing apart from a handkerchief in her coat or dress, but the large black handbag was choked with a variety of articles. The nurse took out an empty matchbox and a small packet of cigarettes. A powder puff and a compact and a bundle of letters came next. In a tiny, blue-lacquered cigarette case were a wristwatch and several little items of jewellery. Right at the bottom the nurse unearthed two intact paper packages. They were from a firm of multiple chemists, apparently purchased over the counter, and printed across both packages were the words POISON POISON, repeated in red block letters. The nurse held up the packages. The young woman had come well prepared for her deed.

'Look at these,' she said. 'Potassium dichromate and bromide potassium. Both deadly poisons.' She shook her head. 'They should never be allowed to sell these to the general public!'

She made a bundle of Bertha's clothing, and, replacing all the articles in the bag with the exception of the poison, gave her belongings to Leon.

'Take these upstairs, will you please? Ward B. Turn left on the first floor.'

Leon was not allowed to enter the women's ward. A sister took the clothes from him at the door with a compassionate gesture. It was extraordinary how kind and helpful they all were, real sisters of mercy. To him it appeared remarkable that they were not upset at all the trouble and annoyance that the girl's action had precipitated. He hurried downstairs back to Michael's bedside. Phineas was seated there alone, clasping his son's hand. The oxygen tube rested in Michael's nostril, and his chest still heaved faintly. His head leaned sideways on his right shoulder, and a froth of yellow mucus was gathered at the corner of his mouth. Phineas turned his tear-stained face to Leon as he came beside him. He picked up Michael's skinny blue arm and as he released the limb it dropped lifelessly on to the bed.

'Dead,' he said faintly. 'Dead and cold. It's all over now...' He roused himself to the sense of his responsibilities as a Jew, his last duty towards his dead son. 'Telephone home,' he said to Leon, 'then go to the Federation Burial Society in Leman Street. Ask them to send down a watcher. From now until he is buried, none but Jewish hands may touch him.'

He returned to the vigil over his son, and Leon, after a last look at the grotesque, spread-eared death mask of his friend, tiptoed from the bereaved parent. He could not but admire the old man's composure at this extremity. Phineas was possessed of tough mental fibre to be able to bear this blow so resignedly; it was not that he did not love his son, but that he realised now that hysterics and heart thumpings would not bring Michael back to life again.

Leon left the hospital and walked rapidly to the nearest telephone box. It was just twelve o'clock.

When he got through, he recognised Rose's voice. 'This is Leon,' he said.

'Well?' came the anxious query.

'It's all over. He's dead.'

He heard a strangled cry, the receiver gave a click and there was a dull thud, as though the girl had fallen to the floor.

'... Hello!' This time it was Deborah.

'Leon speaking,' he repeated. 'He's dead.'

'O – O – O – Ohhh.' A long-drawn wail came across the line and he heard the sharp intake of her breath. 'W – when did he... when did it happen?' she blurted with a tearful rush.

'A few minutes ago,' said Leon. 'Just about twelve o'clock. Bear up, dear, I'm coming home right away.'

CHAPTER XIII

In the afternoon and evening the plague of reporters descended on St George's. Phineas received the first few and gave them a statement, but others arrived every hour clamouring for stories, photographs, snaps of Michael and Bertha. This was news, a hot story, murder and attempted suicide. Most of the reporters were sympathetic young men who tried their best to be delicate about the whole affair; this was their job; they regarded themselves as liaison officers between the victims of a tragedy and the general public. But each fresh question was like rubbing vitriol into raw wounds until at last Phineas could stand it no longer and resolutely shut his door against them. Why did they not allow him to nurse his sorrow in peace? This brand of mental torture was more deadly than the agony he had undergone at his son's bedside; they were tearing him to pieces like psychological wolves – and for what? For what? Had Michael died to make a Fleet Street holiday?

He refused to give them treasured photographs of his son, but by some occult means his favourite portrait of Michael, in cap and gown at graduation, appeared together with Bertha's picture in all the evening newspapers. Deborah was visited by reporters, and Stanley too was pestered for photographs by several young men, who by ingenious sleuthing that would have been a credit to Sherlock Holmes, had discovered that the tragic couple's furniture was stored in his basement. One of them even produced a note purporting to come from Bertha's brother asking Stanley to give him every assistance. Stanley asked the photographer to call back a little later, and in the meantime discovered through a telephone inquiry that Bertha's brother knew nothing whatever about it.

When Leon returned home from the office, he found Deborah distraught. She had just come back from St George's and the spectacle of her father, her sister and her brothers huddled together in the kitchen in their misery had unnerved her. She flung her arms round Leon as he entered and wept on his shoulder, tears more of fatigue and nervousness than grief, for she had cried herself out about Michael long before this.

'It's terrible! Terrible!' she said. 'I see a man walking in the street, and he stops, and I think he is Michael. I sit next to people in buses and trams, and every second one of them is Michael... It's terrible! ... I can't stand it, Leon... I can't stand it!' she sobbed.

Early next morning Leon went down to the hospital. He met Bertha's brother outside the ward, and together they went to her bedside. She lay quietly, her head resting on one side, the lower part of her body encased in an electrically heated basket. Her face was deathly white, her pallor enhanced by the raven black hair that was thrown about the pillow. A strip of plaster was stuck to her right cheek, holding firmly in place the oxygen tube that led to her nostril. She smiled wanly as she saw Leon, and held out her hand. He took it gently between his palms and sat beside her.

'How's Michael? ... How is he?' were her first eager words.

Leon shot a questioning glance at her brother, and he nodded ever so slightly. Hours and days were becoming confused in her head. Apparently she had not yet been told, or had forgotten, but the nod gave him permission to tell her the truth and soothe the restless travail of her mind.

'He's dead,' Leon said. 'He died peacefully, a few moments after you gave him the poison. He died like a child, without any torment.'

She gave a sigh of relief. 'Thank God for that,' she said. 'If only I saved him one moment of pain, I count the rest of my life well spent!'

She writhed in agony. 'He had nearly three weeks of this,' she moaned. '... I have only had two days... I wish someone would do for me what I did for Michael...'

Leon shuddered at the unconscious irony of her words. She had not witnessed Michael's last bitter duel with death, she did not know how he had suffered, and he hoped fervently that she never would. The pain seemed to ease a little. She struggled to a semi-sitting position and began to talk slowly, with laboured breath. She asked about Deborah, and Leon's son, and the rest of her husband's family. Then she was silent for a while, as though thinking deeply.

'I... I hope they're not angry with me,' she brought out hesitantly, at last.

'Of course not!' said Leon. 'Why should they be? You did the best possible, the most humane thing.'

'I... I am glad they understand...' she whispered.

Again she gasped for air and pressed against the pillows, as if by burrowing deep inside them she could find a respite from her torment. With an effort she half raised her beautiful head like a thoroughbred horse dying on the turf, its last strength spent after a gruelling race.

'I... I can't... breathe,' she said. 'I... feel... sick... This horrible... horrible burning in my stomach.'

Leon called the nurse. She adjusted the oxygen tube and Bertha seemed to breathe a little easier. Her head sank exhausted on the pillows, and as she closed her eyes in sleep, Leon and her brother tiptoed quietly from the ward.

The next morning Leon set out for the hospital again. As he passed the barrier at the end of his journey, a placard outside the station bookstall focused his attention. It was the late edition of the morning paper. 'GIRL WIFE DIES IN HOSPITAL' it said. He turned pale and his stomach seemed to twist right over. He hurriedly purchased a copy of the paper, hoping against hope that it might be someone else, but in the Stop Press he found his worst fears confirmed. She had died early in the morning. He thought about telephoning to his wife and Phineas, then dismissed the idea. By this time they too must have known.

It was getting late. He was due at the office. He bought a ticket and boarded the City train. It was sad. Strange and sad, yet somehow so complete. It was probably callous, but he felt that she was better dead. Had she recovered, she would have been dragged through the torture of another 'mercy murder' trial. Her sensitive nerves would have cracked under the intolerable strain. She would have gassed herself or taken more poison, and this time would have made certain. Leon understood now what that stiffening of resolution in the hospital ward had betokened. Her mind had been irrevocably made up. She would not have lived without him. She loved him too much.

At the office, he was unable to do any work all day, and on the way home in the evening the tragedy still obsessed him. It was such an appalling wastage of human life. Michael had been lying disembowelled on a mortuary slab for two days, and by now she was probably there beside him. She had no right to die, but Michael had been doomed from early childhood. At the inquest they would probably find his intestines coated with sodium arsenic, but sodium arsenic had not killed him, he had been dead for years before he had been admitted to the hospital. Poverty had killed him, the result of social maladjustment; that same affliction that had condemned his parents to burrow like troglodytes in a filthy cellar beneath the earth had sentenced him to a lingering, suffocating death on the day that he was born. Amongst the very poor, the weak have no chance of surviving. Those early, dark, airless years had laid their ineradicable mark on him. Years of hungry childhood, years of lean, parched manhood; years of overwork and undernourishment that had weakened his bodily resistance so that when the dread disease had attacked him, he had not the strength to fight back.

At the office, all day, the main topic of discussion had been the tragedy. Little groups of people with set, serious faces had been constantly talking about it. They had left him in peace, knowing of his close relationship to the dead couple, and had dropped their voices to an almost inaudible whisper when he passed, but he knew from their compassionate glances what they were talking about. The women everywhere, in the office and outside, seemed more interested than the men. The men would soon forget it, but it would linger for years in the memory of women. Every woman placed herself instinctively in the position of the tragic young wife confronted by the dying husband, and went through within herself the same futile, heroic gesture. It had hurt the heart of womanhood, pierced deep and left an indelible scar.

For a change, he travelled home by bus. Somehow, he felt that watching the people in the streets would take his thoughts off the tragedy, but it was insistently brought home to him all along the route. Every paper seller had the news plastered on his posters. 'MICHAEL AND BERTHA'. It hammered into him from every street corner. Michael and Bertha, Michael and Bertha. The placards kept shouting at him, as if inviting him to shout back something hysterical in return. Newspapers were held open in front of him, beside him, behind him. Pictures of Michael and Bertha. Incredible that this could happen to a man and a woman so close to him, so intimate with him. Such things simply did not occur to people you knew, your own flesh and blood, you only read about them in the papers, and thought during the reading, if you thought about them at all, 'poor blighters!' and forgot about them...

The man next to him started avidly reading the details of the case, the paper spread wide open so that a page rested on Leon's knee and a photograph of Bertha stared up at him. He felt an overwhelming desire to grab hold of the man's arm and to talk to him. To point to the picture and say: 'You see her? I knew her well. That's my sister-in-law. Michael was my wife's brother. I used to go to the poly with him, and stayed with them once at Slatford. I was at the hospital when it happened. It was terrible, terrible... right in front of my eyes. He could not swallow the stomach pump. "Please... Please," he begged the doctor... And when I went to her, the long black hair was hanging loosely down her back. "Perhaps you could cajole her into doing it," the nurse said... And she said, "What's the use? What's the use?"...'

Leon glanced sharply at his neighbour. The words had rung so clearly through his head that he almost expected to find that he had uttered them out loud, and that the man next to him was eagerly listening for more, but the other had stolidly passed on to the top of the next column. Leon ran his hand across his eyes. Words and pictures indescribably mingled together in some audio-visual compound were shooting across his mind, jumping up and down and diagonally like the erratic thumping pistons of a crazy machine. He saw Bertha and Michael, and the doctor bending over him, and the last ghastly yellowness of his face, and the stomach pumps, and the packages of poison, and the nurse shaking her head and murmuring 'They should never be allowed to sell them... They should never be allowed to sell them', faster and faster and faster like a leitmotiv that held the key to this strange jigsaw of sight and sound. The wild movement abated, the tempo slowed down and suddenly everything fused in blackness and silence. Leon opened his eyes. The man next to him was still reading uninterruptedly. He was glad he was not making an exhibition of himself, and that the hysteria was confined to a formless jumble in his mind. He looked out of the window. Thank heaven he got out at the next stop, before this strange seizure could have a chance to overcome him again.

A young couple sat in front of him, the man about thirty-five, the woman a few years younger. She looked up at the man, her eyes glazed with a gelatinous film of emotion. In profile she appeared to Leon like a woman in a trance, looking at the man, yet seeing beyond him.

'Darling,' she said in a soft voice.

'Eh...?' The man looked up.

'Darling,' she repeated, 'would you do as much for me?'

'What on earth are you talking about?' he asked irritably.

'Would you kill yourself for me, if you knew I was dying?'

The man glanced down at the newspaper in her hands. 'Oh!' He understood now. A grin enlivened his face. 'What's the use of asking me now?' he said. 'Let me see you dying first...'

Deborah went to bed early that evening. She was exhausted by the strain of three days' continuous outpouring of sorrow. Leon shut himself in his study and started to write. This seemed his big chance of breaking into Fleet Street. He sat before the typewriter and began his article: 'I SAW THEM DIE.' All the events of the past few days crowded into his mind, and flushed by a fierce exultation at his command of words, the keys hammered under his fingers like the staccato rattling of a machine gun. The black ribbon pressed against the white paper like the lips of a lover hungry for kisses, and the black words strung themselves out in dozens of parallel lines. This was the finest piece of work he had ever done, probably the best he would ever produce, a slice of reporting in the tradition of the giants, something for the world to remember him by.

His eyes sore and smarting, he tore the last page from the machine and read it over with an intense concentration. He leaned back and lit a cigarette, smug with the contentment of one who has ably mastered a difficult job. Then he began to think, and suddenly his triumph seemed hollow, and worse, even shameful. What could he get for a story like this? Five guineas? Ten guineas? That was, if it were accepted. The thought of it coming back seemed an added shame, like a woman reluctantly exposing her body, then having it spat on in disdain. No! He would not sell Michael for a mess of pottage. His honour was not worth risking for a few pounds. Fifty, or a hundred pounds would be worth trying for, that would be a help for Phineas on whom would fall the whole expense of the funeral, but such sums were paid only to acquitted murderers, or tennis champions, and not to journalists for a journalist's work. He read the article through again. The words seemed dead, ironically lifeless, where before they had pulsed with a fierce animation. With a gesture of disgust he put the pages together and tore them to pieces, flinging the scraps into the waste-paper basket, angry with himself for ever having conceived such a gross betrayal.

Deborah was lying peacefully in bed, fast asleep, when he laid himself wearily beside her. He shut his eyes, but his mind coursed feverishly round the tragedy, recalling the words he had written such a short while before, the phrases recurring insistently, forbidding him the solace of sleep. He saw Michael again, leaning against the pillows, fighting for breath, and at the same time he felt a hot, choking sensation in his own throat. He lifted his hand to his forehead and it was damp with sweat. The shadow of Michael seemed to hover at his bedside like a menacing ghost, his eyes flaming from their deep sockets, an ironic grin playing about his lips as if to say: 'You're next, Leon. It's your turn now.' He suddenly remembered that it was October 23rd, his birthday, and Michael had died on the twenty-first, the day on which he had been born. He lay very still, his heart hammering painfully. It seemed imperative for him to lie silently until the next day; if only he could survive until midnight, the danger would disappear. He was conscious of the perspiration mounting to his forehead, and each breath seemed to have become a painful effort. He moved closer to his wife to feel the comfort of her cool, peacefully slumbering body, and, almost overcome by panic, he had it in his mind to wake her so that she could talk to him until daybreak, and drive away the spectre of Michael. He restrained himself, it would be a pity to tear her from the rest she so badly needed. He braced his nerves and reached out a trembling hand to the bed table for his wristwatch. He glanced quickly at the luminous dial. It was three o'clock – the twenty-fourth! Almost as if by magic, the tumult and the heat were cut off. The twenty-fourth, he was saved! Then he remembered that Michael's birthday had been in the summer, round about June or July. He smiled foolishly in the darkness, strange the tricks an overwrought mind could play on the body! He settled himself more comfortably on the pillows, his brain clear and refreshed, like an invalid who had just passed the crisis of an illness, and dropped into a dreamless sleep.

At the inquest, the jury returned the only possible verdicts, murder and suicide. The male mourners went across the road from the town hall to the morgue where the bodies were lying exposed in their unvarnished whitewood coffins waiting to be screwed down. Their waistcoats were rent in the symbol of mourning, and the six brothers, placing their shoulders beneath the coffin, so light that it seemed incredible that it contained the remains of a grown man, carried it reverently to the hearse. Then they performed a like office for Bertha, and the cortège set off on its long journey to the cemetery.

Michael was buried first. They held a service over him in the tiny synagogue, then, making a circuit round the building, a grave-digger slowly wheeled the body to its last resting place, the family following close behind. The plank was removed from the grave, and two elderly Jews in high hats, whose squat bodies were bent double like gargantuan beetles silhouetted against the clear sky, their black frockcoats flapping eerily in the wind, lowered the fragile coffin into the ground. Each mourner took a turn at the spades, and the black earth spattered in jets over the white wood until the whiteness was obliterated. Israel shovelled feverishly, sobbing bitterly. He remembered how they had played together, how they had slept together as children in one bed, now the dark earth was closing over him inexorably, and no one would ever see Michael again. Phineas's eyes were glued to the remorselessly falling earth that dropped with a dull sound over the coffin like a dark deluge. While there was still a speck of white showing, he felt that he was close to his son, but as the soft black mantle piled higher and higher, a chasm seemed to yawn before him until he felt himself utterly cut off. They walked back slowly to the synagogue and Bertha's body followed her husband's to rest as she had wanted, eternally by his side.

In the evening, the family gathered in the kitchen at St George's. The mirrors were draped with white cloths, and the mourners sat glumly on boxes and low stools, talking in whispers, but for the most part silent. Soon after the evening service they went to bed to seek the blessed relief of unconsciousness, the tall flickering candles on the table burning in solitude, a last tribute to Michael's memory, investing the little kitchen with an unsteady and evermore subdued yellow light. A stifled sob broke out now and again in the darkness, but soon the whole house was silent.

Phineas alone could not sleep. He went over in his mind, again and again, the drama of his son's last moments, and it seemed to him that Michael was not yet dead, but fighting that grisly battle endlessly, to eternity. He could not think of him as a child, as a student, as a young man, but only as a strangled sufferer gasping for life. The lids closed wearily over his aching eyes, and for a moment all was merciful blackness, then with a startling sudden-ness and clarity he saw Michael standing over him. His face was larger than life, and pure white, shining with an uncanny radiance. The vision was so real that he sat up and opened his eyes, but the room was still shrouded in darkness. His throat felt parched, and an overwhelming desire for a drink crept over him. He got out of bed and silently made his way downstairs to the sink.

His thirst slaked, he replaced the cup on the dresser and halted by the gas stove. It would be so easy to obliterate all those tragic memories. Suicide was like a contagious disease; that same after-noon, the taxi driver who had driven them to the hospital had killed himself. The tragedy had even had repercussions in far-off America, and in the House of Lords noble peers were making speeches advocating euthanasia... euthanasia... A merciful release from the disease of memories. Carbon monoxide, quick and sure, the soft candlelight flickering invitingly over the white enamel of the stove.

He shook himself like a drunken man trying to throw off the torpor of liquor. What was he doing to think like this? ... Euthanasia... euthanasia... No... He had a daughter to marry off, and his sons to look after, and David's career to secure. He had to hold on to life. What more could life do to him? Faltering, he climbed the creaking stairs to the leaky attic where he slept, the monument he had built to thirty-five years in London...

The next day a cable came from Biro-Bijan in reply to his wire to Olga and her husband.

'FATHER COME TO US. WE WILL LOOK AFTER YOU.'

He tossed the cable aside wearily and during the rest of the week of mourning never thought of it again. A letter followed soon after, urging Phineas to come to Russia, if not to stay permanently, then at least for a lengthy holiday. Again he disregarded the invitation; he could not bring himself to think of a holiday, that seemed somehow like treachery to Michael's memory. His mind was saturated with Michael, every thought, even every physical movement seemed connected with his dead son. The whole of his life he saw now as a long-drawn-out prelude to this, the culminating point of his whole existence. All his struggles, the death of his wife, the fight to obtain a livelihood, the fight to educate his children, all his failures and hardly won triumphs paled to insignificance beside this shattering blow. Wherever he went, in the faces and voices of his friends and neighbours, he found reminders of Michael, even the very streets evoked recollections of his son.

In time, he thought, the obsession of Michael must grow less strong, the memory of his last death struggle become fainter and eventually expunged altogether, but as he went about his business he found himself inhabiting a dream world with a live Michael, the world of reality around him becoming less real than his imaginings. His family were deeply perturbed at his unbalanced state and united in urging him to take advantage of Olga's offer. Passively, he allowed himself to be swayed by them. Nothing now seemed to matter very much. Years ago he had sent Olga to Russia and she had not returned, now his children were begging him to go and he knew, although he did not tell them, that like her if he went he would never come back.

On a cold Saturday morning in January he took his leave from St George's without even a backward glance at the house that for so many years had absorbed all his vital energies. The boys bundled his luggage into Stanley's car and went off to Hays Wharf where Deborah, Leon and the rest would be waiting. It was a chilly morning, and the white mist of the early hours had darkened into a yellowish fog. The car moved off slowly, greeted by hoarse fog signals from the riverside that grew louder and more frequent as they approached London Bridge. It seemed to Phineas a fitting setting for his exodus. On a cold, foggy day thirty-five years ago he had arrived in England; with such another chill, valedictory salute he was returning home. From Russia he had travelled to Austria, thence to England, America and back again to England, now he was journeying for the last time to the land of his birth. The pattern of his life seemed complete, it had revolved full cycle. The old Russia, the Russia of the Tirchovs and the Voronoffs had spewed him from its gullet like a blob of unassimilable mucus, now the new Russia was waiting to welcome him, if not with a new life, for he was too old to start building afresh, then at least with a secure corner he could call his own.

He embraced his family before he went aboard. Most of them were crying, but his own eyes were free from tears. He walked firmly up the gangway and climbed to the top stern deck. All round him men were busy on the last stages of embarkation. Commands rang out in Russian and were answered in familiar words, the language seeming more intimate to him than the English he had spoken for so many weary years.

The mooring ropes slithered across the lower deck, uncoiling themselves like monstrous black snakes; more hoarse whistles; the deafening escape of steam; and the deck trembled as the boat cast off. Phineas waved to the little group on the quayside until the boat swung ponderously into midstream and made for Tower Bridge, dwarfing the tugs and the squat strings of barges that lay close to the banks. He heard the warning bell of Tower Bridge and the sonorous drive of machinery as the bridge parted and rose to let the vessel pass. He kept his eyes on the grey froth churned up in the muddy water until he heard the mighty throb of mechanism bringing the bridge back into position. Before him the bridge was sinking, ending its yawn like the jaws of a bored crocodile. The grey outlines of the Tower softened and merged into the fog. He had lived in its shadow for thirty-odd years; yet never once had he explored its ancient dungeons. There it had stood at his very doorstep, embodying nearly a thousand years of English history, and he had never felt the desire to get closer to its grey stones. Somehow it had always seemed alien to him. He had never been interested in the boy Princes of the Bloody Tower, in the Armoury, the Traitors' Gate or the Crown Jewels. He had no roots that groped for sap beneath those massive stones; it represented a culture in which he had no part. The Tower he left for his children; its history belonged to them; they might be able to learn its lessons.

The familiar landmarks on either side vanished as the boat moved downriver with triumphant hoots. The shouts of the sailors died down. He pulled the collar of his topcoat about his ears, and his mind swept back more than half a century to the Messiah his mother had dangled on her knee. The one whose fame would go across the world, whose name would be on millions of lips. That was he, Phineas, and ironically the prophecy of Reb David-Moishe had been fulfilled.

London Classics

JEW BOY

SIMON BLUMENFELD

Jew Boy is a novel about poverty and politics in the tumultuous world of London's Jewish East End in the 1930s, where boxers mixed with anarchists and communists, and Yiddish actors and poets rubbed shoulders with gamblers and gangsters. All were united in their hatred of fascism, and were prepared to fight it when necessary. Yet of equal interest is the novel's exploration of the personal lives and thwarted aspirations of young people at this time, both Jewish and non-Jewish. Class means as much to the main protagonists as the older ties of religion and race.

Author Simon Blumenfeld – born in Whitechapel, working its markets as a young man – brings to life the reality of sweatshops and sweated labour, vividly portraying the exhaustion produced by long hours, unforgiving deadlines and cut-throat competition. But this is a story driven by hope, a desire for change, and his descriptions of the exciting culture that existed beyond the workplace help produce a testimony to a unique time and place now firmly embedded in London's volatile history. *Jew Boy* is nothing less than the founding work of what went on to become a unique body of fiction, autobiography and drama – the literature of the twentieth-century Jewish East End.

Ken Worpole, who introduces the novel, is the author of *Dockers And Detectives*, and has played a major part in reviving public interest in the work of Simon Blumenfeld and other Jewish writers from the pre-war East End.

London Books
£11.99 hardback
ISBN 978-0-9568155-1-4

London Classics

DOCTOR OF THE LOST

SIMON BLUMENFELD

When young Thomas Barnardo arrived in London in 1866, he planned to study at the London Hospital before venturing abroad to work as a missionary. The conditions he found in the East End stopped him in his tracks. Unemployment, poverty, overcrowding, alcoholism and deathly diseases were bad enough, but seeing thousands of half-starved children living on the streets broke his heart. Inside a year Dr Barnardo had opened the ragged-school Hope Place and by 1870 the first of his eponymous homes was in operation. His work continues to this day. *Doctor Of The Lost* is the fictionalised story of Tom Barnardo's early years in East London.

Author Simon Blumenfeld grew up in the same streets, his cult 1935 novel *Jew Boy* capturing the magic of the Jewish East End of the 1930s, and *Doctor Of The Lost* (1938) recreates the area in Dr Barnardo's day. Drawing on a friendship with his widow, Blumenfeld brings Barnardo vividly to life, showing the struggles he faced and the battles won. *Doctor Of The Lost* is set in a London of rampant industrialisation, when the few became rich at the expense of the many, and yet this was also a period of charity and good works, when idealists such as Thomas Barnardo were prepared to stand tall and fight back.

London Books
£11.99 hardback
ISBN 978-0-9568155-2-1